Azure Tiger

Desert Sailors Series
Book 2

———

K. J. Frolander

*For all my dear friends who have
continuously encouraged me in my writing.*

1

Judah Wakefield gasped for breath. Her eyes darted back and forth in the dense blackness. "God, just let me get away. Hide me!" Judah refused to give into the hot breath of terror stealing down her neck. She darted up an alley that appeared vacant and tried to hold her breath in silence, but the burning need for oxygen made her pant in hiccupping bursts. She threw a quick glance to her right for an escape in the oppressive dark.

A red digital glow taunted her. 4:17. She groaned and squeezed her eyes tight, her abdomen rising and falling at nearly the same rate as her racing pulse. No hope for more sleep tonight.

The 31-year-old woman pump-kicked her long legs to release the tangle of sheets that had slowed her sleepy run. Rolling up, she snatched her Bible from the unoccupied side of her queen bed. Her gray t-shirt skimmed her thighs as she scampered to the living room to curl up with her checkered quilt in the ragged blue La-Z-Boy her parents gave her when she left for college a lifetime ago.

"You give your beloved sweet sleep," she read aloud. "After three weeks, I am ready for some of that."

Joseph Bartholomew stretched on the floral couch, his head low and his rump high, with his gray paws spread long in front. He sprang from the arm of the furniture into her lap without invitation. Judah buried her fingers in the soft fur around his throat. The cat's rhythmic purr mixed with the ticking grandfather clock to mark the watch until dawn.

She lightly traced the row of 47 stitches on her right cheek with her ring finger. Her mid-night pursuer had caught her in their first encounter. But she had caught him in their next round.

Less than two weeks earlier Lieutenant Commander Judah Wakefield had called in the coordinates for an air strike on her nightmare man's Afghanistan villa. "He's dead. Why does Filasek keep stalking my nights, God? He doesn't have the right!" Judah murmured as she flipped to Ephesians. "If the demonic realm thinks it's going to harass me, they picked on the wrong woman."

She raked her bra-strap-length honey hair back from her forehead. In physical war, the naval officer provided meticulous profiling on enemy combatants and occasionally lined up the sites of a sniper rifle when called upon. In the war of the spirit, she took aim with scripture. "I'll do it every day if I have to," she warned. "Every night you wake me up, I'll be in your face with God's Word." She began to read aloud. At 0545 hours, she allowed herself to gravitate to her morning rite of two cups of strong coffee doctored with two blue Equal® packets and two tablespoons of half-n-half.

Standing over the kitchen counter, she dragged her fingers through the permanent creases in her hair from the navy-regulation bun she wore on duty. Still jumpy, Judah pushed off the counter and retreated to her bedroom with her steaming brew. Judah pulled on crisp dress blues for her debriefing. She straightened the two rows of colorful service ribbons pinned over her heart on the black jacket. A simple twist righted the gold oak leaf insignia adorning her collar. She fingered the sleeve's gold quarter inch stripe between two half-inch stripes. This uniform was her favorite. She buttoned the last brass button. It embodied all that was a naval officer without the effort to keep clean that was involved with summer dress whites.

LCDR Wakefield parked her red Mustang in the secured CIA lot at Langley, Virginia, and entered the outer office of Director of Counter-intelligence Dietz with four minutes to spare. Even when running late, Wakefield was perpetually early.

"It's Wednesday. He'll be in shortly," his day-time secretary, Julia Cravits said and went back to clacking her nails on the keyboard. "You may have a seat."

Judah set her cover in her lap and her briefcase on the thick carpet. She met the secretary's eyes over her computer monitor. Wakefield was used to attracting attention, but she didn't enjoy the wondering sort of scrutiny she had been seeing out of the corner of her eye on this first day she had worn her hair in the military-protocol bun since arriving back from the aircraft carrier. The severe style readily displayed the long, stitched cut that stretched from just under her eye to nearly her jawline.

"What does Wednesday have to do with Dietz's office appearance? Is he human on Wednesdays and takes a day to come in late?" Judah cracked a smile at the thought. Julia Cravits did not.

The secretary shook her tight, salon-chestnut curls. "Every Wednesday before he comes into the office, he spends a few minutes at the wall honoring the agents who have gone before him." The woman was in her mid-forties. Wakefield decided the secretary's perky nose helped her achieve a youthful look despite the fine lines around her green eyes that betrayed her stress over life's details. Her sunken cheeks made her look malnourished rather than model-perfect.

Cravits referred to the Book of Honor stationed at the marble wall in the Agency lobby. Agents killed in service are memorialized on the wall with an etched, five-pointed star. The blue-gray marble wall reminded every agent and support staff member who walked into the building of the gravity of his or her job. And the permanence of a mistake. The death of an agent in service was always a crushing blow to the families of the CIA. Details of the death were rarely shared. Only a name and year inscribed in ink in the Book of Honor, corresponding to an unnumbered star, marked a place of grief. Sometimes not even a name.

Judah didn't find it unusual that Director Dietz would honor those men. He'd known more than half of them personally in his tenure with the Agency.

"Everyone has a religion." Wakefield thoughtfully crossed her ankles under her chair. "It just looks different on some people."

Ms Cravits nodded slowly and frowned. She pursed her thin lips until they disappeared altogether. "I suppose you're correct." The woman adjusted her gaze back to her computer screen.

Wakefield found herself thinking about Dietz as she waited. Richmond Dietz's looks were very well suited to the field agent job that had begun his career 34 years earlier. He was an unremarkable man with medium brown hair, now laced with silver, wide-set, hazel brown eyes, a face that was neither fat nor thin and a small mustache that had gone out of fashion at least a decade earlier. He was a focused man. The CIA was his life, black ops were his family, and each clandestine mission, his new friend. He had the arrogant type of intelligence that never admitted failure, only temporary setbacks in a soon-to-be-brilliant plan. And now, Judah added to her mental image of her sometimes-boss: the wall was his place of worship. In her experience, the idea of God was the only thing that Dietz feared.

Life was an intricate game of chess to him. And he was sure he was winning.

The man occupying her thoughts pushed open the glass door with the Agency seal embossed on it and entered his secretary's office. "Lieutenant Commander Judah Wakefield." He strode over and took her hand in both of his. "Good to see you back in uniform, and with blue eyes again," he commented in a friendly tone.

Judah smiled as large as the stitches would allow. "It's good to be home, sir. There was a little too much sand in Afghanistan for my taste." She chuckled, taking care not to stretch her stitches.

"I thought you military types thrived on getting down in the muck and dusty sand." Smiling, he released her hand to pick up his briefcase again.

"Not all of us!" Wakefield pronounced definitively. The two of them laughed, and Ms Cravits looked up with a bemused smile.

Dietz opened his office door and nodded Wakefield in ahead of him. The light was already on and a couple of starched white shirts hung in clear dry cleaning bags on the lower rung of the coat rack by the door. "Would you get us some coffee, Ms Cravits?" Dietz requested as he shrugged out of his khaki-brown, lined trench coat. "She makes the best coffee in the world, and I ought to know," Dietz said to Judah.

"I remember," Judah said politely. She didn't miss the slightly triumphant rise of the secretary's nose.

The woman rose stiffly from her shiny, cherrywood desk. "Of course, Director. How do you take it, Miss Wakefield?"

"One cream, two blues, please." Wakefield moved deeper into the decadent office.

"I'm expecting Travis Green and Jay Woodstock. Please show them in when they arrive." Dietz arranged.

Ms Cravits nodded mutely and disappeared down the hall.

Dietz's office was attractively Old World, decorated in rich wood with detail work around the high ceilings, windows and chair rails. Appearing antique, reproduction Rembrandts framed in heavy gold hung under spotlights on either side of a stacked-stone, gas fireplace. A heavy, overstuffed, leather living room suite with three extra chairs filled one corner of the large office. Windows brightened the two walls forming the opposite corner, behind Dietz's fully cleared, L-shaped desk.

"I didn't realize we'd have company." Wakefield sank into the loveseat and placed her black Italian leather briefcase with a hand-tooled handle on the seat cushion next to her.

"New company policy," Dietz explained. He flipped a wall switch and a fire sprang to life. "A team of two to four persons must be present at all briefings and debriefings." Dietz sounded like he was quoting.

"Mm," Wakefield nodded. She relaxed back into the seat to wait for the coffee and the other men. "When are you going to ask your secretary to dinner?" She pried as she pressed the smirk out of her lips with her fingertips.

"You are a meddler." Dietz jabbed his first finger toward Wakefield, who didn't miss the slightest bunching of the director's cheeks. "I told you before, I don't have time to date."

Wakefield turned in her seat to look more directly at Dietz. "But you need to get married. You need a life. And she wouldn't take much dating. She is half in love with you already." Judah pressed mischievously.

Dietz rummaged through several manila envelopes in his desk's lap drawer. "She's around me all day. She needs to go to her own home so she can get a break."

Judah decided to drop it, for now. "How did you know I changed my eye color?" she asked.

"Satellite photos," Dietz returned to the seating area with a new package of 90-minute audiotapes to record their session and a half-dozen, high-resolution photos from her recent trip to Afghanistan, which he handed over to her.

She flipped through the 8x10 glossies. The few shots included the six people who had made it out, at various times during their escape. There was a close up of her after she doubled back the black Muslim burka veil over her hair. Her eyes were Mississippi mud brown and her cheek sported red streaks of infection.

"Ugh!" Judah grimaced. "This is a horrible picture. You should burn it!" She spat and then caught her breath as her shuffle uncovered a photo of her partner on the mission, LCDR David Rivers. He was talking animatedly to someone who was out of the shot, and his large grin showed off even, white teeth. A lively twinkle sparked in his blue-green eyes. "Who is Rivers talking to?" Wakefield asked. Dietz would know what had been cut out of the picture to close in on Rivers.

"You," Dietz answered without looking.

Wakefield sucked in her breath again. The picture captured the essence of her mission partner, David Rivers, as she had come to know him: strong in body and spirit, controlled in manner, comfortable with danger, handsome in feature, relaxed with power, and humorous in tension. Rivers was a U.S. Navy SEAL, and he wore it well.

"That last one is my personal favorite," Dietz said.

Wakefield reluctantly flipped to the next picture. It was oriented horizontally, a screen capture of her having taken LT Sands down. She stood bent over him on the ground with one foot on his neck. "How did you get these?" she queried, confused. "I thought the satellite was off-line for maintenance. The navy said they couldn't locate us to send in an extraction team."

Ms Cravits rapped twice, and entered carrying a silver tea tray with two steaming porcelain cups of coffee. Dietz continued speaking. "It was inaccessible when we needed to locate you guys. I went back and traced your movements afterward." Cravits set down the tray and backed out of the room. "This is just a 'best of' series of photos." Dietz said and chuckled at Wakefield's look of dismay.

Wakefield and Dietz talked for 15 minutes before a thin man with shaggy brown hair atop an angular face poked his head cautiously inside the cracked door. "Dietz? Julia said to come straight in." He pushed the door open further when the director motioned him in. Dietz rose from an armchair near Judah. "Sorry we're late. The 6 AM Homeland Security briefing ran over."

Director Dietz made introductions all around. Travis Green reminded her of a 14-year-old who had yet to grow into his arms and legs, though he looked to be in his early forties.

Jay Woodstock was the top profiler in the CIA, Wakefield's counterpart as she worked at Naval Intelligence in the same job. His black suit, similar to the other men's, did little to conceal his powerful chest. His broad nose showed more than a little Native American blood in his heritage. Woodstock was included in the meeting so he could add to the CIA's list of wanted persons and further define those al-Qaeda members already menace enough to be among his current sketches.

Green had brought his own tall coffee in a Cervantes' to-go cup, which he sipped constantly. Wakefield crinkled her nose; Green couldn't be getting more than a taste with each noisome slurp. Woodstock opened his fine black leather briefcase and pulled out a 20-ounce bottle of Mountain Dew. "The breakfast beverage of more Gen-X'ers," he smirked at Dietz's and Wakefield's amused exchange. Woodstock sounded like a commercial. He unscrewed the cap and took a long pull from the bottle while Dietz set up the recording equipment on the coffee table with the new audiotape.

He clicked the red record button on. "Official debrief of Operation 76598 for Lieutenant Commander Judah Wakefield. Operation completed December 25, 2001. Present today, January 2, 2002, 10:13 AM are, myself, Director of Counterintelligence of the CIA, Richmond Dietz and, please state your name," Dietz looked at Woodstock first who repeated his rank and full name.

When Dietz looked next at Green, something shifted in her mind. Even as she spoke her own name rank and naval duty assignment clearly for the tape, she had her first nudging in her brain that this was not going to be the usual debrief she had come to expect with Dietz.

"This interview is taking place in Director Dietz's office." Dietz concluded the opening information for the record.

"Our biggest concern on the outset is Arafeh Filasek." Woodstock stated firmly. Dietz had not even had time to take a breath after his opening statement. Wakefield raised an eyebrow, for Woodstock's age and soda preference, he was all business when it came time for work.

LCDR Wakefield shrugged as she settled into the same professionalism. *Why would they want to profile a dead man?* It seemed odd to curl up with a coffee on deep leather furniture, while discussing matters of national security in terms that might be better suited for a senate hearing room. Usually Dietz and Wakefield ate dinner together with a cassette recorder as she told her story, but this was too high-profile a case. She looked at the director to take her cue from him. He nodded tightly once.

"Filasek lead the party who met us fifteen klicks outside Delaram." Wakefield began at the first meeting in country. "He spoke barely accented American English; He told us he was schooled in Cairo. And I don't know if you could tell from the sat pictures, but he was unusually short. He may have been 5 foot 2 inches, if he stretched. Filasek was short-tempered when we met," she gazed at an Iberian Peninsula-shaped spot on the creamy carpet in thought, "but he would get a lot angrier before we were gone." She hinted softly at the story's ending.

Woodstock spoke up. "Excuse me, Commander. You are speaking of Filasek in the past tense. Is he dead?" Wakefield's eyes darted to Dietz's, and she froze with the last sip of her coffee halfway to her lips. Woodstock went on oblivious, "We were told that someone was pretty confident that Filasek he did not get caught in either of the blasts, his villa or arsenal. It doesn't sound as though you agree."

Judah glanced from Woodstock to Green and landed on Dietz. "What?" Her voice came out deadly calm. No one said a word. *Get a hold of yourself,* she commanded silently to quell her rising panic. She squirmed up straighter on the couch and leaned forward.

"Okay," she said slowly, "give me a minute to think." Wakefield closed her eyes to concentrate under the staring eyes of the three CIA men. Her mind performed a fast-forward blur through the final hours of the ground operation. "I suppose it is possible," she wavered, "but I would not begin to guess at the probabilities. Filasek would have had to have been at a third location or driving between the air strike and the explosion in the mountain. There's no way he could have planned it. *We* didn't even know when Rivers would detonate the bomb he rigged up." Her eyes flashed from man to man, trying to read their eyes and body language as she synthesized the new possibilities.

"There was at least one man who escaped. He had an old Chevy truck. But he is dead now." Wakefield frowned.

"Are you positive that the man is dead, and that he is not Filasek?" Green asked moving his paper coffee cup to his mouth again.

"He's dead." Her voice dropped into its emotionless, cold tone. "I helped carry his body. My partner snapped his neck when the man charged me with a gun. And I know Filasek, up close and personal. He is the one who did this to me." She pointed to her right cheek. "The man Rivers killed was not Filasek." Her voice modulated back to a business as usual tone. "But that man *knew* Filasek. He knew all about al-Qaeda funding. He said he was Filasek's driver and heard Filasek talk to bin Laden on the phone." Wakefield nodded. "I suppose if his driver survived, initially," she looked up, "it's *possible* that Filasek was in the vehicle with him."

"Oh, man," Woodstock smacked his leg, "I would have loved to talk to the driver that heard bin Laden."

"Yes, well, so sorry. Forgive me if I am all you have." Wakefield edged into sarcasm at his thoughtlessness. "He was going to kill me, and Rivers stopped him. It's not like he gave us much of a choice." She heard her voice start to rise and quickly controlled it. "Do you know the source of your tip?" she asked Dietz.

He nodded. "Your partner."

"David? Um, you've talked to Commander Rivers?"

"Yes. He seemed sure Filasek is still alive."

2

A pair of stubby fingers with short clipped nails flew over the keyboard of a laptop computer sitting on an ornate bamboo desk. A breeze from an open balcony door fluttered the edges of a short stack of printed pages pinned under the weight of a new box of .308 slugs.

The clicking of keys stilled and the chair creaked as the typist pushed back. Black eyes scanned the missive. "Yes. It is time we got underway." Lips buried in a fuzzy black beard and mustache spoke in his native Farsi.

"I hope you are ready for this, Dovlatabadi." Arafeh Filasek, age 27, smoothed his beard in a downward stroke with his right hand. He stared at the turquoise waters of the Mediterranean off his balcony remembering the training exercises he had put to the man who was about to receive his e-mail. Forty-two men buried over the course of five years. Each kill honing marksmanship and invisibility skills for this one. This man would be number 43, just like the number of his presidency.

It was not the man himself that Filasek hated, only what he represented.

"Terrific!" Wakefield groaned and touched her forehead. "Why didn't he mention it to me?" She looked from Green to Woodstock to Dietz who

15

shrugged. "When did he tell you this? He's been on an op since we left the ship." She tried to justify David Rivers' lack of communication. She had hoped that he would call. Or something.

"*He* didn't tell us." Dietz told her in an almost bored timbre. "He mentioned it to Admiral Graham, because he's running the war from the USS *Reprisal*'s CIC (Combat Information Center). They sent in some ground troops from Lieutenant Colonel Justice's marine base to see if they could locate him. Graham told us."

"My dad?" her voice rose again. "Rivers told my *dad* that he thought Filasek was alive, and he didn't bother to mention it to me?" She narrowed her eyes at Dietz and unconsciously reached up to finger her scared cheek. "And neither did my father! I talked to both of them, several times over the two days we were back on the *Reprisal* for debriefing with the navy. Why didn't they say something, anything? Why didn't you?" she asked Dietz. Wakefield could feel the angry sea in her eyes. She hoped the three men in front of her drowned in it.

She plunked down her empty coffee cup in its saucer more forcefully than necessary and pushed it back onto the coffee table. She was breathing too heavy, forcing the air through her nose. "This perturbs me greatly."

All the while, her mind was processing what this little revelation would mean to her. There was a spark of something akin to fear in her chest.

Wakefield glared at the three men, as if they could have changed anything. Travis Green spoke up with raised eyebrows that disappeared into his bushy hair. "If you would care to," he took a tiny nervous sip of his coffee, and spoke in a low voice, "we have some anger management counseling available." He gave a tight smile. "It's in-house; it wouldn't go on your military record."

The force of her gaze now pierced the lanky man. She held his eyes captive with hers, unrelenting, until she finished speaking. "I do not need counseling." She spoke overly slow to the man. "You've been stuck in this office too long. I'm not angry, however, since I am sure you are not aware of my position, I will forgive the rudeness." She schooled her features. "Let me explain it to you, Mister Green." Judah realized she was too worked up about this, and she tried to separate her emotion professionally. "I despise being kept out of the loop! Especially when my life could be in danger. I have just been told, more than a week after the fact, that a dangerous and very well-connected man that I perceived to be dead, oh yes, well, he is probably alive!"

Her voice, straining to come through her constricted throat, sounded irritatingly high, even to her. Green was frozen in his seat. He could not bring his paper coffee cup fully to his lips. "Let's go back to something you said—" Dietz began.

Woodstock interrupted him just as Wakefield rolled her eyes. Dietz sounded like a counselor himself. "Why would your life be in danger?" He got right to the point that she knew Dietz was coming to. All three men leaned in for her answer.

Wakefield took a calming breath. She obviously was not walking in as much forgiveness toward Filasek as she had first thought. She spoke detached and calculated. "Filasek was, is," she corrected immediately, "a ferocious man. Last time we met, he exploded at me with an ash-covered knife, and slashed my face—for not wearing the religious veil, the burka. I was in his home, keeping his son alive at the time," she told the men, taking in their varying degrees of concern. "This behavior is completely opposed to the Arabic cultural norm of hospitality and protection while serving as a host. His hate runs deeper than religious fervor against Americans and women. I am both, in case you haven't noticed. Plus I destroyed his house and had his family killed in a bombing run. Whatever the root cause of his rage, he seems to have fixated on me while we were in Afghanistan.

"Filasek accumulated almost as many munitions as one of our large arsenals here in the States. Some were Russian, probably left over from when the USSR came apart, and some were Chinese, however,

17

some...were American. Made in the USA! He has access to us. To me. I have extensive, up-close knowledge of him, his former anthrax plant, and his financing operation. I called in the information that led to the air strike that cost him his family. If he's still alive as you suggest, he will come after me to have his revenge."

Judah rubbed her throat. The muscles felt so tight from holding her voice steady as she profiled Filasek. Why had she had not assessed the man's case against her until she was live with Dietz? She had been able to deliver her assessment with deadly calm. Calm at least by the last few sentences. "I don't know precisely when this became a personal war, gentlemen, but you can bet that it is."

The long morning stretched on, as Wakefield expounded on everything she had observed about Filasek and his kingdom. All three men separately invited her to join them for lunch at the mid-day break. She declined. "I'm going to grab some drive-thru and sit in the quiet of my car."

"If you're that concerned about Filasek's revenge, you should stay with a crowd." Dietz eyes turned down. She felt his empathy.

"Not today." She just wanted to be alone, to be Judah, not LCDR Wakefield, for a moment.

Judah exited the office first. A suited man with fashionable horn-rimmed glasses and black spiky hair stood up from one of the leather chairs in Ms Cravits' office. A #10 envelope tipped in his hand. Wakefield immediately felt herself switched back to professional mode. She knew he was there for her.

The young man indeed made a beeline for her as she stopped in the doorframe. "Lieutenant Commander Wakefield?" he asked in a deep voice that seemed ill-suited for his youthful appearance.

She tapped her plastic, pin-on nametag with a natural, buffed fingernail. "That's me."

"Michael Blackstone from Congressman Silver's office." He introduced himself arrogantly. Your presence is requested at a congressional sub-committee meeting to be held tomorrow. The letter will explain." He handed her a sealed, un-addressed long envelope. The return address area carried a raised congressional seal in blue and gold. "They want testimony concerning the recent intelligence that led to you recommending an air strike and the subsequent massacre in Afghanistan."

Wakefield did not allow her features to reflect her ire. He was probably an intern, fresh out of grad school with governmental-power stars in his eyes. "Very well, Michael Blackstone. I will be there."

She sighed after the glass door shut behind him. "Well, that blows the rest of the work week. I am going to be in the dog house with Admiral Tamburillo when I finally get back." Wakefield let the correspondence in her fist fall heavily to her thigh.

With lunch from a more-American-than-Chinese drive-thru in her lap, Wakefield gazed at the little bit of greenery she found in the evergreens in a small neighborhood play yard. She had eaten here two summers earlier, right after she had been shot and had to spend more time at Dietz's office. Plastic fork in hand, she asked God to bless her food and, "Please give me the grace to get through the rest of this debriefing today without blowing up at the profiler or the other guy with no manners," she blew out her breath through pursed lips. "And help, *please* help, with this congressional thing." She closed her eyes and said tiredly, "Amen." It had already been a long day.

From the tone of the letter which she had read at red lights and again in the food line, Wakefield could not squash the apprehension about her part in the hearing. She could not determine if they thought the air strike was overkill and they wanted an explanation, or if she would be testifying against someone higher up who had made the final decision. She shook her head. "How did they hear about the air strike over the holidays and already convene a committee?" she muttered and thumped the steering wheel in irritation. Bureaucracy was tectonic-plate slow, until there was someone to persecute.

"I didn't want to call in the F-18 Hornets anyway." She had requested ground troops brought in for a specific assault. It was ADM

Graham, Wakefield's stepfather, the point man running the war on terrorism in the Middle East, who had forwarded the intelligence of an anthrax plant in the house of a future Afghani leader to the Secretary of the Navy. The SecNav had made the final judgment. Only the three of them were involved. It did not bode well for any of them.

She was sure of one thing: The congressmen had questions. Congressmen always had questions.

"God, I am so tired." Judah sighed as she maneuvered her mustang between a yellow Beemer and a rusty El Camino in her apartment parking lot at 1735 hours that evening. A lieutenant with short, dark hair in a khaki class B uniform was knocking on the door of her second floor apartment as Wakefield walked the carpeted hallway.

"Ma'am!" the young woman's countenance brightened significantly. "I am Lieutenant Jones with the Judge Advocate's office. I wondered if I could have a moment of your time."

A navy lawyer. *What could JAG want with me?* Judah nodded stiffly without saying a word. The lieutenant's voice did not give a clue as to the contents of her business, but it had a professional distance that made Judah uneasy. A visit from the Judge Advocate General's office was rarely a good thing.

Wakefield unlocked her front door. She had time to pray only, *God, I need more grace,* before inviting the officer inside. She flipped on the light switch and gave the room a quick glance.

Everything appeared in order. After today's revelation of Filasek being alive, she didn't want to take any chances with unexpected guests. "Come on in, Lieutenant. It seems like everyone in the Greater D.C. area wants a word with me today." She gave the lieutenant a tired smile. Wakefield dropped her purse at the door and hung her coat and cover on the coat rack. "Do you want a cup of tea?" she invited.

The younger officer shook her head and waved her left hand back and forth. "Oh, no. Don't go to any trouble for me. I shouldn't be here long, ma'am." She sounded a little off balance. Wakefield felt a smile tug at her lips. Apparently, JAG investigators did not receive invitations to tea very often.

"It's no trouble," Wakefield assured her. "I'm making a pot for myself whether you want any or not." She kicked off her black pumps and wiggled her tight toes. "I've had a day!" She sighed and motioned the JAG lawyer to join her in the small kitchen area. The younger woman might be a naval officer, but after the fiasco with John Garner in Afghanistan being a planted spy, she was not going to trust anyone right away. Nor was she going to leave her back exposed.

"Then I'd love a cup, ma'am. Thank you." The lieutenant frowned and ran her fingers nervously through the ends of her short hair. "I'm afraid I am going to make your day a little worse."

Wakefield went through her cupboards gathering teacups, saucers, spoons, real sugar and cream. She arranged two places neatly across from each other on the lacey tablecloth. "Can it wait until we sit down?"

The lieutenant gave an amused chuckle and nodded. "Of course."

Her brown, steaming beverage sat untouched since LT Jones had begun to ask questions. "So you are accusing me of sexual harassment, conduct unbecoming an officer, and negligent homicide due to culpable inefficiency?" Wakefield's voice was silky smooth.

"No, ma'am. I am not accusing you of any of these things. There was an anonymous hotline call on Friday, and we have to check out all possible infractions. I was assigned to *investigate* the complaints only," Jones explained.

Wakefield's mind raced. Who would have accused her of such things? It couldn't be a joke, right? The caller, when identified, could then be prosecuted. He would be found. It had to be a man, right? With sexual harassment charges. "Who knows these days?" Wakefield mumbled.

"Sorry, what was that?" Jones cocked her ear. Her pen was poised above the yellow legal pad to take notes.

LCDR Wakefield drew her attention back to the table from the watercolor of tulips on her wall that she had been staring a hole through. "I cannot think of a single instance when I could have even been misread concerning the sexual harassment charge. I maintain a strict code of conduct, and I hold myself to a high standard of not even presenting an appearance of impropriety." Judah snorted in disgust. "That charge makes me think the whole call is bogus."

"The dates of the incidents in question are from only a week or so ago. December 20 through 24. Where were you on those dates?"

Wakefield shook her head in a small motion. "I was in Afghanistan." Her eyes squinted. "I can assure you, under no circumstances, did I sexually harass anyone in Afghanistan."

"What were you doing in Afghanistan, ma'am?" Jones asked.

"It's classified."

The younger officer's eyebrows shot up and a look of disbelief crossed her face. The hardened mask of distance from when she was at the door, settled back in place. "I have level two security clearance," she stated evenly.

Wakefield nodded and quietly studied the tulips again as she sorted through the Afghanistan trip for the information she could share with the lieutenant concerning the op.

"Your answer, ma'am?"

"I was there to extract four military personnel and two American citizens from an Afghan prison camp." She gave the JAG her official cover story.

The lieutenant did not even write it down. "What else did you do, ma'am?" A single slim eyebrow arched high. "Hog-tie bin Laden to his camel and grab his missiles and turn him over to the Secretary of Defense?"

Wakefield narrowed her eyes at the impertinent words. She turned coldly to the younger JAG officer. "Why the sudden change of attitude, Lieutenant Jones?" she asked much more calmly than she felt.

LT Jones gave her a pointed look. "There *are* no prison camps in Afghanistan, ma'am." Her voice was low, but not quite accusatory. "Would you care to restate your response to the charge?"

"On the contrary, Lieutenant, there is at least one prison in the southwest quadrant of the Afghanistan wilderness. Or was, until we blew it up on our way out of town." Wakefield could not suppress a tiny smile. "It was a series of caves and I was held there myself for the days in question."

"Okay, ma'am. So there is no evidence because you blew it up after you escaped." The lieutenant's disbelief turned blatant. "Convenient." Jones began to scribble down the story in black ink. "Anything you would care to add? By the way, can anyone corroborate your story?" Jones did not even look up as she continued writing.

"Sure," Wakefield said easily. "Lieutenant Commander David Rivers. He's a SEAL trainer out at Coronado. But wait," Wakefield held up her hand. "He was sent directly on a training exercise in South America. So you can't get him for a while. Um," Judah thought. "Marine Captain Martinez, a helo co-pilot on an LHA, the *Siapan,* was there. He's back on his ship. Major Crenshaw is in recovery at Ramstein Air Force Base in Germany. You could call him. Lieutenant (j.g.) Lewis and Lieutenant Sands—" Wakefield paused. *Lieutenant Sands,* she thought, *he could be the one behind the allegations. He was mad enough.* "They are both back flying off the *Ike.*"

"So there is no one in the States *now* who can testify to your story, ma'am?"

"I suppose not. Is that unusual in your line of work, Lieutenant?"

"What about the civilian who was down. You have accounted for five of the six men you went after." The lieutenant delved for details, trying to pin down Wakefield's cover story.

"Actually, if you will recall, I said there were two civilians. Lieutenant Commander Rivers was my partner."

"I'm glad you cleared that up." She snorted without looking up. "I was having trouble with a SEAL being captured and held in a prison cave."

"Watch your tone, Lieutenant. I am still your superior." Wakefield warned. "One of the civilians was a plant. A sleeper or spy groomed to enter life in the U.S. The other was a female reporter. Jesse Beane. Neither of them made it out." Wakefield felt her face flinch.

"By that you mean?"

Wakefield pinned her with icy blue eyes. "They are *dead*, Lieutenant. That is what that means!"

"Oh! So you deny the sexual harassment but not the negligent homicide?" Jones was undaunted, gaining momentum. She scribbled furiously now.

"Actually, I believe the term would be the 'casualties of war'." Wakefield stared into her still full, cold cup of tea. The liquid had chilled at the same rate as her insides during the JAGman interview. "I think it is time for you to go, Lieutenant Jones." Wakefield rose to show the lieutenant to the door.

"But you have not answered the charges of conduct unbecoming," she began as she readied her briefcase for departure.

"I think that would be a better question for my lawyer. Please see that I'm assigned adequate council." Wakefield handed the brown-haired woman her cover and coat. "I'm sure I'll be seeing you." Judah closed the door behind the investigator.

LCDR Wakefield dumped her cold tea down the drain. It was not appealing now. On autopilot, she went about warming a microwave dinner. She threw herself into the deep cushions on her couch in the living room while her dinner cooked. "God, this is as much as I can stand. Please, no more trouble today." She sighed and dropped her head back against the cushions. What a day!

Before the microwave timer dinged the telephone began to ring. It rang 12 times, and Wakefield had sat down at the table to eat before the caller hung up. She was not taking calls this evening.

3

L CDR Rivers was sequestered with his four-man unit and five other units of SEAL Team Seven in a yellowed concrete block classroom they had converted into a tactical planning room. He walked back and forth at the front of the room as he listened to the report from Petty Officer Foster. Topographical and street maps of both country and region hung, pinned to the corkboard wall. A detailed city map and an enlargement of the fifteen city blocks that surrounded their target, hung against the white board from plastic clips. The target was a wharf warehouse at the water's edge. It was not often that the Teams were deployed inside city limits, especially in metropolitan areas as populated as this one.

Rivers laid down the pointer he had been using to illustrate the route of Plan B's escape as Foster had narrated. Rivers cleared his throat. "I do not need to tell you how important it is that we get this done correctly. Our orders came down from the top. 'Neutralize this weapons shipping warehouse.' Secretary of Defense Shulman does not want another shipment to arrive in Pakistan." Another SEAL Team would rendezvous, unexpectedly of course, with the ship that carried the container of weapons already on the water.

Under Rivers' direction, the men had been using the morning hours of each day to work up conceivable plans for the assault. They had two complete, workable plans already. A third idea was on its way to completion. The afternoons and nights were hands-on training times.

26

The kind that went beyond what they learned in BUD/S—SEAL training school.

LCDR David Rivers, in his khaki naval uniform identical to all the other men's, draped his six-foot-three frame over a barstool. He ran a hand over his recently #2-razor shaved hair. All of his proper insignia, including the highly honored trident pin, were in perfect order.

"Get some grub. Take 45 minutes. A good dinner, people. I want to get the details from individual units in place, so we can begin rehearsals at 0100 hours sharp." He looked over the group. "Dismissed." The entire group came to their feet and stiffened before turning to leave by the door at the back of the room.

The SEAL's original assessment of the newly trained team members of ten days earlier was turning out to be accurate. The team was green. However, in their favor, most of them seemed to realize their vulnerability and carefully weighed his suggestions and correction.

A new lieutenant commander, Will Nicholas, was mentoring under Rivers to run an op of this magnitude. The red-haired man began to fold the maps to put away information that had to remain secret in order to save lives on their operation. "Go get your food, Nicholas. I have a phone call to make first." Rivers told the man. Nicholas raised his eyebrows but did not comment. Phone calls could compromise a mission location.

All was quiet as the heels of LCDR Nicholas' dress shoes died away. Rivers sat down at one of the desks. He shook his head as he hoped that Judah Wakefield would not be the death of him—literally. He could tell his game was slightly off. It took him a fraction of a second longer to react to the details his men suggested. A quarter-second in a shooting match with a weapons runner could mean the difference between life and death.

Thoughts of his partner niggled at the back of his mind. He had decided that whether they ever worked together again or not, in his mind, she would remain forever his partner. He frowned. He didn't approve, but he certainly understood the navy philosophy of a girl in every port. Women could not risk an operation, if they were not on a man's mind.

He dialed an international operator on his cellular phone. It was configured to work anywhere in the world, and he was glad to have one again. His previous SatFone had been crushed in the collapse of a cave ceiling on his last op. "I need the number for a Judah A. Wakefield in D.C., ma'am. Please check all variations. It could be under J. or J.A. as well." He waited 20 seconds for her to search her computer database.

His pen was poised to jot down her number. "Hm." He grunted. "No listing at all?" he confirmed, disheartened. *Ok, backup plan*.

Rivers looked at his watch, picked up his cover, then locked and bolted the door on his way out. He had enough time to drop by administration to do some research. A plan was bubbling to the surface of his mind, and he found himself whistling as he dropped some coins into a vending machine for a cold drink. He turned away, then on second thought, he deposited another three quarters. A flirtatious man bearing gifts was more likely to get help with his search than a man smiling alone. The second soda dropped into the slot with a metallic clunk.

Twenty minutes later and one cold drink lighter, LCDR Rivers walked out of the admin building with the phone number, hand written on a sticky note between his fingers.

He sat down on the cold concrete steps to place the call. It rang and rang. "She should be home by now," Rivers grumbled. He hoped everything was all right. It was 1955 hours in D.C. She didn't seem the type to go out late in the evening in the middle of the week. Twelve rings later, Rivers hung up. Her machine never picked up for him to leave a message. Not that he had anything in particular to say. He just wanted to hear her voice.

Rivers grabbed a roast beef sandwich from the chow line and ate it on his way back to the classroom, while he prayed for Wakefield.

He could not get her off his mind and later would not be an appropriate time to pray.

His men were prompt. All of them were seated, waiting for him. "Let's get down to business," he said. "Is everything on our list available for our rehearsal tonight?"

"No, sir," P.O. Grantham, one of the enlisted men spoke up. The petty officer was heading up the appropriations and had spent four hours gathering the gear needed for the five teams of two men who would be going inside during the op. "We are going to have to substitute some items."

"Well, men, here is your introduction to improvising. You will find it necessary in every mission in which you participate." Rivers told the group. "Let's figure out what we can scrounge up." Grantham read off the missing five items and they wracked their brains. In under an hour, they had come up with a way to accomplish their goal without the items or found a substitution for each thing. "Get some rack time," Rivers ordered. "It will be a long night for all of you."

Twenty brand new SEALS were here for the warehouse black op. There were six more with experience, but only two were seasoned. A group of 28 men that would take out a couple hundred arms dealers that were wreaking havoc on the servicemen in the Middle East. SEAL Team Seven would catch the weapons at the source, before they were loaded with Chinese ammunition.

Lower Level Congressional Sub-committee Hearing Room B-8
Thursday 3 January 2002
0947 hours

A white-mustached bailiff came to the door that LCDR Wakefield had been watching for the past 107 minutes. "Wakefield," he hollered crassly. There were only three people in the hall. He need not call so loudly.

When she entered the heavy French doors, Wakefield looked around in surprise. From the opulence of the marble hallway with arched alcoves where chiseled white marble busts of famous men and women resided, she expected more drama in the meeting room. She had waited on one of several dozen tufted velveteen settees. However, the hearing room was lined with wooden benches that looked as uncomfortable as church pews.

It looked like most of the courtrooms she had ever been in, save the extra-long judge's table where the panel of five committee members listened to testimony and asked questions. Instead of a table for the prosecution and for the defense, there was one polished, wooden table with a microphone pointed directly to the one chair behind it, facing the congressmen.

The skinny bailiff led Wakefield to the hot seat.

Wakefield noted a television reporter she had seen before squirming with nine others scattered among the benches. Because he had been admitted entrance, Judah surmised that Congress was interested only in the navy rescue mission. The CIA objective was still classified super-secret. She focused on those details as she stood beside the uncushioned chair.

"Do you swear to tell the truth?" Congressman Silver asked. He was presiding over the hearing. As his name suggested, he had silver hair, just a fringe of laurel leaves around the base of his liver-spotted scalp. He was overweight, but his large suit coat covered much of his bulk. He had a round face that would have looked jolly except for his sour expression.

"I do." Judah scanned the faces of the men who would be questioning her. She stopped all the way to her left. Congressman DeFore. Her insides clenched. Would he be completely against her after their run-in at the charity Christmas Ball? She hoped he could remain objective.

Congressman Silver led her in the preliminary questions to establish her presence in Afghanistan during the air strike and the time leading up to it.

"This seventeen-hour period that you were separated from Lieutenant Commander Rivers," Silver tapped a piece of paper in front of him. "Can anyone verify your presence on the estate of Arafeh Filasek?"

Wakefield's mind raced. What were they digging for? "Well, there was the little boy, Nasser. I talked to his mother as well. She was Filasek's first wife. The guards who brought me from the cave saw me, but we did not speak because they did not know I spoke Farsi and Arabic. Filasek saw me as well. Oh, yes, there was an old man in Nasser's room for a while, too. He looked to be Nasser's great grandfather."

"And how many of those can we call in to testify that you were present at the villa the entire seventeen hours?"

"I hear Filasek is still running around." She felt the trap jaws closing in on her, and she did not like the direction in which this hearing was moving. Something must have happened during the time she had been separated from Rivers. Congressman Silver's accusatory tone did not help either. So far, no one else on the panel had been able to get a question in. "I'm sure that the marines searching for his location would appreciate any and all help you have to offer," Wakefield added to her statement.

The few members of the press and observers in the gallery teetered a little at her remark. She had not meant it to be funny; it just came out a little sarcastic.

Silver banged his gavel once for order and spoke to Wakefield sharply. "You will answer the questions put to you with no extemporaneous comments, Lieutenant Commander," he instructed.

"Sorry, sir," she said without being sorry at all.

He nodded. "Why can the others who saw you not be subpoenaed to testify before this committee?"

She gave a little look of consternation before answering, "They are all dead, sir. They were killed in the strike."

"The air strike *you* ordered."

"I did not recommend the air strike. I recommended an assault using ground troops, so that the women and children would not be casualties." Wakefield tried to be patient.

"Yes, that is what you say, but you were making the recommendation to your step-father, Admiral Graham, were you not?"

"Yes," she answered slowly.

"He would know, from your tone of voice, what you *really* wanted to do, without resorting to you spelling it out for him. Now, was there *actually* an anthrax lab in the basement at Arafeh Filasek's villa, Miss Wakefield?" His tone was more debasing than it had ever been.

"Hold on just a minute, Congressman Silver!" They could insult her integrity all they wanted, but she would not stand for a good leader like her father being insulted, especially on record, and when he was not here to defend himself. While it bothered her, it also sat funny on the edge of her mind. They *wouldn't* accuse him of such a war crime without him being present.

It was only a split second later that she continued. "Are you accusing Vice Admiral Graham and I of colluding to blow up an ancient monastery full of innocent people to cover up some action, which I can't figure out, that must have happened while I was there? Because if you are, you are dead wrong and treading on libelous grounds. Sir," she added hotly.

The room exploded with noise. The reporters whispered and scribbled her statement. Someone asked loud enough for the whole room to hear, "What? What did she say?"

Silver gaveled them back to order. He did not correct her outburst. He seemed to realize that he was out of line. "I understand you were tired the morning you arrived at your prison cave. Did you sleep the night before?"

The committee member on Wakefield's far right side leaned over to the man next to him and whispered.

"I got about two hours, sir" Wakefield was defensive. "I was caring for Nasser, Filasek's son, who had contracted anthrax—in his own basement, I might add."

"Did you see this alleged lab personally?"

"No, Nasser told me about it."

"Did you ever leave the villa?"

"Only when I was transported to the cave." Judah scanned the faces again. DeFore's face was an impassive mask. The two men on the right seemed to be at odds with Silver, at least with his technique.

"Mr Chairman?" the man on the end spoke up in the brief silence. Wakefield examined his nameplate. *Smitherman*, it said. "This committee would like to know, since you are continuing this line of questioning, how you came across the information concerning Lieutenant Commander Wakefield's state of rest upon her arrival at the prison cave, sir." Smitherman was by far the youngest member of the panel. Wakefield remembered hearing that this was just his sophomore term in office.

"You are correct, I did not." Silver paused and the room silenced waiting for him to continue. He waited so long, it did not seem that he would go on. "My intern took a statement from a lieutenant who was there." He spat rebelliously. It was obvious that he had not wanted to reveal his source, but he did not have the jurisdiction to keep it a secret.

Sands, Wakefield knew instantly.

"May I go on with Miss Wakefield's testimony?" he asked needlessly. If they had said no, he would have plowed right over them anyway. That was just Silver's way. It was how he had gotten his seat in Congress.

"Are you familiar with a Mr Callahan Wilder?" Silver questioned her.

"The American ambassador to Pakistan?" she asked. What did he have to do with anything?

"Do you know of his whereabouts on 19 December?" Silver asked evenly.

33

"Pakistan?" Judah guessed.

"No. He was in a tiny town called Delaram in Afghanistan."

"Well, tiny is right," Wakefield said under her breath. Unfortunately, she was in front of the microphone and her voice carried out to the recorder, which drew Silver's attention to it as well.

"So you admit that you have been there?"

"I flew *over* it, in a helicopter when Rivers and I were being dropped at the original rendezvous location. What about it?" she asked, ready to get on with the questioning.

"That is where an assassin's bullet found his heart." There was a pregnant pause as Silver allowed everyone to connect the dots he had drawn. "Tell me, Wakefield, how are you with a .50 caliber Browning? The trajectory of the bullet was traced to 370 yards away, from a second story window. Could you have made that shot with a scope?"

"Yes, sir," There was no sense in lying. Her confident answer filled her with dread. She could have made a shot like that without a scope. "But I didn't."

"Delaram is merely a three-hour drive from Filasek's estate. We have satellite photos showing two trucks leaving the compound and driving to Delaram an hour before the ambassador was murdered. One truck drove back twelve minutes later, the second drove north into the mountains. "Are you asking this panel to believe that you were *not* on board that transport and did *not* take that shot?"

"Yes," Wakefield said simply.

Congressman DeFore spoke up before the galley erupted. "Yes, you shot him? Or yes, you are asking us to believe you did not?" His voice sounded incredulous and weak.

"I did not murder Ambassador Wilder. I am asking this committee to believe me." To say she was shocked would have grossly underestimated her emotion. LCDR Judah Wakefield was appalled.

DeFore nodded at her. She found understanding in his nod and suddenly knew she had an ally. "I would like to request a recess for lunch, Mr Chairman," DeFore said.

At 1330, the committee reconvened. Wakefield had not eaten. She was sick to her stomach and spent the time in prayer while sipping a Sprite.

"Let me recap and get us back up to speed." Silver said as the room quickly quieted in the panel's presence. Wakefield was beginning to become irritated with the smug expression on his round, clean-shaven face. His squinty eyes were too small for his oversized, fleshy face, and his nose looked as if he had had plastic surgery to correct it sometime in the recent past, Judah judged.

"Miss Wakefield has testified that on the word of a—how old was Nasser?" he broke to question her.

"Seven, sir."

"On the word of a, a baby, she achieved an air strike that dissolved every witness who could have testified to her leaving the estate, placing her in Delaram at the time of Wilder's assassination."

"Or, they could have provided an alibi to clear her," DeFore interrupted.

"Um-hm," Silver grunted a wary agreement. "There is a forensics team at the compound rubble right now that will be able to tell us if she is speaking the truth." Silver cleared his throat and turned a page in his notes. "But that is not the only reason you have been called to testify, Miss Wakefield."

Judah's hand went to her stomach. How could there be more? The crowd moved restlessly at Silver's announcement. Was someone sitting around manufacturing the odd slants on her actions to discredit her? If so, why?

"The second explosion is the one I want to discuss now. According to the JAG office, they are investigating the death of reporter Jesse Beane who was under your care in Afghanistan." The jostling of papers and tiny whispers grew in the room. The name Jesse Beane had not been released yet. The media would be anxious to crucify the responsible party in the death of one of their own. "This committee will leave that to the JAG authority." Judah wondered why he had even

35

bothered to mention it. "I remind you, you are still under oath." Silver gave Wakefield a sharp glance over the half glasses that were barely perched on the end of his nose. "The second explosion, what was the cause?" he asked.

"It was some sort of detonation device that Lieutenant Commander Rivers rigged."

"Under your orders and supervision?"

"I was a little busy at the time he set it up. He did not really need my supervision. He's a SEAL," she stated calmly. She thought that might provoke some laughs in the gallery so she said it as respectfully as she could, but still expected a reprimand. No laughs came.

"Did you order Rivers to detonate the mountain?

"No, sir."

"What were you busy doing?" Silver asked.

"I was shooting out a few of the bars in our prison cave so we could get out before Filasek's men arrived."

"You were successful?"

"Obviously."

"And you had a weapon?"

"We were trapped in an arsenal." Wakefield said and shrugged slightly. "But yes, I had the weapon that Rivers and I smuggled into Afghanistan."

"Did you plan the second explosion to cover up the way in which Beane died?"

"I did not."

"Why not?"

What an odd question. "I didn't need to." Wakefield said with a look as odd as she found the question.

"So you *would* have covered it up with an explosion if you had needed to?"

"No. No one was at fault in her death. I would *not* have covered it up if someone was." Wakefield clarified. He had said he wasn't interested in Beane's death.

"Where did the weapons come from? Besides the one you smuggled in?" Silver made it sound like it was as serious as taking a weapon on an airplane in the post-9/11 USA.

"According to the stamps on the crates and boxes, China, Russia and the U.S., maybe some others."

"What kinds of ordnance were there? How many weapons are we talking about here?" Silver leaned forward as he asked.

Finally, he had moved on. The two of them went back and forth with one sentence question and answers for an hour while Congressman Silver drew a picture of the warehouse for the committee and media.

"Why didn't you call for back up and hide until we could send in troops to appropriate the weapons for our own use?"

"That was not a practical option. Actually, it was a two-fold decision, sir. We had no way to call. Our SatFone had been crushed in the earthquake earlier in the day. And we were—I was—more concerned with saving our lives than with stockpiling more weapons. We already have enough."

Her back was beginning to ache from sitting up, still and straight, all day. The muscles in her jaw and left shoulder were screaming from the tension.

Silver gave Wakefield a depreciating look over his spectacles. "You already stated that you did not find out about the crushed phone until later, after you had escaped and set the detonation device. You didn't need to blow up all those weapons. There were only 300 men there. Rivers could have led the man chasing you directly to the LZ where a ride was waiting to bring you back to the carrier on time. The helo could have taken out your pursuers with no problem. Why did you not think of that Miss Wakefield?"

"That is '*Lieutenant Commander* Wakefield,' sir." She was tired of his derogatory tone that trampled on her authority as a naval officer. "It sounds like that might have worked real well. But, I *didn't* think of it, and I was not *driving.* I was in the back, caring for the men who had been shot."

"Yes. If you had *thought* of it, you could have saved the taxpayers a couple billion dollars. You blew up an arsenal of weapons that could have been transported and redistributed for use against our enemies, not to mention the COD that was shot down with you aboard and the two trips the pair of helos had to make to bring you home. All of that cost money, *Lieutenant Commander* Wakefield.

She carefully controlled her voice. "How much then, are the six lives I saved worth?"

He never answered and no one took notice. "Had we been able to recycle those weapons, we could have diverted the funds assigned to the armed forces to another more worthy cause."

Wakefield slumped forward and allowed her uniformed arms to fall flat on the table. Her cover bounced with the force of her action. "Is that what this is all about? Money?" she was incredulous. "What's more worthy than keeping American citizens alive?" She battered Silver. "Even keeping you alive?"

He didn't answer that question either. "Money is what everything comes back to." Silver gave his logic matter-of-factly.

Wakefield seethed inside. The Congressman had dragged her name through the mud to decrease military spending. "You *know* it's too late to do anything about the weapons in Afghanistan. What did you hope to accomplish with this hearing?" Wakefield could not seal her lips against the question.

"If there's one cache of weapons, there's another. If I can train our military personnel to consider the cost before they blow up billions of dollars into fireworks, then I can reassign the funding."

The quiet in the room was unnerving. Was the press in agreement or in shock? Wakefield was not planning to turn around to find out. That three of the five congressmen on the panel looked perturbed, was enough encouragement for her. "Congressman Silver," she addressed without permission. "I would like to get back to *my* previous question. How many lives are worth the funding you wish to place elsewhere? 500? 100? 50? 7? You obviously find that 6 lives are too few." He glared at her. His fatty facial skin that hung low exploded into multiple shades of red.

No one on the panel said a word. No one in the gallery stirred.

Wakefield reached down for her briefcase. Her presence was not needed. "May I be excused," she said. It was not a question. She was already standing when she spoke to Silver. "May I offer a word of advice?" When the chairman did not reply, she spoke anyway. "Before your next election, I would find some ways that people are more valuable than money." She started to tuck her chair back in, and it scraped across the polished wooden flooring.

"One moment," Silver called the attention of the room back to the high judges table in a choked voice. "Did you testify that you did not take anything out of that arsenal cave?" His voice fluxed to its original, more powerful sound as he tried one last time to make the witness appear guilty. Of something.

"No, I did not say that."

Silver sounded like he growled in irritation at her vague answer. "Did you, Lieutenant Commander Wakefield, personally remove anything from the arsenal that did not belong to you?" He was harsh and direct.

How had he known? "Yes, I did."

"Well, what was it?" Silver exploded.

"It's classified," she said, schooling her features.

"Classified?" Wakefield was glad she was not sitting any closer. She saw actual spit fly past the edge of the shared bench. "I have top level clearance, Commander!"

"Perhaps you do," Wakefield shrugged innocently. She was not giving an inch to this pompous man without a court order now. "But I know they don't." She pointed back over her shoulder to the gallery full of observers with her thumb.

DeFore spoke up again. "I require no further testimony from this witness. If you like, Miss Wakefield, I can have your testimony stricken from the record, or classified, so it doesn't influence your other legal troubles. This meeting was a ridiculous farce, based on narrow-sighted values. I resent the waste of my time, and I apologize for the waste of yours." DeFore took a dig at Silver.

Wakefield smiled as she nodded her thanks to DeFore. "No, I'd like the meeting to stand in the record just as it happened. The things I said were the truth, no matter what slant Congressman Silver placed on them. I'm interested in the public's opinion of these proceedings." It would hurt Silver's reputation much more than it would damage her career. She felt a jab of guilt.

"I make a motion to dismiss," Smitherman said from the right.

"I second," the man sitting next to him said.

I can't ever take it back if I let it stand now, Judah argued with herself. Was the pleasure of seeing this man humiliated worth the displeasure she knew she would feel from the Lord for exacting her own revenge? She had an opportunity before her to show God's love to an influential man.

"All in favor?" Silver said in a dead tone.

"Wait!" The words felt like they jumped out of her heart and missed her lips altogether. "I'd like to strike the record after all."

4

Darkness hung low with the cloud cover. Rivers signaled his men to begin their climb with a small hand motion. He was with five members of Blue Unit of SEAL Team Seven. Two men, black from head to toe, simultaneously tossed two grappling hooks to the fourth floor rooftop. Both made little noise and caught on the first throw. Adams and McCarthy began to climb.

These were his boys. Rivers had been part of their preparation from the day they arrived at BUD/S school. Chief Petty Officer (CPO) Adams, a 27-year-old, wiry black fellow from Detroit, quickly walked up the side of the wharf building as if he was walking flat, not straight up. Petty Officer Stellar, a well-muscled man from California, held Adams' rope so it wouldn't brush the rusting side of the Butler building and alert anyone. The second set of SEALs paired LT McCarthy, who was from Oregon, with PO Little, who was anything but little.

Rivers took Adams' rope when they made it inside. He shimmied up the side hand over hand as if he did it every day. It was actually only every other day.

All five men were inside the building 1 minute 49 seconds later. One second ahead of plan. The office was cramped but tidy, and chilled with the night sea air because the window had carelessly been left open. Just the break they needed. However, if anyone had been paying attention, they would have seen a SEAL of Mexican lineage visit the office just before dusk and pry it open to make way for the SEALs' stealthy mission.

The top half of the two walls that faced the inside of the wharf were glass so the corner crow's nest office manager could easily oversee the progress of loading or unloading the ship in the warehouse berth below.

LCDR Rivers listened at the open window in the dark office until he heard a commotion start around the corner, in the street in front of the warehouse. Drunken angry Spanish carried easily in the moist night air of the river. "I can hear 'em from here, sir," Little said. "I didn't realize Yellow Unit had such an extensive Spanish vocabulary," he laughed.

"They don't. They are just repeating the same curses over and over," Stellar informed Blue Unit.

The wharf occupied prime real estate on a large tributary river that emptied into the Atlantic Ocean less than one kilometer from their location. The wharf, built right on the water, had huge doors that slid sideways to accommodate up to 200-foot ships inside for loading in complete secrecy.

Approximately 50 stevedores steadily paraded up and down a sloping metal ramp, loading boxes into the side-loading hatch of the ship in the slip. A pair of cranes hoisted hundreds of palates and containers one at a time onto the open deck. It appeared that nearly two-thirds of the stock in the building was already neatly stacked aboard.

Little edged toward the door to look out. "Hold," Rivers whispered with a closed fist in the air. Rivers still listened with one ear to the window. The entire plan hinged on precision timing. Yellow Unit's go-phrase Rivers waited for came. He counted down the seconds on raised fingers. Three, two, one.

Silence reigned for two long seconds as Blue Unit waited. A series of gunshots blasted outside. Then an explosion cracked the air.

They were late. But just a little. Yellow Unit's job in that night's mission was to stage a fight out front, in order to divide the men inside by provoking some of the guards and the dock workers to check on the noise. The explosion was the signal for the Blue Unit to begin sneaking down the rickety stairs to the main floor of the warehouse.

The man who seemed to be in control of the loading operation stayed put, but nodded for the men to go check it out. He held a pen and his clipboard of shipping manifests. He looked to be older than the 18- to 30-year-olds who were loading and operating the equipment. About a dozen of the workers hustled outside, speaking in clipped Spanish. Rivers observed the entire scope of workers as he descended.

Red Unit should have arrived by then, so Rivers signaled his team. But a loader spotted them before they were down. Pointing a finger, he yelled, "*Intrusos!*"

Red Unit, six SEALs outfitted in black neoprene wetsuits and fitted with rebreathers, hopped out of the water onto the loading dock. It was fortunate that the tide was in, thus the water level was high on the dock and climbing was unnecessary. But, of course, that was the plan.

The scuffle in subduing the men who had gone outside to investigate the noise went fast. Yellow Unit, another six SEALs, these in civilian dress, entered the wharf. The men stepped through the main, street-side entrance.

On the main floor Rivers watched guns appear in all the loaders' hands. A deafening volley began to echo off the metal walls. Even with 18 SEALs, the battle was not one-sided, because of the automatic weapons and pistols on the part of the loaders.

The foreman was three-quarters of the way up the stairs toward the office, and presumably the telephone, before Rivers noticed his ascent. Rivers had disarmed three men, but two of them would not stay down. The first one was probably unconscious, maybe dead. Rivers threw a hard left at the man directly in front of him, ducked a punch coming from his right, and swept his right leg out as he went down on his side. He scissor-kicked, knocking the second man down with him. The man smacked the back of his head on the concrete floor of the loading dock.

"McCarthy! The stairs." Rivers called, alerting one of his men. McCarthy took the stairs two at a time. The foreman locked the door against the pursuing SEAL and began dialing. Rivers saw him speaking into the phone before McCarthy finished the three-flight climb.

McCarthy kicked the door in.

The foreman dropped the phone and swiftly picked up a revolver from the open desk drawer. He fired at the charging SEAL. McCarthy growled at the man, but all he did was flinch as the bullet passed through his bicep. He kept charging toward the foreman.

McCarthy grabbed the gun's hot barrel and threw it to the ground. The men struggled around the desk, bumping into stacks of paper that fluttered into chaos. McCarthy grabbed the foreman's arm and threw him into the bookshelves that lined one wall. The books emptied into heaps on the floor and the shelves toppled over at odd angles.

The South American stumbled and lunged at the large SEAL. He caught McCarthy around the middle. The thug's momentum shot the two men out the open door and onto the small fourth-floor landing. They grappled back and forth, and McCarthy ended up with the foreman's neck in the crook of his arm.

The South American kicked hard off the wall and crashed into the wooden safety railing. It ripped away from the sides at full speed, and the man tumbled face first toward the cement floor, taking McCarthy with him.

Rivers was reaching for the neck of the man who was charging at him as he saw the two men plummeting in his peripheral. He snapped the man's neck and put a bullet into the heart of the second one. Without waiting to see either of the dead men hit the ground, Rivers sprinted to where his man was falling and stepped under McCarthy before he landed.

McCarthy was a linebacker of a man, even for a SEAL. He weighed in at 242 pounds of bulky muscle and stood a hair over six feet tall. Rivers felt every ounce as his body collapsed under his team member's three-story drop. Rivers slammed into the concrete floor. McCarthy landed squarely on him.

"Ugh!" Rivers grunted as the air flew out of his lungs. His face pressed into the dirty floor. Tiny rock debris, tracked in on people's shoes, embossed his skin. He couldn't breathe.

McCarthy rolled off the officer and hopped to his feet completely unscathed. The sounds of the fight were dying down as more and more of the armed stevedores went down. The battle cry of "Hoo-rah!" frequented the air as the navy SEALs subdued their dockworker opponents.

McCarthy let loose a vile curse as he caught sight of the foreman's death stare inches from his nose. "Sorry, sir!" he said before Rivers' breath returned and he could correct his language "And thank you, sir."

Rivers' lungs screamed at him in protest as they began to re-inflate. He took shallow breaths, but it didn't help the pain much. He grimaced.

"I remember what you told me about being in control, sir." McCarthy said still catching his breath from the exertion of the fight. It wasn't necessary for him to rejoin the fray. "But I was not in control up there. Especially when he took that header through the rails."

Rivers sat up and pressed the heel of his hand into his chest to ease the pain. He felt a trickle of blood on his ear. Not too much though, so he left it. "You ever considered losing some weight?" Rivers rasped.

"Sorry, sir." McCarthy winced. The twin thud of two bodies hitting the concrete floor was followed by a splash as the last dockworker plunged into the water.

Rivers surveyed the warehouse-turned-slaughter-house. Dozens of bodies lay contorted on the concrete floor. Four bodies hung in half over the cable fence at the edge of the ship's deck. The largest crane dangled a tractor-truck-sized metal box in midair with the top half of the former operator hanging out of the chair he was strapped into with one arm slung over his head. Two more Hispanics lay tangled together across the bottom three stairs. They looked like brothers. They shared the same bullet in death.

The great door began to slide to the right. The moist night air moved into the wharf warehouse. "All aboard that's going aboard," Rivers instructed his men. "LT James has the bridge."

"Aye, sir." James said. He had little ship handling experience, but it was more than anyone else assigned to SEAL Team Seven. The rusty bridge on the vessel looked more like a wheelhouse, but she seemed seaworthy.

The rickety ship slipped out of the wharf and into the night.

The only evidence of the SEALs' adventure was the multitude of dead bodies in pooling blood that littered the warehouse.

Judah Wakefield's Residence
Chalfonte Apartments
Sunday 0820 hours, EST

Judah groaned at her alarm clock. "Enough already!" She smacked an open hand across the noisemaker. "I don't feel like going to church." She closed her eyes and curled into a tight little ball. She tried to go back to sleep. Then pushed out her breath in a huff. Dreamworld was not exactly a pleasant place either. The media had enjoyed a field day with her life this weekend. Every time she had flipped on the TV, she was on the news. Her dress whites picture from her recent promotion to lieutenant commander was plastered across all the local stations. She hated that picture. She had even been mentioned on CNN in two different half-hour reports in a row before she had finally growled and turned it off for good the night before.

Her church family could not have missed the allegations floating all over town. Her Congressional hearing, miraculously, had not leaked, but word of her Article 32 set to begin Monday was everywhere.

Judah flipped the covers over her head. She wanted to stay here, buried, away from all the curious, well-meaning questions, and the accusing glances.

She knew she would go though. She was not one to back away from a challenge. And she had an obligation to the children in her four- and five-year-olds class. She never missed a class when she was in town.

Judah dragged herself to the shower.

Pathway Vineyard Church
Woodbridge, VA
Sunday, 0954 hours EST

"Miss Judah, Miss Judah!" five-year-old Sadie had been in her class for nearly two years. She came running at full speed, still swathed in her giant marshmallow parka and furry hat. "I saw you on TV!" She yelled as she hit Judah's knees forcefully and wrapped her arms around her. Judah stepped back on impact and wrapped both arms around the little girl's head at her waist.

Sadie's mom stood smiling in the doorway. "She couldn't wait to see you this morning. She's been so excited."

Sadie tugged on Judah's sleeve. "I've never known anybody who was on TV before. You looked so pretty." Sadie smiled dreamily. "I want to be on TV when I grow up." Judah smiled ruefully. It must be nice to have a child's perspective.

Brian and Jason's dad brought the boys to class. They had seen the news too. They were most impressed that she had gotten to ride in a helicopter and ride the line up from the water. Mr Stiles cleared his throat as he was taking the boys' coats off. "Myra and I want you to call on us if you need anything," he said sincerely. "We're so proud to have a hero teaching our boys."

Judah's chest tightened. "Thank you, John. I may need a friendly face in the next couple of days."

Julia's dad brought her in next. She brought Judah a cupcake. "I made it myself. Momma said you might be sad, and cupcakes always make me feel better." Julie threw her skinny arms around her teacher's neck. "I love you, Miss Judah. Don't be sad."

47

Without exception, all 12 of her students had seen her on television or heard from their parents that she was having a difficult week. By the time Judah drove out of the parking lot to meet the Hendersons at a buffet for lunch, she was juggling three pictures for her refrigerator, a candle, a box of bath salts, a cupcake and had received at least two dozen hugs. Three sets of parents had offered an open invitation to dinner.

It was all she could do not to break down in tears. "God, these people really love me. They care for me." She felt the acceptance, in spite of the allegations. This church was her family while her relatives were in Minnesota.

"I'm so glad you didn't let me skip church this morning," she breathed thanks to her Lord.

Washington, DC
Oval Office
Monday 0949 hours

"What is the problem now, Dietz?" President George W. Bush looked up from a thick stack of papers he was signing as Richmond Dietz walked over the thick carpet in the Oval Office.

"We received confirmation on a hit man who has been hired to kill you, sir. On your trip to Europe. Specifically, the hit is to be made at the stop in Germany."

"Why is this different from every other death threat I receive?" The president's sharp blue-gray eyes did not miss his concern. He raised his pen from the page and gave more focused attention.

"Our man is 98 percent sure that the man contracted is the one called Azure Tiger."

"*The* Azure Tiger?" Bush asked with one raised eyebrow. He pursed his lips slightly. The dignified man in his fifties looked over the top of his magnifying spectacles.

"Yes, Mr President."

"Well, put your best people on it and let's catch this sucker."
When he smiled his upper lip curved curiously.

"But sir...Mr President," Dietz smoothed his tiny neat mustache.
This wasn't going as he had expected.

"Dietz, you know I'm not a man to cower in the closet. This
assassin has been attributed with the deaths of a few of my friends. One
in Japan and a couple from Argentina. I want him taken out. I will stand
as bait if necessary. *You* make it *un*necessary," the president ordered.

The two men talked another 45 seconds before one of the
secretaries knocked discreetly on the door to inform the president of
his next appointment's arrival.

"Thanks for coming by." Bush switched his pen to his left hand
and offered his right to the CIA man. "I'll look for an update as the date
approaches."

5

LCDR Teresa Connor arrived at her office at zero seven hundred to tie up loose ends for the Article 32 hearing she was set to prosecute today. She pushed open the door to the bullpen of administrative servicemen. Only two overachievers were present so far. Glancing at her glass office door, she noticed a tall, chiseled officer with cropped, light hair waiting. He turned when she opened the door and the florescent office lights glinted off a pair of gold wings on his long-sleeved, khaki, class B lieutenant's uniform.

"You are prosecuting the Wakefield case? I have some information for you," he said cryptically as way of greeting.

"Have a seat," Connor offered. She placed her cover on the coat rack before removing her long coat and hanging it up as well. As she smoothed her uniform into place, she caught a cocky grin found only on navy and air force flyboys. "What have you got?" she asked.

Half an hour later, a petty officer knocked on her closed door. The attorney scribbled furiously as her guest leaned back in the vinyl interview chair with one leg crossed over the other at the knee. At Connor's call of enter, PO Milkas said, "Excuse me, ma'am. The JAG would like to see you."

Connor stood immediately and followed Milkas to the Admiral's door. She did not exactly shake in her heels, but the man she was about to see intimidated her more than a little. He was a by-the-book sailor who had graduated top in his class at the Naval Academy a couple decades earlier. He carried a chest full of ribbons honoring his heroism in Vietnam, Bosnia, and the Gulf War. He was on the fast track to becoming the Chief of Naval Operations (CNO). Currently all the lawyers and administration in all the JAG offices world-wide reported to him.

"Lieutenant Commander Connor, reporting as ordered," she said in a strong voice as she stiffened into attention.

ADM Garterbled stood looking out his window at the city street below. "At ease, Commander." He didn't offer her a seat. "Your Article 32 on Lieutenant Commander Wakefield begins this morning, does it not?"

"Yes, sir. Zero eight hundred."

ADM Garterbled didn't turn around. "I know you have a great desire for justice, Commander," his voice carried an odd tone, "but I want to warn you not to let yourself get carried away on this case. Wakefield's step-father is Admiral Graham. I don't need to tell you that he is the man who is running this Operation Enduring Freedom. I want you to tread lightly on this woman's reputation. There is to be no slander, Commander. She is innocent until proven guilty."

Connor stood with her feet shoulder width apart and her hands clasped in the small of her back waiting for the admiral to finish.

He still faced the window. "If she is innocent, I want her completely exonerated with honor and reputation completely intact when she leaves that courtroom." Connor knew it was an order.

"And if she is *guilty*, sir?" she asked masking the edge in her voice. After what the man she had just interviewed had said about Wakefield, there was barely a question in the prosecutor's mind as to the woman's guilt or innocence.

Admiral Garterbled turned from the window, his black eyes pierced the junior officer. "If she is guilty, I want you to nail her butt to the wall!" he said fiercely.

"Aye, sir!" Connor smiled.

"Dismissed," Garterbled barked.

Connor's mousy brown hair and figure were the only things mediocre about her. She pushed the envelope in all aspects of her work and life.

Connor pulled the admiral's door closed behind her. "A three-star's daughter or not," Connor vowed, "Wakefield will be brought to justice. And I will earn my extra half stripe."

Connor pretended not to see the Admiral's yeoman smirk behind her computer. Connor didn't have time to dress down impertinence today. Tomorrow would be soon enough.

Falls Church, VA
JAG Headquarters
Courtroom B
Monday, 1010 hours

Wakefield watched Judge Pella, a navy captain with a gruff appearance, settle back into his chair after the first break. He had begun the hearing at precisely 0800 hours. Only two hours of statements and damaging testimony were over.

Wakefield's attorney, a young cracker-jack, had promised in his snappy opening statement to refute all the charges. His features were too pinched to be called handsome, but he was full of energy. Sims was a lieutenant commander, and one of the better defense attorneys stationed at JAG Headquarters.

The original investigator, LT Jones, sat as second chair for the prosecution. The courtroom was set up with the empty jury box to the right, next to the prosecution's table. There were six long benches in the gallery. Three on each side. A few spectators watched the proceedings. Wakefield was glad only a few people were allowed to attend. She was not sure she could survive another encounter with the press.

Wakefield's immediate supervisor, Captain George Huntington assured her that the press was waiting just outside though. He sat to the right of her pastor, Mark Jacobs, who nodded kindly at her when she entered the court.

Their presence was both a comfort and an embarrassment to her. She hated that people whose respect she desired were hearing such integrity-degrading accusations against her.

"The prosecution may call its next witness." Captain Pella's voice was gentle, in direct opposition to his rugged face. His cheeks were reddened like a man from the Northland. Judah supposed it was the grim set of his ample lips and the manner in which his eyes slanted into slits on the outside that gave his appearance such a gruff exterior. Scuttlebutt had it that he had drawn duty in Greenland for two three-year stints in a row. No one had heard what he had done to rate such a lousy duty assignment though.

LCDR Connor stood, "The prosecution calls Lieutenant Sands."

Wakefield struggled not to groan aloud as her attorney shot to his feet. "Objection! Lieutenant Sands was not on the witness list."

"Your honor," Connor argued. "Lieutenant Sands only this morning came forward. He is an eye witness to the events themselves, not a character witness."

"Objection overruled." Pella ruled in favor of the prosecution. "The defense may have time to interview this witness before cross examination," he told LCDR Sims before he could ask for a continuance. "Call Lieutenant Sands," the judge instructed the marine guard at the door.

6

LT Sands' testimony droned for two hours. The prosecutor asked questions about Wakefield's activities in Afghanistan. Occasionally, Connor let him describe the events in his own words. It was damaging. Sands portrayed her as a weak, indecisive woman, except when making bad decisions. Then she was whiney and demanding.

Sands described to Judge Pella how Wakefield had used her position of O.I.C. to intimidate him and touch him, inappropriately. "She separated me from the other hostages she was there to protect and rescue, and then she forced me into a compromising position on the ground."

Wakefield sat in complete shock, not bothering to hide her scowl at the officer on the stand. She crossed her legs under the table. Her foot swung as fast as she could move it. Judah's jaw flexed with each swing as she held the tension behind her teeth.

LCDR Sims kept glancing at her. She could see he was getting worried about their case. It would take some precision lawyering to get out of the hole the prosecutor was unearthing around her.

"No further questions." Connor returned to her seat with an unveiled triumphant smile.

"I'd like to request that recess now—to interview the witness and to confer with my client," Sims asked the overseer of the court respectfully. His voice sounded as if he were speaking through a spaghetti strainer. Judah saw his left fist open and close repeatedly.

"Very well. Seeing the time, we will dismiss for lunch and meet back here at 1415 hours precisely. If you still need more time, Commander, I will be glad to issue a continuance until tomorrow morning. But don't prolong this hearing needlessly," he warned the defense counselor.

"Understood. Thank you, sir." Sims nodded grimly and sat to retrieve his briefcase. The high sheen wood of the courtroom that had seemed so benevolent on Judah's way in, now appeared hard and unbending. Inflexible like the law. "We will eat in my office, Commander," Sims whispered to Wakefield as they stood together.

He sounded as if he were offering her a last meal outside the "big house."

In his office, Sims let go. "Why didn't you tell me about the incident with Sands? I'm sure my reaction didn't do anything to reassure Judge Pella. His interpretation of these proceedings will determine if you are to be held in confinement while we await a court martial date."

Wakefield sighed. "You don't need to remind *me* of that, Commander." Judah flopped down in the other chair in Sims' overcrowded office. She righted her chicken sandwich from the basement commissary before it slid from her lap to the floor. "What makes you so sure I'll be held over for court martial?"

Sims' intense gaze as he towered over her seated position, made her feel gangly and ungraceful. "Were you just in the same courtroom I was in?"

Wakefield carefully controlled her reaction. "I thought lawyers were supposed to be objective, or at least biased in favor of their clients." She began to unwrap her sandwich from its foil. She could feel herself swelling with anger again at the injustice of it all. The whole proceeding so far had been filled with half-truths and downright lies. Now, even her lawyer did not believe in her innocence. *God, please control my mouth for me, because I don't think I can*, she prayed and took a large bite of her lunch to give God time to work.

The chicken was spicy and fried, but the bun tasted like pasteboard.

"All right, Wakefield," Sims said after an extended minute of silence. He walked around the metal navy-issue desk to sit in his office chair. He left his sandwich untouched on the corner of his desk. "Why don't you give me your version of what happened."

Front Steps of JAG Headquarters
1255 hours

Wakefield walked outside to call her mother and give her an update while Sims interviewed Sands. She sat down on a cold, white brick retaining wall before thumbing through the numbers for *home*. The sky was irritatingly blue this Monday morning. She would rather have gone to the botanical gardens and taken a walk since she was away from her office. She hated to waste such a pretty January day. Like having a particularly sad funeral on a sunny day instead of a rainy day, Judah thought the sky should reflect the dark clouds of depression that threatened her soul, again.

Snow was forecast for later in the week, but as of today, there had been no snowfall this winter in the metro D.C. area, just dreary rain. She pressed the send button on her Nokia and held it to her ear.

It did not ring. She looked at the phone. The display said *no service*. She looked at the meter that measured the battery. There were four lines, a complete charge. The receiver showed that a relay tower was close. Reception was also at four bars. She tried again. Nothing.

"Terrific!" She blew out her breath. "Now I'll have to spend half an hour on the phone with the telephone company to figure out what is wrong with my phone." She rolled her eyes. "What a Monday!"

"Your honor, the defense is ready to proceed with cross."

The marine guard summoned LT Sands back to the witness stand from the waiting area in the hall. Sands looked around the courtroom as he walked to the front, and after a single stolen glance, he avoided LCDR Wakefield's gaze.

Her thin defense attorney smoothed down wispy brown hair, picked up his legal pad of notes, and approached the witness stand. "Lieutenant Sands, how did you hear about these proceedings and manage to make it here from your ship in such a...timely manner?" he asked.

Sands did not appear intimidated in the least. "I was on medical leave, because of my arm." He lifted his elbow to indicate his right arm, which was swathed in bandages. "I have some buddies stationed at Quantico Marine Base, so I am crashing with them while I do a couple weeks of PT at Bethesda. My RIO, Red, uh, LT (j.g.) Lewis called me from the ship and told me about the JAG investigator nosing around about Afghanistan." Sands finally looked fully at Wakefield, "In relation to the Lieutenant Commander here." He shrugged a shoulder in her direction.

Wakefield was incredulous of the air of innocence that Sands was able to pull off in front of the judge. She had certainly under-estimated him. Her father was right when he warned her back aboard the carrier that Sands had it in for her.

"So why choose to spend your leave time here testifying?"

Sands conjured up an odd look. "It is my duty, sir." He lowered his head and looked up through long lashes. His baby blues flashed integrity and virtue.

"What a crock!" Wakefield whispered under her breath. He was playing the entire courtroom for fools with his act. Wakefield watched in disconnected fascination. If she had not seen his natural cocky arrogance in the desert, she decided she would probably believe his act as well. The man was good at what he was doing; to deny that would be like believing there was no hell.

"What did you do upon first meeting the defendant?" Sims began to pace back and forth in front of the witness stand. Wakefield did not know if he was trying to dispel his excess energy or trying to work up some more.

Sands leaned back in his chair and rolled his eyes up to the ceiling. "Well, if I recall, I met the commander at the entrance to the cave and offered to carry her bag."

"And did you also make her a pallet right next to yours?"

"Objection! Leading the witness." Connor jumped to her feet.

"Sustained."

"I'll rephrase, your honor." Sims went on unperturbed. "Where did you first suggest that your O.I.C. spend the night?"

Sands shrugged, "I offered her the warmest place, closest to the fire, sir."

"Right next to your bunk, Lieutenant?"

Sands glanced at the prosecutor who gave a tight nod, before answering. "Yes, sir."

"And did you ever seek extra attention from the commander?"

Sands screwed up his face in confusion. "I am not sure what you mean." He scooted up straighter in his seat.

"Did you ever come on to her?"

"No, sir!" Sands eye brows shot up in perfect arches.

"You never made comments of a sexual nature toward Lieutenant Commander Wakefield? Not in front of anyone else or privately?"

"Objection." LT Jones, the second chair prosecutor stated dully. "Asked and answered."

"Overruled. Answer the question." Judge Pella rubbed his jaw and trained his eyes on the young pilot.

"I object." The prosecutor stiffened in her seat.

The judge shot her an incredulous look. "You object to what? My ruling?"

"Yes, sir"

He shook his head in disbelief. "Overruled. I may be old, but I am not a blind man. The defendant is a highly attractive woman. I don't know of any unattached pilot in the U.S. Navy that would not have approached her. I am interested in Sands' answer."

"It may have seemed that way," Sands said slowly after making eye contact with LCDR Connor again. "But it was really the other way around, sir. She was constantly staring at me and giving me these looks." He raised his brow as if to say, you *know* what I mean. "She would push out her bottom lip and flash those blue eyes at me. It was obvious that she wanted me, sir." A bit of Sands' cockiness shown through the façade. "I knew nothing could come of it, because of the regs, sir. So, I was just flirting back a little. All innocent fun." He shrugged, his face a picture of boyhood innocence.

"Unbelievable!" Wakefield murmured softly.

Sims pushed his thin hair off his forehead where it had fallen. He changed his line of questioning. "When you testified earlier, you said, 'She left Jesse Beane behind twice. Once when she hid her and she was killed because no one was there to protect her, and second when she left her body behind.' Is that correct?"

"Word for word, sir." Sands frowned sadly, but his eyes betrayed him. Wakefield could read triumph there.

"Why do you suppose the commander left Miss Beane's body behind?"

"Objection." Connor did not stand this time. "Calls for an opinion *and* is outside the witness's scope of knowledge."

"It goes to this witness's state of mind, your honor."

"It does call for an opinion, but I would like to know what he thinks his C.O.'s reasoning was." Pella pronounced. "It colors his testimony. Overruled."

"I think she was scared that she would get in trouble for letting the civilian get killed," Sands said. "She's a player on the fast track. She didn't want any bad press. With no body, there was no proof of her dereliction. But," Sands looked to the gallery, "it sure seems like she is getting that bad press now, anyway."

LCDR Sims turned in his pacing to address Judge Pella. "Your honor, would you instruct the witness to answer only the questions asked?"

"You asked for his opinion, Commander. You got it."

Sims looked slightly chastened as he turned back to the witness. His left hand was moving back into a fist again. "Did it ever occur to you, Lieutenant, that the commander only had the time to take people who could walk out of that cave, and she chose to take the live Marine, Captain Martinez, instead of a dead reporter who had no family, no friends to return the body to? No one who needed closure."

"Objection," Connor said lazily this time. She seemed to become more confident in her case by the minute. "Was that a question?"

"It was a proper question." Judge Pella gave her a sharp look. "—Did it ever occur to you?" Pella repeated for the benefit of the prosecutor and the witness.

"No, sir. That did not occur to me." Sands said. His modulation suggested that he thought that scenario was about as likely as the Easter Bunny popping his head in to testify at these January proceedings.

As Judah watched, Sands looked at the prosecutor intently. He had been looking at her quite often. Wakefield noted however, that the look on the woman's face as she returned his gaze, was one designed to keep herself from blushing. As she looked up through her eyelashes, she could not look away. The woman was smitten with LT Sands. He must have turned on the charm with this senior officer as well. *He is out of control*, Judah thought.

LCDR Sims asked a few more questions before returning to his previous line of questioning. "You also testified that Lieutenant

Commander Wakefield separated you from the rest of the hostages after the escape and forced you to the ground where she touched you inappropriately?"

"That is correct." Sands took a sip of the water in front of him.

"Where was Lieutenant Commander Rivers, the 2IC, during this exchange?" Sims acted as if he did not know.

"Uh, well," Sands took a deep breath and tugged his short, jagged bangs forward, "he was standing there, near us."

"Where, exactly, did she touch you?" Sims asked pointedly. He knew what had happened, and he would see to it that the judge did too.

"Uh, my shoulder, my chest, and my neck." Sands answered. He started squirming under the direct questions.

"And didn't those touches come in the form of punches, not caresses, as you have tried to intimate?" Sands did not answer. "And was it her foot that was on your neck once the commander threw you to the ground for repeated insubordination and disobeying orders?"

Judge Pella raised his bushy, graying eyebrows and looked at Wakefield. She could not keep the edges of her lips from turning up into a small smile. The judge's gaze told her that he thought she looked too proper to step on an ant, much less a junior officer's neck.

"No!" Sands started boldly, but quickly deflated as he added, "not exactly," to his statement.

"What, exactly, then Lieutenant Sands?" Sims pushed.

A flush crept up the lieutenant's neck as he struggled with his words. He should have never mentioned the incident. Sims was relentless.

"Didn't you let this woman wrestle you to the ground because *you* wanted *her*?" Sims goaded.

"No way. I did not." He hesitated and then added in a softer voice, "What you said before was pretty much it."

Wakefield tucked her lips between her teeth.

"So, in fact, Lieutenant, Lieutenant Commander Wakefield did not touch you sexually in any way. She subdued you because you were an unruly officer and a constant irritant under her command. Is that correct?"

"I suppose she might have seen it like that," Sands said begrudgingly.

"Is that a 'yes, sir,' or 'no, sir,' Lieutenant?" The defense attorney's phraseology was not lost on the pilot. His eyes smarted to the defense table. It was the exact beginning of the conversation with Wakefield that ended with him flat on his back in the hard-packed desert sand.

"Yes, sir," he said. This time the humility in his voice sounded much more authentic to Wakefield.

LCDR Sims turned away from the witness. "Oh, one more thing. Lieutenant Sands, to what do you attribute your threatened flight status?"

"I'm going to therapy and I'll recover." Sands tossed his head arrogantly. "It's not threatened."

"But if you are not returned to flight status?"

"It would be because the lieutenant commander failed to get us out of the line of fire, like a good officer would to protect his people."

"Nothing further," Sims clucked his lips and sat down.

Judge Pella checked his watch as he asked the Judge Advocate, "Redirect?"

"No, sir," Connor said. Her voice had a touch of impatience mixed with embarrassment. The young lawyer's deportment on this case had ranged all over the spectrum. She needed to pull herself into the game or he would have to talk to ADM Garterbled about having her suspended.

"One moment, your honor?" Sims asked. The defendant was whispering something behind her cupped hand. Sims nodded at his client slowly and turned back to face him. If Pella had to put a word to

Sims' demeanor, it would be reluctance. "I have one final question, sir, if you will indulge me."

Pella shot the defense a dirty look. He was out of order and the officer knew it. But he considered the request. Unless the prosecution had some amazing witness up her sleeve, he was about to dismiss the charges as the vendetta of a hotshot pilot against the female officer who had finally shot him down. "Does the prosecution have any objection?"

"I know I should, but I have no objection, your honor." Lieutenant Commander Connor's tone suggested that she knew she had blown this case by rushing her witness to the stand. She had not built a proper foundation of suspicion against the accused.

Sims raised one slim eyebrow at his client. The blond officer nodded. "It is against my better judgment," Pella heard her whisper, "but, I need to know."

"Go ahead, ask your question, Sims." Pella said.

Sands resettled himself in the witness chair. "Lieutenant Sands, was it you who made the accusatory call to the hotline?"

The look on the young officer's face became indignant. "It was not," he stated hotly. "When I accuse someone, she will know it, as it happened here today. Face to face. I am not some desk jockey who has to hide behind the skirt of an anonymous hotline to speak out."

Judge Pella froze with his lips slightly parted, mid-word, along with everyone else in the room. Apparently, everyone had made the same assumption as he had. The witness's refute seemed more in line with his arrogant character.

The tide had shifted again. With a single question, it was no longer in Wakefield's favor. Sims melted into his leather chair. He had fallen prey to the most basic mistake of cross-examination. Never ask a question unless you know the answer.

Finally, Pella broke the heavy silence. "The prosecution may call its next witness."

He handed Connor a chance to renew her case. The dark-headed second chair pointed out a line on the witness list to her frozen co-council. "The prosecution sent the rest of the witnesses home. We rest, your honor," Connor said heavily. Apparently, she was not thinking clearly enough to ask for a continuance.

The door tapped twice in its frame behind LT Sands as he left the courtroom.

"Defense may call its first witness." Pella growled. He was tired and thought the case was nearly over. Not so now. They could have up to three more hours of testimony today depending on how fast Sims moved along.

The defense had no witnesses. Character witnesses would only help minimally at this point. She had an excellent record; Sims apparently decided that would be enough for an Article 32. "The defense calls Lieutenant Commander Wakefield."

Pella wondered at the curious fresh scar on the otherwise beautiful defendant's face. She rose and walked to the front as if she could hear the executioner's drums beating in her wake.

"Raise your right hand..." Connor swore her in.

7

S ims recapped the last hour of his interview with Lieutenant Commander Judah Wakefield. She had been flawless on the stand. Confident in her decisions, sure of her testimony. She made eye contact with each person in the small courtroom at one point or another.

"It is your contention then, that you did not murder Ambassador Wilder in Delaram?"

"I did not. I could not do something like that," Wakefield answered clearly. She sat composed in the witness box, not wiggling like witnesses in his courtroom usually did.

"Did you leave behind two of the people you were ordered to rescue?" Sims asked.

"Unfortunately, I had to. John Garner, an enemy infiltrator, was killed and buried in rubble, and Jessica Beane, a reporter. She was a casualty which struck me deeply. I could not bring her body home to anyone, and we did not have the hands to carry her out. So, she too, was buried in the rubble of the Afghani cave."

Sims nodded. "Did you sexually harass *anyone* while in Afghanistan?"

David Rivers' face floated before her eyes. If Sands had not called in the complaint, had it been David? They had talked once or twice in a meaningful way. Or, at least it felt that way to Judah. *That almost-kiss in the desert...did he feel threatened by that?* she wondered. She knew she had hesitated too long in answering this question already. "I did not."

"Did you behave at all times in the manner in which an officer should?"

"I had some difficult decisions to make...but yes, I believe I acted in good conscious and as a good leader at all times."

"Did you use your full physical force to subdue an unruly junior officer to maintain good order and discipline?"

Wakefield sat up a little straighter. "I did not," she raised her chin.

The courtroom paused again. She had already admitted to forcing the pilot to do push-ups.

"You *didn't?*" Sims asked as he turned to his client in surprise.

"No." The first genuine smile of the day appeared on her lips. "Like I told the lieutenant when I had my foot on his throat, I went easy on him, because he had a bullet wound."

The whole gallery burst into spontaneous laughter. Even Judge Pella couldn't contain a smile before calling the room to order.

"I see," Sims chuckled, too. "Did you kill Beane inadvertently by not attending to her while you were busy taking out two of the other terrorists?"

"She was my responsibility, and I contributed to her death, but if she had stayed where Rivers put her, she might still be alive."

Sims began to speak, but before he could phrase it, Judge Pella held up his open palm to stop him. "I would like to know where this illusive Lieutenant Commander Rivers is. Why isn't he here offering first-hand testimony?"

The witness answered instead of the attorney. "Rivers is a SEAL, sir. He left the *Reprisal* on an assignment. He has not been in contact since."

"All right," Pella sat back in his leather chair. "Continue, Mr Sims."

"I have no further questions at this time, your honor."

"Would the prosecution care to cross examine?" Pella asked.

"Yes, your honor." Connor said with relish. She smoothed her brown hair in its tight bun at the back of her head as she rose.

LCDR Wakefield's face paled as if her throat had just been bared to a large, snarling dog.

"Lieutenant Commander Wakefield please tell the court of your whereabouts on the afternoon of 28 May 1999." Connor stood ramrod straight and worked without notes.

"Objection!" Sims shouted out without rising. "Relevance? Her question has nothing to do with the events in question here."

"On the contrary," Connor turned on her heels to look at the defense while she addressed Judge Pella. "Wakefield opened this line of questioning when she testified, 'I could not do something like that,' referring to killing an ambassador."

"Objection overruled."

Wakefield's stomach dropped into her ankles. That was one of the worst days in her memory. It still haunted her nightmares. Now, she would have to relive it in front of an audience.

"Isn't it true, Commander, that on 28 May 1999, you were in Morocco?" Connor asked.

"Yes," Judah swallowed hard. She would face this like every other challenge she faced as an officer, head on.

"Tell us what happened."

"I need a moment to confer with my JAG, your honor." Judah addressed the judge.

"A moment only." The judge motioned for Sims to come forward. "Just push the microphone away."

Wakefield quickly whispered to Sims, "This info that is about to come out is classified, super-secret. The press needs to be removed from the courtroom. I was assigned to remove the Moroccan ambassador who was selling military secrets to the Chinese and about to make a run for it.

"Sims face blanched white. "By 'remove' you mean, kill?"

"Yes." She replied.

Sims nodded succinctly. He backed away from her, and she couldn't tell if he was done talking or if he was revolted by her actions. She didn't blame him. It still sat on her conscience from time to time. It still seemed like there should have been another way, but Dietz had been insistent. So she had followed orders.

"Your honor, a sidebar?"

The judge nodded and wiggled his shoulder boards before motioning Connor to his perch. "Go on," he said, when both lawyers were standing in front of him.

"We need to clear the gallery. And double check everyone's security clearance before moving on." Sims stated. "I'm also concerned as to how the prosecution came across the information she is about to disclose."

Connor huffed a bit. But since the question was not asked directly and the accusation not made in specific words, the judge could not compel an answer or explanation.

"Any objection?" Judge Pella asked Connor.

"No sir, I suppose not."

"Then let it be done." He raised his voice and spoke to the marine on guard duty. "Please clear the room of all persons without super-secret credentials or higher."

It went fairly quickly and Judah was sad to see her support walk out the door with all the others, though not so sad to see the row of reporting hyenas that had doubled in number after the lunch break slink out the double courtroom doors. She composed in her head how to frame her recitation of that awful day.

When the quiet had resettled, there were only four spectators left in the room who were not part of the proceedings in the front.

"You may answer the question, Commander Wakefield." Judge Pella prompted.

She drew a breath of strength. "I was deep under cover as a shop clerk in Marrakech. Under the direction of the CIA, joining with Naval Intelligence, I was brought in as a sniper and...and I killed an ambassador who had turned traitor on his country."

"Go on," Connor instructed.

"I saw the evidence myself, there was mounds of it, and I reported it up the chain of command. He was planning to make a run for Russia after the meeting he had set up for that afternoon. As you know we have no extradition treaty with Russia. He was meeting with a bookseller across a busy intersection from where I was on location. It was near noon—no shadows, no wind—when I took the shot. The ambassador was headed into the store. He was going to sell military secrets concerning the Stealth B-2 to a Chinese official he had met there on two previous occasions."

Wakefield finished her explanation. The prosecutor would have to pry the details from her: the blood spatter from the middle-aged man's brain that had decorated the young mother walking beside him on the sidewalk. The way the ambassador's body nearly crushed the baby riding in the carriage when he collapsed into it. The screams of pedestrians on their lunch breaks as they ran for cover as if she was a random, cold-blooded killer. The bright blood spot mixed with grey brain matter that dripped down the stone wall.

"How many shots did it take to kill him?"

"One shot, one kill," Wakefield stoically repeated the phrase that the marine sniper who had trained her had always used.

"So contrary to your previous testimony, you *could* kill an ambassador. You *did* kill an ambassador," Connor smirked evilly. "It stands to reason that you killed Ambassador Wilder."

Wakefield could feel her breathing speed up. It was more from reliving the horrors of that May day, than the anger she was feeling toward LCDR Connor. *How did she even know about it?* Judah wondered as she practiced control techniques. It was supposed to be classified as super-secret in Dietz's CIA files. Now it would be in the record of these proceedings for everyone with clearance to stumble across. With the media flurry surrounding her, she was sure the transcript would not disappear under the rug.

Sims spoke when Connor paused. "Is the prosecution planning to ask a question?"

Connor wisely left that subject. "How did you know when to leave the cave where you were imprisoned?"

Wakefield groaned on the inside. The nightmare of a day was quickly moving toward becoming a night terror. *If only it was a bad dream.* Wakefield knew what the councilor referred to, but the prosecutor had not phrased the question easily. "We didn't have much of a choice. The earthquake opened a passageway in the back and we stumbled upon an al-Qaeda terrorist guarding a huge cache of weapons. It was a now-or-never kind of situation." Wakefield re-crossed her legs and wiggled back in her seat a little. This witness chair was not designed for sitting for long periods of time.

"Let me be more specific," Connor frowned. Her lower lip stuck out, oddly flat. "Why did you not break out earlier?"

Well, here it is, Judah readied herself for the depreciating humor she was sure would follow. "I had a dream the second night I was there," Wakefield paused only a moment. She was not ashamed that God spoke a warning to her, why should she act as if she was embarrassed by it? So what if the people in the room thought she was a kooky religious nut? There weren't many people left anyway. She knew what was real and what was temporal.

Judah leaned forward, she would not be defensive over this issue. She leaned into God's strength, the strength of his reputation. "I feel it was a warning from God, not to leave the cave before the appointed time."

The whispers did not start. Judah guessed she shocked them speechless with her unforced admission.

Connor theatrically allowed the silence to swell in the room before asking derogatorily, "So, God speaks to you?"

Calmly she answered. "Yes, Lieutenant Commander, he does." Judah held her pose and kept any trace of arrogance out of her voice. *God, help me out here!* Judah pleaded.

Connor's eyes snapped waiting for the thrill of the kill. "So you have an exclusive 'in' with God then, Lieutenant Commander Wakefield? What makes you think you are so special that God would speak to you?" she asked in degrading tone. Connor was not even looking at her. Her back was turned to Judge Pella, but Judah saw the profile of LT Jones' lips turn up in a sad sort of good-luck smile toward Sims.

"There is no exclusivity with God." Wakefield said confidently. "He speaks to anyone who will listen."

Connor turned to Wakefield with a canned smile. "Anyone?" She raised her eyebrows comically high. "Even say...me?" she lashed out. "I have never heard God say anything to me."

"Yes," Judah smiled sweetly. In a moment, Judah saw the struggle that Teresa Connor—the woman, not the prosecutor—was having with the concept. "Even you. In fact," Judah paused wondering if this was the right time and place for the revelation she had just received. "God tried to speak to you last night. Twice."

Connor had been starting to turn back to her table, finished with the self-incriminating witness, but she whipped back around faster than Wakefield thought possible. Teresa Connor gripped Wakefield's gaze with her steely brown eyes.

Judah did not pause, but looked directly into the prosecutor's heavily scarred soul. "First, through your mother and second in a dream." Connor, along with the rest of the room, simply stared at the naval officer sitting contentedly on the stand. Judah raised her eyebrows waiting for a response. When she received nothing but the shocked stare, she went on. "The dream concerning the man you are currently involved with and considering trapping into marrying you?"

71

Wakefield decided that was plenty of information. Ugh, nope. Probably too much.

The prosecutor opened and closed her mouth three times, looking very much like an aquarium fish, but she still had no verbal response. Her body language was enough to tell Judah, and the rest of the room's occupants, that the words were true.

Connor cocked her head to the side in wonder, but still did not speak. Sims was shocked silent as well.

She had never received such a non-response. Her voice was gentle though. She did not goad the woman whose heart had just been laid bare before a group of strangers. She just wanted the prosecutor to know she was telling the truth. "Did you need me to further describe the dream that ended up with you in a mall parking lot dead by a machete attack?" Wakefield asked.

Judah often received words of knowledge and words of wisdom during church ministry time. It was nice to know that the gifts of the spirit, as found in Ephesians, were not elevated to "Sunday-use-only." Judah hesitated, rethinking the situation. Maybe she *had* gone too far. The gifts were given to up-lift and encourage, not tear down prosecutors in front of a crowd. Wakefield gave a little cough. "You know, the plans God has for your life are much better than trying to get your own way, because He loves you very much."

Judge Pella cleared his throat. Wakefield snapped her mouth shut.

Finally, Connor shook herself from her stupor. "You do *not* need to go on." She turned, obviously shaken on a deep level, to get her notes from the table.

"Do you want me to take over?" LT Jones asked her lead council from the second chair in whispered tones while Conner stalled at the table. The quiet room did nothing to shield the question from the courtroom population.

"No!" Connor said sharply. "I've got it." By the time Connor had recovered her footsteps to reclaim her position in front of the witness stand, her previously guarded visage was firmly back in place. It was no holds barred.

"Commander Wakefield," she began. The quiet clacking of the court reporter resumed. "Were you ever alone with Lieutenant Commander Rivers?"

8

"**Y**es, on several occasions," she nodded. It was obvious where the attorney was going with this line of questioning.

"How close did the two of you have to get when he stitched your face for over an hour?"

"Objection, relevance?" her defense attorney finally found his voice.

"I am afraid I have the same question. Approach." Pella instructed the three lawyers, and motioned them forward with a crooked finger. "Where are you going with this, Commander?" Wakefield could hear him ask the prosecutor.

"I will show that the defendant was, at the very least, emotionally involved with Lieutenant Commander Rivers."

"Your honor, that is not breaking any regulations, and if it were, she is not charged with fraternization." Sims spoke up in whispered tones.

"But, sir, she was the O.I.C. Any involvement with a man under her command is outside the boundaries of good order and discipline. It's conduct unbecoming. It goes to pattern, your honor."

Pella weighed the arguments for a moment. Then sided with the prosecution. It was probative, but needed to be brought to light, if it was true. "Back away," he said. "Overruled. You may answer the question."

"Do you need me to repeat the question?" Connor asked with a self-congratulatory smirk.

"No, thank you. My face required 47 tiny stitches. We were within inches of each other, but we—"

Connor cut her off. "And when the two of you went skylarking off into the desert, back to check the alleged fire, how long were you alone?"

Wakefield felt emotionally worn down. She did not know how much longer she could hold up under the continuous questioning. There had been so many highs and many more lows during the course of the day. How much longer until they were dismissed? "Nearly two and a half hours," she said. "The fire was very real. It was recorded by NASA from the shuttle's recorder if you'd care to verify it," she offered.

Connor ignored the comment. "Two and a half hours? What were the two of you doing that could have possibly taken that long?"

"I don't like what you are implying." Wakefield pierced her with a gaze.

"Nevertheless," Judge Pella spoke from the bench, "you must answer the question."

The courtroom door in the back opened and in strode a familiar trench coat-clad figure. He walked confidently toward the front without taking a seat. "You are in the wrong courtroom, sir." Pella told him.

"No, I'm not. Mason Pella?" he asked even though the judge's name was etched on the brass nameplate on the court side of his desk. The newcomer looked at the officer on the witness stand and smiled conspiratorially. "Lieutenant Commander Wakefield has been reassigned, TAD, effective immediately."

"Not before this hearing is over," Connor said, alarm raising her pitch.

"Who do you think you are bursting into my courtroom like this? Marine, restrain him. We will talk in my chambers when I am through here." Pella snapped.

"Richmond Dietz. Actually, you don't want to do that." Dietz spoke quickly. He dug into the inside pocket of his coat he as continued forward.

There was a whimper from the front row of the gallery and several people slipped down in their seats. LT Jones ducked under the prosecution's table. Even Sims turned a little green. Judge Pella flinched. A pair of marine guards responded to the threat with valor. They were on him immediately. "Jeez! You people are tense!" Dietz shook of the guards. "Relax." His eyes rolled heavenward. "It is just a letter." He waved a single sheet of high-quality stationary around in the air. "And I believe the signatures outrank you, Captain," he told Judge Pella.

"Approach," Pella instructed Dietz, who was coming forward whether the judge liked it or not.

Wakefield watched the action with open-mouthed surprise. She was in the middle of an Article 32, people did not get released for duty in the middle of one. What was Dietz thinking?

She gave him a strange look, but, she did appreciate his timing.

Dietz handed the letter over to the judge, and the whir of whispers filled the room as the officer of the court read.

"I *strongly* object," Connor put in her opinion of the disruption and possible disappearance of the defendant whom she was quite sure was guilty.

Pella looked up and his eyes darkened at the CIA director standing impatiently in front of him. "I object, too, Lieutenant Commander Connor, but it seems we have both been out ranked," he said. "We will reconvene at a later date, while Lieutenant Commander Wakefield attends to 'a matter of classified national security'," he read from the paper.

"But, your honor..." Connor whined. Then she regained her composure. "I believe the prosecution has demonstrated evidence enough to hold these charges over for court martial."

"Be that as it may, the defense has not finished presenting its case, Miss Connor. They will receive a full and fair hearing—when Wakefield returns." Pella turned his gaze to include Dietz. "I expect to be notified when she returns to the country. We *will* complete this hearing."

Wakefield sat stunned, listening to the men. The judge handed the stationary to Wakefield. She saw three signatures scrawled at the bottom before Dietz said, "Oh, you can keep that. It is your copy. Wakefield has her own waiting in my car."

Pella cleared his throat. "It seems you are free to go on your own recognizance, Commander. For the time being. But if I hear that you are back stateside before you report in to me for a new hearing date to pick up where we left off, I'll have your oak leaves!"

"Yes, sir!" Wakefield smiled broadly, though she could feel the tightness of the skin on her scarred cheek. She stood and followed Dietz out of the courtroom.

Her pastor was standing to greet her as she saw that he had waited for her in the hallway all this time. "Thanks so much for coming to support me," she whispered to Pastor Jacobs before disappearing out the double doors. "I can't stop right now." She begged his understanding.

In the elevator by themselves, Judah turned to Dietz. "What was that all about?" she teased. "I didn't realize you rode a white horse."

"Don't count me as your knight yet!' Dietz warned. "I lied." He reached inside his jacket's inside pocket again.

"You lied? To a judge! Are you crazy?" Wakefield was flabbergasted.

Dietz smiled at her vehemence. "I have your orders right here." He unfolded another piece of thick white stationary. "It is not in the car."

Wakefield grasped the paper from his hand and stared at the signature line. "The Secretary of the Navy, the Secretary of Defense and," Wakefield paused as she looked up at Dietz, "the President of the United States? My word!" she exclaimed. Wakefield rubbed the blue bottom signature. It was real.

"Yes, I've had a busy day," Dietz commented slyly. Wakefield scanned the contents of the letter. "Germany! It is freezing and so gray there this time of year," she commented. "Sorry," she amended, "I don't mean to sound ungrateful.

Dietz led her out a side door with a crash bar to the parking lot. "But," Dietz held up one finger and raised his eyebrows laughably, "it is better than a court martial for next week, right." He sounded rather proud of himself.

She laughed aloud with relief. "Yes it is!" She leaned over and gave him an unprofessional peck on the cheek.

Dietz put a hand to his jaw, "Already, Miss Judah?" he pretended to swoon. Wakefield laughed merrily. She would bet her whole savings account that none of Dietz's other agents ever joked in such a silly manner with him.

"Thank you for saving me from that prosecutor. I thought she was going to eat me alive. You were the answer to prayer for someone who was almost a martyr, Dietz." She loved to tease this man about spiritual things. Theirs was an odd relationship.

After six years, Dietz seemed comfortable with her strange little ways. "But I haven't even told you the best news yet!" His thin mustache curled up on the corners.

"There's more? Why, sir!" she batted her eyelashes at him and pretended to preen her long hair that was still back in a solid bun. "I don't know what to say."

"Oh, you! You've got to quit putting me on that way. You never know when an old man like me is going to take you seriously and fall for a pretty young face like yours," he told her.

"That could be a good thing, you know." Judah kept up the act. "Maybe you'll stop sending me into places where I get shot!"

She glanced sideways at the career CIA man. Maybe there was more truth to his statement that she had first thought. He was walking awfully slow. Was he prolonging their time together? *Nah, he's just a spy good at misdirection.* "Here's my car." He took the keys she had fished out of her purse and unlocked the door for her. "What is the other news?" she asked expectantly.

Dietz smiled again. It had to be some kind of record for him. "Lieutenant Commander Rivers is on his way home. His *training exercise* was successful and he will be joining you again on this assignment."

Wakefield closed her eyes briefly in relief. One of the stressors in her life was over. David Rivers had lived safely through his mission. When she opened her eyes again, she interpreted Dietz's smile accurately. "I know how much you like him and all," Dietz teased her.

Judah huffed, hoping to hide her blush. She swatted the CIA director's chest. "You are as bad as my father!" But she could not hide her bunching cheeks. "I do not have a crush on Lieutenant Commander Rivers, no matter what the two of you may think." She slid into her driver's seat as the sky was turning pretty shades of purple, pink and orange with the setting sun. The Mustang's powerful V-8 engine roared to life.

"I know you don't have a crush on him, Judah," Dietz placated her with an open hand. "Be at my office for a thorough briefing on Wednesday, I'm still trying to get him there too."

"See you then. Thanks again for your impeccable timing," Wakefield shut her car door, and he could see that while she backed out of the space she was still snapping her seatbelt into the buckle.

Dietz watched her pull up to the guard shack and wait for the mechanical security arm to rise so she could drive out.

"I know you don't have a crush, Judah," Dietz repeated to the icy air. His words made white puffs of frost. "I think you may be falling in love with him." Dietz let a half-frown rest on his face for a full twenty seconds before returning to his vehicle.

9

Wakefield pulled into the home-bound traffic and reached for her cell phone. She wanted to call the Jacksons, who had invited her to dinner. Kelly was a terrific cook. "Well, Kelly said she didn't need any more notice than me walking through the front door." Judah couldn't imagine having an unexpected guest for dinner. "One more microwave meal, I suppose," she snorted at her own deficiency in the kitchen.

She dialed information and waited four seconds for the operator to pick up before she remembered that her phone was out of service.

The naval officer debated whether to go or not for ten minutes as she crept along the Beltway. "I can't believe I am going to crash someone's dinner!" she said aloud. She directed her red sports car to the line of vehicles leading off the exit ramp.

She had attended small group at the Jackson's home one semester on Tuesday evenings, so finding it was not a problem. Ringing the doorbell at 6 PM, hoping for a friendly reception, and knowing that she needed it, was a bit more difficult.

Timmy from her Sunday School class answered the chime. His freckled face lit up in delight and he left the door wide open to the freezing January air while he took a few backward steps toward the kitchen.

Kelly came around the corner drying her hands on a dishtowel. "Who is it?" she called at the same time.

"Oh, Momma!" Timmy whispered sounding awe struck. "She really came!"

His voice did not have much volume, but his excitement was genuine.

Timmy turned back to the door at full speed and launched himself into his teacher's arms. "I am so glad you came. I've been praying all day for you to come. I want to show you my paper, and we are having my favorite dinner." Timmy's bangs fluttered into his eyes, and Judah smoothed them back.

She gave the boy a tight squeeze. "Then I'm glad I came too," she told him. She looked up to find a smiling Kelly watching the two of them.

"Perfect timing, Judah." She motioned her inside. "Timmy," Kelly warned in her best 'mother' voice, "Let Miss Judah take her coat off first and give her some breathing room."

"Okay, Momma. I won't talk too much. Just like you said. I just have to show her how I can make the *J* now." The four-year-old wiggled out of her arms and went running to the kitchen.

"I'm glad you came, too." Kelly said. "I could use an extra pair of hands to tear the lettuce for salad."

"I'm on it," Judah said hanging her coat and cover on the pegs by the door. She had forgotten she was still in uniform. Kelly was wearing an apron over a pair of faded designer jeans and a blue Duke sweatshirt that had seen better days. Kelly's appearance reminded her that though the two women were the same age, they led very different lives.

"Timmy learned how to write a *J* today in K-4." Kelly explained proudly. "When I told him the J starts your name, he started praying right there in the car that he would get to see you today." Kelly smiled broadly. Her cherry lips were full and colorful without lipstick.

The authentic grin did wonders for Judah's heart.

She dropped the half torn head of lettuce into the bowl and went around the counter with tears threatening to spill down her cheeks. "I can't tell you how much I need friends today." Judah's chin quivered.

"That bad, huh?" Kelly asked. She wrapped her arms around Judah's waist.

"You have no idea." Judah snorted, returning the life-giving hug.

The oven timer buzzed, and the two women giggled.

"Welcome to my life," Kelly said. "With a four-year-old, a two year old, and one on the way, it seems like it is always one thing bumping into another. Baked pork chops, garlic bread, salad and iced tea, how's that sound?" she asked.

"I wouldn't care if it were stale white bread and water with no ice." Judah went back to tearing the iceburg lettuce. "I didn't know you were expecting." She smiled fondly at the woman.

"Nine weeks. We haven't made an announcement yet." Kelly smiled widely, and Judah wondered how she had missed the glow earlier.

Wednesday 9 January 2002
Dulles International Airport, DC
1745 hours

"I can't tell you how happy I am to be flying civilian, Dietz," Wakefield said. She looked much more relaxed than last time he saw her. She was dressed in comfortable flared leg, black pants that had a permanent crease sewn into the length of the leg and a black cotton/lycra shirt perfectly fitted to her figure. Tiny embroidered rosebuds embellished the fabric.

"Those passengers holding business class tickets and first class tickets on flight 8253 for Paris may now board," the announcement came over the loud speaker in a French-accented female voice.

"That's you," Dietz told his companion and uncrossed his legs to stand.

Judah peeled herself out of the molded plastic chair, picked up the strap of her laptop case and folded her thigh-length mohair coat over the computer. "Thank you, Dietz. I appreciate what you've done for me." She smiled softly, her eyes giving her message legitimacy.

The older man tried to shrug it off. This woman sure knew how to get to him. "Company upgrade. You deserve it." Gratitude made him uncomfortable. Maybe it was because he had seen so little of it in his profession and in his life that he did not know how to respond to it.

"I didn't mean the seat." Judah's blue eyes glowed with warmth. She flipped her straightened, honey blond hair over her shoulder. It was just at the length where its long layers slipped forward against each other like living silk. "I meant sitting here with me, waiting for my seat to be announced." Judah chuckled. "There is probably not another man in the country who would do that," she corrected herself, "who *could* do that."

Dietz had thrown around his weight as the Director of Counterintelligence of the CIA a little bit at the security checkpoint. He had to flash his badge for the managing lieutenant before he was searched and allowed through ticketless. Life was fun every now and then.

The pretty intelligence officer stood eye to eye facing him. "Also, thank you again for your particular timing in that hearing." Her face was open with gratitude. "Now, if you can get the rest of the hearing cancelled and the court martial charges that are sure to follow, dismissed while I am away, I think we will be just about even. And I would be eternally grateful."

Dietz chuckled. He quickly sobered and looked away. He stared at a framed poster boasting the castles of the Rhine River. "I did not come with a purely selfless motive…"

Dietz's mouth twitched from side to side in an awkward mannerism. His thin black mustache moved too. "You need me to reassure you that I will be fine on this mission." Wakefield understood. "Dietz you know God will take care of me." They went through this every time he sent her out. To Judah it had become a tradition. One where she was able to freely share her faith with the rarely-receptive, influential man. At these times, he almost begged her to tell him about God.

Dietz's face hardened slightly at her words. "That's what you said last time." His eyes cut to her cheek. "Look what happened then." He looked like a sullen little boy who had been disappointed.

Judah knew that that was exactly what the man before her was: a boy who was taking baby steps in his heart toward Christ. Dietz had trusted God with Judah's well-being, and he felt let down when she came home hurt.

Suddenly, it did not matter if she missed her plane or her connection with Rivers who had flown out to Berlin from California earlier in the day. She had to help the disappointed boy inside Dietz understand. "You know one of the things I appreciate and admire most about God?" she asked. Judah rested her coat-covered laptop in the plastic seat.

"What's that, Wakefield?" Dietz wrinkled his brow.

"I appreciate that His ways are higher than my ways. I don't always understand why things happen, but I know that God allows certain things, even bad things, to happen for my ultimate good." Judah broke off.

"Go ahead. You better explain that statement," Dietz remarked. He was candidly open for a man who did not misunderstand many things.

The airline began calling passengers by rows in coach. The bustle rumbled around them as passengers rushed to be first in their assigned seats, but Dietz concentrated fully on her face. That was a miracle in itself. Dietz was a man trained to listen to whomever was speaking, but observe his surroundings.

"One of the ways I understand God is to see Him through what I understand to be His two major goals: to draw all men unto Himself, and to seek a deeper relationship with the ones who already know Him."

"I follow you so far," Dietz nodded. His eyes creased around the edges as he concentrated on her words. He seemed to want to understand.

"God allows things that are hard, things that are ugly," she pointed to her healing scar, "things that we cannot fix on our own, to give us a reason to draw close to him, to rely on his strength and wisdom. See, to me," Judah said thoughtfully, even as she drew her own conclusions, "this cut on my face, is God saying, 'I love you Judah. I want you to remember that I saved your life on this day. Will you trust me? I will bring you through.' It is also God's way of saying to Satan, 'This one is mine'." Judah sighed softly.

"That is where I lose you, Commander." Dietz frustration was evident in his voice and jerky mannerisms. "How can a God who loves you, allow you to go through life scarred like this? I mean sure, there is plastic surgery, but not if it had been a hundred years ago, heck, even 25 years ago. It doesn't make sense."

"Looking at it from a beauty versus ugliness stand point, no it doesn't," Judah agreed. *How can I make it more clear?* She prayed for help. "When an artist signs the bottom of his painting, though it mars the picture, does it detract from its beauty? Is it up to the sculpture to advise the sculptor on how to chisel it? What if as a result of my beauty, I became vain and turned away from God? Then beauty would be a detriment, would it not?"

"That wouldn't happen to you, Judah." Dietz rolled his eyes at a suggestion he considered ludicrous.

"God is the only one who can decipher the intricacies of the human heart. Sometime I wonder...no one is above denying Christ. It is just finding the right price. I would rather not risk it. Only God knows the full impact of good this scar will leave upon my life. Even though God doesn't do evil things and does not desire them for us, He turns bad things that happen because of human choices—whether ours or someone else's—into good things. I have already found myself much more compassionate toward others with disfigurements."

"But you're not even married yet, how do you expect—" An announcement on the overhead cut him off from making a hurtful blunder.

"Last call flight 8253," the flight attendant called in French, German and then English. "Miss Wakefield, everyone is on board except you." The words came out of the loud speaker.

Judah turned around to the check-in desk, shocked. The woman shrugged and smiled as they made eye contact. "Cross-reference on the passenger manifest," she explained—not on the microphone.

Judah shook her head, amused. "I am coming." She picked up her laptop again, pulled her ticket out of the front pocket and swung it up on her shoulder. "Do me a favor and just think about it," she said to Dietz.

"I'll do that," he said. "Miss Wakefield, you are in the right business. I think I should amend your service record to read that you speak 10 languages, and add Christianese to the list."

"Oh, you're funny!" Judah smiled fully. "I've still got a lot to learn. Besides, I am thinking of tackling Chinese or Japanese next."

"Good evening," Judah told the attendant who was in her forties. "Thank you for waiting. It was quite important."

"Not a problem. You're still on time. And I can see it was important. Your man is still waiting to say good-bye." She offered a knowing smile.

It was easier to smile and wave good-bye to Dietz than to explain their complex relationship to the happy-to-be-a-facilitator-of-love flight attendant.

10

J udah had to change planes in Paris at 0625 local time. It was smack
in the middle of prime sleep time for her at home, 0125 hours. She
tried to blend in with the tourists as much as possible. With this
case profile, and the constant threat of Filasek, one could never be
too careful, but still she hurried. She was not sure she would still have
time to stop at the international terminal bakery before having to board
her next flight. She visited the owner, Monsieur Beauvais, every time
she was in Paris.

Her layover was only 50 minutes, but her mouth watered for
the long baguette of fresh crusty bread. It was always warm. Thick
crunchy crust with billowy clouds of yeasty softness inside. She greeted
the man behind the counter. He did not recognize her out of uniform.
"Mr Beauvais. It is me, Judah Wakefield. I am sorry I am in such a hurry
I can't stop and chat. I need one of your long baguettes. I have been
dreaming of it since Washington," she smiled pleasantly. She had a
thought. "No, make it two." She decided Rivers might like to have one,
too. Hers wouldn't last the short flight from Paris to Berlin.

"Of course. Hurry, hurry. It is always a pleasure to see your
lovely face. Mademoiselle Wakefield. Make some time to talk to me next
time you are here, eh? No charge for such a beautiful lady." He
motioned emphatically for her to put the debit card away. "Just do not
tell the other customers our secret, eh?"

"Thank you a million times, Monsieur Beauvais. We'll have
coffee next time I'm in, and I'll buy!" She hurried off to make her
connection.

Tegel International Airport, Berlin, Germany
0900 hours

Judah was anxious to claim her bag and grab a taxi to the center of town where one of Dietz's secretaries had secured Rivers and her two single rooms. Wakefield, once her penchant for French bread was satiated, thought a shower and a good nap, until 1400 hours, sounded like heaven.

She could miss a night's sleep when necessary, but she always felt a little punchy. So when the job did not require immediate attention, she liked to take a few hours and get a fresh start.

Wakefield followed the signs to the baggage claim carousel while announcements blared on overhead speakers in German, French, English then Spanish. "The only problem with speaking so many languages," she murmured to herself on the second escalator into the belly of the airport, "is listening to them." Most travelers would be able to tune out at least half of the redundant messages about parking in the drop-off zone and leaving baggage unattended. She could not.

LCDR Rivers stood near the bottom of the stairs that led from the terminal to the baggage area, so he would not miss her. His flight had gone through Frankfurt and arrived nearly an hour earlier. He decided to wait for Judah so they could go to the hotel together.

Most of the people coming from the international terminal, which was practically everyone at Tegel Airport, walked as singles. He had to scan hundreds of faces. Business men and women arriving from Paris to work for the day, students returning to school, as classes resumed on Monday, a pile of 25 tourists who must have been on their first European experience all came down together. They all spoke in unmistakably loud American English, and took pictures of each other and the airport.

Rivers shook his head at their antics. "If you've seen one airport—" he said under his breath. "Then what?" he asked himself. The

SEAL despised laziness, including the laziness of speech found in clichés and common cursing. "Then...you are likely to see another one," he finished, pleased with himself.

He nearly missed Wakefield as she tagged along at the end of the tourist mob parade. He caught his breath. She looked different than he remembered. He studied her while she walked, unknowingly, toward him. She looked more cultured, more continental, than he had thought. Maybe because he was comparing her to the garish Americans she was walking with. Her blond hair was different from when they were in the desert; it was modernly ruler straight instead of falling in waves down her back or being secured in a regulation tight bun.

And she certainly was not in uniform. Or that awful abaya.

By the time River's gaze landed on Wakefield's sea blue eyes, she had seen him, and a wide grin was quickly spreading across her lips.

"Hey there, sailor!" she broke away from the crowd to greet him.

"Good morning," he said returning her toothy grin. He looped a finger under the strap of her computer case and swung it over his shoulder, reminiscent of when they were boarding the COD to leave the USS *Reprisal.* "Do I know you, ma'am?" he asked with a twinkle in his blue-green eyes.

"I sure hope you don't greet women you *don't* know with that smile. It's lethal!" Wakefield commented lightly. "Come on, let's keep me moving. I am about to fall asleep on my feet." She flipped her hair out of her face with two fingers.

They moved into the crowd around the moving belt that spewed mostly black suitcases of every size, shape, and age. "So...you like my smile." Rivers said while they waited.

She turned to him slightly, but did not look at his face. "I didn't say that," she told him in a flat voice.

"So you don't like my smile?" He frowned unconsciously. Women were always commenting on his smile. He had only assumed she would like it too.

"Relax, Rivers." She snorted slightly. "I didn't say that either. Why are you still here, by the way?" she questioned finally looking at him.

"I thought you could use a ride." He decided to use the safe answer. She was acting a little strange.

"That was courteous of you."

Was she teasing or not? "What can I say? I am a courteous gentleman."

"Yes, you are. And I missed you too." Wakefield reached over to squeeze him in a familiar sideways hug. "What's wrong?" she pulled away quickly at his sharp intake of breath.

He hadn't meant for her to find out, especially this soon. He shrugged. "I cracked a rib or two a few days ago."

Her face lost some of its color. "While you were...out of the country?"

"I feel like I am always out of the country these days. But yes."

"Can you tell me what happened?" she asked concern written on her features. "Or is it classified? Hey! There's my suitcase." The navy blue bag with the light blue scarf knotted at the handle tumbled onto the belt.

While they waited for it to come around, he told her about McCarthy. "He felt really bad about it, and I told him to go on a diet."

Wakefield shook her head. "I am glad you didn't lose your man, but do you always have to play the hero?"

Rivers recognized the rhetorical question for what it was, and wisely he kept his mouth shut.

"Where is your luggage?" Wakefield asked as Rivers wheeled her bag behind them on their way outside.

"I already stowed it in the rental."

"You rented car?" she asked with a perplexed expression. "Transportation in Berlin and on the trains and trams is a cinch. Germany has one of the best transportation systems in the world."

"True," Rivers nodded agreeably. "But, now, we can go on our own schedule."

"I know you," Wakefield smiled impishly and teased, "you just don't want to be out of control." Wakefield's tone sounded accusing. "When you are driving, you are in control, just like back in the desert. Go ahead, deny it." She challenged even as she put a hand over her mouth. In a single glance Rivers could see regret on her features so he waited a beat for her to amend the attitude. But the apology didn't come.

Rivers snorted and shook his head, deciding to continue on with the strange light banter that he didn't quite understand. "No way. I learned my lesson with you, Miss Wakefield. I will choose the battles I know I can win. I agree; I do like to be in control." Rivers began to shove her suitcase into the tiny white vehicle.

"Is it going to be an issue on this assignment?"

"What? I don't know. The only issue I have is whether both we and our luggage will fit in this vehicle at the same time. Why are you being so argumentative?" he asked her. This is not how he had imagined their reunion.

"I am not being..." She cut herself off before arguing that she was not arguing. "Sorry. I'll try to do better. I guess I've had a hard week or two."

Rivers snorted divisively again. "*You* have had a hard week? Try again!" he snapped. "Ugh, why won't this hatch close properly?" He slammed it shut forcefully. He hated being out of sync on an assignment. Especially in the beginning and especially with Judah. The sound echoed all around the parking garage. This time it did stick, only a strap hung out. "There!" he was satisfied. The strap could be a tail. He was not going to open the hatch again for a four-inch nylon strap. "I think my week has probably been a little more stressful than your cushy desk job at Naval Intelligence."

Wakefield's expression blanched. "Are you driving?" she asked evenly. Her eyes, so full of life a few minutes earlier, were now icy daggers. She folded herself into the passenger's side, arranged her computer flat on her lap, and buckled in mechanically.

Rivers watched her actions from the back of the vehicle in shock. How had their conversation nose-dived toward the ocean floor? He took a deep breath as he felt a nudge about his previous comment. He got inside the tiny mini and fastened his own belt. Their knees were up to their chests and there was no personal space. "I am sorry, Commander," Rivers said as politely as he knew how. He was still smarting about her unusual hero comment. "I am sure your week has been difficult, too. I apologize for making little of your job. Do you want to talk about your week?"

Her posture lost a fraction of its rigidity, but she did not look at him. "You could not do your job if I didn't do mine so well," she said.

"I realize that," he said slowly, trying to figure out her frame of reference for such a statement. "So what was your week like?" he prompted again.

She was still locked down. "I'd rather not talk, Commander. Could we go ahead and check into the hotel please?"

"Kinda early," Rivers looked at his digital watch already set to Western Europe Continental time. "Only ten hundred hours. Most hotels don't accept—"

"I know," she interrupted. "But please," her voice was steely, but then dropped off as her tiredness broke through, "let's try."

Hotel *Askanischerhof*
Ku'damm 53, Berlin
Thursday, 10 January, 2002
1045 hours

Judah nudged the door closed with her heel and wheeled her suitcase past the private bath. Walking into the main European-sized room, she let the luggage swing back upright with a dull thud. Her eyes bugged out. "It's got to be about 40 degrees in here," she said as she blew warm breath into her cupped hands and looked around for the thermostat.

After flicking the small switch from *off* to *high heat*, Judah eyed the overly floral bed and then her watch. She could take a couple of hours to unkink and rest her eyes.

She peeled back the bedspread so that the corners met and then folded it back on itself again, picked up the whole pile in the middle and folded it sideways in half twice more on the way to the small wardrobe. She tossed it on top.

Still in her coat, Judah laid down flat on her back and closed her eyes as she sank into the mattress. Her muscles and bones felt like she was falling slowly toward the floor as she forced them to relax. How long had it been since every muscle had loosened at once? Before the flight, certainly before the hearing when Dietz saved the day—or at least postponed the day of reckoning. Perhaps it was just before LT Jones had showed up for the investigation? "No," Wakefield whispered, as she went even further back in her memory. "Even in Dietz's office more than a week ago for the debrief, I was holding this tension."

Wakefield stretched her still-shod feet toward the wall and the crown of her head toward the headboard. She heard Rivers bump something heavy through the connecting door in the next room.

"Rivers." She sighed. "I haven't been fully relaxed since I met him on our little adventure in the desert."

"Oh," Judah groaned in embarrassment at the fresh memory of the airport carpark. She threw her cold, stiff, coat-covered arms over her chilled face. "Lord, everything kept coming out wrong. Then everything he said just made me madder." She blew her lips out in a little horsey blubber of disgust at her response. "I was such a jerk. Why bother getting offended at such a little thing. He couldn't have known about the hearing. I should have just told him instead of pouting about it. Stupid."

Judah kicked off her shoes as she tried to quiet her soul. *But he didn't need to take such a high and mighty tone.* She could not be still and so stood, pulled back the blanket and sheet and crawled into the bed, coat and all.

David ran the sink water next door. *The walls sure are thin,* she grumbled. *Does he really think I just sit behind a desk all day? Eighty to ninety percent of my job is fieldwork analysis. And I do a good job.* She shook her head as the irritation smarted again.

She rolled to her right side and pinched her eyes shut against the light that permeated the curtain. "Lord, he is normally so kind and considerate. Why is he getting under my skin like this?" She tried to be still, to examine her heart for what was missing that she seemed to be expecting David Rivers to fill.

Everything was quiet. No answers falling from above.

The pressure began to build again. *I don't care what anyone thinks of me. Why do I feel such a need to be perfect in front of him?* She growled while clenching her teeth and flopped over to face the wall. "I just need to sleep for a little while," she moaned wistfully. Though she knew that would not bring resolution, only, hopefully, a clearer mind to sort through the emotions.

11

U.S. Embassy, Berlin
Neustadtishe Kirchstarsse 10117
Fourth Floor CIA Station Chief's Office
Thursday 10 January 2002
1520 hours

"Welcome to Berlin, Lieutenant Commanders. I'll show you in." A business-like executive assistant rose from her desk to open an inner-office door on the fourth floor of the U.S. Embassy. David Rivers and Judah Wakefield stepped into a dark office paneled in rich wood. Expensive fixtures and furniture lined the walls.

"Your team from the States has arrived," Ms Marshall said by way of an introduction. "Coffee and kuchen are already on their way up from the kitchen, shall I send for two more?"

"Yes, please." A man in his mid-forties stood to greet the naval officers. "I'm Paul Nelson. And this," he gestured to the younger man rising next to him, "is Chad Wellingham." Nelson offered his hand first to LCDR Rivers and then to LCDR Wakefield. He was of average height, with salon-styled hair that was graying at the temples. Grey also laced his well-kept full beard and mustache. He seemed physically fit and comfortable in the three-piece suit he wore.

Quite obviously, Chad was the agent and Nelson was the Station Chief. Chad Wellingham looked to be in his mid-twenties with stringy, long, black hair that was too flat a color to be natural. Wakefield wondered why anyone would do that to his hair on purpose. He had three facial piercings that Judah could count. His oversized clothes hung off his body in all the wrong places. Chad's cheeks were ruddy while the rest of his skin looked pasty—probably from the bad hair dye, Judah decided.

His firm handshake was a surprise, as was his refined voice. "A pleasure to make your acquaintance," he said. Chad Wellingham sounded as if he was from the eastern seaboard without the whiney nasal tones found in the Boston and New York areas. "I've not met many sailors who look like you, ma'am."

He said it with such awe that Judah laughed. "I'll take that as a compliment," she said with a genuine smile. She folded her hands together in front of her.

"So, Mr Nelson," Rivers interjected. "Nice office you've got here."

"Yeah," Wakefield looked around. "It looks remarkably like Director Dietz's office at Langley." She admired the smooth brown leather furniture in front of stacked stone fireplace and away from his desk area.

"Perhaps because Dietz was the West Berlin Station Chief from 1984 until 1990, when he was promoted home after the Wall came down. I was moved in after an interim chief was here," Nelson explained as he shifted from one foot to the other.

"I didn't know that." Wakefield said absorbing the news. As CIA Chief of Station, Berlin, Dietz must have been intimately acquainted with the world-changing events of November 9, 1989.

"I wasn't aware that the CIA would be housed in the same building as the State Department at the Embassy," Rivers raised an eyebrow as he commented to Nelson.

"Well, they did relegate us to this corner of the fourth floor. The Ambassador's offices and his staff take up the first three in their entirety, plus both wings and the back-side of the courtyard. It's actually quite a large operation. However, it is not secure enough for what we've brought you in for. So, I am glad Dietz sent you both over. We can use the extra help."

"Why exactly are we here?" Rivers asked. Dietz had told Wakefield that he'd given Rivers the gist of it over the phone, but the details he would leave to Nelson.

"I'll let Chad explain." Nelson brushed a piece of lint from his suit with long, slim fingers.

Ms Marshall rapped twice on the door before entering and announcing the snack. Her light brown hair was cut in a conservative bob, that did little to enhance her features, which, if highlighted, could have been pretty.

"Coffee and kuchen is a German tradition much like the British afternoon tea," Nelson explained. "Just much less formal. We usually serve at 1500 instead of traditional 1600 hours teatime. Coffee with a cake-like sweet. Similar to American pound cake, but more dense and sometimes has flavored fillings or toppings." Nelson reached for a plate with a large slice of kuchen and a silver demi-spoon. "I'm afraid over the last decade or so, I've become hopelessly addicted," the ambassador grinned as he patted a slight paunch unapologetically.

Wakefield returned his smile in their awkward little standing square. Then she broke to lean forward and dress her thick black coffee with cream and sugar. She took a sip. "Wow!" she gulped. Her voice was a little horse. "Tastes like marine coffee, except smoother."

"Ahem," Rivers cleared his throat after taking a smaller sip of his coffee that had been diluted with three spoons full of sugar and plenty of thick cream. "That'll make your hair stand up," he agreed.

Nelson gestured to the chairs. "Let's sit."

Chad took them back to the reason for the officers' assignment. "I got a tip from one of my contacts, who had heard from one of his inside men, that a hit has been ordered on the president. While according to Chief Nelson, that is not unusual, it's not just anyone who has been hired. We believe that Azure Tiger has been contracted for the hit.

"There is a CIA dossier on him, but no picture. We believe him to be responsible for several high-profile deaths. But since there is not a picture, or even a drawing, of him on file, there is nothing to pass on to border control. The only identifying markers we have are that he is a Hindi extremist from India. Perhaps a rogue officer from the Indian army, or he may have been kicked out of the royal family." Chad said. He took a sip of his coffee.

"That's a pretty big difference," Rivers brow creased. He held his coffee to rest high on his chest in a relaxed pose, too enthralled with the agent's details to drink.

Wakefield nodded in agreement. She classified the details methodically, to clarify his persona in her mind. An officer would be organized, methodical and weapons-savvy. A royal would be unpredictable, and probably high-strung in his movements because he had not had any formal "warrior" training.

"I know." Nelson sighed heavily. "What's more, we have five suspects. Each of them entered Germany through Berlin in the last seven days and their passports threw up red flags. We have people following them. Credit cards and bank activity have also been flagged."

"It is a lot of information to whittle down," Chad said. "I have been cataloguing it myself when I am not out on the street."

"Probably too much." Wakefield set down her coffee cup. "Could be a smoke screen. Do we have a history on these five suspects? And how confident is the source that the hit will take place in Germany? I mean why not England or France? The president will be stopping there on his tour as well."

"We're back-tracing the movements of the five men for the last six months. Be a couple of days, maybe a week." Nelson slurped the dregs of his coffee.

Chad seemed to be staring a hole in the wall as he concentrated. Wakefield thought it incongruous with his appearance. Finally he spoke. "The contact seemed sure. I am trying to recall his exact words, because that is what convinced me." The young agent sighed. "Um, I cannot recapture it, but my contact heard that Azure Tiger chose Berlin, because of the new Embassy to be built at the home of the original one that was bombed out during World War II. The proposal for funds is on somebody's desk in Washington, pending approval," Chad explained. "To frustrate the effort, he wants to build American suspicion against Germany. He does not want the Embassy at Brandenburg Gate reconstructed."

"So he must have some background contact with Germany. Do we have a copy of the file on Azure Tiger?" Rivers asked Nelson.

Chad stood and retrieved a thick manila folder from Nelson's desk. "This contains the headlines, reports, and notes on the cases of all the deaths we have attributed to him." He handed the file to Rivers.

"She's the profiler," Rivers passed the file over to Wakefield. "See what you can make of it," he told her.

Judah settled back into the fat leather chair as she opened the front cover. "First, who compiled this information?" She glanced up at Nelson.

"As you'll see," Nelson ran a hand over his mustache and beard to check for stray crumbs, "the hits are scattered over the last seven years, when we were first aware of his activity in the West. I've done a lot of the compilation myself. A couple of aides added tips from Langley to it."

"But that's only since we were made aware of Azure Tiger's existence, correct? Who is to say that that is when his activity began?" Wakefield pondered aloud.

"You've done this before. I'd not considered that he had killed before." Nelson frowned.

"It makes sense that a top-notch assassin would not have begun with high profile cases." Chad pursed his lips and nodded his assessment.

"What was the classifying evidence, Chief?" Wakefield asked as she gave the file's pages a once over. "What made you attribute these particular deaths to the same man?" She looked up to find all three men looking at her. "I'm sorry." She broke off at their surprised faces. "Has no one ever questioned your data?" She smiled and hoped they all knew she was teasing the station chief.

"Actually, no." he said pleasantly.

"I suppose as this investigation goes along, we will all question everything. It is the truth we are after, correct?" Chad commented in his cultured tones.

"Only if the truth leads us to the assassin." Rivers grunted.

Wakefield raised her eyes from the file to glance at Rivers and then lowered her gaze back to the page in her lap. "On roughly two-thirds of the cases," Nelson explained, as he glanced between the two officers. "We found a fingerprint, or a partial, at the shooter's nest. Over ninety percent of the deaths occurred in town. Always by a double tap to the heart."

"A double hit is a pretty common mode," Wakefield dismissed. "You said, 'shooter's nest,' how often has the trajectory come from ground level?"

"Never."

"Interesting." Rivers commented. "Has ballistics traced a common caliber?"

"He likes big guns. Mostly a .50 cal on his long distance stuff. A .44 and a few .45's and .38's. In 1997 and 1998, he used exclusively .308's. Eighteen kills in that period, Commander. And he has only gone back to that size twice since then."

"What uses a three-ought-eight?" Wakefield turned to Rivers' expertise.

"The M-1 model rifle. Either a M1D sniper rifle or the M1A bush rifle are the most popular and readily available."

Wakefield thought in silence for a moment as she digested the information. Both a royal and a military man would have access to many types of weapons. In her experience, a killer usually favored a particular size or make.

"None of the ballistics match, if that was to be your next question." Nelson announced with a perturbed grimace.

"Never?" LCDR Wakefield looked up. Nelson shook his head. "He either has a collection or a source then," she said. "How many?" she waved the closed file in the air.

"One hundred seventeen in there," Chad answered for him.

Rivers' eyes bulged. "That's huge. Even during war time, professional marine snipers don't do three times that many."

"I guess you could say the man is a prolific hit man," Nelson commented wryly as he smoothed a hand over his coiffed hair.

"The fingerprints would have been left purposefully." Wakefield said. "Azure Tiger is too professional for it to have been accidental. It leans toward arrogance too. He wants recognition for his kills. Perhaps he's been building a resume."

"Not on my watch," Nelson spat.

The foursome discussed Azure Tiger for another two hours before parting for the night with plans to plow through the money trail the next morning.

12

Judah pulled the mascara wand through her lashes in a final swipe. She halted the applicator over her left eye as a knock sounded on her hotel room door. Rivers was early? She slid the applicator back into the tube and critiqued her appearance in the bathroom vanity mirror.

"I still have 30 minutes, Squid." Judah spoke as she flipped the bolt and opened the door with the odd, old-fashioned key, used as a handle.

"Squid?" A good-looking man with a British accent smiled at her. He was a hair over six feet tall with loose, dark brown curls, and skin the color of tea with cream. His long oval face of baby-soft skin gave him the look of a romantic poet. Obviously not LCDR Rivers.

When he smiled, Wakefield swallowed.

"I have been called a good many things in my lifetime," he spoke again confidently, "squid is not one of them. Especially by a woman to whom I am bringing breakfast." The man held out a Styrofoam cup of dark-brewed tea and a pastry on a paper plate with the logo of the bakery she had noted just past the hotel. "I apologize," he said, moving the plate to balance on top of the steaming tea. He held out his right hand. "James Yates, British Intelligence," he said and smiled again. Judah didn't hide the fact that she was sizing him up as they shook hands.

"LCDR Judah Wakefield, U.S. Navy," she returned.

"Naval Intel," he corrected.

She felt strangely off balance and suspicious, but only for a moment. It must be that hair, she decided. Yates' large curls were longer than the usual close-cropped military style she was used to and had a glossy sheen about them that tempted her to touch them. There was not a strand of silver to his dark locks, even though his face placed his in his very early forties. It wasn't fair to waste hair that pretty on a man, she thought. "How do you know that, James Yates, British Intelligence?"

"'Tis our business to know." He smiled again, cryptically this time. He had beautifully-formed strawberry lips. Judah wanted to keep him smiling. "May I offer you breakfast?"

Wakefield eyed the plate of fluffy strudel-topped sweet in his hand, "If breakfast is that pastry that is making my mouth water, you certainly may." She held out her hands but was trying to decide how, diplomatically, to tell him she would not be inviting him into her room.

"I will just wait down in the lobby for you and Lieutenant Commander Rivers," he said, seeming to read her mind. "I want to lend a hand in catching this Azure Tiger bugger. Nelson failed tell you I was coming?" he smiled knowingly.

She shook her head and allowed her closed lips to offer a modest smile. "Give me ten minutes." Wakefield said. She set the steaming cup on the table beside the door.

"You don't need ten minutes, but I will wait." Yates' eyes twinkled at her and Wakefield watched him go.

She gave Yates twenty seconds to depart the hall, before she scrambled, barefoot, to knock on Rivers' door, next to hers.

He opened the door as she was still knocking, holding a half-eaten pastry like a slice of pizza.

She'd brought hers too. "I see you've made a new friend as well." She smirked when he took giant bite which she matched.

"Don't you just love Deutschland?" She sighed around a mouthful of sweet layers of bread.

Richmond Dietz sat in his office chair looking out at the low early-morning, clouds. Traffic had been murder on the commute. "Twice inside 18 miles," he muttered, his lips barely parting. That he missed plowing into the abrupt stop of a semi-truck was unbelievable enough, but when he jerked his wheel to the left, in the left-most lane, to avoid a drifting SUV driver on her cell phone, and he did not end up at the bottom of the ravine and crash through the ice in the river, it was nothing short of a miracle. He had seen exactly what would happen in his mind's eye. Then suddenly he was back in his lane, completely behind the black SUV, and the driver following him was at the same distance behind. He didn't remember turning the wheel back right.

"Judah would say it's a miracle. That God was trying to grab my attention." Dietz whispered. He twitched his tiny mustache. But then miracles happened to her all the time. "Miracles don't happen to people like me." His voice sounded cynical, even to him, even as his heart dared hope, *why not to me?*

The door to his office flew open at the same time as the intercom on his desk came to life. "Admiral Tamburillo of Naval Intelligence is here to see you," Julia Cravits sounded irritated.

Dietz was startled out of his trance, but calmly twisted his chair away from the window to face the charging one-star. It was not a social call; Dietz couldn't remember ever seeing a black man turn red in the face.

"Admiral," Dietz stood to greet the man. "What a surprise." He walked around his desk and met the officer halfway. His hand was outstretched in what he hoped looked like a friendly manner. "Won't you sit down? Can I get you a cup of coffee?"

Cravits mouthed, "Sorry, sir," from the doorway as she traced Tamburillo's warpath. Her green eyes belayed her worry. Dietz shook his head at her in a tiny motion, and she pulled the door closed softly.

He should have warned her that the admiral was likely to make an appearance this week.

"No coffee. No small talk. No seat." Tamburillo growled. His dark eyes flashed. "What do you mean sending Judah in after Azure Tiger? *No one* who pursues that man lives to tell about it!"

"Judah?" Dietz could not help questioning the man's use of his subordinate's first name.

"Yes, *Judah*! Lieutenant Commander Wakefield if you prefer. My people are important to me. Her especially. It's my responsibility to see that my people stay alive!" His flaming eyes pierced Dietz. "*You* are making that very difficult."

Tamburillo's square jaw flexed in and out as he struggled to maintain a semblance of control. His black hair and bushy black eyebrows seemed to form a scary mask as he leaned in to stand eight inches from the director's nose.

"Judah is one of the best agents I have. She's cool and collected during danger and can hold her own in a fight—guns or fists. Her language skills are unbelievable." Dietz modulated his voice to try to calm the angry sailor in his office.

"I know that. Who do you think trained her?" Tamburillo responded to Dietz's soft voice and dialed his own volume down a few decibels. "But that's just it. You don't have her. She belongs in my office, and if this assignment endangers that, it's your head on a platter at the next Congressional subcommittee meeting! I'll see to the carving myself." The admiral sucked in a breath as if he was reloading "I haven't gotten over the *carving* you allowed on the last assignment." His voice was dangerously low now. The quiet voice scared Dietz more than Tamburillo's raised one. So he stayed silent, absorbing the verbal assault of a navy two-star admiral.

"Speaking of the last assignment, how dare you sneak her out of an Article 32 before she could clear her name—which was only barnacled because of you!" Tamburillo narrowed his eyes. Dietz straightened his shoulders, determined to take everything the admiral shot at him.

But then it was time to fire back. "In case you were not aware, she was drowning in there, Admiral! From what I read of the transcript, the hearing officer would certainly have preferred the charges to court martial. Where were *you* in her hour of need?" Dietz allowed the guilt he felt to ricochet back at Judah's C.O.

Tamburillo lowered his brow and looked fiercely at Dietz. His snapping coal eyes nearly disappeared underneath his wild black eye brows. "How did you read the transcript of a closed, on-going judicial proceeding?"

Dietz lowered the corners of his eyes "I *am* CIA," he said, as if that explained everything.

"I wish, for once, you would not sneak around like a—like a, I don't know. I can't think of an animal except a snake that is as despicable as you are. Allowing a noble woman to take your hits, and in the courtroom." Tamburillo snorted and turned to leave.

Now that Judah was in the middle of the assassin investigation, neither of them could do anything, short of ordering her home. Dietz wasn't even sure how much weight his order would carry, as the Commander-in-Chief had signed her previous orders.

With his hand on the door, the admiral turned back to Dietz, who still stood in place. "You get her back A-sap, and unscathed this time, or I'll see to it that you are promoted to retirement. Even if I have to go to the press to do it."

ADM Tamburillo slammed the door. The sound echoed in the room until Miss Cravits' voice came over the speaker again.

"Director, you have a call holding on line four. It is an Admiral Johnson, out of Coronado. Says he is Lieutenant Commander Rivers' C.O."

"Terrific!" Dietz mumbled as he returned to his desk. "Two admirals in under 20 minutes." He forced his breath out on a huff. "I need a drink!"

13

Wakefield slowly stood up from the long wooden table in the D-3 conference room to stretch her back. "I need a break and some food. No offence Yates, but that pastry from breakfast didn't sustain me. And it's been four hours since coffee and kuchen." The team of four had been pouring over documents and computer files and printouts all day. She walked to the window and looked down at the street below. *Glinkastrasse.* It teemed with people this time of day. All different ages and coat colors, but everyone was pretty much the same thick winter shape and all walked at the same no-nonsense German clip. Wakefield let her mind wander. *Where were all the people were hurrying to, the market or walking home from work, or kids out for a little fresh air before the evening meal?*

She touched her slender palm to the glass pane. "Temperature's dropping. You guys want to send out for dinner?"

"Sorry, can't." Chad told her. "But if you place an order for take-away, I will pick it up on my bicycle," he offered.

"What's close?" Rivers looked up and took the last pull from his sports-top water bottle.

Chad retrieved his backpack from under the table. Unzipping the front pocket, he pulled out a fistful of menus. Most were copied onto plain white paper, lists of offerings in black ink, though each of them seemed to have their own logo as a heading. "There is Persian—very hot food, and vegetarian sandwiches on a long roll," he gestured with his hands, "What's the word? Oh, sub sandwiches. Italian—pasta only." He laid their choices down one at a time on the table, sliding the pages toward his teammates. "Another Italian—a little spicier and they have meatball sandwiches, too. These guys do great pizza—thin crust only though. And Thai—unusually good take-away." He shot the last page down the table. "Oh, yeah, there is always brauts in a bun with or without curry from the street vendor two blocks down. Only if you are ready for a typical German taste though."

Rivers lifted the left half of his face in what almost looked like a grimace as he glanced at the menu in either hand. "I could eat any of it, I suppose, but, none of it sounds especially thrilling," he said, effectively leaving the decision to the others.

Wakefield watched him just a moment while he read the offerings again. The air between them had mostly cleared, but the day before had just been ignored. The easy camaraderie of the end of their pervious mission was missing. Maybe it was for the best. "Well, all of it sounds good to me, as long as there is a lot of it," she said. "I'm starving. Do you have a preference?" she asked Yates who sat opposite her and a few feet down, next to Rivers.

Yates shrugged gently, studying a menu. "Um, I don't care for spicy food much, but pasta or pizza or Thai…" he smiled and nodded in the affirmative. Yates placed each menu on the table as he mentioned it adjusting the page bottoms until they lined up with the table edge.

They called in an order for a large pizza with everything and two large pasta dishes to share.

Rivers watched Wakefield walk back to the window a few minutes later. She giggled as she leaned far into the glass. He couldn't see the source of her amusement, but she whipped around and enlightened them with a saucy grin. "Chad really does have a bike," she said. "Just not what I pictured. He's riding a little-old-man bike with a wire basket on the front!" She turned back to watch.

Rivers smirked at her back. For all her travels, culture studies, and languages, Judah Wakefield was distinctly American in her perspective. She adapted quickly to new surroundings, he knew that from their cave experience, but her initial thoughts would always be American. "What did you expect? A black BMX?" He hid his smile by returning his gaze to focus on the tedious paperwork. But he had to put his finger on the page to mark his place, because he was not really reading. He heard Judah turn from the window in surprise.

"Well as a matter of fact, yes." In his peripheral vision, Rivers saw her force her mouth closed.

Yates was up and out of his seat. "What? I must see this." He had to step over five piles of paper on the floor to get to her.

Rivers could feel Judah's eyes still on him and finally in an exasperated voice she said, "You're not allowed to that, Lieutenant Commander Rivers.

"Do what?" Rivers' twinkled his eyes with merriment. He knew what.

"Read my mind, Commander."

Rivers' lips formed a small O. *If only, Miss Wakefield, if only I could*, he thought. He said nothing, only continued to stare at her shape against the dark window behind her.

She held his stare for a full five seconds before looking down. It was progress. She looked as if she was afraid he really would read her thoughts.

Yates moved into the tall window next to her. "Where is he?" he asked, looking up and down *Glinkastrasse*.

"Right there," she pointed out, "just kicking off on the sidewalk into the traffic." She followed his progress with her pointer finger to the left.

Yates leaned into the window to see better in the reflecting light, bringing him closer to Wakefield. He was practically looking over her shoulder. "What is that thing he has on?" His voice carried a tenor chuckle.

"I wondered the same thing," Wakefield said. "It looks like a green garbage bag. It must be to keep the wind off."

Rivers had seen the get-up when Chad arrived that morning. It was a vinyl sack-like coat that had a drawstring hole for his face and arms and it covered down past his knees while he was seated.

"I hope it's functional," Judah laughed, "because it sure is not attractive."

Rivers watched surreptitiously as Yates put his hand on Wakefield's far shoulder, effectively wrapping her in a loose embrace. "Hey, look at that," Yates pointed to something on the street.

"How sweet," she said. Yates almost imperceptibly tightened his touch. Unnoticeable, except that it was SEAL-precision measuring the movement.

Here comes another LT Sands, he thought. He waited for Judah to put the forward Englishman in his place, the way she had rebuked LT Sands' come-ons in Afghanistan. This was not France after all. Rivers expected such behavior from them, but not a Brit.

Twenty seconds later, she drew back with a simple, "Excuse me," and she returned to the worktable.

Rivers' felt his eyes go wide. *Is she actually blushing?*

U.S. Embassy
Fourth Floor Conference Room D-3
Saturday 19 January 2002
2050 hours

Rivers looked up slowly as Chad smacked his timeline notebook on the table. His black hair jerked forward with the motion. "Ugh!" he groaned. "We've got to get a break soon. Nine days of paperwork." He shoved his chair away from the table and slunk down in his seat. "My fingers are beginning to chap."

The young agent's eyes bagged dark against his pasty skin. Wakefield and Yates both leaned back in their chairs. They'd worked fifteen- to nineteen-hour days, checking, double checking, reading printouts, looking for discrepancies, or connections. The only similarity Rivers could see was that all five had entered the country, through Berlin, within seven days of each other. Information he and Wakefield had been *given* the first day.

Rivers stood up from where he was sprawled on the floor with a poster board chart and colored markers. What he needed was more coffee. He picked up Wakefield's cup on the way to the carafe.

"Thanks," she mouthed. He loved the grateful, but tired, smile she gave him. "Chad, why don't you go on home." She dug her fingers into her right shoulder muscle. "You've put in a lot of work on this. In fact, I think you guys should take a long morning. Meet here at 1100 tomorrow," she suggested. "Yates, you should go on, too. This isn't your battle, yet you've been so kind to help us wade through this information."

Yates leaned into his straight-backed, wood chair. Resting his elbows on the arms of the chair, he laced his slender fingers across his flat stomach. "A Yank battle is a Brit battle. Solidarity and all that," he said with a tired up turn of his rosy lips. "However, I believe I'll take you up on that, Judah. I'll be back at 1100. With more of those pastries." He looked at Judah. "Cherry or blueberry this time?"

"Cherry." Wakefield nodded with a smile barely turning her lips. Rivers watched the exchange as he returned her coffee cup. "Two sugars, one cream," he told her. The scar on her cheek stood out against her pale skin and her eyes looked heavy.

"Are you sure your embassy can continue to spare you?" Rivers questioned Yates.

Yates shook his head in a circular motion. "It is not a problem. I am in Special Projects. I'd say ridding the world of a hideous assassin/terrorist is a special project."

Rivers nodded. "Pick up a couple of those almond-covered soft pretzels for me, will you?" he said. Rivers moved his poster from the floor so he could stand over the table. Yates took his leave, but Rivers saw the special smile the Brit left with Judah.

The squeak of Rivers' green marker was the only sound in the room. Then that stopped too.

Wakefield glanced up briefly to check on him, and found him studying her. She raised her eyebrows in question. He did not look away. She couldn't read his expression. "What is it, Commander?" Her words came out softer than she had intended, almost a whisper, yet they resounded loud in the still air.

Rivers dropped his forearms to rest flat, one in front of the other, supporting most of his weight on the table. He cocked his head to the side, presumably to see her better. Wakefield was sitting in the chair that had become hers that first night, on the street-side of the room, away from the door. Rivers was across the table and perhaps four feet closer to the door.

"I was wondering something," he told her. She gestured with an open left hand for him to continue. She kept her pencil point in the column of figures on the table. "Does your face still hurt?" A look of compassion touched the SEAL's face as he asked. He hurriedly added, "I never had stitches in my face, but I know that weeks after the stitches in my arm were removed, I could still feel it if I moved a certain way. And then when I got shot...woo," his breath swooshed out, "I could feel that for a *long* time."

Judah reached up and traced the now-familiar scar. She smiled softly taking in his whiskered face. "Do we need to go over that no guilt speech again?" she asked gently.

"No," he said too quickly. "I mean, you *know* I'd do anything to go back and prevent this, but that wasn't what I was getting at. Does it still hurt?"

His intense gaze from across the table felt almost as if he was touching her. "Thanks for the concern," she said simply. It was nice to know he was aware of her continuing saga with the cut. It was refreshing to be asked instead of people looking quickly away.

She felt Rivers pull back slightly from her. When he looked away, she realized that her words sounded like a dismissal. "No. *Really*. Thanks for being concerned," she said more strongly. Now she sounded like she was overcompensating.

Rivers' hand moved back toward the green marker he'd put down.

"Yeah, I feel it," she said. "It doesn't hurt, but I can feel it." She felt like she was talking to herself.

Wakefield could not figure out this man who was so daring on the battlefield, so powerful in hand-to-hand combat, so confident in his abilities, so self-assured. Initially, on several occasions when they had talked, he had been so open about his feelings toward her, only to retreat suddenly. Sometimes, Judah wondered if his open heart could become a closed fist in 1.2 seconds. Or was he simply taking a compassionate interest in a fellow Christian officer and she was misinterpreting his looks?

Usually, as in the airport, she allowed the misunderstanding to remain. But this time, she decided to pursue the risk herself.

"Commander." She changed her approach. "David, I meant what I said." Her heart rate doubled, pounding in her throat, and in the very wound they discussed. "I *do* appreciate your concern for me." He finally looked at her again, but his eyes were guarded. "Do you know what it is like—" she couldn't believe she was going to tell him this, but there it was, falling out of her mouth, "—to have people afraid to look at you?" Her voice tremored. "One of two things happens everywhere I go, since I was cut. Even at church." She laid down her pencil unconsciously, and spoke out of her pain. "People never ask. Either they turn away, embarrassed for me, or they stare. Some of the looks I've gotten..." she shook her head, trailing off.

Judah did not realize how deeply she hurt until she spoke.

She felt her chin begin to quiver and her eyes watered. Her nose began to sting. Wakefield bit the inside of her lip. She refused to cry in front of him. *God, please, I don't want to cry*, she prayed silently.

She stood and went over to the window to look down on the street lamps that blurred and streaked together in her vision.

Rivers straightened from where he was leaning over the table at the same time as she rose. He was not blind to her fight against the tears. Finally, he was seeing some emotion from this beauty of a partner of his who was so concerned with being accepted as a competent officer that she forgot that the uniform was made to fit a person, a woman in her case.

He enjoyed her company more when it was just the two of them. Her guard was lower and she was much more pleasant than when she tried to divide her attention among the three of them.

He admired her silhouette against the dark window for a moment. Even layered in cable knit and cords she made an attractive figure. He appreciated the curve of her waist and hips.

Rivers sensed her need, but he also wanted to respect her privacy. To tear down her strength as an individual and as an officer, or offer help where it was unwanted, would be disastrous, as he had learned in the airport.

This was the longest stretch of time the two officers had spent alone since their arrival. Even the drive to and from the embassy only lasted 12 minutes, sometimes 14.

Rivers stood frozen in place; he felt like he was the high-wire walker in a circus, trying desperately to balance concern with respect.

The small sniffle from the window finally tipped him over.

Rivers walked slowly around the table. He laid his fingers on her shoulder and saw her eyes start in the window reflection. He turned her around and drew her lithe body to his chest. That she came willingly told Rivers all he needed to know about her emotional state.

"I'm sorry." She put her forehead against him. "I didn't think I..." She sniffled. "I just...I am ready to be normal again," she exhaled the words. Bringing her hand up to cover her face, she broke. Judah leaned into his strength, and he could feel her shake with her silent weeping.

"It's okay," he whispered and smoothed her long hair, keeping one arm securely around her back.

Their connection lasted one silent minute. She didn't have a period of collection, but immediately began to struggle against his grip as soon as she stopped crying.

"Just stay put, I haven't prayed for you, yet," he commanded.

"Uh, it's my nose," her voice wobbled. "I'm going to drip on you, if you don't let me go," she said with a light, spontaneous chuckle.

"Oh...okay. Wait," he said. Rivers fished in his pocket for the two tissues he had picked up that morning before leaving his room. He pressed the folded Kleenex into her hand and released her.

"Would you really pray for me?" she asked in a small voice once she had wiped her nose in the close quarters.

"Right now," he stated surely. Judah closed her eyes and peeked them open as he took her hand.

"Holy Spirit, please give me the words you want to pray over Judah." He paused to wait. "God, please comfort that deep part of your daughter that feels rejected by all the people who have seen her scar and not known how to react or what to say. Cause her to learn all that you have for her out of this experience. Give her rest in her soul and joy abounding in her spirit. Fill her mouth with words to set others at ease. God, thank you for...sparing her life that day. Thank you for accomplishing your purposes in her life, for bringing her to the place that fulfills all that you have for her to do and to be."

14

Judah bobbed in the presence of God that filled the room and her being. She felt the true healing, beyond forgiveness, begin. "Wow!" she said softly letting go of his hand to wipe tears off her chin.

She saw him smile tenderly at some far off thought as he moved his gaze from the window where he was staring. His concentration came to rest on her face. They stood rooted to the same spot.

Rivers brought his left hand up to touch her face. "May I?" he asked before laying his SEAL-work calloused fingers on the scar.

His touch was as hot as a branding iron. He was the only one who had touched it, besides the intern who had removed the stitches. She couldn't speak.

"You know," he said softly as he massaged the skin, "if you stimulate the nerves and keep the blood flow circulating freely in the skin, the healing will be more complete. And faster. You can minimize the raised scar tissue by stroking the site in the direction of the scar." Rivers demonstrated as he spoke.

She shook her head in the smallest of gestures. His hand followed the movement.

He stopped and removed his fingers, leaving Judah feeling chilled. His gaze dropped from her eyes to her lips and back to her eyes. Surely he would kiss her this time. Her heart still stung from his last rebuff. She wouldn't say a word this time. She held her breath. Waiting.

He brought the same hand that had held hers during his prayer up to his lips, and kissed his first finger softly. He reached out toward her. He tapped the tip of her nose in an intimate gesture. He smiled, his eyes saying what his lips would not.

Judah felt her whole body rocking under her tremendous heartbeat.

"Can, ahem," he cleared his throat and started again. "Can I interest you in some chocolate from the vending machine on the second floor? I didn't see any M&Ms, but they probably have Cadbury chocolates, though I prefer the former." His voice hummed deeply.

Rivers' voice was smooth in her memory-transcript of that fiery night they spent in the desert. *"Have I told you how women are like a bag of M&Ms?"* Despite the storm of swirling events, he had spoken as if they were walking down a Paris street in early spring.

"Did you see the commercial before we left advertising a bag of all purple M&Ms?" His powerful presence had been distracting on that walk. *"Whoever buys that bag wins a million Japanese yen. The commercial doesn't say how to recognize the winning bag though. It can't look any different from the rest, or people wouldn't buy M&Ms in the quantity that the marketing company is counting on. You can't know you won unless you look inside the bag, but the value of the prize is eliminated if the bag is tampered with. It's a catch 22."*

She remembered smiling at his comparison.

"But the general population doesn't think ahead. They buy M&Ms to feed their sweet tooth immediately, and tear into the wrapper. Right?" His insight amazed her.

"So, you see every woman as a prize and you won't unveil her secrets—uh, sleep with her or mishandle her—until she officially belongs to you in marriage because that would devalue her. And rob you of a prize."

"Uh, sure." Judah snapped back as she backed up half a step and bumped into the windowsill.

"Okay, but then back to work. Or do you want to go home, too?"

"No." she said quickly. "I want to stay. I felt like I was getting close. But give me a minute, huh?" she asked.

15

Judah Wakefield slowly pushed her empty coffee mug toward the middle of the conference table. She blinked and looked again. "Those numbers look so familiar." She was only aware she'd spoken aloud when she heard her voice. She felt cross-eyed tired, there had to be a break in the case soon. She pushed herself. She needed a lead to follow, something that would pinpoint which man was the contractor. They couldn't afford to arrest the wrong man.

She was about ready to say, "haul 'em all to gulag and we'll sort it out later." Though all five men had sordid pasts, there was never enough hard evidence to put any of them away. Only two of the men had even done time. The deadline for the president's arrival was approaching. 25 January. Six days. They were no closer to identifying Azure Tiger than when they had arrived.

"Wait just a minute..." Wakefield tapped her first finger to her lips. Her fatigue vanished.

"What is it?" Rivers looked up from his stack of papers.

"I'm not sure. Yet. But," she trailed off. She shuffled through some papers in a different stack to her left. "Here it is," Wakefield pulled two sheets stapled together away from the others. She traced the column of numbers down the right side of the page. "Yes!" she burst out. "Just what I thought."

"What is it?" Rivers repeated more adamantly. His voice reflected her excitement.

"Just a second, I'll show you. Help me. I want to lay out all the bank statements on each account from December 2001 in rows classified by each man. Just the deposit listings if there is more than one page. Uh," She looked around for a clear place in the messy room with reams of paper in stacks everywhere. "I guess here, on the floor." She demonstrated.

Most of the men had three or more accounts. One man had seven. "Okay, watch this," She got down on her knees to see the printing on the statements. "December 31, 2001. The most recent statement from each bank." She went down the list and pointed out, "a deposit for 21,000 euros on this account." She moved to the next statement belonging to the same man. "Nothing on this account for that day." She picked up a third statement. "This one shows 14,000 and 10,000 on the same day, same account. Check out the routing numbers for all three figures." She passed the papers to her partner who was standing over her.

While he compared the numbers she went on to the next man. "Now this guy," she said with a snort. "He has nothing deposited on this account since February of 1999, then out of nowhere, on December 31, 2001, he acquired a wire transfer for 19,000 euros and a *second* one for 17,000 euros." She raised a single eyebrow suspiciously. She ran through three other accounts belonging to the same man without coming across any suspicious activity. In the last account she found it. "Okay, here he has a 19,000-euro deposit for the same day. Routing numbers all match." She shook her head. It was too obvious.

"This third total of 45,000 is where it hit me," she picked up the second statement in his row. "He has three accounts but all five deposits landed in one account. On the same day." Wakefield pointed it out to Rivers. "See, 5, 5, 17, 7, and 9,000 dollars, I mean euros. Thirty-one December."

Rivers took the offered paper from her in wonder. "These others have the same 45,000 figure too?"

Wakefield shrugged. "If they follow pattern. If we are lucky though, all but one will have the same transfers. That would mean he's our man."

Rivers had squatted down next to her to hurry along the process. "This one equals 45," he said while she picked up the last row.

"Well, it's here, too," she huffed in disappointment. "Oh, well. Nothing easy is worth doing."

"This gives us a connection among the five men though." Rivers tapped the edge of one of the statements against his palm as he thought. "They all received a total of 45,000 euros on the last day of last year," he repeated. "That tells us...that they are...suspect," he finished in a delayed huff trying to piece the implications together. "But we knew that," he sighed, "because, they also have the common denominator of being here on our floor."

Rivers frowned and rubbed his hand back and forth his dark stubbly hair. It was getting longer. He rested his square, muscled jaw in his palm and crossed his arms.

"It also tells us they were all hired by the same source, or one account was used as a holding escrow account for the money. OK, why multiple transfers each though? Probably a smoke screen. And it worked! The whole thing has wasted days." Wakefield huffed.

"So we trace the account and we have our man...or someone who can lead us to him."

"Finally some action!" Rivers was already moving toward the computer in the corner. It was on a satellite Internet connection, keeping record of the bankcard activity of all five suspects.

Wakefield did not move. She had no need to. "Except that this number of digits and this starting sequence indicate that it is a Swiss account.

Rivers stopped in his tracks, he shoulders slumping. He groaned, "Not our dear Alpine neighbors to the south! They're more closed-mouth than the NSA."

"Oh, yes. Even if the CIA coerces the account holder info, the account can be listed under a false name or even a series of numbers and letters."

Rivers turned back to Wakefield his blue-green eyes glazed, "202,500 euro. Either we have an expert negotiator on our hands or these transactions didn't originate in this currency. Our man is Indian, why the euro not the pound or dollar or the...what is the currency used in India?" he asked.

"The rupee. I don't *know* why?"

"Hmm. That would build the house I picked out. Not in California, but I could get started."

"You're going to build a house?" Judah looked up at him as she stood. The idea of a permanent dwelling did not reconcile with her perception of the on-the-move SEAL she knew.

"I *want* to," Rivers corrected, but declined to expound.

"Well, 200 K may be a lot on an officer's salary, but though it pains me to say, it's chunk change to Azure Tiger. His hits start at 3 million these days."

Rivers whistled through his teeth. "Maybe I should change my designator."

Judah smiled, "Thinking of becoming a hit man, there, Rivers?"

Rivers lifted his shoulders in a non-committal gesture that suggested, perhaps. "You could quit the navy," he invited with a conspiratorial smile, "and we could go into business together. With your aim and my stealthy ways, we would be the most prestigious team in the world." She giggled at his lofty plan. "We could both move to the islands, and live in hammocks until we went out on assignments from there." He nodded as if he had been thinking of it for some time. "Of course, we would keep the money in an off-shore account as we live the high life of danger."

"Of course," Judah nodded laughing lightly.

He told his whole plan straight-faced, which only made her giggle more. "Only one problem," she said when she regained her composure.

"What's that?" Rivers asked, sounding eager to correct any delay in their venture.

"I prefer the mountains." Judah said. Rivers snorted and they both laughed

Just then, the computer beeped twice. Rivers walked over, still chuckling, to check it out. "Awful late to be spending money." He bent over the small card table to study the screen. "What are you boys up to?" he asked. He scrolled back through the recent transactions on two accounts.

Wakefield joined him. Rivers didn't look up, but spoke as she drew close. "You may get your break after all. It seems two of our boys have just gotten together. Two authorizations made at the same hotel. *Rotes Ross* in…" he hesitated over the foreign name. "Halle. I wonder if that is where Halle Berry got her name."

Wakefield glanced at the screen. "Uh, I don't think so. It's pronounced HU-luh," she corrected with the soft u that rhymes with *duh.* "I wonder…"

She left Rivers standing in front of the computer and went to her laptop case that she had been carrying back and forth every day. She reached in the front Velcro pocket, withdrew a postcard and flipped it over to read the back. "Yep," she said with a smile. "I think it is time for a fieldtrip, Commander." Her grin widened as she held out the card, picture side up.

"Tonight?" he glanced at his watch.

"I suppose our bandits are staying put for the night. We could leave extra early in the morning." She acted as if she was relenting. She hadn't meant now anyway.

"I thought you just gave us the morning off." He smirked.

"I gave *them* the morning off, not us," she replied innocently. "Besides this is the good part. You wouldn't want to miss it." She sat down at the computer and in a few clicks she was printing driving directions. "Seems like that car rental was a good idea after all, Commander," she finally conceded. Every morning as he drove in, she mentioned what a nice morning it would have been for a brisk walk. However, she never said a word when she dropped into the passenger seat for the late night rides home through the narrow dark streets of Berlin.

"So what does this," he flipped the post card back and forth in the air and made a whipping sound, "have to do with...Halle," he pronounced, imitating her sounds.

"Nicely done, Commander," she complimented. "Tomorrow's Sunday. And I want to go to that church." She pointed to the postcard. "A friend of mine in D.C. said if I ever got to Halle in my travels, I should visit this church. And well, here we are, and on Sunday to boot!"

Rivers shook his head in a teasing manner and frowned. "It must be a sign. We'll leave around 0500," he said. "Unless that is too early for you, Gunsmoke."

Wakefield allowed a small curl of her lips to show. He had not called her that since she was on the fantail of the aircraft carrier when they had tied in a high-scoring shootout after they first met. "Very funny. I'll be ready when you are. I'm the one who is on time, you know," she said superiorly.

"How could I forget? You are always there first to remind me."

She chuckled. "Shouldn't we get Chad and Yates to go too?"

"Nah, we wouldn't all fit. Why don't you just leave them a note on the computer? We should be back before 1500, um, maybe 1600." Rivers said.

16

A short man with a tidy black beard walked out onto the balcony of his white adobe villa in Poros, Greece. Arafeh Filasek. He tightened the belt of his plush dark blue bathrobe. Barefoot, he looked out to sea in the gentle island night, and moved his cordless telephone to his ear. He could barely make out the glow of Athens, 31 nautical miles northwest of his villa. "Come on, pick up the phone," he ordered in his native Farsi. "I know you are there."

After six rings, the receiver finally connected. There was a clatter and some shuffling as the handset was dropped on the other end. "Hullo?" came the greeting, in sleepy, perturbed tones.

"Asleep already, Dovlatabadi?" Filasek skipped a greeting, and spoke in Hindi to the man in Germany. "That is no way to set up an assassination," he admonished.

"Ugh!" the sleepy man groaned and replied in Hindi as well, "Not you again. I thought I told you not to call me here. If it gets traced, I am a dead man. Then what will you do?"

"What attention would an incoming international call bring in a capital-city, five-star hotel? Believe me, I would not put our plan at risk." Filasek stroked his beard in a downward motion with a light hand. A moist breeze fluttered the bottom of his robe against his legs.

"What do you want then?"

"To explain my next project."

"Look!" The tone of the awakened man was edgy. "You hired me to take care of someone for you, not talk to you. Leave me alone to do my job. You'll know when it is done. You can wire me the other half of the money and our *relationship* is over," Dovlatabadi growled.

"No. *You* look. I am paying you more than enough to talk to me. Obviously I know where you are. I wonder what the local police would do with an anonymous tip about an international assassin under their noses. I could fax them a copy of our work together."

There was a grating silence as the assassin contemplated. "I never did ask how you got this number, did I," he finally said. "Go ahead." He sighed, resigned to listen. There was a rustling of what sounded like sheets.

A steely calm dropped over Filasek as he gripped the salty white iron railing of his balcony. "I want to destroy a woman completely. I want to shatter her reputation, cause her grief such as she has caused me. I want the world to despise her with me. I want her dead on the inside, yet alive to feel the pain when I finally take her life."

"Okay, Filasek, man," Dovlatabadi's slow voice came over the line. "What did she do to you? Why don't you just kill her and be done with her? This kind of revenge will eat at your soul even after she is dead."

"Do *not* presume to tell me my business! And this coming from a low-life hit man that I created." An ironic laugh filtered from Greece to Germany. "Besides where is the fun in killing her right away?" He cleared his throat and loosened his white-fingered grip of calculated rage on the railing. "I want you to set her up to take the fall for this hit. She is a sharp shooter, could have been a sniper. Apparently, she is going to take the fall for our little indiscretion in Delaram last month without my help. I want the world to believe she killed her own Commander in Chief. She is already in Berlin with you."

Another rustle sounded over the phone connection. "Give me a name."

"Lieutenant Commander Judah Wakefield." Filasek spat out the bitterness of her name on his lips.

There was a sharp intake of breath on the line. "You want me to take out a low-level U.S. military officer?" The voice was no longer sleepy. It held a note of disbelief.

"Yes. With the suspicion level surrounding her currently, you should not have to plant hard evidence, unless you want to try to lift her fingerprints. She is a marksman, under suspicion, in the same city, the same day, the Pre—as the killing takes place. That, with one hair placed at the scene of the shooting should be enough to convict, if not in the courtroom, at least in the press." Filasek laughed, low and guttural. He could almost taste the headlines.

"You know, I *hate* being told how to do my job. That's why I am...self-employed. I will do what I can." The killer had a hard edge to his voice.

"You are not *self*-employed. You are in my employ. She had better take the blame for this death. If I have to break the hint to the press myself, your name and picture will also come out...perhaps as her boy-toy lover, too soft to pull the trigger for her."

Filasek disconnected Dovlatabadi with a sharp jab to the talk button on his receiver. He tossed the phone six feet to one of the thickly cushioned loungers on the balcony. Gripping the round iron rod of the bannister with both hands wide, he leaned over as far as he could at his diminutive height. "Hmm," he mused aloud. "Not a bad idea. If that came to light it would give her a bad name at that church, too. Disillusion the little brats she teaches in *Sunday School*," he mocked. "Very nice. Far reaching."

He nodded. "Allah will be pleased." A sneer spread across his face, but it was hidden by his heavy facial hair. He knew he did not do this for Allah; his ultimate goal was to surpass the worldwide fear associated with his father's name, bin Laden. To have the name *Filasek* overtake the man who refused to give him his name though it was his right, all while his father yet lived to feel the shame.

Arafeh Filasek pounded the railing a single time with his fist, and turned toward the lit interior of his newly purchased villa. The old man needed to experience the shame of being bested at his own power game of fear. Filasek found it fun to create and manipulate another man to accomplish his next step in a long-time-coming goal of destroying a U.S. President, while at the same time bring revenge upon a woman who dared disrespect him. It was an added bonus that he would receive a reward in the afterlife for the death of some Infidels. If, of course, that religious hooey was actually true.

On the days when Filasek's own quick-minded ideas powered through his veins, Allah sounded more like a crock of lies to be used to manipulate a growing population. Filasek tugged the triple-wide sliding glass balcony door closed behind him and shrugged. He would wield whatever tool needed to bring satisfaction to his hunger.

Hotel Askanischerhof, Berlin, Germany
Sunday 20 January 2002
0440 hours

Rivers was up and showered. After four hours of solid sleep, he felt completely rejuvenated. He still could feel the deep emotional bond from the previous evening between himself and the woman next door, who was, hopefully, getting ready to go, too.

Rivers combed his short hair with his fingers more out of habit than necessity. He wished that the American tradition of in-room coffee had jumped the puddle to Europe. Looking at his watch he did some calculations, as he resigned himself to wait a few hours until they could find somewhere to stop. If anything was open.

He frowned in thought, wondering if the three and a half hour time difference between Germany and the Arabian Sea would be enough to allow Admiral Graham to be available for a phone call. He weighed the risk of waking a three-star on a Sunday morning to ask a favor against waiting for the next 15 minute time slot that he might have available during day light hours on this side of the world.

He dialed, "Shore-to-ship operator, please." When a young man's voice came over the speaker of his satellite phone, he said, "I need the USS *Reprisal,* a person-to-person call for Vice Admiral Graham."

Rivers' line transferred to the communications room of the mammoth U.S. naval aircraft carrier. "I'm sorry, Commander Rivers." The lieutenant who answered the call spoke clearly into the phone. "The admiral is speaking in the Protestant service this morning."

"He is preaching?" Rivers asked, amused. "What happened to the chaplain?"

"He came down with laryngitis. He asked the Admiral to fill in for him. The brass attracted a huge crowd, too! I think half the ship is down there this morning."

"Impressive. Listen. Give him a message that I called. No emergency, I will call him back when I can."

"Yes, sir. I've got it down."

Rivers turned off his phone and placed it with the other things he was packing to take along. "Guess that answers that question, huh?" he said aloud. "I see you will arrange it in your timing." Rivers prayed with a casual laugh. "You take this God-business far too seriously," he grinned as he caught sight of himself in the mirror. His expression was funny. "And I love you for it."

Rivers strode over to the wall between their rooms and tapped out R-E-A-D-Y-Y-E-T, in Morse code.

Y-E-S came her reply.

17

They met in the hall and Wakefield whispered, "Good morning," with a comfortable smile. She felt more at ease with him now than she had the entire time they had been in Germany. "I can't believe you're early, Squid." She felt her eyes glint with teasing. She felt bright and refreshed even this early. "I'll buy you a cup of coffee as a reward...if you can find me coffee to buy." She waggled her eyebrows suggestively.

"Therein lies the catch." Rivers said. They walked down three flights of stairs as quietly as they could. "This is a European Sunday. They still observe it as a holy day. Which is good...except that the stores don't open. I wouldn't get my hopes up for coffee."

She knew that, but Rivers could do all kinds of miraculous things. Finding coffee in Berlin did not seem as monstrous as finding nuclear weapons in Afghanistan.

"But it worked when I got my hopes up for you," she said sweetly. Rivers stood slack-jawed, staring at her over the roof of the tiny white mini in the carpark across the alley from their European residence. "Relax, SEAL!" She giggled at his reaction. "I meant, I hoped that my punctuality would rub off on you, and it did."

"Oh."

"Could you hurry?" she snapped the locked metal door handle a couple of times. "It's freezing out here."

"Sorry." Rivers snapped out of it and hurried around the back of the car and unlocked Wakefield's door for her.

"Thank you, Commander," she said formally, even more impressed when he waited for her to settle herself and shut the door after her. She reached over and pulled up the knobby lock on his door.

The lieutenant commanders drove an hour out of Berlin, half way to the mid-sized town that had only been in the free world since 1989. Halle was actually an ancient city though, built on the river Saale. Originally known for salt mining and more recently, well the 1600's, for being the home of the university named for the father of the Protestant Reformation, Martin Luther.

"Why is it that we are going here?" Rivers asked as he guided the car along the quiet small lanes of the autobahn.

"To follow our lead: the two guys who are in Halle together when all the rest of them are scattered all over the country." She shook her head in wonder. As if a SEAL could forget their objective.

"I know that." He stated with a snort. "I don't have old-timers. I—"

Wakefield interrupted with a small laugh, "Old-timers? You mean Alzheimer's?" She could not contain herself.

"My niece, Lauren, calls it old-timers. Her great grandfather on her mom's side has it." He returned easily to his previous thread. "The guys already have tails, what are you planning to do? Go peak in their windows and look for a presidential itinerary sitting out on a desk."

She frowned and gave a sarcastic look. "Hmm, I hadn't thought of that." She hadn't really thought it through. She looked over at him through lowered lashes. "Maybe," she shrugged. "I wanted to get a look at the men in person." She hoped that their demeanors or body language would somehow give her a clue. It hadn't hurt that the men were sleeping in the one city she had wanted to visit.

"I think," Rivers met her gaze, "that you were going just as stir-crazy as the rest of us sequestered in that room for nine days straight." He returned his eyes to the bumpy roadway between Berlin and Halle. "Am I wrong?" he teased when she did not reply.

"Not completely." She pushed her head into the headrest as she admitted it.

They drove into the sleepy little city minutes after sunrise. "Interesting statue," Rivers commented. A large bronze stood near the roadway. It was four fists of men, raised to the heavens in both anger and demand. There were many dates inscribed on the sculpture itself.

"Mm-hm," Wakefield twisted backward in her seat to look at it again. "I bet there is an interesting, painful story locked up in the heart of that artist."

"And the city, if they want it as a representative of themselves to visitors here at the city's edge." Rivers added. "Are you ready to navigate?"

Wakefield picked up the folded directions pinned under her thigh for safekeeping. Eight minutes later, she gave the final instruction. "Turn right at the next intersection. It is *Leipziger Strasse*. We are looking for number 76."

"Yes, the *Rotes Ross*. Sounds like a dive." Rivers rolled his green eyes. "You would think making €45,000 for one job, they could afford to splurge a little."

"Oh, you!" She bumped her shoulder against his in the small car. She did not have far to go. "It is probably not that bad. Look. Here we are now."

"You were saying?" Rivers asked dryly. A bit of humor touched his voice. The place was not falling down in ill repair, it just looked like it could use some maintenance: paint, sidewalk cleaning, window washing, a new sign.

"Don't judge yet," she warned just as humorously. "It could be much better on the inside."

"Or worse," he laughed. Why did she feel the need to defend a hotel she was not sleeping in, had never seen before? She finally laughed in concession. "Now what?" He slowed in front of the yellow stone building.

"Go on up a little further and park. We'll walk back."

"Looks like everybody just parks on the side of the street." Rivers commented.

"Or sidewalk..." Wakefield pointed out a car that had not had room to parallel park, so the driver had simply pulled in straight, until his tail was out of the street. It left his front tires squarely on the far side of the sidewalk.

"Funny," Rivers scoffed.

Langley, VA
12:10 AM

Director of Counterintelligence Richmond Dietz sat at his desk with his jaw balanced in his palms, elbows on his desk. His days had been stretching into monsters all week. They usually did when approaching crisis level at Langley.

No word from his team in Germany in three days. Only five days until the president was scheduled to arrive, and the world's top assassin-for-hire was loose on the cobblestone streets of Berlin.

His telephone trilled in the darkened office. Dietz didn't know why he didn't go home. Melissa, his night secretary buzzed him to say, "It's Andrew Donnelley, head of the Secret Service, for you, Director."

Dietz groaned aloud. This would not be pleasant. "Thanks, Missy." He depressed the speakerphone button and turned down the volume a fraction. "Dietz," he said shortly to let the man know he was there.

"Glad to see you're still on the job. Help me out, Dietz. The president is breathing down my neck. What've you got?"

"I doubt that. You just don't want to lose your job. Or a president," he added after a brief pause. "I have nothing," he said. "There is still a credible threat, but my people have not been able to come up with anything solid. Nothing is panning out." Dietz noticed that his voice had taken on an old, papery quality. When had that happened?

"Honesty, Dietz? From the CIA, how refreshing," he said, sarcasm deeply etching his tone. "But it's not enough. I need something concrete, like cuffed wrists and ankles in a concrete cell."

133

"I cannot produce that at the moment. It is my recommendation—" Dietz hesitated. *This failure will echo implications around the world,* he thought. *Better a black mark on my record than a dead president on my record. Whispers of this administration*—he did not allow himself to continue the thought. He finished his statement with a confidence he did not feel, "I recommend the trip be postponed."

Donnelley cursed, railing the CIA's incompetence from every angle Dietz had ever heard. When he finally got his Irish temper under control, his last words echoed. "You get to tell him." The connection clicked, and a steady tone droned until Dietz punched the speakerphone button.

"Oh, boy," Dietz blew out his breath. He was suddenly beat. He did not wait. "Missy," he pressed the intercom button. "Cancel my morning appointments, and see if you can get me into the Oval Office."

"Yes, sir," came the strong reply. Dietz plucked his long, lined, trench coat from the rack by the door. He was going home.

18

"But you don't have to speak German," Wakefield explained in the voice Rivers had identified as her lieutenant-commander, don't-argue-with-me-I'm-right voice. "Their names will be spelled the same way they are on their credit cards. I will get the attendant out of the office and you search the computer records."

"How are you planning to do that?" he asked skeptically.

"You don't want to know," she stated, not leaving any room for questions.

Rivers eyebrows shot up. What was she planning, and more importantly, who put her in charge? He wondered, but before he could open his mouth to ask, she was stripping off her coat.

She turned around completely, folding her coat as she twirled. Finding no place to stash it, she shoved it at Rivers. "You'll have to keep this for me." He accepted it without a word. "I need to hurry. The shift changes typically at zero eight hundred." She smoothed her hair and unbuttoned the top three buttons of her shirt. She slid her snug black pants down on her hips a few inches, leaving a revealing gap between the waistband and the hem of her fitted shirt.

Rivers swallowed hard. He could see the kind of assault she was planning. Poor man. She added some red lipstick to complete the ruse. "Wakefield...Judah," he tried again. "Please, be careful," he finally said.

Wakefield looked at him and decided that he meant well. "David Rivers, I am a lieutenant commander in the United States Navy. You

135

know, first hand, that I can handle myself, and anything any man might try to pull," she couldn't hide a forming smirk. "Including yourself. So, don't get any ideas from this—" she looked down, "rendition of this outfit."

"Yes, ma'am," Rivers threw her a mock salute. "You are getting cold, let's get this *show* on the road," he quipped.

"May I have the keys?" she asked. He handed over the set of four keys on the rental ring.

LCDR Rivers hid himself around the far corner of the building as Wakefield donned her new persona, complete with a suggestive gait and thrown back shoulders that enhanced her curves. Three minutes later, the night-shift attendant walked outside with her. Judah's little-girl voice sounded fake, even though he didn't understand the German words she spoke. He wondered how any man could fall for such an obvious help-me plea.

Rivers had his hand on the door to enter the building when he took a last look at the pair. Wakefield gave a theatrical shiver and the hotel man brought his arm up and around her shoulders.

Rivers passed the night manager 14 minutes later on *Leipziger Strasse* as he headed back to the car and the manager walked back to work. They nodded to each other. The manager wore a large grin that Rivers did not see often on German streets. Germans were generally a reserved people, especially those who had been part of the Communist GDR.

The manager also wore a perfect imprint of red lips on his cheek. Rivers held back a smirk that played at his lips as long as he could.

Judah sat in the driver's seat with the motor running, using a tissue to rub off the excess color in the rearview mirror, when Rivers folded himself into the passenger seat. "You don't fight fair," he chuckled.

"What?" She gaped at him.

"What did you do to that poor boy?"

"I asked him to help me get my car started. He fixed a loose wire that I pulled while he was, uh, preoccupied with my anatomy. Then I kissed his cheek...as a thank you." Her eyes narrowed questioningly. "It was as simple as that."

"I *saw* that," he remarked blankly.

"The kiss?" she squeaked.

"No. The *evidence* of the kiss. I wonder how many people will see him before someone tells him?" His look crossed mirth with amusement. "I do not think your friend is a mirror-friendly type. That's just mean," he said with an approving grin.

"I notice *you* didn't say anything to him," she commented.

"And undo all of your fine mission planning? No, ma'am."

Judah rolled her eyes and they laughed.

"Don't laugh," she smoothed the wrinkles in her pant legs, "that lipstick will probably increase his social status among his lecherous buddies."

"That may be. However, returning to the subject of mission planning for a moment," he jutted his chin toward her shirt. "You may want to button up before you catch cold."

Wakefield tilted her chin down. Her shirt was still open. "Oh dear," she gasped. "Sorry, I was just—" she stopped short as a pink color spread across her cheeks. "So what did you get?" she asked as she buttoned the three small buttons.

"Well, do you remember that part about not needing to speak German?" he asked with a frown. She nodded. "Their names were recognizable, but the rest of the screen was in German."

Wakefield's face fell, "So you didn't get a room number."

"I didn't say that," he drawled.

"Well, spit it out. We're burning daylight."

"They're in 22 and 27. And," Rivers paused for effect, and Judah sighed at his antics. "I thought to look at a map of the hotel's layout."

"I hadn't thought of that. Excellent idea." She took her coat from where he had folded it on his lap. She pulled the keys from the ignition and passed them back. "Here you go, Lieutenant Commander Control Freak. I saw you eyeing them. Let's go take a peek." They got out of the tiny car. "It's on the second floor?" she assumed.

"Nope," Rivers said cheerily. "Third floor. They count the ground floor as zero and use single digits. The first floor is on the second story using teen room numbers, the second floor is on the third story. You know that."

Wakefield stopped four steps down the cracked walkway. "I forgot. How are we going to look through the third floor windows?"

Rivers was amused. "If you'll slow down a minute, I'll show you." He opened the hatch and unzipped the bag he had brought down from his room with him. "Have you done any repelling?" he asked with a smile as he held up some thin nylon rope in one hand and a pair of carabineers and safety belts in the other.

Wakefield broke into a beaming grin. "I sure have." Her words were slow. She cocked her head to the side and her lips parted in a grin.

Sunday morning worked well for their unusual reconnaissance. No one stirred on *Leipziger Strasse*.

The pair climbed the fire escape with ease. "Remind me not to stay here," Wakefield grimaced. "It is not very...secure."

Rivers looked up from the rope he was knotting tightly. He shot her an incredulous glance. With raised eyebrows, he merely nodded. He squashed a small snort of laughter once he returned to his task.

Wakefield fastened the buckle of her harness around her hips. "Here you go," he said and tied the last knot. He handed her the threaded metal clasp. "I don't suppose you need help, do you?" He arranged his face in a particularly wolfish grin.

Wakefield missed it all together. She was securing her long hair into a loose ponytail and didn't look up. "Nope, I got it." She snapped the hinged carabineer onto the D ring on her harness and spun the bolt closed with her fingertips.

"Go down here." Rivers pointed over the edge. "We are directly over room 22. You will have to descend three floors. I will take a look at

27. Then you can hop over," he indicated pushing off the wall with two feet by curling his first two fingers, "when you are ready."

She nodded succinctly, backed up until her heels were hanging three inches off the ledge of the roof, and looked over her shoulder. "You forgot to remind me to avoid the gable," she smiled. She let the rope slide through her leather gloves and kept her knees straight until she was at a 90 degree angle with the hotel's outside wall. Walking backward, she gave the rope slack, her body weight made the descent smooth.

Rivers was impressed with her form.

19

There was no sound as Rivers flawlessly moved down the wall about 40 feet from Wakefield's rope, a nimble spider.

Wakefield looked back to the top to count the floors. This was the one. She popped up into a sitting position and caught the rope with her leg. The curtain's position revealed only a three-inch crack to peer through.

Brown beer bottles and cigarettes butts littered the surfaces of the room. A man lay face down with his feet hanging off the bed in wrinkled clothes. He had the heavy-sleeping look of a passed-out drunk. A pack of playing cards lay in a discarded heap on the floor next to a straight-backed kitchen chair that lay on its side. Clothes oozed out of a closed suitcase like too much jam on a PBJ.

The place made Wakefield shudder with disgust. It must smell horrible. She didn't even have to see the man's head beyond the striped curtain's obstruction to know. This man was too unstructured to be their assassin.

She looked over to Rivers. He motioned her to go all the way to the ground instead of bouncing over. He would go up. Lithely, he climbed the rope as easily as when he had descended. The muscles of his arms bulged in his black, long-sleeved, turtleneck.

Wakefield walked down the wall to the ground in a straight line, but she was paying more attention to the view above her than the ground below. Fortunately, she had no problems.

"I guess you couldn't see in the window?" Wakefield asked her partner when he returned to the mini a few minutes later.

"Oh, no, the curtains were wide open," he replied, not giving her any clue as to his actions.

"Then why?" He could be so cryptic.

"I was able to do your case profiling for you and save you a horrible image on your brain. This man was not our hit man."

"But how do you know? Was he dead or something?" Wakefield pushed. "Describe the room to me."

"It was pretty clean, not much out of place." Rivers described. "Except the sheets. They were in a tangle on the floor. Soaked in half a bottle of red wine."

Wakefield's breath sucked in, "Are you sure it was wine, not blood?" The words popped out of her mouth before she remembered who she was talking to. "Sorry. Of course it was wine. Go on."

Amused, Rivers eyed her from the corner of his eye. "That's pretty much it."

"What about the man?" she asked.

"Uh, he was sprawled out on the bed, face up, naked as a newborn and just as filthy. That's what I didn't want you to have to look at. He was lying in his own vomit," he paused. "The single half-bottle of wine does not fit with his wasted position though."

"He probably helped himself to some of the alcohol consumed in room 22. It was a wreck." She sighed. "Well, two down, three to go."

Rivers started the car and maneuvered onto the narrow, bumpy street. Ancient cobblestone and brick were still the paving options of choice in Halle. While their beauty in pictures was remarkable, and the longevity of their wear was unquestioned, they were murder on the rear ends of people driving rental cars with bad shocks. "What are we going to do when all these men are eliminated as being Azure Tiger?" Rivers asked turning back onto *Glockenstrasse* toward the center of town.

141

"Is that what you think, too?" she asked, gripping the door handle and the edge of her seat to keep from jarring too much. She had not noticed the bumpiness on the way in; she was too focused on their information gathering ahead.

Rivers nodded thoughtfully. "I cannot reconcile myself to the idea that these small-time thugs are anything more than a smoke screen. I feel like we are chasing our tails in researching them."

"But what else are we going to do? It is the only connection we have. The only break we can hope for is that one of them will unknowingly let something slip."

"They are hired low-lifes. What could they know to let slip?" Rivers asked.

Her frustrated sigh billowed through the car. She pressed her head against the headrest. "So what do you propose?" She knew he was right. "And where are you going, by the way."

"I am going to find us some coffee—even if it is at a filling station. You still treating?"

She turned her head on the headrest. "Mm-hm. Just use that petro-station coffee as a last resort, all right?"

"Yes, ma'am," his face was impassive as they drove through the quiet streets. A few people were stirring. They would need to find the church soon. "I don't have any specific plan, but we need to draw him out, get him to incriminate himself."

"So we offer him something he wants...something he can't refuse." Wakefield was on the same wave length—to a point. She deflated suddenly. "But what is that? Who knows what motivates an assassin."

Rivers gave her an incredulous look and narrowly missed an oncoming car before concentrating on the road again. "Money." He gave the obvious answer.

She sat back in her seat. "We hire him to kill someone and set him up?" She tensed forward. "Are you crazy?" Her voice filled the small vehicle. Rivers tensed slightly at her loudness. "That is illegal!"

"Not if he does not actually kill anyone."

Wakefield was beginning to squirm in her seat, which was not easy in the little car. "Haven't you seen his stats, Commander?" she asked, definitely back in military mode. "A 100 percent mortality rate. If Azure Tiger is hired to kill you, you *are* dead!"

"You don't know that." Rivers' voice was uneasy with dissension laced through it. "At Naval Intel you would only hear about the ones who were dead, not the ones he failed at."

"I suppose you must be correct. Nobody has a 100 percent kill rate," she relented her stance.

Rivers did not take his eyes from the road as he said softly, "I do."

Wakefield looked back and forth at nothing out the windshield. "You've killed everyone you've ever gone after?" she asked just as softly, mentally, she was trying to tally how many that could be, over the lifetime of a SEAL.

"Unless ordered to bring them in alive, yes."

"What about Filasek?" she asked. "You threatened him." She did not know if he realized that she had heard his statement. In the desert, when the two of them met the Afghani man, Rivers had promised to kill Filasek if he hurt her. Then the man had filleted her cheek.

"I have not gone after him. Yet." The flat tone of his voice scared her.

"David," Wakefield appealed, "you have to let that drop. You cannot exact your own revenge. It's wrong. You are more godly than that."

"Do not put me up on some pedestal, Judah." His voice did not sound humble, but filled with disdain toward himself as if he had seen his own heart and found it lacking. "I do not belong there."

The sound of the car on the bumpy road filled the silent air. Rivers broke it first. "Why did you call me "Commander Control Freak" back there?"

Judah pressed back in her chair. "I was just kidding." She shook her head and then realized the body language she was sending and stilled her body while staring down the dashboard clock, but not seeing it so she could focus her peripheral vision on David. "I'm sorry if I offended you," she added when he didn't reply.

"Is that really what you think of me?"

Wakefield felt her heart pounding and her face heating as she transitioned to the jack-knife in the conversation. "Um, sometimes. But—" Judah trailed off as she tried to know her own heart, and get down to the root of the emotion and thought while at the same time not offend David further.

"But what?" He asked. "I've worked hard in my life to become as disciplined as I am. Not just in my professional life, but in my heart and spirit." Rivers signaled and slowly edged the Mini Cooper around the end of a stopped rusty-red mini-bus full of children with one little pig-tailed girl waving out the back window. Rivers fluttered his fingers back at her. "I do like to control myself. I think it honors God. But I know that there is no way to control my environment. But I want to always control my *response* to my environment."

"Hmm." Judah felt like she should engage in the conversation even as she felt blind-sided and was trying to determine where Rivers' words were coming from and why she was having such an emotional response to them.

"But if I give people close to me the impression that I need to control everything, then I have failed."

Wakefield looked up sharply. His voice sounded desolated. "It's not that." She tried to reassure him. "It's just that sometimes I want to drive too. I am good at it. You're not always better at things than everybody else."

Rivers' head whipped toward her and his eyes narrowed in on hers in the briefest of moments before he turned back to the highway and she felt like her soul had been read. "I am not better than everybody. I've never thought that."

He sounded more hurt now. Great.

"What do I do or say that makes me seem that way?" He asked. "I'm serious." She saw him glance back over at her. "I'm around the same kind of personality all the time. All my buddies are SEALs and besides my brother, no one has the gumption to see me and really talk to me like you do."

Wakefield struggled to keep her eyebrows from reaching toward her hairline. She shrugged. "Well, you always have to drive for one. You always have to be the leader, like when we headed to the bridge on the ship last month. If the conversation turns to weapons, you always know more. Or you can do more or run farther and faster. You talk like you're invincible sometimes. And you don't like Yates. Just because he likes me."

"That could be true about Yates. And I am not trying to show off my weapons training. I just specialize in weapons and physical fitness in my work. I am a SEAL. It is not *just* what I do, I became a SEAL because of who I am. But I really just like to drive. Especially on the autobahn." He grinned. "But in the desert, the guys needed you to doctor them up, that's why I drove. I can only do so much with that sort of thing."

"Well." She breathed hard as his words made since. "Sometimes I like to drive too. Especially on the Autobahn." Judah echoed.

"You and I are alike, you know." David said. "More than I thought. You're not used to having someone who can keep up with you. Not used to being around someone who is just as capable of leading and doing things and knowing things as you are."

Wakefield was quiet, struggling. *Do I really like to be in control as he seems to, Lord?* She asked silently. *Is that why his problem bothers me so much, because I subconsciously recognize my own weakness manifested in him and he handles it better? Why is everything a competition with me?* Finally, she cleared her throat. "You know what?" she asked in a light tone. "We don't argue very well. I think I take offense too easily."

Rivers was too wise to agree with her. She smiled. The agreement looked as though it wanted to jump out of his eyes. He simply tightened his jaw against the urge to speak.

"This conversation actually hurt your case earlier though. Not this topic, but the one before," Wakefield decided aloud getting back to the safer topic of business. Even the business of hiring an assassin felt safer than the emotional waters they had been treading. She pulled the ponytail holder out of her hair and smoothed her stick-straight blond tresses back into order again. "If *you* have a 100 percent kill rate, then Azure Tiger could too," she equated.

Rivers swung their white Mini into a parking place suddenly. He stopped the engine, removed the keys and placed his hands smoothly in his lap. "Has he ever gone head to head with a U.S. Navy SEAL?" he asked with a confidence that frightened her.

"Oh, no you don't!" Wakefield grabbed his arm as he was getting out. She was surprised at her own strength. "Where do you think you're going! We're in the middle of a conversation. You can't make an announcement like that and then run off!"

"Coffee." He pointed to the McDonald's sign a block away. It was nestled on the bottom two floors of one of the not-quite-white buildings that stretched six stories to the greyer sky.

"Oh." She got out, too. "I didn't realize your hero complex went so deep," she whispered as they walked but her voice was not quiet. "You think that because you are a SEAL that a *bullet* can't catch you! I will not allow you to do this."

"You may not have a choice," he said. She sped past him. She could not think with him acting so ridiculous. He had sounded so humble a few minutes earlier and now his power-play was on full display. There was another way. There had to be. She ground her teeth.

"Don't walk away," he said as he caught up with her. "I'm open to suggestions," he tried reason. She did not speak. The thick soles on her black shoes clunked dully on the cobblestone sidewalk.

He stopped and touched her upper arm.

"Don't touch me, Commander," she snapped and jerked away from him.

"We are here," he opened the glass door and invited her to go first with a simple hand gesture.

Wakefield retraced two steps and walked inside. She inhaled the warm air, heavy with grease from sausage patties and frying oil for hash browned potatoes.

"Are you hungry?" she asked. Distance and chilliness tinged her voice. She couldn't risk allowing him close if he was going to go off and get himself killed. There had to be another way; she just needed the time to figure it out. She needed space to think without his larger-than-life presence crowding her.

And now she was also doubting her own personality. *Do I need to be in control all the time? If that's true, why?* Wakefield wiggled her right ankle in her shoe as she pushed the question back to peruse the menu. Pictures accompanied the posted German menu, so Judah didn't bother to translate for David.

20

Inside McDonalds, Judah watched a little girl playing with her small brother in the plastic balls of the second story play area partitioned off inside glass doors. Both children had kerchiefs tied around their necks to keep them warm in the cold Deutschland winter. Judah suddenly thought of her third sister, Melia. She had a feeling she would be announcing her second child soon. Judah prayed, *Please give her a safe pregnancy and a healthy baby,* and she tucked the information away.

The children's mother in the play area had brought a book along to read. She slouched against a wall, sitting sideways in her chair with the open book propped up on the table, but she was not reading. She watched her two children play with each other, a small smile touched her plain, unmade-up face.

Judah sighed. *Eventually,* she promised her heart again.

She turned her focus back to Rivers. He crumpled the paper that had wrapped his breakfast. They drained their paper coffee cups simultaneously.

"How do you plan to finance your little hero fest?" she asked quietly, in case the woman watching her children understood English. It was easily possible since most of the world did.

"Our expense account," he shrugged. "I will either have the money back by the time anybody reconciles the account, or I'll be dead. They can't do anything to me then."

His charming smile made the words seem less harsh. *Rivers is definitely a weapons expert. He knows exactly how to wield that smile.* Her heartrate increased, much to her chagrin. *See, I'm not a control freak, I can't even control my own reaction to him.* She wasn't exactly sure whom she wanted to observe that little trait though.

"Your idea stinks, Commander," she said, feeling more resigned than hostile now. "Let's go find the church; I don't want to be late."

Rivers gathered their trash and separated it into the appropriate collection containers.

Halle
Bartholomausberg Kirche
0940 hours

The organ bellowed out an ancient, gut-moving hymn. Its sound encompassed so many layers of music that it sounded nearly like an orchestra in itself. "Sorry," Rivers mouthed as if he was the reason they were late. She shrugged half-heartedly. It wasn't his fault her directions took them on a complete tour of Halle before depositing them on *Kirche Strasse.*

Voices raised in song filled the entryway where they stood removing their coats. The back door to the sanctuary opened and a man dressed in several layers walked toward the outside door. "*Welkommen,*" he said, in his native German tongue. "You may want to leave on your coats. It is quite cool inside the church. Please sit anywhere." He went back and opened the door for them.

Wakefield shrugged her coat back into place and Rivers followed suit. He took the lead and directed Wakefield to the second to last row of chairs. He motioned his partner in ahead of him and a beautiful young woman with long mahogany-colored hair said, "'Scuse me," as she gathered her purse and Bible and scooted toward the middle.

She spoke in English.

It wasn't until that moment that Wakefield realized that Rivers was not going to be able to understand the service. "You're American?" Judah whispered with a smile.

The girl nodded. "So are you." She grinned widely showing white even teeth. "You don't know how good it is to hear a voice from home." She pointed out the hymnals and the numbers listed on a changeable sign on either side of the raised podium.

Wakefield touched Rivers' upper arm and pulled him down closer to her mouth. "Do you want me to translate for you?"

"When we get to the teaching." He told her. "I can worship in any language." He straightened up and his eyes closed. Though his lips did not move, he seemed to be breathing in the majestic music.

Judah found the words for the song just as it closed, then found the next one more quickly. In a culture that was so different from her own, deep in the throes of intrigue and searching for an assassin, and in the midst of she-didn't-know-what with Rivers, Judah found herself able to relax in the commonality of worshipping the same Savior as her brothers and sisters in Christ. God's personal presence was the same in any locale.

The pastor, dressed in elaborate clerical robes, walked to the front and began his exposition. Judah leaned in close to whisper the English to Rivers. The big SEAL swung his arm over her head to rest on the back of the chairs and leaned in closer to her. She felt warmed by his arm's heat on her back.

As the officers moved to leave after the service had concluded, opting to skip the coffee and kuchen offered, the girl who had been sitting next to them caught Judah's arm lightly. "I'm Melody. What brings y'all to Halle?" she asked in a friendly manner. She looked to be just out of her teens.

"I'm Judah Wakefield and this is David Rivers. We're in the navy. U.S. Navy," she added quickly.

One of Melody's sculpted eyebrows arched high. "Y'all are a long way from the water," she commented with a chuckle. They did not answer her unspoken question. "Listen, I wanted to say thank you for interpreting today. I don't speak German yet, and I really needed to hear this message about trusting God's care. I was ready to hop on the first plane home, even though I know God wants me here."

"Where are you from?" Rivers asked. "Got to be south of the Mason-Dixon line."

The girl's laughter tinkled merrily above the soft waves of conversation around them. "Birmingham, Alabama." It sounded like she exaggerated her slight southern accent. "And it is so good to hear unaccented American English," she sighed and rested one knee against the cushioned seat.

"I understand exactly what you mean," Rivers shook his head.

"How did you end up here? We're a little off the beaten path." Wakefield smiled at the girl.

"I am an *aupair*—a nanny," she explained for Rivers benefit. "A local family hired me to watch their two children and teach them English. Which is a good thing, because like I said earlier, I don't speak much German yet. It is a *lot* different than I thought." Her smile seemed to be one of resignation. "God deals in purposes we've never dreamed of. Sometimes we just can't see what he is up to."

"It is always good though, isn't it?" Wakefield asked.

Melody nodded thoughtfully and stood straight again. "Do you want to meet Pastor Katzmann?" Rivers shrugged and Judah nodded. "He doesn't speak much English," Melody told Judah, "so you'll want to address him in German."

They walked the few steps to the back door in a line. "Then how do you know him?" Rivers asked.

"His son, Jan, speaks English and translates for me," she looked over the top of her stylishly small glasses at Rivers, "when I'm not late."

Pastor Katzmann personally invited them to stay for coffee, but Wakefield made their excuses of having to get back to Berlin without even translating for Rivers.

"Seems like that message was more for me than for you," Wakefield commented to Rivers as he opened her car door. "I guess I will have to trust God to take care of me…and you."

"Well, I was not going to say anything," Rivers exaggerated his casual shrug and large eye roll. He went to the driver's side first to unlock the door. She stood at the bonnet and adjusted her scarf as he kneeled and leaned across to pull up the lock on the passenger door. Standing back up just as she started toward the passenger door, Rivers jingled the keys. "Well, do you want to drive, or don't you?" Then he tossed them across the top like he was making a free throw.

Judah's lips cracked open in a wide toothy grin. "Oh yeah. I'm so ready."

She folded herself behind the steering column and buckled up while Rivers walked to the passenger side.

"Trust has always been difficult for you, hasn't it?" He asked as she turned the engine turned over.

"Most of my life, yes, I suppose it has been hard. I've tried so long to produce the best that is in me, independently, it is hard for me to change that and realize, like Pastor Katzmann said, 'a two cord strand is not easily broken, and three…' well, I had always equated that verse with marriage. I thought, being single, that I was at a disadvantage, so I pushed harder and clung more tightly to my second strand—God. But marriage, though it can be applied there, is not the point. It is about accountability and being open with any other person in your life about your weaknesses. Being strong together," she explained her epiphany as she negotiated the narrow streets back to the highway, not taking the city tour this time. "I think that is the same thing you were trying to tell me this morning." Judah frowned and it made her scar pull strangely at the side.

"I wonder why I have such a hard time trusting. It's a simple concept," Judah mused. She seemed to be putting the sermon into practice. She was never this open about where she was spiritually.

Rivers glanced over at her perplexed look. "You really don't know?" With all of her experience as a profiler, he thought she'd have better insight into her own life. She shook her head, staring through the glass. "For starters," Rivers told her, "two-thirds of the most important men in your life left you—without warning."

Judah turned slowly to look at him. Rivers sensed her openness and continued. "First, your father died when you were young and then your college boyfriend left you. He was more than that, really. You had effectively already committed to be his wife, if you were expecting a ring, like you told me. So, you lost a father and a husband. Either of those two traumas alone would be enough to make trust a difficult issue, for anyone. Even a strong, independent lieutenant commander such as yourself. Listen," he paused. "Are you hungry?" They were passing an *Intermarche* grocery store that was open.

"Would you mind waiting until we get back to Berlin to eat?" she asked. "I think I have more than enough to digest right now," her voice was soft and introspective.

"That's fine. You're the one who didn't have any breakfast."

"I'm okay. You know, I never thought of those," Judah broke off seemingly searching for words, "events as traumas. They were just a part of my life, you know, something that happened. Graham has been as much a father to me as my real dad was. Maybe more in some ways." Her soft tones did not indicate that she knew she was speaking aloud. "Hmm."

Rivers was content to drive in silence for the duration of the trip and was surprised when 25 kilometers outside Halle, Wakefield spoke again. "I am ready to tell you why I had such a bad week in Washington," she volunteered.

Rivers changed mental gears and cautiously asked with a bright tone, "Why's that?" He consciously relaxed his rigid shoulder muscles.

"It started in the Afghanistan debriefing with Dietz, when he told me you said Filasek is still alive." Rivers started to speak, but snapped his mouth shut when she held up a slender open hand. "Then I had to appear before a Congressional subcommittee that was hell-bent on turning me into an example to military servicemen who waste appropriated funds by blowing up millions of dollars' worth of weapons that could be reconfigured for our use. Not to mention that they accused me of murdering an ambassador."

"What?" It exploded out of Rivers' mouth before he could stop it.

"Oh, I'm not done yet," she warned. "I am currently in the middle of an Article 32 hearing with JAG. I stand accused of conduct unbecoming, sexual harassment, negligent homicide due to culpable inefficiency." She ticked them off on her fingers." Oh, and they tacked on murder one. I feel sure it will go to court martial."

"What!"

"Yep," she said in his stunned silence. "I told you I had a week."

"True," he was incredulous. "But that much…stuff…would constitute a bad *year*." Rivers called on his years of military bearing to force himself to remain calm. "Why—when—how—" He stuttered trying to decided which question he wanted an answer to first. He took a calming breath. "How are you on a mission in the middle of an Article 32 hearing? When are these things supposed to have taken place?"

Wakefield explained as much of the hearing and Dietz's well-timed entrance as she could during the remainder of their drive.

"They did the investigation already? No one talked to me." By the time they reached the outskirts of Berlin, Rivers had a good picture of what had taken place in the courtroom. "Count on me to come testify for the defense as soon as we catch this assassin," he promised.

Without asking directly, Wakefield eliminated Rivers as being the one who had phoned in the hotline complaint. *Sexual harassment...who was left? Who called it in?* she wondered.

"Speaking of assassins, do you know how to hire a hit man?" she asked. Her heart pounded hard in her chest, unconsciously she reached up to still it with her hand.

"No. I just kill them." Rivers screwed up his face at the way his words sounded. "You know what I mean."

"I bet Chad would have a contact or an e-mail address for us." Wakefield suggested. "According to the call log, he was the agent who phoned in the threat."

"So you think we should let them in on our plan?"

"I don't think we have a choice," she balked. "They need to know they are risking their lives being with you."

"Point taken." He looked thoughtful. "But I don't trust Yates."

Wakefield snorted in her throat. "You just don't like him because he likes me better," she teased.

Rivers didn't look at her. "We should get started right away. Who knows how often he checks for new jobs."

21

"So, I just click on this spinning icon?" Rivers moved the mouse on the computer to point to a small triangle in the bottom right corner of the screen after moving the page as far to the right as it would go.

"Correct," Chad said. His long, course, black hair hung onto the officer's shoulder as he leaned over Rivers to check the screen. "It will take you directly to the message board. It does take a while to load, though," the young agent warned.

The message board was tucked away on an unseen part of the screen attached to the *About Us* section of an obscure club for lovers of the praying mantis. Quite obscure in itself.

"It's up." Rivers said when the blue screen finally had a title. There were maybe a hundred tiny pictures of praying mantises in an unusual shape. It almost looked like letters. "What is up with the bugs?" Rivers asked. "I thought he was called Azure Tiger." The message board was empty so Rivers clicked on a button that appeared, hopefully to enter a new message. The words were in what looked like Sanskrit.

Wakefield came and bent over Rivers' left side. She smelled like the tropics today. "He would not call himself 'Azure Tiger.' That is just a name some office worker would have come up with in order to classify the killer so he could be filed both manually and on the computer database. Since there was no name or picture, whoever filed him six or seven years ago, came up with that name to tie him in with the only info we had: India."

Rivers nodded; he was already typing.

"I had wondered about that," Yates said in his high British tones. He was seated at the wooden table reading through the five men's bios again, for perhaps the hundredth time.

"Could I get some breathing room?" Rivers' hands paused on the keyboard, and he straightened his back. He felt buried underneath Chad and Wakefield.

"Sorry, sir," Chad backed up. Wakefield laid a hand briefly on his shoulder and returned to her place at the table.

"I suppose the message board is empty because he deletes it after returning and replying." She flopped back in her chair. Wakefield did not pretend to be siphoning through more paper and information. She seemed drained from their morning trip, more emotionally than physically.

"Okay, how does this sound?" Rivers pushed the rolling chair back a few inches from the keyboard and read the form he had filled in with his message.

The room was on alert. They quietly absorbed every word.

"I understand from a mutual friend that you are in Berlin. I have an opportunity for you to make some extra cash. There is a United States Naval officer in the same city that I would like to see in Arlington, Virginia instead. Name your price, but only if you can comply in the next four days." Rivers read.

"I hope he speaks English," was Wakefield's dry comment.

Rivers turned to look at her sharply. "Do you think he wouldn't?" His brow furrowed.

"The message about the president was in English," Chad told them.

"There's always an on-line translator program if he doesn't," Yates put in.

Rivers nodded once and returned to the monitor. "So, I should post it?"

Wakefield seemed to pick up on his hesitation. He could see her out of the corner of his eye. She bit her bottom lip. "Change, 'comply' to

157

'carry out,' and 'four days' to the actual date—24 January." Wakefield suggested.

A few more clacks on the keyboard, then Rivers double clicked the mouse. "The invitation is in the mail." He leaned back heavily in his chair causing himself to roll a few inches away from the computer desk.

"What happens if Washington gets wind of this?" Wakefield asked of their unorthodox plan.

"How would they know, unless one of us tells them?" Chad returned.

"Aren't they monitoring the website?"

"No," Chad told her. "I promised my source that I would not reveal it. If the site starts to get too many hits then the webmaster will get suspicious and shut down the site." Wakefield nodded and pursed her lips. "I will leave us logged on," Chad continued, "and the screen will refresh automatically every 15 seconds. We can see his reply in real time."

Silence held the room in a tight fist.

"Do you really think this will work?" the Englishman sputtered like a wind-up car. "I mean what are we supposed to do? We cannot leave you alone, but we could die as a result of being near you. What if he succeeds? We will be accessories to murder." His breathing had become ragged as he realized what he was getting into. "This is rubbish." He mumbled under his breath.

"And I'll be dead. You can do whatever you want." Rivers pushed further away from the terminal. "Yates, if you were having trouble with the way we are handling this, you should have spoken up before I posted the hit request." Rivers voice was edgy. He stood and walked to the black window.

Rivers watched the interchange behind him in the glass.

Wakefield looked at Chad and then him. She looked to Yates who seemed to be formulating a response that would not cause a blow up. "Sorry," she mouthed to the Englishman.

He nodded and winked at her, a strained smile on his face. His dark curls bobbed slightly with his gesture.

The wink stirred a tightening in Rivers' throat.

Judah walked toward him and placed a calming hand on his back.

The SEAL turned into the room in the opposite direction from the side where she stood, effectively shaking her off. "Look, we are not going to get anything else accomplished tonight. I know it is early, but I think we could all use the rest." If he examined his motivation honestly, he just wanted a break from the interplay between Yates and Wakefield.

"But it is not even 1800 yet." Yates' voice grated Rivers like a whine. He was lining up their markers in rows on the table. It wasn't like he was doing any life-changing work, yet he went on, "You and Judah have only been back for three hours."

"You can stay if you want, I am going back to my hotel," Rivers told the smooth-skinned man. He stared at the paper-covered table. "I can take a cab or a bus back, if you want to keep the car, Commander," he offered his partner.

"No, I'll go, too."

"Very well." He moved for the door. He was suddenly in a big hurry to get out of the claustrophobic room. "See if you can procure me a large map of Germany before you go back to your flat, Yates."

"I already have one," Chad volunteered.

"Great," Rivers donned his coat and reached for the door. "I have an idea for tomorrow. 0700." He was out the heavy wood door, but left it open for Wakefield to follow. He heard her scurry to pick up her coat. What does she think, that I am going to leave her?

"Wait up, Sailor," she called to him.

"What's that, Gunsmoke?" his voice echoed in the hall. "Can't keep up?" She clicked the latch on the door shut.

Hotel Askanischerhof
Ku'damm 53, Berlin
David Rivers' Room
1845 hours

David waited with his SatFone radio held out in front of him as the *Reprisal*'s comm officer rang ADM Graham's stateroom. He paced in the small room. Even though Dietz had put them up in a very nice hotel, even by American standards, the size was still very continental.

"Mr Rivers," The admiral's voice came through the tiny speaker with remarkable clarity, though the two men were separated by two thousand miles. "I understand you've been looking for me. Is everything okay with Judah?" Anxiety colored his voice.

"Yes, sir," Rivers smiled. "She is fine. But she *is* the instigation behind my call, Admiral."

"Oh?" Now that he was assured of his daughter's safety, his voice relaxed. Rivers thought he had not sounded surprised at the call.

"You see, sir, I well..." Rivers had never been at a loss for words, but he was close. "I would like to take her out to dinner and perhaps dancing afterward."

"And?" Graham gave another one-word response.

"And...I wanted to ask your permission to pursue a relationship with her." He spit it out all at once and then halted his pacing as he held his breath unconsciously awaiting the aftermath.

"You are stationed in Coronado, California, Commander. How do you propose to do that?"

"Well, sir, I have not worked out a solution for down the road, but, we are currently both TAD in Germany." Had she not told him?

"Hmm, have you decided where you are going to take her?" Graham's lowered voice sounded almost conspiratorial.

"Uh, no, sir. I did not want to...get my hopes up before talking it over with you. How did you know I am at Coronado, sir?"

"You're a SEAL, Rivers. There's only two places you could be stationed," a jolly laugh filtered over the connection. "I suppose I should confess: after you left here at Christmas, I checked your service record. I also got a credit report, did a criminal background check, and I even got a hold of your psych eval."

"You did what?" Rivers asked in shock before he could stifle the question.

"A father knows," Graham did not apologize. "You seem to have ordered your life well, Commander, as an officer and as a Christian. You have my blessing to date my daughter. If she agrees."

Rivers had to sit down on the end of his bed to keep from falling down. He stared at the black box in his hand that was quickly coming to be his favorite item.

"Can I assume your silence is shock, Mister Rivers?"

"Ye...yes, sir. How did you get my psych evaluation out on the carrier, sir?

ADM Graham's laugh was filled with mirth "Admiral's privilege," he retorted. He seemed to enjoy a bit of mystery in his command. "Now I'd like to offer a few suggestions if I may."

Rivers had been about to hang up and let the man get back to his business of running the War on Terrorism. "Of course, sir, please." Rivers perked up.

"First, don't pursue this if you are not intending to make this a permanent relationship. She has been wounded by one man already and can be, shall we call it 'prickly' when it comes to men asking her out. In short, she does not trust men's motives."

"Yes, sir. I've seen that first hand. She told me about the college situation. Sir, permanence is my intent." He took a deep breath. He had not even realized it himself in concrete terms, until he said it aloud. He wanted to be with Judah forever. And not just in heaven.

Rivers eyes bugged out as he glanced at himself in the mirror. Was he truly having this conversation with Judah's father? If he had realized before that this conversation would have so many life-long implications, he would have been much more nervous to place the call. He was glad he hadn't known.

"Good," Graham said in his simple, to-the-point manner. "Now second. You need to have a plan and tell her what to expect on the date. Surprises embarrass her. The only time we ever threw her a surprise birthday party, when she turned 17, it was a disaster. Don't do surprises, Commander."

Rivers felt like he should be taking notes on a battlefield plan of attack. Instead he rose from the bed and resumed his pacing.

"Her favorite foods are Chinese lo mien, steaks—but only grilled, not broiled or fried—the only seafood she likes is popcorn shrimp, no fish. And she loves all things Italian. Her favorite music is thirties and forties, the old love songs and big band music. She took swing dance lessons and enjoys that best. Judah despises club scenes and loud, rough music. I believe she once said, 'Anything with an electric guitar gives me a headache.'"

"I am beginning to get the picture, sir. She has very definite opinions."

"True. But she would never tell you that she didn't like something."

"She is too tactful for that." Rivers nodded as he looked at the string of streetlamps outside his window. "But then how do you know all of this, Admiral?"

"I am her father, Rivers." He chuckled as if it was an obvious answer. "I have lived with her since she was eleven, except for my shipboard billets. I am sharing this with you, because I like you. And I think she does, too. You would be good for her."

"Yeah? You should tell *her* that." Rivers commented wryly.

"She would not appreciate the intrusion, believe me. She'll figure it out on her own. It is part of what makes her Judah."

22

Suite 1216
Sunday 20 January 2002
2130 hours

Walking to his window, a man took out his 'handy,' as the Germans call their cellular phones. He spoke in clipped Hindi to the leader of his diversionary men as he studied the wide hotel with the flags of 70 nations adorning the second story across the street from his room. The conversation was not long. Maybe 45 seconds. Including ringing time.

He sat down at his computer, clicked on the spinning triangle and formulated a response. His lips curled into a smile. This was turning into a very profitable month.

Hotel Askanischerhof
Monday 21 January 2002
Wakefield's Room
0545 hours

Wakefield heard the shower in Rivers' room shut off. "Why are you up so early?" she moaned. "You are a man. It should only take you 15 minutes to get ready." She rolled over and put the flat pillow over her head. It was too late. She knew she would never be able to go back to sleep. A nice long bath would be a relaxing way to start the day.

She glanced in the mirror on her way to start the water. "Ugh, What I really need is cucumber slices or tea bags," she frowned at her reflection. Her eyes were puffy from lack of sleep. They had come back to their rooms early enough, and Wakefield had even settled herself under the duvet by 2100 hours. But she tossed and turned for hours before drifting off to chase a blue tiger in her dreams. It was when the tiger turned to chase her that she forced herself awake.

Wakefield heard Rivers secure his door as she turned off the water. She waited with her bathrobe in her hand for his knock. It never came.

She shrugged and stripped her nightgown over her head. She stepped into the steamy water and immediately felt the tension in her shoulders lessen.

"Where is that man going?" She bit the inside of her lip. They had agreed that except their private rooms, he would not go anywhere alone. "So much for that idea." Rivers was a man to do his own thing. She ducked her head under the water. The heat stung her ears, eyes and scalp. It helped to move her mind, if only for a moment, off the man who preoccupied her thoughts far too often in her opinion.

She blew out her breath making bubbles in the water when she remembered that Rivers had listened to her suggestion about not being alone, but he never made any promises about taking company with him.

Woolworth's Department Store
Berlin
0605 hours

Rivers melted in with the few other early morning shoppers at Woolworth's two blocks from the *Hotel Askanischerhof.* He was on the candy aisle, having no luck. He asked three people before he found someone who would admit to speaking English. He needed a suggestion on where to find M&Ms.

"*Aldi,*" a wrinkled woman suggested with a heavy accent. "It is a grocery market. They carry foreign candy. But this chocolate," she pointed out a square of *Ritter Sport* chocolate, "is much tastier."

"I am sure it is, ma'am." Rivers respectfully inclined his head to the hunched over woman. Her skin sagged in places that Rivers did not know would hang. She looked old enough to have been an adult at the same time as Hitler. "But I need M&Ms."

"I see," she said. Her expression clearly stated that she did not see. "*Aldi* is three blocks south, two blocks west."

"Thank you, ma'am," Rivers offered her one of his toothy grins and winked.

"Oh, go on," she swatted at his arm, a blush creeping up to her wrinkled ears.

Rivers reentered the increasing flow of people walking to work or to the tram stops and subway stations. Three blocks south and two long blocks west. *Aldi* sat on the oddly-shaped corner of *Potsdamer Strasse* and *Fontaneplatz*.

He walked across the aisles until he saw baking supplies and went down that one. At the far end, near where the butcher was putting out his cuts of meat and cheese for the day, Rivers found the chocolate section. He traipsed up and down three times before he saw on the bottom shelf a sticker that said, 'M&Ms 4.77.' That seemed high even when converted to euros, but he would pay any price. The shelf, however, was empty.

"Terrific," he growled under his breath. "Who knew it would be this hard to lay my hands on some simple candy."

He left *Aldi* and tried the only other two establishments that were open before heading back to the hotel. Neither store carried more than the obligatory check-out area candy.

He glanced at his watch. He had three minutes before he was due to pick up Judah to go to the embassy. He saw a BP petro station as he started to open the hotel's front door. It was a block away. True, they were British, but maybe...

On the dusty bottom shelf of the front counter was a half-full box of plain M&Ms, no peanuts, no almonds, no special colors, but they were gold to him.

Rivers waved them at the counter clerk and tossed over a two-euro coin onto the counter. "*Danke!*" he said and booked it back to

Judah's room. He did not even care that he had just forked over $1.96 for a 60-cent package of old M&Ms. He put the crinkly package in his coat pocket and double-timed it to pick up his partner.

Elevator Bank
U.S. Embassy Lobby, Berlin
0707 hours

"Good morning, Luv," Yates greeted Wakefield as the three rode up to CIA territory on the fourth floor. *Where does he get off calling her Luv?* Rivers seethed. They were late, but even Wakefield did not seem annoyed by the tardiness, only anxious to check the message board.

"We left last night around 10. There was no reply yet," Yates offered an impotent update.

Rivers touched the M&Ms in his pocket, wondering about an opportunity to give them to her. She stood between the two men, chatting it up with Yates. Rivers stared at her light honey hair. Today it had all kinds of waves that were so shiny that they almost looked wet. He wanted to touch them. He turned the brown bag of chocolates over in his pocket instead.

When the doors slid open, Chad was waiting. He burst out, "We have a reply." He motioned them to follow him. He hitched up his low-slung pants as they walked. Rivers felt as if he was walking in his own funeral processional.

They all four leaned over the back of the chair in the doorway, to read the text, even though Chad had already read it aloud.

"It's cheap," Wakefield straightened up first and moved to put her laptop down. "I've not heard of any of Azure Tiger's hits going for under a million. This is only a quarter of that." She looked at Chad. "Are you sure it's the right man?" She was already shuffling through her paperwork for a list of account numbers to cross-reference with the account list. "The numbers look familiar."

"I don't know who else it would be, ma'am. Who else is there?"

"Do you suppose he knows it is a trap?" Rivers asked. What would that do to the dynamics of the chase?

No one spoke, so they all heard Wakefield's sharp intake of breath and her soft moan as she rushed over to the computer again.

"Yes, I think he knows it is a trap." Her face had blanched white. "I also think he is willing to play a game of cat and mouse to prove he cannot be caught. He is getting bold. That means he feels secure, untouchable. That is not a good thing for us."

The four occupants were spread out all over the room now. Yates and Chad joined Rivers in staring at Judah.

"How do you know all that from that little message?" Chad asked.

Rivers strode over to the computer again. It had to be something in the note. Maybe the phraseology or...what else was there, the time and location of the message's origin? The note asked for a name and gave an amount in the same currency as the other deposits, and a routing number for the account.

"The account number," she said softly, dropping her weight into the rolling computer chair. "It's mine."

Melia Wakefield Morris's Residence
Wisconsin Dells
6:20 AM CST

"Hey big sis, it's me, Melia," Judah's youngest sister said into the phone. "Where are you? I didn't think you would have left for work yet." She tucked her highlighted, light brown hair behind one ear. "Jake and I have some good news, but I can't possibly leave it on the machine. I want to hear your reaction. Call me at home when you get this message. Day or night, it doesn't matter. Jake is out of town all this week, so it is just me and Lilly. Listen how are you? Mom told me a little about the Afghanistan trip. I feel like it has been ages since we've talked. Maybe you could fly out for Lilly's birthday. She'll be two in three weeks. I really miss—" The machine beeped in her ear and cut her off. Melia hug up the phone with a sigh and put it down on the couch beside her. She touched her flat belly. "Just you wait until you meet Auntie Judah. You'll love her. She is lots of fun. You can ask your big sister when you get here."

"Mooommy!" a high voice called from the bedroom. "Up now!" Lilly called firmly.

"Coming, sweetie," Melia called. She put her lukewarm mint tea on the side table and hauled herself to her feet. "She had better call me back *this* time."

Oval Office
Monday 21 January 2002
8:10 EST

"My team is doing all they can, Mr President. But the assassin has been hiding for more than seven years, quite successfully."

President Bush nodded in an easy manner. "I suppose, even though you have assigned Wakefield, I should not expect a miracle in less than two weeks. What is it you want to do, Dietz?"

"I want you to help us set up a sting, sir."

"A what?" Bush asked. His square mouth turned up at the sides in a tight smile. He seemed to be struggling to contain his laughter.

"We want to catch him, Mr President, and the only way we can do that is to allow you to go on...or someone who *looks* like you to go in your place."

Bush laughed aloud. "Don't think I don't see right through your little scheme, Dietz. My ego does not need stroking. I would be no more a part of your 'sting' than the queen bee is in gathering pollen."

"Well, probably not," Dietz smoothed his suit pants. "But if you would postpone your trip without letting the public know, we would be able to sleep better over at Langley."

"Are you saying the secret service can't handle the risk?"

"I am saying, why subject them to the risk? This man will shoot to kill. When one of your men steps in and dies for you, how will it make you feel to know your decision today could have kept him alive?"

"The men know the risks when they take the job," he said calmly. It was as if he was referring to himself in the same sentence. "I'll wear Kevlar, but I'm not rearranging months of scheduling because of this threat."

Dietz's face fell. He had the list of people to be notified in his breast pocket. "Kevlar doesn't go on your head, sir. Respectfully." He didn't sound very respectful. "Though I suppose a vest would be an improvement, sir." His head started pounding.

"Now go on. I have a breakfast scheduled with my girls, and I'm late."

"Of course, sir." Dietz scurried out the door behind the most powerful man in the world.

His secretary caught Bush's attention. "The president of France's secretary is on the line, Mr President." She raised her eyebrow in question.

"Tell him I am late for breakfast with the three most beautiful women in the world. He's French, he should understand the consequences of that." He gave her a closed mouth smile and a quick eyebrow waggle.

The three female secretaries in the outer office tittered as Bush waved over his shoulder and he left with his marine guard in his wake.

Dietz moved his head side to side. The man certainly had priorities. Which was a good thing when running a country, except when those priorities clashed with staying alive.

23

Poros, Greece
Filasek's villa
12:30 PM local time

"Zreik, can I count on you to do this exactly as I've said?" Filasek mooned into the telephone in Farsi.

"You pay me good, Boss," the young man on the other end of the line said. He was in New York. "I'll do good work. I'll get to D.C. today and get the process going."

"Very good. Check in with me tomorrow morning, your time...Did you write down the address?"

The young Arab sighed. "I've been workin' for you five years, Boss. Of course. '21 C Chalfonte Apartments, 1601 Argonne Place, Northwest, 20009,'" he read off the information.

Filasek hung up and immediately dialed again. "Hello, this is Judah Wakefield, he said pleasantly. "I am moving tomorrow and I need to have the cable shut off."

"Certainly, sir. Your address?"

Filasek recited Wakefield's Washington address, her social security number and her mother's maiden name.

"It will be terminated as of 3:00 today, sir. Thank you for your business."

"You are welcome," Filasek hung up. He did the same thing with Washington Gas Line, Potomac Electric, and then AT&T.

The elaborate idea had come to him while he was on the phone with Sprint shutting down the Infidel woman's cell communication last week, but he was just getting around to implementing the details. After the president was dead it would appear as if she had planned to take the money and run. It would be the final nail in her coffin.

So far, the woman at the phone company was the only one who had any concern over the last minute shut offs he had arranged. She could take care of the line with no forwarding number without even visiting the apartment. Apparently, people left D.C. overnight all the time. "What about the messages currently collected on your service, sir?"

"Don't worry about them," Filasek told her. "If they are important people, they will receive my new number and can call me again, right?" he laughed casually as he improvised his story.

"Right you are, sir. I've just deleted the messages and shut off your service. What about forwarding your last bill?"

"Let me give you my visa number." He rattled off Judah's 16-digit number from memory.

Filasek hung up and went to eat lunch on the wide marble balcony off his bedroom. He loved to eat in the warm salt air. The next call would be a little trickier. Talking to Mrs Levesque needed to be after she got up, say 10 AM in Washington.

U.S. Embassy, Berlin
Conference Room D-3
Monday 21 January 2002
1420 hours

After returning from lunch, the group sat around the conference room. They abandoned their previous efforts. Yates had straightened all the piles of printer paper and sat in his ladder-back chair with his PDA, working on a project for his meeting with the Irish coming up in a few days. Judah and Chad tossed cards into a pile between them on the floor in an elaborate game of War. Rivers sat at the cleared conference table and tried to tune out the noise.

At the next 15-second refresh, the computer beeped as it added a second return message. Rivers was the first one to the screen. He read the short message and sighed. He felt the weight of what he'd done settle on his neck like a choke collar. For once, he allowed himself the ease of using a cliché to communicate. "The point of no return," he enunciated slowly.

"What did the guy say?" Chad turned to face the inside of the room. "You know, I never considered that this could be a woman."

"What? No way this bugger is a woman." Yates shot him down. He shook his head emphatically.

Rivers frowned in thought focusing individually on each person in the room. "Why not?" he asked.

"Well...well, because..." the Englishman sputtered. His palm slapped the table with a smack. "I mean look at what we know. He is a rogue out of the Indian Army, he is said to have ties to the Maharaja of India. Look at the shots he has made. Double hits to the head or chest. Some of the shots were taken from half a mile away, one from 1,926 meters, over a mile!" Yates shook his brown curls like a little boy, refusing to give in, or even speculate. "Azure Tiger is obviously a man. No woman could make those shots."

Wakefield cleared her throat, "No offense, Yates, but I could make those shots. I don't think it is unreasonable to consider that our hitman might be a hit-woman."

"Why didn't we consider this earlier? Does it change anything?" Rivers wandered over to the map that Chad had thumb-tacked to a corkboard. He was lost in thought, his hands on his waist, looking at the map, but not seeing it. He wanted to occupy his conscious thoughts so that his subconscious could tackle the revelation and revision. Conversation buzzed around him like white noise.

"You...you can shoot a man in the heart from over two kilometers away?" Yates asked. Rivers smirked as he classified Yates' tone as half-incredulous, half-admiring.

"Don't challenge her to a duel," Rivers warned. He heard her shift her weight from one foot to the other and chuckle deep in her chest. He took it as a sign of pride.

"I take it you tried, Commander?" Yates asked, a chuckle evident in his voice. Rivers could hear the corners of the man's mouth crackle as they turned up.

"She is a crack shot." Rivers moved some of the colored push pins around on the map. "The crew of the *Reprisal* call her 'One-shot Wakefield'." Rivers' back was still to the group.

"You're joking!" Yates exclaimed. "This I must see! Maybe you would like to go target shooting? Tonight? I could take you to dinner first, my treat." He offered. "You could show me your secrets. I've never been any good. Chad, could you keep an eye on Rivers? Maybe take him to a pub?" Yates asked before Wakefield could use babysitting as an excuse.

"Sure, whatever." Chad agreed. When Rivers turned back to them, Chad was already watching him. He probably had no idea that he had agreed to help Yates maneuver in on the female of their happy group. "What did the message say?" Chad asked again. He raked his fingers through his scraggily black hair and leaned low in his chair with his feet stretched out in front of him. He looked relaxed, but Rivers noticed the tension in the way he held his shoulders up close to his ears.

"Just that he had received our down payment and would post a reply when the job was complete."

"Great, I hope that is all he took out of my account," Wakefield complained quietly.

"What are you doing then?" Chad asked.

"Yes, what are you doing?" Wakefield had taken up Rivers-watching as well, after accepting the date with Yates.

Rivers had turned back to the board in a precision military turn.

He was in his element. Thinking about three aspects of his objective at once. He stepped back from the board. "Bring me the last three day's printouts of all five men's bankcard movements." Rivers said instead of answering Chad's question. The field agent was already getting out of his chair. That the young man found the correct folder inside two minutes amazed him. After two weeks of following a paper trail, their conference room had a higher mass weight of paper than it did of body weight.

Chad slapped it into the officer's open hand. "I want to try tracing the movements by name and time and place all at once. They are all on the move again. And I want to see the pattern."

Over 15 minutes, Wakefield called out names and locations, Yates handed the appropriate color of tack to Chad and Rivers who found the locations on the large map. Definite patterns began to develop. Most of the patterns were in semi-straight lines, headed in a southerly direction, and two of them were traveling together.

They all stood back and stared.

"What's in Munchen?" Rivers asked.

"Apparently the 2002 Bad-Guys Convention." Wakefield raised a single eyebrow and stared at the city as if that would cause the map to reveal the secrets they were trying to find.

"Except this one line here. It does not connect." Chad pointed to a second green line of tacks.

"Does that mean that, uh," Yates double checked the name, "Dalhlinger could be our man?" The excitement in his voice was unmistakable.

"We probably have a stolen credit card," Rivers suggested. "And Dalhlinger hasn't noticed yet. See the two green lines?"

Chad chuckled, "Maybe we should ring him up, you think?"

Washington, DC
Chalfonte Apartments, second floor
Monday 21 January 2002
12:49 PM

A neatly dressed man in his late twenties knocked on the door marked, 8 B. He was clean-shaven, with a light brown buzz cut. He touched the iron-on purple emblem on his long-sleeved, button down shirt that introduced him as the manager of Intercontinental Moving Company. He rounded the bill of his ball cap in his hand again and again.

As he knocked again, the door opened three inches under his knuckles. "Mrs Levesque?" he asked the gray-haired woman who behind it.

"Yes?" Her voice whispered like a wasp nest.

"Did you get the call from Judah Wakefield's commanding officer a few hours ago, ma'am?" he asked respectfully. He was in big trouble if Filasek had not made the call yet.

"Oh, are you here to move her already?"

"Yes, ma'am. She told me to pick up the key from you."

The door clicked shut and reopened after the woman removed the safety chain. "Wait right here, young man, while I get her keys.

"And the cat, ma'am." Zreik called softly.

"Joe, too?" Her voice came from the kitchen. Apparently, there was nothing wrong with her hearing.

"Yes, ma'am. Ms Wakefield asked if I would mind bringing the cat to her."

"That's strange—" Mrs Levesque returned with a gray striped cat in her arms. She baited him by dangling the two keys in front of his paws while he lay like a baby, "—you taking Joe." She lifted her eyes to his face.

"We are a full-service moving company." Zreik puffed out his chest in what he hoped looked like pride. "Confidentially, though," he lowered his voice and put a hand to his mouth as he leaned toward her, "this is the first time I have ever moved a cat to another country."

"So she is staying in Germany then? I wondered."

"Germany? Oh, yes. That is where we are shipping all of her things. I will be taking care of Joe myself, on the...ship."

"I thought that the navy usually sent their own out for moving their people." The old woman suddenly pursed her lips and narrowed a crinkly eye at him.

175

Zreik shifted from one foot to the other. "New policy," he nodded forward. "To generate income and boost the economy, the federal government told the forces to start handing out moving contracts for transporting personnel to new duty stations. But the servicemen get to pick who they want." He explained while thinking that his explanation had more holes than a target ship.

She accepted his words with a single nod. "I know about a bad economy. It is too bad she can't come say good-bye, at least." Mrs Levesque frowned a sigh and handed over the set of keys and the cat. "I'll leave his food and the litter outside. Your men can pick that up on one of their trips out."

Zreik had to put his cap back on to take the squirming cat. "You know Uncle Sam. He wants you where he wants you, *when* he wants you." They both chuckled. "I'm sure she'll give you a call. I'll mention it to her," he promised.

He backed up to the door. "We'll try to be quiet, ma'am. Shouldn't take more than a few hours, then you will have quiet until the first of the month." Zreik smiled at the wrinkled face.

"That will be nice, though Judah was always a quiet neighbor." She started closing the door. "What a nice young man," he heard her mutter.

Zreik smirked. "Easy as pie," he breathed.

24

C IA Berlin Chief of Station Nelson knocked once on the wooden door of the conference room he had assigned for the visiting team and stuck his head in the door. The four people he came to see were all standing at the far side of the room with their backs to the door, talking in staccato, hushed cadences. "I've got coffee and kuchen," he said by way of announcing his presence. They must not have heard him knock. He set the tray down on the conference table, and it was the clatter that finally drew their attention. "

"Great bunch of field agents you all are," Nelson chastised their startled expressions. "I knocked and announced myself. What's so intense?" he asked. He walked over to view the map where they were arguing.

Wakefield's smile looked too tight. "Why don't you explain," she nudged Rivers with an elbow. She moved toward the tray he had set down, and poured five cups of coffee from the silver carafe while Rivers explained his theory by tracing the five suspect's routes.

"I don't see the problem, Commander. Why would a trip to Munich be any different than following any other lead?" Nelson asked Rivers. Why wouldn't they just follow it up?

The SEAL shook his head once. "I do not see the problem either. Ask Wakefield." He jabbed a finger at the thin blonde across the room.

She looked up mid-slice, and lifted the knife out of the cake to gesture with her right hand. "What he didn't say, is that he wants to interrogate some of them. Probably all of them, and with—" she cut

177

herself off with a choking noise. She looked down and continued slicing the cinnamon kuchen. "And that is not safe. We should bring them in, question them on our own turf." Her words sounded edited.

"The four of you shouldn't have any problems if you talk to one or two at a time." Nelson tried to diplomatically reassure the woman. He'd not seen her display fear. According to the chats he had with Dietz, she never did. But today it was clear in her long-lashed blue eyes.

"That is the other problem," Wakefield appealed. "Yates is hosting some diplomats from Ireland. They requested him, and it has been on the schedule for eight months. It is important for relations between England and Ireland to have him there." Yates shrugged and offered an apologetic smile. "It is only a day," Wakefield continued her arguments, "but according to Rivers, we have to go right away. I realize we only have three days until the president is here, but still…" She jerked her thumb toward the young field agent in the room. "Chad has a monthly meeting with a contact tomorrow that he has not missed in four years."

"I can assign two men from the embassy to go with you," Nelson offered. He was quite familiar with Chad's contact. He came through with some of the best tips and information, including this assassination contract. Nelson did not want to compromise that relationship.

"No, thank you," Rivers interjected. "The two of us will attract less attention. I will re-appropriate the men's priorities one at a time, and Wakefield can watch my six." The SEAL had it all planned out.

Nelson looked at the female naval officer. There was no way on earth she would not attract attention. Her beauty was too striking, her scar too mysterious. He was interested himself. And he had not been interested in a long time.

"That is just it!" Wakefield touched her coffee cup back to its saucer with a rattle. "What if I can't watch your six?" Her jaw muscle worked in and out as she stared down the other officer. The gauntlet had been thrown down and the men in the room all recognized it. But it was only her partner's reaction she seemed to be gauging.

Rivers seemed to intuitively understand. He set his coffee back on the table without even taking a sip. "May I see you outside?" he asked, all arrogance aside.

She marched to the door without replying. Rivers closed the door behind them.

"Boy what I wouldn't give…" Nelson started. He gulped his black coffee.

"Me, too," the other two sounded wistful.

Wakefield glared at Rivers. "We've been getting along great for the last couple days," she tried to keep her voice on an even keel, but lost the battle. "How dare you call me out here like an elementary child going to talk to the principal!" She was embarrassed at being shamed in front of her colleagues, and at losing her temper with Rivers. He had never been on the short end of her wrath, but he was about to experience it. Her head boiled. "I am not—" she paused to control her rising voice. "This is *not* the way to my good side, Commander! I—"

"This is not about you, Judah," he told her softly. The sound of her given name on his lips did more to begin calming her than anything else would have. How he knew exactly when to keep his calm to save her from going over the edge, she would never understand. Oh, he made her angry for sure, but in those times when it was deadly important, or in front of others, he soothed her instead of riling her. "We have to catch this man. Our Commander in Chief's life is in more jeopardy the longer the assassin stays alive. This is the only way. I think you know that." He paused. "We have to give Azure Tiger a place to attack."

She moved her defiant stare from the opposite wall to look at him. She had to lift her chin to see his face because he stood toe to toe with her.

He studied her eyes, first one and then the other. She refused to protect her soul by looking away. She wanted him to know what this

K.J. Frolander

surrender cost her. "Maybe this *is* about you," Rivers said almost inaudibly.

"What do you mean?" she couldn't help asking.

"You are more than capable of watching out for me; you have already established that. There is no one I would rather have looking out for me. I don't think you doubt your abilities for a minute. But," he touched the back of her arm and brought her closer as an office aide approached them with a stack of documents in his arms, "I think you are dealing with trust issues again."

Wakefield felt her heckles rise again, but she held her tongue. The aide's passing gave her time to clarify her thinking. He was right. It made her feel irritable and vulnerable that he figured it out before she did.

She calmed herself before speaking. "How is it that you seem to know me better than I know myself?" she asked.

Rivers seemed to sense that her question meant more than speculation. "I have an inside track?" he asked with a small smile.

Wakefield liked his small smile better than his large happy grin. "Are you saying that God told you I don't trust him enough and that is why I am acting like a five-year-old?" she didn't try to hide the self-depreciating smirk on her lips.

"Nope." Rivers patted her arm before lifting his hand away. "You just did." Her eyes rolled up and over. "I recognize the same symptoms in me, I just overcompensate with my need to control—as you so often point out."

"Oh," Wakefield stated without making a sound. Her lips paused in the small shape.

"And are you not the one who always points out that God knows what he is doing, that he has our best interests at heart, Miss hot-shot-officer, One-shot Wakefield, Take-'em-down-with-one-punch Profiler?"

"All right," she halted his attempt at compliments. She touched the door to go back in. "but if you get yourself killed, don't come complaining to me!" Rivers laughed as she thought, *because I'll already be complaining to me enough for the both of us.* Then she berated herself and prayed silently. *God, please help me to refuse to partner with this fear. I know it is not irrational fear from the world's standards, but I want your standards. I choose to trust you completely.*

Judah inhaled strength from the Father's heart as she walked through the threshold. "We're going to Munich in the morning," she announced back in the conference room.

Three sets of eyebrows arched toward the ceiling as if rehearsed at her dynamic change of attitude, and the three men looked to Rivers behind her.

"But I am not giving up my shooting date tonight," she assured Yates. "I need to shoot something, and this will keep me from shooting my partner," she told them all with sugary-sweetness dripping from her voice.

Nobody dared laugh until Rivers did. "Why don't you find Azure Tiger and shoot him instead?" Chad suggested.

"I plan to shoot him, too." Wakefield played along as the tension eased. "But I'll just wing him. I wouldn't want him to miss the rest of his life rotting in the jail cell that is waiting for him."

Hotel Askanischerhof
Ku'damm 53, Berlin
Wakefield's Room
1856 hours

Rivers knocked on Wakefield's door. Chad stood behind him. The two were headed to a pub that Chad recommended for dinner and to kick back a few. At least that is what Chad had issued the invitation for. And Chad probably *would* guzzle German beer all evening. However, alcohol dulled the senses, and Rivers refused the disadvantage.

Wakefield opened the door and looked questioningly at the two men. "I thought it was a little early for James," she said before Rivers could find his tongue. He tucked his hands in his jacket pocket and fingered the lumpy bag of M&Ms. Another day, he decided. He did not want to share her with James Yates.

"I just wanted to know—you to know," he corrected, "that we were leaving. This is the name of the bar where we will be." Rivers pressed a hotel stationary postcard with a name and phone number into her hand.

It was then that Chad was able to put together a semblance of a sentence. "Wow, ma'am! You look stunning!"

She smirked and her eyes darted to Rivers. "Thank you, Chad." Her chuckle sounded melodic. "You guys have fun, and Chad, bring him home in one piece, huh?"

Chad just nodded, unashamedly taking in her feminine figure. Rivers turned to go and caught the young man's expression. He cuffed him lightly on the back of the head. "Quit staring at my partner, Mr Wellingham," he warned. Even Rivers himself did not know if he was serious or kidding.

25

"The sight must be off." Yates yelled to Wakefield over the gunfire. "I've never been this bad!" The red light at the end of the range blinked three times in rapid succession, and Wakefield and Yates, along with the other shooters, laid down their weapons and removed their ear protection. A man called, "Cease fire," in German over the loudspeaker. The line of targets began to automatically move forward on the pulley system suspended overhead.

"I think you missed the target all together on one," Wakefield laughed as she removed Yates' bull's eye. There were only four bullet holes on the small paper.

Yates reached across to pull Wakefield's target down. He paused. "You only have one hole in yours. What went wrong? Are you losing your touch, One-shot?" Yates flitted the paper in front of her. His cute mannerisms intrigued her.

An announcement began. "It seems we have an expert on the field tonight. Number 11, please step forward."

"Um," Wakefield interrupted Yates' casual flirty grin. "They're calling me." She gestured to the field. She hadn't expected to be put on display. She opened the Dutch-door to the hallway behind her shooting stall and stepped three feet out. A picture of her target with the center '5' neatly punched out flashed on the overhead instructional monitors. The black ring around the number had not even been tattered as all five bullets passed cleanly through the bull's eye.

She waved awkwardly and stepped back inside as a few people applauded weakly. The speaker continued, but she wasn't listening.

"They are giving you that round free? You made a perfect score?" Yates translated loosely. He pulled her close and planted a kiss on her lips in exuberance. "That was wonderful, Luv!" he said releasing her. He stayed close by and whispered in her ear as people began replacing their ear protection for the next round of firing. "I guess I should be more careful around you, Miss Wakefield. You certainly *could* be our assassin."

"Oh, you!" She tapped him lightly on the shoulder.

A-Frame Jazzclub
Pestalozzistrasse 105, **West Berlin**
2210 hours

"Isn't this a hoppin' place?" Chad yelled over the loud jazz band playing in a lit corner of the dark club.

Rivers had to cup his hand behind his ear to catch the words. He looked at the crowd. Some were rowdier than others. He sat at their bar table with his back purposefully to the dance floor. The gyrations were too provocative for him to enjoy watching. "Interesting place, anyway, Chad." Rivers nodded, though it was not in agreement, just assessment.

Rivers watched Chad drain his third pint while he nursed a single cup of coffee after their meal at the eatery next door. The waitress in a tiny black uniform kept warming it up for him, and he had to adjust the cream and sugar each time. It was excellent coffee though.

"Chad, just ask her to dance, will you?" Rivers instructed. He had been watching the young man eye a woman at the next table for over an hour. "I am about ready to go."

"Go? We just got here. Did you want to try something a little more..." he made an emphatic gesture to suggest something more wild.

Rivers frowned with his eyes wide and shook his head. "No. This is plenty. I have a long drive ahead of me tomorrow. I want to get some sleep."

Chad studied him for a few seconds and then gave him a knowing smile. "Right." He nodded. "You just want to be there when Yates walks your partner to the door. "Make sure he doesn't get—"

Rivers halted the black-haired agent with a scathing look.

"It's okay, sir. I get you." Chad implied that Rivers' jealousy was understandable.

"I do not think you do, Chad. Wakefield is not like that anyway. She handles herself with integrity. Look," he was sounding exasperated. "Go have your dance, and let's get out of here." Rivers did not want to discuss the intricacies of his relationship with Judah Wakefield with anyone. Except her.

Thirty minutes later, the woman he had danced with, accompanied Chad to drop Rivers at his hotel before the two of them went on to another club she knew.

"Promise me you'll stay inside. Wakefield will kill me if you get shot tonight." Chad told him with a pleading look at the glass lobby door.

"Very well," Rivers snorted in disgust. "I promise not to get dead on you tonight." The SEAL rolled his eyes. *This babysitting routine is overkill. If a sniper was going to take a shot at me, having a warm body standing next to the target is not much of a deterrent.*

Kurfurstendamm Strasse, Berlin
2315 hours

"This is pleasant, isn't it?" Yates asked. He and Judah were walking down *Kurfurstendamm*, near *Alexander Platz*, a small town center plaza that Yates showed her. He had his arm draped over Wakefield's shoulders. Though Yates was effeminate in his poet's features and lanky figure, he was tall, like Rivers, and it was a comfortable fit to walk together.

"It is a nice night, James. It feels warmer than normal, and not as windy as it usually is in the city." She glanced up at him to find his eyes on her, too. "It's nice to not have my hair blowing in my face." She pushed her hair back out of habit.

"You have beautiful hair, Judah." Yates smoothed the wavy curls with his slender fingers and then dug in to squeeze the nape of her neck. She shivered.

Wakefield looked in the shop windows as they passed by them in the lamppost light. Yates was good company. Actually, she had enjoyed a delightful evening of his attentiveness. The Brit was knowledgeable on many subjects from Biology to the history of China to the location of the best coffee houses in Europe to Russian poets. He was humorous without being crude and very conscientious of her preferences and comfort. *I could get used to this attention. He is not afraid to touch me like Rivers is.*

He talked about a rat in his flat while she window-shopped and nodded in the right places. She was comfortable enough not to listen.

When she focused again, he was saying, "...so then they decided it was high time to fumigate our entire building. But the manager was kicking and screaming all the way to the office to make the call. He would have rather lived with rats than be away from his precious collection of seashells for three days." She laughed with him.

"Here we are, *Kurfurstendamm* 27. Pretty lofty building, huh?" Yates sounded excited. He checked his watch. "Her Majesty sprang for a pretty nice suite to be my home away from home, because I will be entertaining the Irish while they are here, tomorrow afternoon."

Judah nodded as she took in the opulence of the place. "Wow! This is nice." A regular room probably didn't go for under 300 a night.

"You should see my suite. It covers half of the top floor. It has the most amazing completely marble bathroom, a bed fit for a king, a crystal chandelier in the foyer. The closet is as big as the lounge in my flat." They were passing the revolving door and she peered into the brass and glass lobby with scarlet accents that screamed wealth. "In fact," Yates pulled them to a stop, "Why don't you come up and have a look?" he invited. "I guarantee you have never seen a German hotel room as large as this one at the *Kempi.*" He called the place by its local nickname.

Wakefield looked longingly at the rich lobby. She took a step back for strength. "As much as I would love to, I can't." Unconsciously, she brought her fingers up to her lips where Yates had kissed her in excitement hours earlier.

"Judah, you don't need to be worried," he chuckled softly. "I didn't mean *that.* Really. The invitation is for a tour, maybe some wine, or coffee if you'd like. That's all. Come on," he sounded like he was begging, "it is so beautiful. I want to show it someone. To you."

"I'd be lying if I said it was not tempting," she spoke softly. He heard her with no problem. They were standing close. "But, the best intentions are sometimes the ones that cause the most trouble. Thank you. I'll pass." She made her decision. "Please tell me you understand." She looked up into his eyes apologetically. She did not want to jeopardize their friendship or working relationship with a misunderstanding.

He moved her closer to him, guiding her away from the light that spilled out of the doorway. "I think I understand," he replied, his voice almost a whisper. "But I want to understand more." His face leaned in to hers. "I want to understand all about you." He touched her lips lightly with his first finger. "Your secrets," he kissed her forehead. "Your strength," he looked at her eyes almost teasingly, then kissed her chin. "Your beauty." Finally, his lips found hers again.

Judah was the one to break it off, breathless. She let her fingers trail over the shadow on his jaw and she pulled away.

She had to swallow before she could find her voice. "I need to go home," she said simply.

James Yates took her hand, threaded his fingers through hers, and put their hands in his coat pocket. He turned them around, content to walk the few blocks back to her hotel in silence.

One block from *Hotel Askanischerhof,* a police car raced past them. The blaring siren pierced Judah's ears. But it was the second car that caused concern. The undulating sirens stopped abruptly after turning the corner.

The corner was the entrance to the *Hotel Askanischerhof* lobby.

Judah's pulse began to race. *Surely it couldn't be.* She wanted to dash ahead and see, and at the same time, she dreaded knowing.

Yates touched the length of her fingers soothingly. "Relax," he intoned calmly. "What are the odds that it is Rivers?"

They turned off the main street into the side street entrance of her hotel. Two small police cars and an ambulance parked at awkward angles in the small area. The ambulance waited backwards, within a few yards of the door. The air was eerily silent with all the emergency workers inside. The flashing lights threw shadows on the downtown Berlin buildings.

Wakefield felt as if she was watching a scene from a horror movie with the sound muted.

She tore herself loose from Yates saying, "Highly probable, considering what we let him do today." She ran down the uneven sidewalk only to be stopped by a beefy uniformed arm as she tried to enter the building.

"I am sorry, ma'am," he told her in German. "No one is allowed inside the premises right now." He firmly blocked her way.

"I am a guest at this hotel," Judah shot at him in a clipped, dismissive tone.

"You may wait just outside, but don't go far. If you are a guest, we will need to question you." He crossed his arms over his puffed chest.

She was quickly losing her temper; she could feel it rising. "Will you at least tell me what room number is involved?"

"How do you know it was a guest?" the policeman asked as his arms moved to a fist on each hip.

Judah blew out her breath in a huff and could not disguise the small roll of her eyes. "It is like 350 to 1 that it is a guest in trouble. There is only a night check-in manager on duty. And who would have called you if it was him who was...in trouble?" She spoke jerky sections of speech, not caring if it helped or hindered her accent.

"Please back away from the door, ma'am. I don't want to ask you again," the burly officer stated.

She felt Yates presence behind her as he walked up. He touched the small of her back to pull her over to the side where the officer indicated. She twisted out of his grasp and remained steadfast in front of the officer.

"I am not leaving until you tell me the room number," she challenged, stepping loser to him. She held her breath.

She could see Yates out of the corner of her eye, watching her with a glint of amusement playing at his lips.

"Four hundred seven," the officer said, but held his ground.

"Oh, God, no!" she tried to barge past the policeman. He caught her by her elbow and threw his weight into her, effectively stopping her charge. "That's my partner in there. You will unhand me, Officer!"

"All right, lady. Let's see some ID." He led her to the far side of the hotel's entrance. His large hand fit around the whole of her upper arm.

She flipped out her leather ID with her driver's license on one side and her military ID on the other, and her military passport. "I am sure you don't want the entire U.S. Navy breathing down your neck, so I know you are going to let me through to check on my partner in room 407. See, here's my key. I'm next door, 409." She dangled the key in front of his face.

"Fine, you can go up," he relented, "but stay out of the way!" he called after her retreating back. "We are professionals. Let us do our jobs, the same way you would expect to."

Yates followed her at a quick pace.

"Not you," The policeman stopped him.

"He is with me," Judah took a few steps back and tugged Yates' other arm.

"Of course he is," the guard swore under his breath, but released Yates to follow her.

Wakefield ran up the four flights to their floor instead of waiting for the lift.

Another policeman stood sentry at the stairwell door. Wakefield headed off his protest with a professional, hurried toss of her hair. Her simple phrase, "Lieutenant Commander Rivers is my partner," seemed to be the magic password when paired with another flash of her military ID. The uniformed man directed her forward to the room without argument. Police all over the world seemed to understand the complex feelings associated with a partner.

Wakefield's mouth felt like she had tried to swallow the entire dust bowl region. The paramedics were backing out of the room with a stretcher and she had to wait. It was empty. Would there be a body bag instead? The smell of fingerprinting dust laced even the hallway air. Had Azure Tiger waited for his prey in the man's own room?

"*Nine!*" She heard the irritated voice of her partner growl. "No!" He repeated in English. At least he had picked up some German. "I do not want any shots or medication." His fierce voice carried menacingly into the hall.

Judah sagged against the wall. Her heart pounded in her ears blocking out Rivers' further heated complaints and threats against the emergency crew. He was still alive.

Yates touched her shoulder in a comforting gesture. She had forgotten he was there. The Englishman had seen her expression. It showed in his eyes.

"I'm fine," she touched his hand. "I think I have this under control, why don't you go home and get some sleep before your fighting Irishmen get here tomorrow."

Yates nodded and kissed her cheek. "Be safe, Luv. I...really like you."

Judah looked away with a peculiar turn of her lips. "Good night, Mr Yates. Thank you for the lovely evening."

Judah steadied her breath and rolled her body around to the inside of the doorframe, still supporting her weight on the structure. She felt her knees could give way any moment. If Rivers was refusing treatment, maybe the paramedics could see to her—*Is there a treatment for near heart failure?*

She surveyed the room. Except for the fine black powder that covered every surface and the extra people, everything was normal. The room was tidy. Rivers' deodorant, aftershave, comb, gel, and water bottle lined the desk under the mirror. There was no blood, no broken furniture, no sign of a struggle. It was cold though.

The flutter of the open curtain behind Rivers, who sat on the bed with two men fussing over him in German, caught Wakefield's eye. The left section reflected the movements and lights of the room. The right side was a flat black color.

Wakefield crossed her arms, fixed a mock glare on her partner and waited for Rivers to look up. She cleared her throat. "I hear you are giving these men a tough time, Commander." She was grateful her voice sounded calm.

"Hey! Judah A. Wakefield." His face lit up like a little boy. "Am I glad to see you! Will you please tell these monkeys that I do not want my ribs taped or any pain meds." He pushed the shorter of the two away again.

The other medic turned to Judah and explained Rivers' condition in German. Judah chuckled in spite of herself and then spoke to Rivers. "They understand you perfectly. They are ignoring you," she pursed her lips comically, "because you are being a pain in the rear— though that is not a direct quote. Your blood pressure is too high. Let them give you something." She managed a pleading expression that did not even feel close to a smile.

Rivers gave his partner a look of betrayal. "If you understand English so well," he directed his comments to the two medics, "understand this: my blood pressure will drop as soon as you leave me alone. It has nothing to do with being shot at. He missed. I do not think you guys understand that. It is not a big deal!"

Wakefield covered an amused snort and pushed herself slowly away from the wall with her hands. "Maybe they would believe you if you tried a more neutral tone of voice," she suggested, walking closer.

Rivers sat bare-chested in the direct path of the cold air. She tossed him his undershirt and then spoke to the pair of paramedics. It was the revelation of her experience as a corpsman in the navy that finally convinced them that she could handle Rivers alone. The man digging the bullet out of the wall completed his regimen of picture taking, and he left with them.

The night manager had called the general manager who paced the length of the hall back and forth. He passed in front of Rivers' room every 14 seconds. The finger printer had lifted a hundred prints from the room. He gathered his documentation kit and bade them farewell. The general manager collided with him at the door. One steadying moment kept the hundred slicks of prints from contamination on the floor.

Wakefield motioned the manager in. He came in talking. Wakefield just wanted quiet. "I am so sorry. Nothing like this has ever happened at *Hotel Askanischerhof* before. I will clean the mess myself. I apologize that your trip to our lovely country is marred by this. The rest of your stay will cost you nothing..." He apologized all over himself. The man bent over at the waist to make his impassioned plea as close to Rivers as he could come. It embarrassed Wakefield for him.

"Herr Hermann, please." Judah stood and reached out to straighten the middle aged man. "There is no way you could have foreseen this. We will not allow it to color our view of your fine country or your hotel," she promised him in his native tongue. Even though it left Rivers out of the loop, she thought the manager would feel more at ease conversing in German. At his current level of stress, it might even prevent the bursting of a blood vessel.

"Do you have another room where we can move Commander Rivers until the glass can be replaced in the window?" she asked politely.

"Alas, we have no more rooms." His head began its apologetic wag again. "We are all full from your president's visit this weekend. But," he brightened largely and showed his teeth, "I have one more cot. I will bring it into your room, yes? He can sleep there for one night?" He clasped his hands together with a popping sound.

Wakefield frowned and glanced at Rivers. He pulled his t-shirt on over his muscled chest. She could still make out the green and light yellow bruising from the South American incident. "No," she told the manager regrettably. "That will not work." Her mind raced with options as she rejected each one.

"Oh," the manager frowned. He obviously wanted his idea to work. "You are both adults, yes?" Herr Hermann asked. "Surely one night..."

Wakefield closed her eyes, frustrated. "We are both adults, yes." She sighed. "*That* is the problem."

"I have another idea. He can come back to my house with me. My son can move into bed with my wife and me. He can have my son's bed." He nodded seeming pleased with this alternative.

Wakefield smiled gratefully, but she knew Rivers would never go for it. Herr Hermann was trying desperately to accommodate them. She saw that. "You have a couple of options," she told Rivers. "I can't make this decision for you though. None of them are ideal in my opinion."

Rivers nodded for her to go ahead. He leaned back on his palms. "The hotel is full, so Herr Hermann has offered to move the last cot into my room." Rivers raised his eyebrows and smiled. Her disparaging look stilled him. "He also offered his son's bed at his own home. Or there is Yates. He is only a few blocks away at the Kempinski. He has a gorgeous, huge suite there with plenty of room. I'm sure he wouldn't mind the company."

Rivers eyes narrowed and his mouth moved to one side. "Why does James Yates have a hotel suite? And how do you know what it looks like?" he questioned.

Judah felt her face flush pink. "He described it to me," she squeaked in a tiny voice.

Rivers let out a belly laugh that startled poor Herr Hermann. "Then I am sure he does not want *me* as a guest." Rivers chuckled, suggestively wagging his eyebrows at his blushing partner.

"Probably not," she choked out. "Perhaps I could recommend a nice cardboard box for the street corner." She pretended she was not flaming red. "What do you want to do?" she tilted her head toward the bewildered looking manager who stood waiting.

"Do you think you can procure some plastic sheeting and duct tape?" he asked Herr Hermann directly.

"Of course, sir. What—You are not thinking of staying in *this* room tonight." It was more a statement than a question.

"You bet I am!" Rivers was emphatic.

Wakefield was almost disappointed that she did not get to explain why he couldn't stay in her room. On second thought, she decided she probably wouldn't like him so much if he didn't already know.

26

"Thank you for not pushing us to get on the road at oh-dark-thirty this morning," Wakefield sighed. She pushed her blond hair out of her face where it seemed determined to remain this morning. "I am still so tired."

"Didn't you sleep well?" Rivers asked glancing at his partner out of the corner of his eye while maintaining his vigil on the darting traffic crammed into the narrow lanes of the A-4. They narrowly missed several crashes because of Rivers' quick instinct and jerk of the wheel.

Wakefield unconsciously pressed her foot into the floor where the brake pedal would have been, had she been driving. The release of her white-knuckled grip on the door handle was the first indication that she had resigned herself to life or death. If they stopped on the heavily trafficked roadway, it would be death for sure. She was too tired to care.

"Oh, I slept fine. Once I finally got to sleep. I kept thinking about last night," she admitted. "Last time I looked at the clock it was 3:47." She yawned until could hear the skin on the sides of her mouth stretch. She gulped another shot of her morning ritual. "Sorry. You probably slept like a baby," she accused jealously. He was alert this gray, foggy morning, almost chipper.

"Exactly. I woke at 2, 4 and finally at 6, I got up." Rivers cracked a rue smile.

"Very funny," Wakefield commented in a flat voice. "You never told me how you happened to be practicing to be the wrong end of a bull's eye," she prompted. Whatever the circumstances, they had to be better than the scenarios she had dreamed up between midnight and 3:47.

"When I came in, those ugly curtains were wide open. I distinctly remembered closing them to change before meeting with Chad. I knew someone had been in the room." Rivers shrugged, his chest pushing against the seatbelt. "I checked the bathroom, the closet, under the bed. We have platform beds, in case you wanted to know. There was no sign of anything. Just those misplaced curtains.

"It took about two seconds. I dropped to my knees as I realized that the sniper had probably opened the curtains to take his shot through the glass. That's what I would have done. Makes an easier escape." Rivers explained. "I was going to belly crawl over to close the drapes, but not a split second later, the glass shattered and a single bullet buried itself in the wall where my head had just been."

Wakefield sucked in her breath with a shwooshing sound. She coughed as the coffee in her mouth started down the wrong way. Rivers would have become another statistic correlated with Azure Tiger if it had not been for God's protective hand. Wakefield felt her chest tighten in recognition as she pictured God's hand shoving the mighty SEAL to the hotel floor.

"The glass shattered. It was all over the place and loud, too. I think that is what drew the attention of the night manager."

"Actually, no," Wakefield remembered aloud. "I overheard him giving his testimony to the police when I bullied my way through the front door." Rivers gave her a quick glance of amusement. "He was outside taking a smoke break. Some of the glass fell on his head." Wakefield chuckled appreciatively.

"Interesting." Rivers snorted. "What are the odds of that happening? Do you suppose he could be involved? It would explain the lack of signs of forced entry."

"I suppose it's possible," Wakefield frowned in concentration as she stared at the knobs of the heater in their mini. "But I don't think he would have stood in a glass shower on purpose. I mean that would be pretty difficult to judge, anyway."

"Maybe he was *lying* about that. Maybe he was coming upstairs to look for the body." Rivers suggested.

"Ugh! Don't say it like that," Wakefield scowled in protest. "It seems to me that he had a cut on his forehead and his ear. That would support his story," she rallied.

"Hmm. What if he cut himself, just for that purpose?" Rivers tone and cadence of speaking suggested that he knew he was reaching.

"Then," Wakefield sniffed indignantly as she searched for words, "then he is fanatical enough to deserve another chance. Have you been checking for a tail?"

"Don't need to."

"Why not?" Wakefield whipped her head around to stare him down.

"Because we have a tracking device mounted under the bumper. I thought it prudent to check for a bomb, based on last night. You know, no sense in you going with me."

"Not funny, Commander." *How can he joke about death so easily?* "What did you do with it?"

"I left it there."

"What are you thinking!" she exploded. "You left it there?" Her voice was as thinly spun as cotton candy. "Why?"

"I figured we should all end up in the same place. Make a nice and cozy trip to Munich. And," he offered a closed mouth grin, "it keeps Azure Tiger out of Berlin."

"Great! Just great." Wakefield's shoulders bunched up tightly. She felt like she was sitting on a bomb. She took great interest in the brown countryside enclosed and dotted with evergreens. Why did the SEAL feel the need to shake a stick in the face of Azure Tiger? *The man attracts danger the way that a fresh notebook attracts ink.*

Chalfonte Apartments
Washington DC
Tuesday 22 January 2002

Zreik eyed Wakefield's living room. Joe rubbed his gray forehead head against the toe of Zreik's scuffed right Nike.

Zreik shut the door forcefully behind himself with his other foot. He had been wandering around the bedroom, bathroom and living area for hours while considering his plan. It deviated from his instructions, but would accomplish the goal.

For months he had been searching for a way to get Filasek to move him up in priority, in responsibility, in leadership. "Filasek never appreciates my effort, my attention to detail. I am not some itinerant field worker."

He took one last lap through the tidy apartment. The Bibles and Christian literature teased his senses like camphor. Sitting on her bed, he pawed through the silky lingerie, picking out a long black nightgown and pair of skimpy purple pajamas to take home to Jerra. Zreik packed the electronic equipment and small appliances in her thick bath mats and luxurious sheets and stowed them in his truck to sell. Her silverware wasn't worth much. "What kind of woman doesn't keep at least a little jewelry around for special occasions?" he asked Joe, who mewed at him in every room.

Zreik stopped in front of the painting hanging on the dining room wall. "I have U.S. citizenship and a degree in civil engineering." Zreik's chest puffed out. "This time, he will take notice," he promised himself. He touched the oil shape on the large canvas.

Tulips. Bright and proud on green stems of pearlessence. They appealed to him. The artist had only signed initials. A black, scrolly *P.E.W.* adorned the bottom left corner of the 26X30 gold-framed canvas. He had never come across that artist before. Zreik could picture the painting above his whitewashed, brick fireplace. It would be great!

Stowing it in the front seat of the yellow Ryder truck, Zreik patted his pockets before returning to Wakefield's apartment for the final trip. Matches and knife both accounted for. He picked up a brown, cardboard box and a milk jug of yellowish liquid. Zreik did not hide his pleasure. This would be his first quest. "And I will be successful."

Hotel Askanischerhof, Berlin
Wakefield's room, 409
2010 hours

A tall man bent over the keyhole on the outside of Judah Wakefield's Berlin residence. His hands deftly controlled the slim lock picking instruments. The lock was uncooperative. He was able to get three of the pin's tumblers, but the forth was stiff.

The lift door pinged in the quiet hallway. The man swore colorfully, glad his mother could not hear him. He jiggled the fourth tumbler with all the effort he dared to use. A woman's voice bade her fellow elevator companions a good evening and flounced toward him.

She stared at him openly and curiously. "What are you doing?" she asked from two doors down.

He spoke to her in English but pronounced the peculiar chokes and high pitches of his native language more distinctly. Hopefully, it would charm her to distraction or throw her off balance. "I am trying to get into my room." He felt the last tumbler click. Finally! "Good. There we go." He twisted his hand to the right and shouldered the door open. "I have the most stubborn door in Berlin," he told the woman who was closing in on him. He slipped the thin metal rods into his suit coat pocket.

The woman eyed him suspiciously. "Is that why you were using a lock pick?"

He smiled, faking a bit of embarrassment. "Oh, you saw that did you?"

"Mm hm," she was neither charmed nor intimidated.

"What is your name, beautiful lady?" he emphasized his accent again.

"I am *not* giving my name to a stranger!"

He pressed an open palm to his chest as if he were disappointed. "Then, alas, I cannot share my secret with a stranger." He did not drop her bold eye contact, neither did he open the door to Wakefield's room further.

"Secret?" she finally bit.

"I am very sorry. Thank you for your interest. Perhaps when we meet again, we shall not remain strangers." He picked up her hand from her side and brought it to his lips. She withdrew her hand slowly. When they were no longer touching, he shut the door in her uplifted face with a soft click.

The legendary assassin pressed the heel of his hand into his forehead. "I have too many ships at sea," he berated himself. He wanted to blame Filasek for making him incriminate the naval officer, but it was his own fault, he knew, for accepting a second, time-critical job in addition to a myriad of other things he was doing. He had not even brought his pistol. "I would have had to choke the nosey woman." He frowned thinking of her chatter. *That might not have been a bad option*, he decided. "I could branch out. A different means, same result. Nah. I prefer the cleanliness of being far off."

He collapsed on the double bed and exhaled all his breath heavily. A large black suitcase sat on the floor with its top open invitingly against the wall. Wakefield had not taken all of her belongings with her.

He ran his hands over the tidy rows of rolled clothes. The shirts were rolled to eight-inch lengths on the top row, organized by color from light to dark. Pants and skirts were rolled in twelve-inch lengths with the same organization.

Something glittered between a lavender button-up shirt and a green and white checked seersucker blouse. Methodically, he stacked each article of Wakefield's wardrobe in order on the floor in front of the suitcase. He shook his head. "And I thought I was a systematic over-achiever who was freakishly neat." He cackled. "Not anymore."

He picked up the shoulders of a red-sequined ball dress. The dress shimmered as he rose to his feet, the dress unfolding to its full length. Azure Tiger gave a low catcall. His eyes widened," What could the woman who can fill out a gown like this have done to envenom Filasek so monstrously?"

He placed every article back with the same precision rolling and squaring that the original packer had used. He wandered through the bathroom, taking his time. A small, clear hotel glass reflected in the vanity mirror. A single print of berry-colored lipstick stained the rim of the glass. "Perfect!" he intoned. Several long strands of blond hair lay in the sink and some in the bathtub. Upon close examination, some still had the root attached. Unarguable DNA evidence. "Not so freakishly neat in the bathroom," he rebuked his unknowing host.

He narrowed his eyes. Demanding a bonus from Filasek was now a given.

27

Zreik shifted from foot to foot in the long line at the post office. His brown paper-bag-wrapped shoebox rested on his right hip. Conversation buzzed around him like flies on dead meat. Couldn't these people just wait quietly like normal people?

He moved the package to his left hip. It wasn't heavy. About four pounds. He wiped one sweaty palm on his Wranglers. He touched his brow, then wiped his hand again. *Is it hot in here?* No one else in line, even in heavy winter coats, was sweating.

A third fire truck screamed down 28th Avenue. The post office was far from sound proof. Speculation rose to a higher pitch in whispered tones. "Do you think it is the doughnut place or the apartment complex?" the voice came from behind.

Zreik's whole body reacted to his startle. Heat flashed through him. He juggled his hold on the box to keep from dropping it. The voices still did not quiet. Finally, he could not stand any longer. "Ugh!" he choked out an explosive scream. "Why don't you people just shut up!" he cursed. "You don't know anything! You won't until after the 6 o'clock news in your yuppie little homes. Just shut up about it!" He lowered his voice a bit. "Just give a man some peace, would you?"

He could feel the silent, cowering stares.

A four-year-old boy standing next in line clamped his hand over his open mouth. Wide brown eyes stared impudently at him. "Ooh!" he drawled. "Mommy! That man said lots of bad words. He must have a very wicked heart." The tiny black-haired boy pointed at Zreik.

He switched the box to the other hip again and wiped his palm. Zreik glared at the boy and then at all the patrons in case one of them was looking in his direction.

The child was not intimidated in the least. The others only breathlessly moved their eyes to see the exchange.

The mother, a young woman, heavy with her second child, looked ready to dissolve into the linoleum flooring. "Give Mommy your hand," she commanded. "What did I tell you about pointing?" her thin voice shrilled.

"I don't know," the child shrugged. "Will he get in trouble?" his face lit up with his hope for justice.

"Next." The desk assistant became available.

"Let's let that man go ahead of us. I don't think he feels well." The young mother prompted her little boy loud enough for Zreik to hear her and she nodded him to go ahead. None of the eight people in between them in line protested.

"That's not fair!" the little boy crossed his arms and pouted. Zreik moved quickly to the front of the line. The statistics of postal workers going ballistic did not surprise him. This place gave him the creeps. Now it was quiet. Too quiet, like death. He set his package on the counter. His scalp prickled and a bead of sweat trickled down his spine.

The child's voice came from behind him, "Coals of fire on his head? What's that?" the sound echoed through the painted cinder-block lobby. Zreik could not make out the mother's answer, but he decided that was exactly what it felt like. His head felt like it was on fire. So did his hands.

"Sir" the worker got his attention. "When do you want this to arrive?"

"As soon as possible."

"Global Express will put it there by Thursday, 10 AM."

"Good. It will be a cash payment," Zreik pre-empted her next question. His chest felt like it was swelling. He was having trouble breathing in the confining space.

"Do you want to insure it or certify the delivery..."

"No. I don't care!" Zreik rashly pulled a crisp hundred out of his wallet. "Give the change to the kid." He jerked his thumb over his shoulder at the boy.

Zreik charged the door, blindly mopping his face as he went. His goal was the outside. He ran for the fresh, breathable air.

Only he inhaled acrid smoke instead. He choked, clutching at his throat. He threw his head left and right looking for a clear way of escape.

Berlin Chief of Station Nelson's Office
Wednesday 23 January 2002
1307 hours

Director Dietz's voice filtered hollowly over the speakerphone in Nelson's Berlin office. "Chad," the director addressed the young agent, "I need you to go over every detail, every nuance of your conversation with your contact," Dietz instructed.

"Like I told Mr Nelson, the contact told me that Azure Tiger accepted a time-sensitive hit in the last couple of days. Set to occur before the president arrives."

"Before? Who?" Dietz was terse. Tiny scratching noises beamed from the Virginia office to the office in Berlin.

"The hit was ordered on Lieutenant Commander Rivers, sir," Chad raked back his stringy black hair. Keeping the commander's confidence would depend on how the director's next question was phrased. He would be truthful, all cloak and dagger aside. Lying to the CIA was like signing your own hit request.

"Have you traced the money?" Dietz pounding his desk came through loud and clear in Germany. His voice sounded constricted.

"We went through several banks. Starting with Lieutenant Commander Wakefield's account again, sir." Chad bit the inside of his cheek. "It is a similar pattern to before." It was true. They had patterned it that way purposefully. "We lost it in the Swiss system."

"Good try, Mr Wellingham. I'll put one of our hackers right on it. He's had some success there." More scratching. "Give me the numbers and names."

Chad recited the Swiss account number from memory.

"Is Commander Wakefield available? I have some news for her." Dietz moved on to the second purpose of his call.

"No. She and Rivers are in Munich tracking down our suspects for an intense interrogation." Nelson joined the conversation.

"I can probably get a message to her," Chad offered. "A contact of mine is going to meet with them this morning in Munich, sir."

"No. Not a good news item to pass along while they are investigating. When they get back, have her call me, would you?"

"Of course, sir." Nelson made himself a note. "Anything I can do?"

Dietz picked out compassion in the normally emotionless director's tone. "It's best coming from a friend, but," the director hesitated. "The Fire Marshal called her C.O. last night. The admiral called me."

"What is it, sir?" Chad held his breath

"Her apartment building burned yesterday afternoon. The investigator believes it started in her apartment. That was the site of the greatest damage. An accelerant was used." Dietz exhaled heavily. "The Fire Marshal and the insurance adjuster want to speak with Wakefield as soon as she can talk."

Nelson and Chad looked at each other with wide eyes. "They think *she* did it?" the chief asked dumbly.

"I don't think they are both looking for a date." Dietz replied harshly. "Have her call me ASAP. Not a word, you two." Dietz disconnected. The room echoed a dial tone for a couple of seconds until Nelson smashed the speakerphone button with his first finger.

Munich, Germany
Deutsches Museum
Wednesday 23 January 2002
0958 hours

Rivers followed the map he picked up at the Smithsonian-like museum's front entrance. There was no straight shot to the Stone Age tools display. He and Wakefield were supposed to meet Chad's contact at ten hundred.

Something in the man's voice when he called had heightened Rivers' SEAL sense the night before. In stalking mode, LCDR Rivers completely absorbed his surroundings, cataloguing every movement, every face, every glance of the people wandering the museum this Wednesday morning. Touring classes of small children were something he had not factored into the game plan. Overall, it was a secure site. The wide aisles between displays and categories of exhibits were ideal for avoiding priceless pieces on loan if their meeting came to blows.

"Too bad I cannot say the same for the B&B where we're staying, in case it comes to blows with Wakefield when she realizes I left her behind." Rivers cringed at the thought of Wakefield angry with him, again. "But I would rather have her angry than dead if this guy ends up being the assassin." He mumbled softly to himself. A habit he had only picked up since meeting Wakefield.

It was an impressive display of tools from ancient times—if bits of chipped rock can be impressive. Rivers secured the area first. No one else in Germany was looking at Stone Age tools that morning. Not the contact either.

"See, what is the point in being on time for a meeting?" Rivers griped aloud. "If there are two people involved, one is going to be late." In training future SEALs at Coronado, Rivers stressed timeliness to the second. Missions could be blown for a breech in some of their split-second timed actions.

1003 hours. Still no sign of him. Rivers paced like a caged panther continually watching both the side entrance and the front that he had used.

1009 hours. Rivers breathed an irritated sigh with his growing suspicion. The contact was not going to show. He froze as a nightmare occurred to him. What if it was all a ruse to separate him from Wakefield. Was she the one in trouble? The contact had known so many details.

1012. The tension got him. "Ugh! Where is he?" Rivers exploded in exasperation.

"Where is who?" a familiar voice asked from the side entry.

Hotel Isartor, Frauen Strasse, Munich
9:25 AM

Three men surrounded a table in the haze of a cheap hotel room. They had lost count of the number of hands they had played and the number of rounds of bourbon they had downed. The alcohol had run out around six, they had been playing since two. Since they could still hold the cards, they were still playing. The stubs of half a dozen stogies lay in piles of ash in two hotel glasses.

Their only common thread was the source of their paychecks. One of the three was planning to collect an extra paycheck today. One hundred thousand euros for a simple killing. True he had missed the first time. Today there would be no reflecting glass barrier between his revolver and the new sailboat he planned to buy with his 80 thousand euros in earnings after expenses. He could already taste the thick salt air. Maybe it was musty cigar air. "Time for me to catch some shut-eye. Getting too old for these all-nighters." He chuckled to himself at how easy it was to ditch the others. Ganitopoulos stood and swung his leg over the back of the chair tucked in close to the small table. His dull friends had never noticed that while he poured them two fingers each round, he poured himself one. Or less, just a splash.

His head was clear. He felt ready for target shooting. What fun.

28

Rivers froze. He didn't dare turn around. The voice was cool like the long barrel of a shotgun. "You are late." He put together a sentence.

"*You* left me behind."

Rivers pivoted on the balls of his feet. Not even his SEAL nerves could steel him to look his partner in the eye. "I thought it best."

She was a stiff silhouette in the doorway. "What happened to the SEAL code? *Never leave a man behind.* It doesn't apply to me?" Her sharp tone did not scare him. It was the deadness in her voice. She sounded resigned.

He opened his mouth to fill the silence. He snapped his teeth shut. It would not be a wise move to explain that the SEAL code referred to leaving a partner in danger, not *out* of danger. He was hoping to secure a future with her. She may have trained as a sailor, but to him she would always be a woman.

However, it was the iron-sided officer that was tapping her toe with a fast rhythm on the marble floor. He had to go through the officer to reach the woman. "I thought it best," he dumbly repeated. It sounded weak as it echoed through the room.

"You thought...*you* thought it best? What about what *I* think?" Her tone was no longer the cool barrel, but the heated flash pan. She moved toward him. "We were partners in this. Fifty-fifty. Then you go off. You're just like all the others."

"Keep your voice down. You are going to scare away our contact or bring in a bevy of guards. Probably haul us off to the brig."

She turned her flashing blue eyes on him. Ouch. "At least there, I wouldn't have to run you down or wonder if you are still alive." She did lower her voice, but it did not have the positive effect Rivers thought it might.

He cut his eyes to look at Wakefield. Her hair darkened toward her temple. His hand came up of its own accord. Her hair was damp. She jerked away, restored her hair, and crossed her arms over her chest. Her jaw clamped and she lifted her head in defiance.

"Sorry." Rivers lifted both hands. "You *ran* down here?" His words were slow as he absorbed the impact himself.

"Give Sherlock a doggie biscuit," she spat. "What was I supposed to do?"

Rivers shrugged his shoulders. He grimaced and reached up to massage the tension out. "Take a cab?" The problem had a simple solution.

Wakefield leaned in, her hands moved to her hips. "With what? My good looks?" she drew back. "*You* have the petty cash. *You* have the car keys. You even have the stinkin' *maps*! I had to get directions from high-strung Mrs Smith who insisted I take a map for every attraction in Munich." Her eyes flashed dangerously. "You need to get this control problem under control, Commander."

His jaw muscle twitched. How dare she! "Perhaps the reason it bothers you to such a degree, *Commander*, is that," he forced the air through his teeth in an effort to maintain a level of decorum. He was failing. "You recognize the same personality snag in yourself."

"Don't even go there. My problem is you. I do not need to be in control to feel validated." She tilted her head to the side. "I would need to be included first, for that."

"Mm," Rivers touched his chin.

"Ugh!" Wakefield growled at him. "You're impossible. She

threw her hands up. "Does it fulfill some hairy-man-need in you to bait me, Commander?"

Rivers face pinched. How did things get so screwed up?

"Look," her features tightened and she re-crossed her arms. Rivers watched her fight for the same restraint he was clinging to. His stomach constricted as she turned her back to him to find it. "Chad's contact isn't coming. It's 1033. We need to round up the guys for questioning." Her voice dropped to a whisper. "Or is that an I-job, too?"

He studied the rigid line of his partner's back. How had he managed to scuttle his entire future in 15 minutes?

"What is this?" she burst out.

What now? Rivers wondered as he looked at the display in her line of vision. A large wooden barrel rolled to the top of two thin boards functioning as a ramp. He tipped his head to the right. "I don't know." The display did not go with anything else in the room.

Wakefield whirled around on one foot. "I don't know?" A note of disappoint was short-lived in her voice. "I thought you knew everything." Innocence dripped from her tongue like cake batter.

"Cool it, will you?" Rivers was getting tired of this game. It was seriously out of hand. "Quit over dramatizing everything."

"Oh!" She gasped with wide blue eyes and covered her mouth with her hand like a heroine in a 1917 speechless film. "You're right."

Rivers ignored her theatrics. "We need to interview those five men, I think two at a time, but I would like to look at the aviation display I passed on my way in. They have hang gliders and parachutes used in World War I and II."

"Whatever you think is best, Commander," she chaffed sweetly. "I'll just go see if I can find the collection of dresses and maybe there will be cooking utensils from ancient times. 'Cause that would be a delight."

"Sarcasm does not become you, Commander."

"As if you'd notice."

Her stiff departing body chilled Rivers' skin.

Hanish Ganitopoulos stood on the bridge, 150 meters downstream from the long Duetsches Museum located on a landmass in the middle of the River Isar. His eyes roved adjacent *Zweibrucken Strasse* for the best vantage point from which to earn his pay. "Only one entrance and exit. He'll have to cross the walking bridge." He touched the Glock 17 pistol in his coat's outside pocket. He glanced around to see if anyone was watching and then slyly moved it to the small of his back. The cold metal against his skin honed his focus.

The trees lining the river walk would be perfect. A single Red Oak beckoned him to hide in her low branches. It was half the distance between the museum's pedestrian bridge, *Bosch Brucke,* and the alley where he parked his Vespa scooter.

He walked toward the tree. He would wait there until they came out. According to Dovlatabadi's description, Ganitopoulos looked forward to recognizing his tall target by his blonde companion. It would not be as clear as a hotel room window, but he preferred a challenge anyway, and the easy attempt had only failed due to the luckiest ducking he had ever seen through a scope.

He lifted his face to study the branches. His stomach rumbled. "As soon as I'm through," he promised himself. The limbs were more scant than they had seemed from a distance. He tugged on one 1.5 meters off the ground. "Hmm," barely any movement. "It'll work. Just can't go too high."

A finger tapped his shoulder. The Greek swore loudly and convulsed. His insides began a frenzied dance as the uniform of the German police registered on his brain. Where did he come from?

Deutsches Museum Ladies' Room

Wakefield pressed a cold paper towel to the back of her neck in the room marked "dames." Rivers infuriated her like no one else could. "God, give me grace." She groaned as she replayed the scene in her mind. "I am acting a fool. I thought we were finished with the abandonment issues." She closed her eyes in pain. *Is a lesson ever really over?* She felt tears well up as she answered her heart's question. "Not if it still hurts." Her chin trembled.

"It is not my fault. He got what he deserved." She raised her eyebrow at herself in the mirror. "How can he treat me like this?" She felt her old nemesis rise again. Anger built up in her belly, unchecked.

"Breathe, Wakefield." She used her drill sergeant voice on her reflection. She looked away. Her hands begged for something to do. With three long-legged strides, she threw away the compress and depressed some lotion from the dispenser. "Ugh, it smells like toilet water." She gagged and reached for another paper towel to wipe it off. "Lord," she paced in the ladies' room, sometimes it helped to walk it off, "give me something else to concentrate on. Please. Anything." She counted her breaths. A picture formed in the mist of her mind's eye.

Rivers stood with his hands in his pockets just outside the museum. Wakefield stalked to the street ahead of him. A muzzle flashed. Rivers' body jerked once. He dropped to the sidewalk. He rolled off the curb and crumbled into a pool of red. Wakefield kept walking.

"NO!" Wakefield startled the woman pushing open the restroom door. The lady backed out and disappeared. The door crashed to a close.

Judah covered her face with her hands. "Is that the root of this...this...outburst. Is that what you are telling me? I am afraid of Rivers dying?" She threw the lotion-covered towel onto the counter, and relished the splat. She exhaled all her breath.

Her chin dropped to her chest. "God, you're right."

"Officer?" The Greek raised his bushy eyebrows in what he hoped was an ignorant tourist expression.

"Identification." The young officer bent one beefy arm to reach his hip, nearer his nightstick. He shifted his bulk on fidgeting feet.

Ganitopoulos noted the officer's shallow breathing. The man was nervous. He held out his hands in an air of innocence. "My passport is in my left breast pocket."

"Reach in slowly." The policeman was hyper-alert and triple checked the picture against his face. "Visiting from Greece? What is the nature of your business?"

Did the uniform think he was on border patrol? "I am here on pleasure, officer."

"Alone?" The officer's light eyebrows rose nearly to his hairline. He leaned in as if he could smell a lie.

Ganitopoulos looked to the river. "My...my wife," he cracked his voice to sound emotional. "She was supposed to come with me, but she died two months ago." He pressed a hand to his eyes as if to relieve the pressure building there.

The policeman returned the passport and motioned him to turn around. "I am sorry to hear that, Herr Ganitopoulos. Arms out." The policeman's voice had softened a touch, but he was still planning a thorough inspection. "Feet shoulder width apart."

Grateful at least that he was no longer *facing* his detaining officer, Ganitopoulos could not help rolling his eyes, perturbed at the lengthy intrusion. The Greek looked up and down the street. It was not overly busy for the time of morning. Would it be better to run along the river and disappear into the *Markt* square three blocks west when he finds the gun, or run back to the Vespa and hit the open road? He calculated the distance. It was a toss-up.

Maybe the policeman would enjoy a nice chilly swim. The fall alone would probably kill him. Greek smiled at the thought of the officer's large, meddlesome body floating with the ice chunks in the River Isar.

The man's hands were heavy but fast as they patted down his sides and outsides of his legs.

Ganitopoulos looked at the population of the street. It was virtually empty. The river felt like his best option. His sailboat wavered in his vision.

Deutsches Museum

Wakefield's shoes squeaked against the polished marble floor. She spied the woman who had opened the ladies' room door towing a guard in the wake of her animated speech. Wakefield turned and found herself face-to-snout with a fire-breathing dragon from the 700s A.D. An ancient vase depicted legends more ancient. It fascinated her until the woman towing the guard passed without recognizing her. Then she sped to the aviation wing.

When Wakefield finally spotted him, Rivers was moving around underneath the hang-gliding man display, examining it from every angle. He said he would be there, and he was, but, he did not look as tall as he used to. She watched his boyish fascination. He was probably figuring out a way to try on the gear. Wakefield approached him and cleared her throat.

A middle school class, restless from listening to lectures, moved to the full size helicopter next to the hang glider. Wakefield lowered her voice so as not to distract the children. "We need to get busy." She knew she owed David an apology, but she was not ready to ask forgiveness yet.

She spun on her toes, enjoying the squeak as she started to leave. "Just a minute. I have not seen the Luftwaffe aircraft yet."

"We don't have all day to play." Turning with another squeak, Wakefield cocked her head and raised her eyebrows.

"If I recall, we wasted a whole day on your church service excursion," Rivers leaned forward while whispering. "I think another 10 minutes for me to read about a German airplane will not alter the world."

"Fine," she shrugged. If he was going to be catty, she would show him she could remain reasonable. *Even if it kills me.* She straightened her shoulders.

Wakefield read the placard description of a steam-powered automobile from 1892. Then reread it. Her spirit stirred within her an urgency to leave. The picture of Rivers rolling over on the concrete bridge replayed often enough to nauseate her. She placed a hand on her rolling stomach. "We're staying until he begs me to leave." She gripped the placard.

"One more second," Rivers held up his first finger and kept reading. "Huh," he grunted and looked up. He smiled as he caught her eyes trained on him. "Did you know that in 1945, the Germans had a bomb capable—"

"Tell me on the way." She looped her hand through his elbow's crook and led him prisoner-fashion toward the coat check. *It would be vain for me to wait for him to beg.* She hated waffling females, but sometimes a change of mind was best for all concerned.

29

The policeman squatted to pat up the inside of the Greek's legs. *Now,* Ganitopoulos told himself. *There is no reason to wait.*

"All right. You're clean." The burly officer's red face stood out against his short greying hair. Bending with his belt cutting off his air supply did not seem to agree with him. "I don't know what it is like in your homeland, but in Germany, we do not climb public trees." The policeman's jaw moved to the side as if it was disconnected. The double chin underneath followed a noticeable fraction of a second later. "Nor do we allow our guests to do so."

A strange sensation worked its way up from the Greek's lower abdomen. The tightening felt almost like joy. He turned around, a jubilant smile pegged on his face. "Oh, I understand, sir. No, sir, I won't be climbing any trees. Beautiful trees they are."

"Good," the policeman's voice sounded as if he had just reformed Himmler himself. "Move along then."

Ganitopoulos walked, pretending tourism with hands held up thumb to thumb in L's to practice picture framing. While the police officer watched him from behind, a new plan took shape in the Greek's mind. The pistol securely in the small of his back was his inspiration. He would wait. He would pace the sidewalk until his target emerged from the shelter of the museum.

He walked past the pedestrian bridge. It was 20 meters long. It would take eight to ten seconds to meet his victim half way.

Deutsches Museum Pedestrian Bridge-*Bosch Brucke*

Wakefield breezed through the door he held open for her. *Why is she suddenly in such a hurry?* The sunshine pierced the back of his eyeballs. By the time his focus had returned, Wakefield was eight steps ahead of him. He shook his head at her. Lieutenant Commander Full-Speed-Ahead. A chill pricked his scalp. It had nothing to do with the weather.

He rounded his back and scanned the faces of the crowd as he shifted his mind into his oiled SEAL mode. Something was not right. *Where are you, danger? I can feel your breath. Come on, speak to me. I dare you.* His eyes worked twice as fast as his head doubling up the scans of the area.

There.

He identified what had set him off. A man had simply turned around and walked in the opposite direction out on the main river walk. Rivers continued a slower version of his earlier walk as he replayed the turn in his mind. Something in the mannerism suggested a pattern. It was not his first turn around. *Probably just waiting for someone.*

"Judah," Rivers' raised voice attracted several turned heads. A gray haired woman on her way into the museum made a guttural sound of disapproval not quite under her breath. Reserved Germans did not yell on the street. Only a vulgar Yank, or maybe an Aussie would do that. He stepped up his pace as Judah steamed further away.

Rivers sighted the waiting man again. He had a determined look on his face. And he was staring at...him.

Rivers' eyes cut to Judah's back and then back to the man who was still staring, but had moved a pace closer.

The shooter.

He would never reach Wakefield in time. She was between him and the threat. *She will not be injured again because of me.* He found his feet in an all-out run before he remembered sending the signal to his brain. "Get down!" His voice carried onto the river.

The shooter ran to intercept them. The man reached at an awkward angle to the small of his back.

Gun!

Wakefield turned around with a small upturn of her lips, "I thought you were right with me." She stepped backward. Her expression fell flat.

"Gun!" Rivers yelled his warning to every English-speaker in the vicinity.

The shooter reached the corner of the wide pedestrian bridge before Rivers could get to Wakefield. Rivers ripped his keys out of his coat pocket and let them fly. Years of yelling baseball coaches paid off. A perfect strike.

The shooter's gun discharged.

Rivers dove forward catching his partner's waist. He heard her panicky cry and reached one hand up to cradle the back of her head. He twisted their bodies in the air so his crashing weight would not crush her.

The bullet pelted into the concrete guardrail. Chips of gray needled the pavement. The impact forced the air from Rivers' lungs. Again. He grimaced against his urge to grunt in pain. His ribs. A second shot came off. Then a third and fourth before Rivers' keys made contact. Even a 93 mph fast ball couldn't compete with bullets.

A primal yell split the air. It quickly cut off. Rivers rolled with Wakefield in his arms to absorb as much of the impact as he could. He gasped as he felt them roll off the curb. His insides compressed.

Rivers was able to see three men dressed in black set off in pursuit of the shooter. The rest of the witnesses stirred themselves into a frenzied pandemonium. Some children whimpered, others cried, while mothers and nannies rushed them inside to safety. Others scattered to a safe distance to watch. Everyone ran. All away.

K.J. Frolander

The sudden quiet after the extreme noise jarred Rivers' senses. He collapsed into the softness of the body under him.

"Rivers?" The form under him pushed at his aching chest. *Just be still*, he begged silently. "David. Let me up. I can't breathe. We've got to go after him." She shook his shoulders.

He tried to speak or move or something. His body would not respond to his command.

Her voice notched up to shrill in his ear. "Talk to me." Her lips were five centimeters from his left ear. She managed to roll him back against the curb enough to scoot out from underneath. Now his shoulder dug painfully into the unyielding concrete. The ground pressed back against him. *Has concrete always been this hard?*

"Oh God! Somebody call an ambulance!" He tried to tell her she was speaking in English, not German. He could not make his mouth work. "You're bleeding. Can you tell me where you were hit?" His partner's fingers felt icy on his face. She spoke some nonsense language that he did not recognize as she pushed open his coat and ran expert hands along his arms and neck and legs.

Finally, she switched back to English. "I can't find the entry wound." Her tender voice wavered. "Don't you dare die on me, Commander. I'll order you to stay alive if I have to."

She pressed on his collarbone and followed his sternum down checking his rib cage for steadfastness.

He had no breath to cry out, but she found the problem. "Lie still," she instructed. Her voice was comforting. "You have two or more broken ribs. I don't want you to puncture a lung."

His lungs were bursting for lack of air. Breathing was like trying to suck up strawberry milkshake with fruit stuck in the straw. He struggled against his need for oxygen as he sucked in with all his might. His throat rasped as he tried to take in air.

Two shots rang out.

Rivers coughed in the top of his chest. He choked out, "If they killed him, I will kill them.

"Quiet now, and wait for the paramedics to arrive." His partner tossed her hair over her shoulder and leaned in close to him. He could smell her perfume. Today, powdery soft musk.

Rivers squirmed his face away, but ran into the curb at his back. "Either help me up or move out of my way." His voice sounded harsh even to him. "Please."

Running footsteps moved toward him, but he could not see because of his angle. "Sir, you've got to come now if you want to talk to him." The man was talking as he jogged toward them. He recognized him as the agent with no lips from Idaho who had been tailing one of the six suspects for three weeks. "He's almost gone."

"Help me up, Matthews." Rivers lifted on hand. "I'm not shot, Wakefield. Just bloodied from the fall." He wanted to pre-empt her objection. "I feel like an old man." The two men wrapped their palms around each other's wrists and Rivers let out a growl as Matthews pulled him forward.

"Careful for his ribs," Wakefield coached. Rivers concentrated on her bottom lip between her teeth as he rose to a standing position. *Maybe things are salvageable after all.*

Matthews cleared some debris by scraping his foot across the drive of the bridge. Rivers' stomach dropped as he recognized the sound. He touched his jacket pocket. He came away empty handed.

Rivers looked down his body to see Matthews' black, steel-toed boots sloughing his tiny M&Ms into the gutter. The paper wrapper tumbled over and skidded away in the light breeze, a gaping hole torn in its side.

Brown and orange and green and red and blue dots scattered all over the sidewalk and bridge.

His hand flopped down to his thigh. It felt as heavy as a gallon of milk. He chanced a look at Judah. Her pained eyes followed the course of the symbolic chocolates. *Yes, she remembers.*

"Cancel the ambulance," he said mildly. His face twitched with the effort of walking, but he pushed himself to keep going.

Wakefield picked up the wrapper and flattened it between her fingers as she straightened up. She felt a lump in the bottom of the brown bag. Tilting it, the last two M&Ms slid out of the ragged hole into her waiting palm. One green, one purple. "I'm the green one," she whispered as she closed her fingers over them. Then she popped them both into her mouth.

It was not an effort to catch up to Matthews and Rivers. Trotting along behind them, Wakefield had to assume that Rivers had called in the CIA field agents earlier without her knowledge, too. Rivers hobbled like a thrown cowboy.

She folded the bag into quarters and hid it in her pants pocket. She stooped to retrieve their rental car keys from the pavement.

The two men were talking ahead of her and most of the words drifted back to her. "We had to shoot him. He was climbing over the embankment. Going to take a header into the river."

She furrowed her brow trying to go back to the vision she had seen in the bathroom. There was a connection, she was sure. But the point of view was different. *Thank you, God, the outcome was different.*

She could hear Rivers hold his breath as he leaned over the man whose black hair fell over one eye. The thick hair did not completely obscure the bloody dent in his forehead. The keys Rivers had thrown. A stream of blood flowed from his leg and chest; it filled a crack in the sidewalk and found its way to the street. The dripping spatter pattern on the embankment wall separating the sidewalk from a steep fall to the river below reminded her of Morocco.

Wakefield saw everything in slow motion. The man's death gurgle brought her attention to his face in time to see spit leave his mouth aimed at Rivers' face in his dying breath. Rivers' fingers flexed garishly and his arm surged forward. He grabbed the man by the throat. "He's gone." Rivers made the announcement flatly.

Wakefield was mistaken. He had been reaching for the man's pulse, not to cut off his life. The fog crept in on her brain as surely as if it had floated in off the dank river. *I can't think. Just sit down,* her autopilot instructed her. *Now!*

Wakefield made a controlled crumble to a seated position with her legs crossed Indian-style under her. The outsides of her ankles pressed into the age-old brick. She reached up to touch her heart through her unfastened coat. "What did you ask him?" Her voice carried softly.

"Nothing." Rivers shoulders sank. "I told him something."

"Hmm?" To form actual words required too much effort.

"What he had to look forward to in eternity." The SEAL hunched over and wrapped his arms around his ribcage. His head lurched forward as if he had suddenly lost the energy to hold it up.

To Wakefield, David Rivers' precision-edged posture looked to be forever curved. The fog must have enveloped him too. She reached out to touch him, to comfort him. She could not reach him.

30

"Filasek, you must leave me some peace. How am I supposed to get my work accomplished with you calling me every other day?" Azure Tiger stood at the slatted window on the sixth floor. The wide-slat plantation shutters cast horizontal stripes of sunlight in the darkened room. He flipped one slat up with a slender finger to view the hotel across the lonely street. Two in the afternoon did not lend itself as a popular time to peruse *Ku'damm strasse.*

"Peace. You want peace?" Filasek's voice sounded mysteriously calm. The assassin in Berlin wondered what explosion he was about to get caught in. "No more than I want peace. I want the kind of peace that lets me live in my own home with my own family. I want to own my own business in the field of my expertise, and to speak freely about the things on my mind." Filasek's deep voice worked up a growl. One that sounded as if it could reach through the phone and grab him around the throat. "Americans are stupid children. They whine then tattle to the U.N. They threaten to take their toys and go home or to blow up their enemies like little boys who have just learned to play with matches. Freedom, ha! Only if freedom is red, white and blue."

The assassin's eyes widened as he wandered away from the window. He ran a finger along the top of the television to inspect for dust. He was pleasantly surprised.

His conversation partner continued his verbal diatribe. *Bin Laden would probably thank me personally, if I quiet the this man permanently.* "How can they spout freedom and force me to conform to their version of freedom?" Filasek's view parroted most of the extremists from the Middle East that Azure Tiger had interacted with, but the man made a nuisance of himself. "Perhaps when their way of life outlasts all other regimes to date, people will listen."

Ah, a pause. He wants feedback. Azure Tiger quickly replayed the tape in his mind. "It will never happen. Ideals are always compromised. They will see the glory of power and thirst after the world's salaams. Probably before they reach the age of a quarter-millennia." As much of an irritant as Filasek was, he still wired the money that financed his life.

"I have another assignment."

"Don't you mean business proposition?"

"Call it what you will. You have never turned down my assignments yet."

"Why do I feel like a puppet?" the assassin huffed. *The man has to go.*

"You are. You're a regular Pinocchio."

"Does that make you the foolish Ghepetto?"

"I made you who you are today."

"I made myself. You paid me along the way." He felt his hand tense around the receiver and forced himself to relax. He switched to the other ear, taking his time about it.

"And I'll pay you again, until you are of no more use to me."

Only until I am ready to pay the price for my peace. Filasek's life would be the final trophy. He envisioned the torn out headline of the local paper: Miser Murdered in Sea-side Mansion. He would post it on his bathroom mirror next to the one he planned to laminate about the American president. Maybe he would collect newspaper headlines in all different languages and create a scrapbook to send to his father in India. That would show him what his pride had done to the world.

"I faxed the list," The assassin tuned back in to hear Filasek's most recent words.

"A list?" *Of what? I should not have tuned out.*

"It should be coming up to your room now." Sure enough, a cream-colored hotel stationary envelope slipped under the crack in the door. "You remember your Greek alphabet don't you?"

He looked around the room for a video camera. Filasek's timing was uncanny. He seemed to have a spy in every venue, now even his hotel room. "My Greek tutor would be displeased you even had to ask." He slid his finger under the seal—ugh—It was still moist. He followed along as Filasek read the names.

"The first five are a family here. They are being rather tight-fisted with my new bio-chem plant."

He swore under his breath. Filasek with biological and chemical weapons scared him. *It should scare the world*, he excused his fear. His voice squeaked pre-pubescently, "You already have a new plant up and running?"

"Already? No. It has been in operation for four years. The one in Afghanistan that the Americans imploded was 15 years in the making. The other two people on the list, let's just say they, together, have become a source of irritation for me."

Irritation? The assassin's eyes bulged. He sat at the antique white iron desk to examine the list under the desklamp. "I want 1.5 million. Each."

"Too much. I happen to know that you just accepted a U.S. naval officer for a quarter million."

Azure Tiger's long face tightened. He looked around furtively for a spy camera again.

"I have spies in your head, Tiger." Filasek's chuckle filtered over the lines. "I am offering 2.5 mill for all seven."

What was this, volume discount? "Fine," he agreed in a hurry. His fingers itched to get off the phone. "I'll be there in a week." Chills ran down his spine. He beeped off the phone. Without good-byes. Without the pleasure of slamming the receiver back into its cradle.

His palms were sweaty and he felt compelled to get out of the room. Now the puppet master could read his mind. He had to get out. He tucked the fax inside the lining of his gun case. The gun he always disposed of, but the case he had stolen from his father. It would remain with him always, a constant inspiration of fresh reasons to go on with his life's path.

Zweibrucken Strasse, Munich
1100 hours

The shooter was dead. Where was the satisfaction in a job well done? An ambulance siren wailed a couple of blocks from the Isar. What an unexpected outcome. What happened to Chad's contact?

The siren motivated him to life again. Rivers reached into the dead man's pockets one by one. The passport, he examined. "Nice picture." He handed it behind him to Wakefield who looked as shell-shocked as he felt. He returned to pat the rest of the man's pockets.

His shirt's breast pocket crinkled. Rivers reached in with two fingers and withdrew a torn off strip of notebook paper bearing a name and number: *Kempinski 089/59-79-23.*

"Finally." Rivers breathed softly.

The surging howl grew louder and was joined by another screaming undulation. The police. Rivers jerked to his feet. His ribs cursed him. The paper burned like hot coal in his hand. He crushed it in his fist; the few scratches on the strip branded into his brain.

"*Kempinski* is a hotel in Berlin, right?" Rivers addressed one of the agents who paced while looking like he wanted to fade into the sidewalk.

"Yes, sir. The *Kempi* is across the street from *Steigenberger.* You know, where the president will address Europe tomorrow."

Rivers felt his eyes grow large as he saw how the assassin planned to execute his objective. Three steps back toward Wakefield. He would not have the phone number of his own hotel in his pocket. No way this man lying dead on the brick walk of Munich was the feared Azure Tiger. The assassin must have farmed out the contract on him. "We were never here." Rivers made sure the agent understood.

He thrust out his hand to his partner. "We have to get back to Berlin. Now."

Wakefield ignored his help and pushed herself up. Dusting her hands, she cocked an eyebrow at Rivers. "You wanna let *me* in on our plan?"

"On the way." He gripped her slim shoulder and turned her around with his empty hand. "Otherwise the police will haul us in for questioning and we won't get out of the keep until Easter. 2004." He left his hand on her shoulder to guide her to where he had left the rental car.

At the back of the parallel-parked mini, Rivers paused and touched the hatch. "Underneath, near the tailpipe, there is a metallic black box. Can you grab that for me?"

Wakefield's seasoned gaze found the truth in his eyes. "Your ribs hurt too much for you to bend over." She isolated the problem. "Is it magnetized or bolted?" Her voice muffled as she scooted low and moved under the car.

"Magnetized. Twist and pull." She lay on her back, her long legs propped up at the knee to keep them out of the street. Her head disappeared under the white mini.

"I can't—" She grunted. "Never mind. I got it." She held it up. "Do you want to do the honors?" She motioned toward the River Isar on the other side of the concrete blockade.

"I thought we should attach it to the car back there," he motioned with his thumb over his shoulder.

The idea blossomed in her eyes. "The one with the Spanish license plate?" Her half-grin grew.

Great minds...well, it is nice when they come in a pretty package, too. "That's the one. I thought we should keep our pursuers entertained."

"Okay, but then we are going to a hospital."

One look at the line of her body told him to argue later. But he could not help himself. "Why? Are you sick?" he called after her.

"No. You are." She tossed a saucy glance over her shoulder, daring him to contradict her. Her hair whipped around her face in a gust of wind. She held it back with one hand.

I'll take that dare, he answered in his mind with a challenging look of his own. He opened the driver's door as her head disappeared under the red BMW with Spanish plates. "I feel fine." He ducked inside the car before she could come back.

The sharp pain sliced through his lower chest again. "God, forgive me for lying," he whispered the soft prayer as he reclined the driver's seat as far back as it would go and still allow him to see out of the windshield. He held his breath. That was bearable. If only he did not require oxygen.

Wakefield plopped into the passenger seat, her right leg on the sidewalk in the open door. The whole car jiggled. "David," her voice was loaded with compassion. He knew the double barrel was coming. "You cannot hold your breath all the way to Berlin."

How did she know that? "I'm not holding—"

"Don't insult my intelligence, too. You've done enough damage for one day, don't you think? We aren't under the time constraint anymore. If you feel you must drive, drive us to the hospital." Rivers started the engine. She slammed the door with a delighted smile. "See that was not so hard."

He had no intention of going to a hospital. It was more time-efficient to argue on the road. She did not realize that Azure Tiger was still at large. "All they can do is tape me up," he said as he pulled away from the curb. "You know that."

"There is also pain medication."

"I don't need any." He set his shoulders. *How is it that my whole body connects to my rib cage?*

"It wasn't for you." She crossed her arms and flexed her jaw.

31

"**A** better view of the side door." Azure Tiger mused in the room that had already been cleaned for the day. Room 516 offered a perfect view of the kitchen entrance. Suite 411's access to the front entrance was only bested by the penthouse suite. The band and red carpet would be set up out front, but it depended on where the limousine dropped the leader of the free world. If he went to the side door, this room's unique angle gave a side view of the stately *Steigenberger*.

Room 327 actually offered the most interesting approach. Directly across from his window in that room, the assassin could train his sight on the two-ton crystal chandelier through the third floor glass. He smiled, considering the headline of taking out the entire presidential entourage. Those two bullets would probably make the American Smithsonian Museum as the most valuable bullets in history. It could be interesting. Different. He curled his upper lip. "Too dramatic. One double shot. That's more me."

Room 017 was his refuge in case they searched the hotel guests for the killer. Of course, he would be questioned. Everyone would. That room's view was of the ground floor garden. A shaggy spruce stood over half of the window. If the worst came, he would squeeze out that half window and disappear.

Airforce One
39,000 feet above Maine

"I understand the risks, Dietz. How many times do we need to have this conversation?" George W. Bush kicked back in his stocking feet in the alcove of leather recliners used for in-flight briefings and switched the boxy telephone to his right ear. This chair remained his favorite of the identical seats that faced each other like four pair of stern Highland soldiers ready to fight to the death. This corner chair had the best view out the window, with no wing obstruction. Even better still, he could still see the television and those who happened to be present.

It was in this chair that he absorbed details of the 9-11 attacks, as they came to light. He caressed the smooth leather in remembrance. It was the longest flight from Florida to D.C. ever with stops in Louisiana's Barksdale AFB and Nebraska's Offutt AFB.

"One more, sir. Always one more." Dietz finally sounded resigned to his going anyway.

"I asked Laura to stay behind. That should count for something." He switched the SatFone to the other ear and loosened his light blue tie at the first button. The Secretary of State, strode in, dangling a single sheet of paper between two fingers. A deep frown lined his dark, round face.

Dietz droned in his left ear while he carried on an eyebrow conversation with the Secretary of State. The two rarely agreed situation handling. It didn't look as though the fax Secretary Tyler held would be outside their norm. Bush held up one crooked finger to ask him to wait. The man turned to come back later. Dietz still talking away in his ear gave him no choice. He had to clear his throat to get Tyler's attention. He pointed an inviting hand to the leather chairs that surrounded him and motioned the secretary to sit.

Bush finally heard the CIA man take a breath so he filled the brief quiet. "Director, if you are so worried about Azure Tiger assassinating me, why don't you hop a plane and come stand in front of me?" *That should quiet him down,* he hoped.

231

"I considered it, Mr President." A chagrined voice followed, "I thought you might have me shot yourself."

His belly laugh bounced off the walls in the small alcove. There was little to laugh about these days in his profession. It felt good. "This isn't North Korea or Iran, Dietz." His laughter dimmed to a small grin. He touched the corners of his mouth where the skin stretched. "Do whatever you think is necessary, short of canceling the speaking engagement." In the short pause, he could hear the gears spinning in the director's mind. "It does not matter who is surrounding me, when my time is up, I am leaving this world. Nothing can make me leave before then, and nothing can keep me here after that time. Until then, I am doing what God has purposed for me to do: protect the United States and her interests."

Dietz's voice softened thoughtfully, "Commander Wakefield said something similar to me recently."

"Maybe God is trying to get your attention." Bush felt Tyler looking at him. It was not often he took to proselytizing. "Listen to him, Dietz. It is the most important mission you'll ever undertake."

Dietz delivered slow words. "Thank you, Mr President." He sounded profoundly struck.

A click sounded in his ear. Bush drew his eyebrows close and touched the crease that formed in his forehead. "Hello?" His thin lips curved up slowly. "I think the director of counterintelligence just hung up on me."

"That's a good thing?" Tyler's bass voice boomed.

Trying to place the feeling, the president pushed out his thin lips. "It was rather human." He reached for the fax Tyler held. "I have not been hung up on since—" he searched his memory. "Since Evelyn Carter in the tenth grade."

Tyler's whole body shook with laughter. "I bet she is sorry now."

"Probably not. I deserved it." The contents of the fax cut off his self-depreciating chuckle. "Saddam Hussein again? I don't know why the Iraqis don't shoot him. The man is becoming a whole briar patch in my side."

"We could send in a SEAL team, sir." Tyler suggested, his jaws jiggling.

Bush wasn't sure if he was kidding or not.

"No. I'll send the UN a new resolution. I don't want to go at him alone. He has to destroy the weapons of mass destruction. We will try diplomacy again. I will not have the world afraid of us. We are humanitarian peace makers, not pre-mature gun-jumpers. That would make us just like the terrorists."

33

Wakefield had long since realized Rivers was not going to the hospital. They parked in the street in front of their bed and breakfast. "Pack your stuff and I'll settle with Frau Schmidt." Rivers gave her a hopeful look.

"You had better not call her that to her face. She'll skin you alive." Mrs Smith was a feisty school marm from Pennsylvania who followed her 60-year dream of running a European inn. She had not left her snappy demand for respect stateside. She made a good German.

In her room, Wakefield rummaged through the front pocket of her tag-a-long suitcase. "Gotcha." She pulled out a Ziploc bag of medical tape and underwrap. "David," Judah called out as he passed her open door.

Stepping backward, he bent his head back into her doorway. "Are you ready?"

"Mm-hm, except this," she held up the baggie for his inspection. She hoped for an easy agreement. "Come on in. I won't bite."

She watched with hidden amusement as his eyes flew back and forth between her face and the clear baggie three times. "You might not, but that tape will." He fudged at the door. "How do you happen to have medical tape?"

"How did you happen to have rappelling equipment?" She quirked one eyebrow high.

"A SEAL is always prepar—" he cut himself off and poked out his lips in a seven-year-old's pout.

She felt victorious. "Yes, well, I should have been a SEAL. Take off your shirt. I have underwrap, so it won't stick, Commander."

Rivers took a step in the door and grasped his shirt by the back of the collar and, leaving it buttoned, pulled his shirt and round-neck undershirt off together. His tin dogtags hung over his heart. *Has he finally grasped when to keep his mouth shut? Maybe he is getting tired of arguing.* "I am," she sighed moving toward him.

"You am what?" Rivers tossed his double-layered shirt on her unmade bed.

Her eyes darted to his face. "Going to use this tape on your mouth if you argue with me about driving back to Berlin." She snapped the springy underwrap at shoulder-width.

"Are you sure you'll have enough?" Rivers smugly tipped his jaw higher.

"Well you do have a big mouth, Commander." She tapped the tape roll. "But I think I can manage. There is at least 30 feet left on this roll."

"Very funny."

"Yes, it was, wasn't it." Her cheeks felt tight as they bunched into apples with her grin.

"I meant enough to tape my ribs."

She wrinkled her nose. "It is not as funny then." She exaggerated a pout and tore her gaze from his wide chest. "Arms up." He complied

She traced the maroon welts across his ribcage, willing herself to remain professional. "Why won't you rest?" She measured every breath. The shallowness of respiration spoke volumes to her once-practiced eye. He was in tremendous pain taking air into only a quarter—maybe a third if she was measuring generously—of his lungs.

Wrapped in a cocoon of tan stretchy wrap, he swallowed. "I cannot rest. Not until Azure Tiger is caught or dead. This pain I can deal with, but—" he caught his breath at the telling moment. "I couldn't deal with knowing I could have sucked-up the pain, but instead, our president lies entombed prematurely."

She understood. Judah still wondered, in quiet moments, if she could have saved Jesse Beane or others like her who had died under her watch. Their caring went beyond required duty standards. Rivers was fulfilling excellence in ancient traditions. It was a quality of character that they shared as naval officers—a vowed bond to protect and defend if it cost them everything.

Wakefield reached for the white 1.5-inch tape from the spindly table at the doorway where the two officers stood awkwardly. She ripped the cut end away from the roll. "Judah." Rivers caught her hand that held the sticky end. "Will you forgive me?"

Her heart thudded in her ears.

He captured her jaw with his other hand. His movement messed up the even lines she had created. His feather soft touch felt like a struck matchhead.

"I am sorry I left you behind."

She rested the anvil weight of her head in his fiery palm. She studied the textured wallpaper stripe: a 10-point size cream paired with a 25-point mauve-pink.

She could not meet his eyes. He could not be allowed to see how much it had hurt. Rivers' action had wounded her pride as LCDR Wakefield. She could contain that pain, but the act had seared her soul as Judah. It was the part of herself she did not allow anyone to touch.

"In trying to save you physical pain, I caused you greater emotional pain. I'm sorry I broke the tenuous trust we were building."

It was a moving apology. She did not feel like moving.

Judah twisted her neck upright anyway. Secretly, she loved that his hand followed her movement. "I went from wanting to kill you this morning, to watching you almost get killed." She sniffed dryly. "I did not like it. Please, don't do it again."

She ripped more tape away from the roll, and they were no longer touching as she reached behind him to catch the end.

"I can't promise that." His voice softly begged her for something she could not identify.

She reached around him and wrapped even lines of white medical tape to hold his ribs in place. Reached and wrapped. Reached and wrapped. "I know."

Fourth Floor U.S. Embassy, Berlin
Nelson's Office
1430 hours

Nelson started violently enough to dribble coffee on his tie as his secretary buzzed his intercom. "Lieutenant Commander Rivers is on line one, Chief." Ms Marshall intoned.

"About time." He grabbed for his desk phone. "Where have you guys been? The president will be here in 21 hours. Do I still have a killer on the loose or not?"

Rivers cleared his throat before speaking. "We've been a little busy, sir. We wondered if you have talked to Chad recently."

"Chad?"

"We can't seem to raise him on his cell. He and Yates have both gone MIA."

"Commander, do I still have an assassin on the streets?"

"There is one less than there was." The officer's low tones did nothing to reduce the churning in his stomach. Nelson closed his eyes and reached for his desk-top jumbo bottle of Tums. "One of our five suspects, the Greek, is on his way to the morgue."

Nelson groaned. *Public relations nightmare, here we come.* "And you don't think he was Azure Tiger?" He tucked the receiver between his bent neck and shoulder and fought with the child-proof, yellow cap.

"No, sir. There is nothing definitive to suggest a conclusion either way, but the assassin always fired two rounds. Ganitopoulos shot one the first time, if that was him, and five this morning."

Nelson peered into the bottle with one eye cocked and shook it to rearrange the few anti-acid tablets left. The red ones and the green ones were gone. He frowned and shook three yellows into his damp palm. "Did you not have enough to do tomorrow? Wait. Don't tell me." Nelson dropped the Tums bottle back onto his desk with a hollow rattle as the truth dawned on him. "You had to draw him out, so you used yourselves as bait." *Stupid amateurs*, he huffed. "You hired him yourselves."

"Not both of us. Just me. Can you get Chad for us? I need him to follow up on a lead. We're headed back. Probably arrive around 2200 hours."

"I assigned him to the sweep team with the Secret Service. They are going over every scenario a third time and need the help." Nelson narrowed his eyes at Rivers' sigh. He felt his stomach lurch again as the part-time field agent requested a favor. "Contact Yates at the British—" It sounded like Rivers moved the phone to talk to his partner. "Does Yates work from the Embassy or the Consulate?" He could not hear Wakefield's reply. "He's at the Consulate. Should be working in-house."

Nelson tapped his pen on his desk. "What do you need, Rivers." He prompted the officer.

"I need him to talk to the manager of the Kempinski Hotel and get the security tapes of the check-in counter for the last week—make that two weeks, Wakefield says—ready for us to view. Our man has to be on that tape. Tell Yates any cross-referencing that he wants to start would be appreciated."

"Do you have a room number?" Nelson scribbled while talking. His pen stuck. He shook the ink and tried again.

Rivers laugh sounded rye over the line. "That would be simple. *Nothing* about this case is simple."

"The info will be waiting for you if I have to get it myself," Nelson dotted his note forcefully as if his pen was a dart. The point made a hole in the paper. "Just hurry up and get home."

34

Filasek's bare feet slapped the cool stone of his villa balcony. Each step was ginger, but deliberate. Glaring at the black phone that lay like a broken mockingbird on the cushioned lounger, he willed it to ring. He passed it again and glided to the white stone and iron barrier that overlooked the steep cliff into which the villa nestled. When he was at the farthest point possible, the phone jingled. Filasek scurried, his callused feet scuffing against the stone. He dove forward to capture the phone. It did not break silence again.

He cursed. "Must have been a stupid seagull. Curse all seagulls, their bothersome noise, their pesky begging, their inopportune droppings." Filasek held the phone to his ear.

A static dial tone greeted him. "No wonder!"

He clicked the button off and threw it with another curse back into the cushion. Promptly, it rang. Filasek cut short his tirade.

He dove after it again, the top of his toes scrapping the stone floor in his haste. *Finally. Finally!*

It rang in his hand. *What will he think? I can do it on my own.* His lids closed over half of his eye. *It would swifter though to use the men already in training camps.*

Another ring.

He straightened the collarless white shirt on his shoulders and smoothed his beard. When his fingers touched his newly clean-shaven chin, he shook his head at his own ritual.

Fourth ring. Filasek punched the oval key. He answered in Farsi, "Hello?"

A-376
In route to Berlin
1509 hours

Wakefield gripped the steering wheel and looked at Rivers' sleeping form. A smile softened her features. He had finally relinquished control enough to fall asleep with her at the wheel.

A sign announced an interchange ahead. *Nurnberg or Regensburg?* Judah rubbed her lip. *Which city did we come through on the way south?*

She looked at Rivers again. He would know.

The road split in one kilometer. The overpass stood against the horizon.

She looked at her partner again. She reached a hand over to shake him awake. The smoothness of his face caused her to hesitate, hand held mid-air.

She dropped her hand to the gearshift and frowned. The man trusted her to make the right decision. She would do it. "God, which way?"

The exit lane widened to her left. She leaned toward staying on their current route. The cut off was 30 feet out. In one smooth, controlled motion, she held her breath and swung the wheel to ascend the ramp. "Don't let me get us lost," she exhaled the prayer.

Rivers shifted deeper into the reclined seat and settled his palm over his broken ribs with a horsy blubber of his lips.

35

N elson twisted the key in his desk drawer. He drained his coffee cup on the way to the door. Pocketing his keys and grabbing the collar of his long winter wool, he grunted a good-bye to Ms Marshal.

"Chief," the secretary's chin bounded up, "this package came for Miss Wakefield. What should I do with it?" With wide eyes, Ms Marshall fingered the line of tape that held the brown paper wrapping in place.

"I'll take it with me. I'm meeting her and Rivers in a few hours." Nelson strode over and exchanged his coffee mug for the brown package. "Hm, the postmark is Washington." He hefted it. *Too much weight for papers.* "Probably a present from whomever she is seeing socially. Take care of that cup for me, would you?"

Nelson traipsed toward the elevator bank hefting the box to guess the contents. *Four pounds of chocolate?* Nobody would be stupid enough to send American chocolate to a woman in Germany, would he? *It's weeks from Valentine's Day. Too heavy to be clothes, at least the kind a significant other would buy. Maybe a couple of thick novels.* Nelson snorted. *As if she has time to read.*

He set the box between his feet to button his coat. It was cold out, but at least it wasn't raining. Poor Yates, according to the Consulate, he was in London, and it rained every day in that gray town.

Nelson shrugged. He knew he was too valuable in the Agency to be doing such a menial task, but he'd promised Rivers. Nelson pushed open the heavy doors to the embassy. He smiled at the added benefit of setting himself free from the chains of his desk that was still drowning in paperwork and pink phone slips.

Poros, Greece
1545 hours

"So you like the idea?" Filasek shuffled his feet and rolled his fingers as if he was counting paper money. His fidgeting made him feel like a 10-year-old on his second visit to the headmaster's office in the same day.

"I did not say that." The voice on the other end sounded cryptic and cultured. "I said that it has the potential to be a boon to our cause and our recruitment numbers. The location is ideal. The data is raw though."

Filasek looked up without moving his head as the voice continued to instruct. "Figure out how to guarantee that your construction company will receive the bid for the bridge repair and then I will work through the details and help you choose the men."

Filasek cleared his throat. "I will do this myself. I have a contact inside the trade committee. She can give me the numbers and I will underbid the lowest time estimate by a month. Keep the money the same. I just wanted to bring in help that has already been through training. I thought you could recommend a camp with some experts that will be ready before the deadline."

Filasek had finely combed every detail already. It was a perfect plan. He touched his bald chin again, stroking the dip just below his bottom lip. The smoothness felt strange.

San Francisco, the City by the Bay. Filasek scratched his palms with filed nails. *Soon, part of it will be* in *the bay.* He could not control the half-lidded smile that came at the thought of personally scarring some 15,000 American families, irreversibly. Maybe some of them would be some of his mortgage holders and he would get to repossess some homes. Fire or water. Water or fire. His heart rate accelerated. It made no difference to him how they went to their mass grave.

True, he mused, *the construction company might disintegrate. But this is why I began building its reputation four years ago.* Filasek tapped his chin. He was enjoying the company's profits. He grimaced slightly as he looked out over the sparkling Mediterranean blue waters from his white, third-story balcony. With the right spin from the CEO, and the loss of many employees, the company might even survive. Working on the Golden Gate would automatically include bumping up the insurance coverage. That would be a dandy payout.

His jumping eyes gave away that he had forgotten he was still on the phone with America's Most Wanted man in history. "Perhaps coordination of our current efforts would cause a better effect," the man was saying when Filasek honed back in.

Filasek frowned. "Which one?"

"Operation Endeavor in Florida and Knox Blox in Kentucky. Hmm," the man slurped air through his teeth in thought. "I like it. A joint effort to hit the southeast, midwest, and west coast simultaneously."

Filasek ran his finger between his collar and his neck. The fabric must be shrinking in the sun. It felt like the man's voice was crawling under his very skin.

"It might disrupt your 7AM timing for the bridge. We would have to wait for the shuttle to take off and then detonate at perhaps 20-minute intervals after that." Al-Qaeda's terrorist god warmed to the idea as he processed it. Filasek could hear it in his voice. "Keep working on the details. I'll call you in a week."

Filasek's stomach lurched, and he gritted his teeth. "Very well."

"A word of warning: give up your obsession with pinning the blame on the woman. We need to claim all three for maximum impact on the Great Satan. You will divide your focus. A divided man fails in both his efforts."

As if he would know. Filasek pulled the phone away from his ear as it clicked off. He rolled his eyes. "Whatever you say, Bin-y boy." Stretching back in his sun-warmed lounger, Filasek released his breath.

The man knew nothing, never acknowledged who he was. Osama bin Laden spoke to him as if he were any other operative living and planning destruction abroad for the cause of Islam. He had never understood or cared for him as their relationship stipulated. The phone on Filasek's stomach moved up and down as rejection raged, and he went over his plan again.

His eyes drifted closed as he wondered how to implicate Wakefield in the Golden Gate's downfall after she was imprisoned for the president's death. Now if the jury went death-penalty quickly, he wouldn't need to put forth the effort, but otherwise, they'd need a clearly concealed email trail that would lead back to her. Physical evidence could always be manufactured and planted.

His one well-placed call had begun the damage to her reputation. The noose of a hotline worked wonders; now, to knock the foundation box out from under her feet. He ached to see that woman profusely destroyed, found guilty of terrorism and treason by her own people. It would taste wonderful to attach those two words to her name forever.

Filasek smacked his lips in his slumber.

The Kempinski Hotel, Berlin
2050 hours

Wakefield tossed her keys to the valet at the door of the five-star hotel. "Hope he doesn't look at those keys too closely." She squinted one eye at Rivers as they pushed through the glass door at the same time. Wakefield entered first.

"Why? Still caked with blood?"

"Yep." Wakefield gawked like a tourist with her head tilted back to view the fantastic red and gold lobby.

"Wow." They spoke together.

"And to think," Wakefield teased her partner with a serious face, "you turned down staying here to cover your dinky window with plastic."

"Huh," Rivers snorted and got them walking again, "If you had mentioned that it looked like a king's residence, I might have given it a second thought. I bet it was hard for Yates to move back to his German flat after this poshness."

Wakefield watched the closest of the three concierges replace the handset of his telephone and glide toward them. "Lieutenant Commander Wakefield," the tuxedoed man spoke in French-accented English. He offered her his elbow. "Lieutenant Commander Rivers, Monsieur Nelson requests you join him in the viewing room."

Wakefield tentatively grasped the man's arm and was spun 90 degrees to the left. "How does he know we are here?" Her chin moved forward as she searched for the station chief.

"State of the art video cameras. Fifteen. We monitor all common areas of the Kempinski. And here we are." The polished Frenchman reached his hand forward to the gold-handled door. He closed it behind them on silent hinges.

Nelson spun around in his chair that faced a large monitor. "Ah. The navy has arrived." He pushed up his rolled shirt sleeves on his elbow. A boyish grin flashed in his tired eyes.

"And you've started without us." Rivers noticed aloud. "Where are Yates and Chad?" he sounded curt to Wakefield, and she wondered why. She searched the darkened room. Monitors lined one wall and provided the only light.

Nelson did not respond to Rivers' testiness. "I'd forgotten how much I loved field work. Berlin's station chief's face reflected the colored movement on the screens. "My secretary has been calling my handy every 20 minutes. I finally told her I was never coming back." He grinned. "Meet Gustav," Nelson gestured to them. She and Rivers had halted just inside the door. "He can do anything on film."

"Tape." Gustav corrected the station chief in German. He rose to a crouched position over his chair and extended his hand. "We tape the security areas with these cameras. Film is used for movies and television dramas."

Wakefield shook his pasty hand briefly and watched as Rivers did the same. The German security man was younger than she had first thought. Maybe 26. His ears stuck out too far and were accentuated by a short hair cut in the front that lagged longer in the back. He did not appear concerned about his presentation, but was enthusiastic about one thing. Film, or tape rather.

"Pull up a chair." Gustav motioned to a stack of metal folding chairs stacked haphazardly against the hall wall.

Nelson spun his chair back to the largest monitor where he and Gustav resumed scanning the tape on fast forward.

"No more spin-y chairs, sorry." Gustav had apparently seen the incredulous look she had exchanged with Rivers behind Nelson's back.

She smiled knowingly at the youngest member of their group. "Quiet all right. One seems plenty in this limited space." Wakefield slide a brown box to the side and laid her coat over it to make space for the chairs Rivers brought.

"You will not believe what some people do in public." Nelson pointed to the screen. A man in a three piece suit at the check in counter reached down and scratched himself. The guys laughed; Wakefield rolled her eyes. "We've been through three days on fast forward since I got here at 1600. Nothing suspicious yet.

"What day is this," Rivers threw his hand in the direction of the picture. He reclined back as far as possible without falling out of his chair. She hoped it helped him to breathe, because it hurt her back to look at his position.

"One week ago. Seventeen January."

"And you've looked at 14, 15 and 16?" Wakefield stared at the images moving like Charlie Chaplin.

"Just 15 and 16. This is the end of day three."

An hour later the four stared at the check-in desk video that covered 0100 hours on the eighteenth. Wakefield felt her eyes cross. It was taking longer and longer for her eyes to reopen when she blinked.

Eight hours of driving did not couple well with sitting in a dark room with only the sounds of shifting bodies and an occasional cough.

"I think I'm numb," she told the men. "I'm going to go talk to the maids. See if they noticed anything unusual." The three men, glued to the monitor, gave identical single nods. She closed the door while squinting against the hall light.

Screen figures from Saturday afternoon wobbled around the lobby on the tape. "Oh," Nelson looked up. "Where did Wakefield go?"

"She left." Rivers looked at his watch. "Twenty-five minutes ago." Gustav joined him in a chuckle.

"Where were you?"

Nelson jabbed a finger at the 32-inch monitor. "In the lobby." His eyes seemed soldered to the pictures, never distracted. "Somebody remind me when she gets back, she is supposed to call Dietz and she got a package from her boyfriend this morning.

David Rivers felt his heart protest beating. "What boyfriend?"

"Didn't know she was seeing someone, Commander?" Nelson nettled. He released his gaze from the large monitor for the first time in hours. Nelson fixed his eyes on him instead.

Rivers squirmed. It was painful. "I can call Dietz." Rivers sucked in his breath, leaned forward, and began to move toward the SatFone in his coat pocket.

"It's personal, Commander. He needs Wakefield."

"Then I'll go get her."

"Hey!" Gustav pointed one finger at the monitor and flipped the switch under his right hand to pause.

Nelson spun back to Gustav's equipment. "I've seen that guy before." Nelson's words tangled with Gustav's, "He's already checked in."

Rivers dropped back into his chair, his ribs screamed profanely at him. He squinted to focus on the monitor instead of moving closer.

The man filling the screen did look somewhat familiar. *Something about his nose.*

"Up the sound and rewind to where he comes up to the counter."

"We don't record sound. Sorry," Gustav touched his Adam's apple as he rewound the tape with the flip of a toggle on the board in front of him. A line rolled through the screen as the action resumed at regular speed. The man, about 6 foot 1, with Albert Einstein hair using a silver-handled cane entered from the left of the sidewalk. He switched a briefcase to his cane hand and opened the door with his left hand. He did not have a pronounced limp as he plodded across the open space with his cane to the desk.

Nelson pursed his lips with a tiny smacking sound. "Gustav, get the general manager to cross-reference the time of check in with the room number and name. Credit card info too. While we continue to look." He smacked his lips again. "How long do you suppose it's been? Two, maybe three hours since the other guy checked in. I think it must have been two tapes ago."

"No, sir." Rivers squirmed in his hard chair. "It has to be since I got here. He looks familiar to me, too."

Gustav scribbled the time to the second and picked up the black rotary phone next to his station and let out what sounded to Rivers like a string of curses in hot German. "Sorry." He gave the others a sheepish glance. "The phone is out again." He stood up to go speak to the manager in person. "I don't know how they expect me to warn them, if they don't buy me a phone that works." The door slammed and shook the room.

Rivers lips turned down. "It does seem incongruous to have a million-dollar surveillance system and a telephone left over from the Third Reich."

Nelson snorted. "That's just Germany, my boy. Why replace something that is not broken."

"It's broken now."

36

Kempi Housekeeping
Readyroom/Breakroom

LCDR Wakefield marched into her battlefield. The locker-lined room smelled of antiseptic-covered must. Eight maid buggies formed a double line of vigilance against the back wall. A lone woman with a dark ponytail hanging to the middle of her back stood next to the canvas buggies stuffing her large laundry bag into the shoot that presumably led to the washroom in sublevel two. She hummed softly between grunts of lifting and stuffing.

"Excuse me," Wakefield announced her presence.

The woman whipped her ponytail around as she turned in a jerky motion. It ended up over her shoulder. "*Hallo.*" She cast her eyes to the painted yellow concrete floor after a brief glance. She was not yet 20, and had luminous skin. Her haunted coal eyes betrayed her startle at the interruption.

"Do you have a moment? I'd like to ask you some questions?" Wakefield moved forward and placed one foot on the long wooden bench that ran the length of the room separating the two rows of lockers. Leaning forward, the officer stretched her tired back muscles and crossed her arms, resting them on her raised knee.

"No to speak German. To hear only." The young woman's halting speech and use of infinitives gave credence to her statement.

"English?" Wakefield tried her native tongue. No reply. "*Francis?*" She looked a little French.

The girl shook her head in a tiny motion and studied the cracks in the floor paint as if they were placed there by Monet himself.

"Where are you from?" She tried again in German. She spied a tiny Russian flag on her apron's neck loop. "Oh, I see your pin." Wakefield spoke in formal Russian.

The girl looked up and her face brightened. She stepped back and looked back at the concrete. "What did I do wrong?" Her voice trembled softly, her hands moved behind her back.

Wakefield could feel the girl's fear from 20 feet away. "Nothing." She added a more friendly tone. "Nothing." She plopped herself down to straddle the wood bench. She decided to deviate from her original head-first approach. She did not want the girl to close down completely. "You're a long way from home. You must miss it a lot."

Tears flooded the girl's black eyes. Wakefield recognized something of herself in the young woman as the Russian blinked rapidly to clear her vision without shedding the tears. "I do miss it. My sisters most of all."

By the time the girl put her bag away, they were chatting about tough jobs and strange languages. Tatiana joined Wakefield on the bench. "Have you noticed anything unusual about the rooms you've cleaned in say...the last three weeks?"

"I am not sure what you mean. I am tired all the time. I work two shifts a day to get money to go home again. It is a beautiful hotel, but they have messy guests. I must get home to Pater again." Tatiana's eyes flooded again.

So much for a simple interview. The president would be here in nine hours and this woman needed counseling. Wakefield felt like taffy inside. Her job obligation pulled against her purpose in life.

Jesus, help me make the right choice. She touched Tatiana's rough hands. The girl burrowed her chipped nails into the folds of her apron. "Tell me what happened to you, Tatiana." She could literally hear her watch ticking.

It seemed that the kind interest was the Russian woman's undoing. The dammed tears started as a trickle and broke through into a silent flood. She made no whimper. Finally, hunched over and refusing to make eye contact, the younger woman spoke. "On my 16th birthday, my father discovered me with the son of his most hated business enemy." The girl darted a glance at her. The expression begged understanding. "I loved Pater," she choked, "more than I loved my father. I refused to stop seeing him, even after he threw Pater out of the house."

Wakefield felt compassion rise in her chest. "I don't know how it feels to have my father pitted against my lover." She hoped she never would. "But I do know how it feels to lose both." Wakefield tangled her fingers together on the bench in front of her.

She reached for Tatiana's hand again. This time the younger woman allowed the touch.

Tatiana's words came in halting sentences. Some words she spoke slowly as if each was a knife, some she speed through. Wakefield wondered if speaking faster hurt less. "My father bought a one-way train ticket, and sent me as far as his money would buy. I did not get to say good-bye to Pater. My mother stayed home." She withdrew her hands to wrap them in the safety of her apron. "My two sisters came. They begged my father not to send me away."

Wakefield watched the collar of Tatiana's white blouse absorb the steady track of water. "I miss them so much. It aches inside to think of them."

Wakefield reached out and squeezed the girl's knee. *God, let your love flow in and heal her hurts.* "I am sorry such painful things have happened to you." She felt a single tear work its way down her scarred cheek. "Parents don't tell us when we are young, but love is the most painful emotion there is. It can be the most exhilarating and motivational, but it also causes the most pain."

Tatiana sopped her face with her fingers and then the back of her hand. It didn't help much. She chuckled at her own efforts. "I'm sorry. I usually don't break down in front of strangers."

251

"You probably never had a reason to." Wakefield saw the blush creep up the girl's neck. "Please don't be embarrassed. We all need to release our stress to someone."

Judah's watch ticked.

Tatiana straightened her back. "I have done it on my own for two years. I will earn enough money, and I will return to Pater." The gut-spilling session seemed to have fulfilled its catharsis. "What was it you came to ask me?" Her black eyes still shimmered. Wakefield admired her determined posture.

She fed off the younger woman's resilience as she transferred back into lieutenant-commander mode. "I am investigating a man who may be residing in this hotel. I don't have a physical description or room number though." Wakefield inclined her head to the side. "Have you had any suspicious or just unusual guests in the last few weeks?" Wakefield ticked off the descriptive items on her fingers. "He would be excessive—either obsessively tidy or tornado messy?"

Tatiana squinted one eye and leaned in to interrupt. "What is tornado?"

Wakefield spun her hands in a circle. "A whirlwind. Very messy. Belongings everywhere. He would be keeping a low profile, no visitors, few phone calls—foreign probably. He might not even leave his room. He either orders in all his meals or never orders. If you ever ran into him, he would either be exceptionally charming or absolutely silent. This man is extreme in everything he does. He probably drinks very little or not at all. We know he has a computer. He may even have a high powered weapon in his room." Wakefield stopped her description. That was all she knew.

Tatiana tipped her head back and forth and her eyes studied the ceiling tiles, as she thought. "Excessively neat I have not seen." She smiled ruefully. "Excessively messy describes ninety percent of my rooms. Most people here, this week especially with the American president coming, receive and make foreign calls. All of the business people have their laptops and handys."

The girl stared at the wall behind Wakefield. She drummed her fingers hollowly on the wood bench they shared. "I think I remember hearing something." She bit the ragged nail on her ring finger. "Some of the girls were talking about some strange rooms they have been cleaning. Some brothers."

"How long ago?" Wakefield spat.

"I think maybe three, four days past. I may be wrong. Because of the language."

"Think Tatiana. Who was it? Who should I talk to?"

"It was that group from Guatemala. Marta maybe. But she quit. Moved to Switzerland day before yesterday. Alejandra or Lupe-Maria, or one of the others might know."

Wakefield felt her head lighten. A name. Two names. "When will either of them be in again?"

"Shift starts at five o'clock." She looked at the break room clock. "In four hours. Can it wait until then?"

"I hope so."

"Don't call them at home." Tatiana shook her head. Her features scrunched together. "Lupe-Maria is a big, fat, mean woman. She'll stare you into a puddle on the floor if she thinks you've been talking about her, even *thinking* about talking about her." She emphasized with a closed fist.

Wakefield hid a smile. She had never considered the hierarchy involved in the maid service.

37

"Where have you been?" Rivers burst out when his partner's silhouette filled the doorway to the stuffy monitoring room. "I looked everyplace I could think of. Tell me next time you decide to disappear for three hours."

"He's been driving us crazy. Please tell him next time." Nelson put in from his rooted spot. He lifted one hand in greeting, but did not turn around.

"I told you where I was going. You weren't listening. You two don't make a very good surveillance team."

Rivers watched Wakefield's left eyebrow quirk up in a way that was becoming as familiar as her half-smile. In Afghanistan, he had assumed it was because of the injury to her face, but she had a particular half-smile. It seemed reserved for times she was annoyed with herself or others and trying to maintain diplomacy. This eyebrow quirk crossed curiosity with amusement in him. "You're supposed to call Dietz." Rivers brought his fingertips together. He was proud of his carefully honed vocal control.

"Oh? Did you call back?"

"Apparently it's personal." Rivers leaned into his heel and felt his knees lock. "Where were you?" He crossed his hands behind his back.

Wakefield stepped closer and folded her arms across her chest, imitating his stance. He could not tell by her protruding jaw expression if she was imitating him on purpose or not. "Is this a game of Let's Trade Secrets?" She cocked her head to the side. Her long straightened hair fell away from her face silkily and down her shoulder.

It was definitely on purpose. "Is your previous location a secret?"

Nelson snorted from his monitor. "Commander, if you are going to argue with her, at least let her open her package first. You're dying to know what's inside, too."

Rivers watched his partner's eyes light up in the reflection of the monitor's moving light. Her posture straightened and she dropped the armored stance. "I got a package? From Yates?" Her eyes searched the darkened room. Her tone was so syrupy she may as well have added, "Aw, he's so sweet."

Rivers knew the moment she found the shoe-box sized package behind him on her radar. Her face registered a curious frown.

She stretched out her hand as she walked in River's direction.

"No," Nelson interrupted Rivers' reply. His voice sing-songed, "Your boyfriend sent you an early valentine."

Her eyes darted between the back of Nelson's head and the package. Just behind him, short of the package, Rivers felt his partner freeze. "I'm not seeing anyone. You're sure it's not from Yates?"

She moved in on the package and Rivers turned to see.

"D.C. zip code. Yates got shipped back to London. Didn't I tell you that on our way here?" His spirit felt uneasy. He tried to separate his jealousy from a possible warning. He couldn't do it.

"Oh, it must be from my C.O. or Dietz."

Nelson swiveled his chair silently. "Maybe it has something to do with what Dietz wants to talk to you about." Wakefield lifted her head to look at the chief.

"I am supposed to call him?" she prompted.

"He said it was of a personal nature."

There was some expression in Nelson's eyes that Rivers did not like. The way the chief looked at his partner. *I'd characterize it as pity if I didn't know better.*

"I'll open it before I call him." She hefted the package and studied the postmark. "It's marked with my zip code. I wonder what Dietz was doing there."

Rivers stared intensely at her fingers as she slit the glass tape on one end. Her fingers stilled and he glanced up to find her eyes on him. "Did you want to check it for a bomb or anthrax?" She asked with that half-smile he liked so much. It felt like she was teasing this time.

"Already did," he tipped his nose up. "Not a bomb. No powder residue from anthrax."

She opened the other end just as easily. A pink and grey Adidas tennis shoe box slid out of the sleeve.

Gustav opened the door splashing light inside. "Hey guys." His voice was jolting and brash. "I got the info on the three men. Wakefield, you're back." Rivers wanted to wipe the goofy smile off Gustav's face.

Tegel Airport, Berlin
0310 hours

Air Force One touched down on the tarmac as soft as a mother smoothing her newborn's hair. No jarring. No welcoming fanfare. Only a still black night.

George W. Bush turned over in his sleep, subconsciously aware of the change in pressure and movement. But he knew there was no need to wake. The toughest fighting force this side of heaven kept watch for him: The United States Marines.

He sighed and sank back into deep, unconcerned sleep.

Kempinski Hotel, Berlin
Suite 1229
0310 hours

Assassin Azure Tiger flopped to his right on the firm mattress. He kicked off the covers. *Why won't the thermostat regulate the accursed temperature?* He touched his warm forehead and dragged his bony fingers through his matted curls. He blew out his breath.

It was not too late to take the first half of the money and run.

Turn it into cash and disappear, something inside prompted him.

As far-reaching as his puppet-master was, there were places for hiding. Maybe it was time to cut the strings. Filasek could not have bugged the entire planet.

Tomorrow will be too late, he heard a voice inside resound.

He rolled to his left and punched his pillow up.

Kempinski Hotel Security
0159 hours

"Oh, sorry. Didn't mean to interrupt your early Valentine's Day. Gustav nodded for her to continue. "This can wait a moment." Wakefield dropped the brown paper onto the floor.

Wakefield eagerly returned her focus to the box. Size 9. The sketch on the end looked identical to her new running shoes. *Weird.* The box top lifted from the side.

The door opened again, another pool of light spilled into the security room. "The computer is free now, if you want to do some cross-referencing." It was the daytime manager who poked his head inside. Wakefield noted his casual dress. Someone must have called him in, but his customer service smile was firmly in place.

The lid fell back into place at the interruption.

Gustav swore in colorful German. Judah's felt her eyes smart wide. It was a good thing Rivers did not understand the language.

257

"What is that smell?" The young man fanned the air in front of his face with his hand.

Nelson was further away. "What did he send you? A rotten cabbage." He chuckled and laced his fingers.

"Ugh." She got her first whiff. Her stomach churned at the rotting stench. She wrenched her face to the side looking for clean air.

Gustav chuckled low in his throat and gagged. "That is bad!"

"I am going to kill Dietz if he was so thoughtful as to send me the contents of my dairy drawer."

"Open it. Open it." Rivers' impatience rang in his voice. He had shuffled a few feet away.

"I am working up to it." She took another side breath. That air was not fresh anymore either. *What could possibly smell so horrid?*

With one finger, she flipped the cardboard lid back.

The impact hit her breastbone. "Oh Jesus, help." A wave of white heat flashed through her vision.

She could not draw a breath. She could not speak. She could not tear her eyes away.

Joe.

Her vision blurred. She blinked and blinked again. *Why Joe?*

Rivers' words stirred the sludge in her brain. "Judah, what is it?'

The four men stared. She could not look at their concerned faces directly. Her skin began to feel too tight. Without looking back down to the box, she snapped the top closed and shoved it toward Chief Nelson. "Have your people run this through the lab. I want everything printed and analyzed to ID the sender."

Nelson gapped like a fish. "It wasn't Dietz? What is it?" He tried to cover his grimace. The chief must have gotten a snoutfull.

The box sat on his stiff, raised arms away from his body. "It is Joseph Bartholomew Wakefield. My cat. His throat was slit and he was disemboweled."

"What? Here in my hotel?" Faulkenburg, the Bulgarian day manager pulled at his thinning hair.

"Relax. This happened in Washington." Wakefield willed him to be calm. Her nerves were frayed. She could not handle a scene. "Rivers, could I use your phone to call Dietz?"

He was already moving to her. "Of course." He unclipped the phone from his belt. "Are you—okay?"

His fingers felt wide and warm on her elbow. The initial heat wave had turned to a deep cold that settled in her toes. "I am sorry," he told her, "that seems inadequate."

"No. I don't think I'm okay. I will talk to Dietz, and I would like to take a walk. Alone." She added before he could volunteer to accompany her. She needed space. It was too cramped in the security room to breathe.

He slapped the phone into her hand. "Auto dial four is the office. Five is Dietz's home." Rivers opened the door for her. His fingers trailed down her back as she tottered toward the outside.

The night air, though it smelled as cold as her insides, felt crisp. It was not heavy or moist like it normally felt in the city.

She brought her partner's SatFone close to her face in the circle of lamplight. It smelled like him. Woodsy, spicy, clean.

She did not have to calculate a time difference. A presidential assassin was on the loose; Dietz would be *living* at Langley.

Three rings before the harried evening secretary, Melissa, picked up. "I'll put you through immediately, Commander Wakefield."

38

Rivers smoothed his hands over the wall beside the door and then patted the other side. "Where are the lights?"

Gustav hit a switch on his chrome control panel.

Florescent lighting flooded the room.

"That's better," Rivers strode across the room in five large steps, avoiding the manager. He snatched the paper up from where his partner dropped it. His breath caught in his throat.

Thrusting the stiff brown paper on top of the box in Nelson's long arms, his words shot out forcefully. "Take this with you."

Nelson adjusted his hold and caught the paper before it fell again. "This paper was touched by hundreds of people by the time it got here." He shook his head and grimaced.

"And the killer had to touch it too. Have you ever tried to use scotch tape with gloves—even latex gloves—on your hands? His prints are on that paper, too. The lab can isolate them. Or I'll learn how and find them myself." The growl he uttered felt good leaving his throat.

Rivers could feel his hands tremble. SEAL's hands do not tremble. He shoved them in his pockets.

"Go after her, Rivers." Nelson stood from his swivel chair and straightened stiffly. The box teetered. "She is about to find out that her apartment building burned down."

"What?" Rivers yawped. In one giant step, he was in front of the station chief with the man's rumpled shirt collar in his fist. Nose to nose. "What else do you know?" The man's coffee breath and stale body

260

assaulted Rivers' senses. Nelson's muddy brown eyes shivered back and forth.

"She is the number one suspect," Nelson squawked.

Rivers shook his fist with Nelson in tow. He dropped the man. "CIA," he muttered, "why can't you speak up like everybody else. This is somebody's life here."

Nelson shook his shoulders straight and righted the box. "That's right, this is somebody's life. George W. Bush's life." The commander did not acknowledge the glare the station chief sent in his direction. "And don't ever touch me like that again."

The man's scornful voice grated against Rivers' raw nerves. "It is about Judah Wakefield at the moment. It is about the president tomorrow. Don't ever speak to me like that again."

"It is tomorrow," Rivers heard Nelson mumble.

The slamming door punctuated Rivers' exit.

Kempi Surveillance Room
0230 hours

"Please forgive the commander. He can be hotheaded concerning his partner." Nelson blinked slowly trying to regain his dignity. He inclined his head toward Faulkenburg. "What were you able to dig up for us?"

The Bulgarian manager's thick black mustache twitched. Unfolding a printout with a center crease from top to bottom, he delivered it to Nelson. "The two men are indeed related. They are brothers," he recited. "There is a third also here in town. I checked him in myself, earlier that Wednesday."

"Was there anything unusual about that one?" Nelson smiled at the easy way with which he found himself slipping back into the hunter mode. "Did you hear about any disturbances or oddities about any of the brothers?"

"In speaking with the eldest, I can say I found him to be genuinely excited to visit with his brothers. He asked that they receive rooms with the best views, even if they ended up in different locations.

Of course, their rooms were already assigned, and they were on three different floors. They all requested particular rooms in their reservations. I guess he didn't know about that."

"Anything else?"

"He seemed surprised that we are full. He did not know of your president's visit."

"Maybe he's not a TV watcher." Gustav interjected from his chair at the console. "I wouldn't have known except for the staff meeting day before last." He shrugged. Nelson thought he looked a little embarrassed. "I watch screens all day at work. I do other things to relax at home."

Nelson faced the manager. He refolded the paper and flapped it against his open hand. "May I see the records for the entire length of their stay for all three men?" Nelson felt some connection. "There is something there, I just can't put my finger on it. It will come to me."

"Of course. Come to my office. It is quieter than the front desk, even at 2:30 in the morning."

"Say," Nelson flipped open the pages as they clipped down the hallway, "what are these brothers names?"

"Um. They were foreign. Dovlata, I think. Look in the top right corner. Sounds Indian, like that prince, but they didn't look Indian."

"It sounds more familiar than that."

Ku'damm Strasse
0245 hours

The street felt endless, as if she could walk all the way home.

"Do you need me to come, Judah?" Dietz voice squirmed into her brain.

"No, if I start to buckle under the pressure, Rivers is here." She tried humor. She could not fool herself or the director of counterintelligence.

"Still, if you need anything…"

"Can you put a man on the investigative team with the fire marshal? If this is deliberate, I want the name of the person responsible."

"Already done. The second report from the fire marshal's office is that regular car gasoline was used as an ignition accelerant. My man has confirmed. It was certainly deliberate."

"Oh." What else was there to say? She looked down. She did not remember when she stopped walking. The cobblestones had tufts of grass growing between them. Even in the limited light, she could see the bright green color. In January. Very tenacious grass.

"Who would want to destroy your home, Judah?"

She figured he was trying to be kind, but his voice came out pitchy, and it squeezed her nerves.

She touched her forehead, urging her brain to move. "You'd have the records of all the people who don't like me."

"There's no disgruntled boyfriend or ex-husband that slipped through the cracks? I'd need to know."

She smiled sadly, with her lips only, at the director's hesitant tone. "No skeletons, Dietz." She was confident only of that. "Tell the fire marshal that I'll be home in a few days, one way or the other. I'll speak to him right after Judge Pella."

Judah thought she could hear the man shaking his head on the other end of the line. "I never thought you would have these kind of people lined up to talk to you, Wakefield. You've always been my good kid."

"Me neither." She sighed, feeling she had shrunk three inches since she walked outside. *All my uniforms altered for the correct length are gone. It will take weeks to have those done again.* "I need to go." She tried brightening her voice, but it came out squeaky. "Thanks for telling me personally. I know it was hard for you. You are a kind man. Whether anybody else believes it or not, I know it."

"Stay safe, Commander."

"I'll help our president stay safe, sir." She broke the connection and punched the power button.

"God, I," her voice shook and she dropped the phone to her side. "I can't take any more." Her utterings dropped to a whisper. "You promised. No more than I can handle. I'm there."

She heard the words resound in her spirit more than heard them in her ears. *I am your strength. Lean into me.*

"I will hold you to it."

Poros, Greece
0450 hours local

Filasek blinked away the sleep in his eyes as the numbers cleared once again on the page in his hand. *I will sleep while the world cries in outrage. "Tomorrow."* He smiled widely.

His team working in the bio-chem plant had finally broken through. The hollowed out cliff beneath his neighbor's house was finally productive.

He shook his printed e-mail. The results of eight months of research after he had given the scientists the combination of chemicals he wanted to use. The lab tests showed that death resulted in 20 to 30 minutes, 15 seconds at close range, and had a 98 percent fatality rate in rats.

The poison gas was a mix of three bare elements. The elements had to be broken down from other forms and stored separately before being combined together to form his very own weapon of mass destruction. The combination sped like a rocket-propelled jet engine when exposed to oxygen. Skin contact did nothing, but once in the lungs, the air passages began to close in minutes.

Short but painful. Filasek touched his bare chin.

Colorless, but not odorless. Filasek squinted in the light from the single torchiere behind his Queen Anne chair. The spike on the odor chart showed a definite chemical combination that mixed two scents. Typed over the graph were two Greek words: *lavender* and *honey.*

Filasek chuckled deep in his chest. It was better than he had hoped. *Who could resist inhaling deeply and repeatedly at those springtime scents?* Perfect. Sixty grams could spread at a lethal concentration to a 10-mile radius with no wind in approximately two hours. *Unheard of.* His teeth tapped together.

The best was saved for last. This poison did not have to be shot into an area on a detectable missile. It could be added to products that sprayed. Hairspray, deodorant, cooking spray, perfume, anything with an atomizer to propel the atoms in their first movement.

The properties would also bond with the oxygen contained in drinking water. *Perhaps a trip to the headwaters of their Mississippi River is in order.*

Filasek reconnected his laptop to the Internet pipeline and sent a reply: Begin mass production immediately. Forward projected costs to me.

He leaned back in his chair and drummed his fingers on the closed computer in his lap. "I may postpone Azure Tiger's newest hit for a few weeks." He grinned as he stared into space. "At least until they get a couple more batches completed."

39

Rivers exited the brass and glass lobby into the circles of lamplight that seemed to puff the crisp blackness of night away from their safe haven. He peered up the street as far as he could to the left. One pair of brake lights disappeared around a corner. No civilian foot traffic. The night was just as quiet to the right.

West. He began a limited trot. Maybe she instinctively walked closer to home.

Thirty seconds into his search, he saw her frame in the distance. He quickened his silent pace.

Her shoulders drooped forward, her back was to him and it looked as though her head hung forward. Her arm flopped to her side with the energy of one who has just come from surgery. "God, let me be your arms of comfort." Rivers prayed.

He reached a tentative hand toward her. She still had not moved. Fear stirred his belly.

There. He could hear the soft rise and fall of her mutterings. An uncontrolled quick breath pushed more air out than it brought in. Rivers felt his heart quicken at the depth of her anguish.

She had to be freezing. He withdrew his hand to spread her coat wide so he could wrap it around her shoulders. The length of the coat had not touched her body before she sprang.

She spun to the inside and her right arm chopped him in the ribs. His arms were up, leaving his broken core unprotected.

His breath left him. His head felt light.

A sharp pain pressed behind his knees and he felt them give way. Suddenly the cobblestone was under his six. As his head snapped back, he saw her knuckles coming closer and closer to his eyes.

"Ahh! It's just me!" He threw his face to the side in avoidance as he was sitting half-laid-out on the sidewalk. He curved his back to absorb the anticipated blow.

She seemed to have the presence of mind to know who "me" was. The blow stopped short.

Rivers dared open one eye to a squint. He peeked through his lashes just as she made contact. Her first finger flicked him on the forehead. "Ouch."

Her face was only inches from his. He could feel her weight pinning his legs flat. *Interesting position.* Her brow wrinkled into three lines. Her lips twitched as her chin flattened upward. The scar on her right cheek reflected a light glowing in a first floor storefront across the narrow street.

Her tongue darted out to moisten her lips.

Her eyes. Where are her eyes? What is she looking at? The blue orbs, like the sea of forgetfulness, studied his eyes watchfully. She was looking for something.

"Didn't they teach you anything at BUD/S?" Her lips glided into the slightest arc.

What does that minuscule smile mean? "I learned a lot of things in BUD/S."

"How to subdue a target and take him into custody?"

"We did not practice the custody part very often."

"Just the capture and subdue?"

"Mm-hm." He felt his head nod slowly as he peered inside Judah's soul.

"You did not do a very thorough job tonight, SEAL Rivers."

He matched her slight lip movement. "I don't know about that." He released her eyes and looked pointedly at her leg. "You don't seem to be escaping to me."

"Escape…" She looked down at the ancient round cobbles. Her eyes tipped down. She exhaled and her voice was barely audible. "That would be ideal."

"Judah?"

"How much is one person supposed to take?" Her sea-eyes saw the tide come in. She seemed to beg for an answer.

Her chin struggled to control its tremble.

"Nelson told me what happened. Do you know how much I admire your restraint right now? In the last month, you have dealt with more bogies than an entire flight squadron in a week of war. Yet you are handling it."

She leaned forward and groaned. Her shoulders shook as she rested her forehead against his shoulder. His ribs groaned in protest at the additional pressure. "That's just it," she mumbled, "I'm not handling it."

"Oh, come here." He drew her to him. He sat up straighter to combat the pain. It didn't help much. Her body felt small under his arms. "Tears do not constitute failure. You have to put down your colors. There is no white flag in your personality."

His fingers traced her spine. He could distinguish each bony vertebrae through her shirt. Her coat lay in an unreachable heap four feet from them.

Her hair was a satiny pillowcase as he buried his face and touched the ends that hung down her back.

"My real dad's pictures and uniforms were all at my house. God, what about Mrs Levesque? Did she make it out? If they got Joe, they would have had to contact her. Ugh. My new bed. I just bought the most comfortable mattress in the world. It took months to choose, and it was on clearance."

David listened with vested interest to her blubbered mourning. It gave him a unique perspective on her heart.

"All my pictures from childhood, college, my duty stations. Ugh, my address book. How could they be so cruel?" She fell silent with a stuttering sigh.

Rivers licked his top lip and risked a question. "Who is they?"

"I don't know." Her voice sounded far away and her head burrowed deeper into his shoulder. His ribs' earlier protests had now turned into a screaming match. He had to move. Soon. "It seems like one thing after another. Like I am being attacked, personally. I feel like I have a bull's eye on my forehead."

Footsteps clunked on the cobblestone a block away, coming in their direction.

Rivers touched Judah's forearms and glided his hands up her arms to rest on her shoulders. He tugged her gently away from his body. "Sorry." She shivered as she looked down to the right. She wiggled to back off his lap, to get her feet back under her.

He pressed one hand against her shoulder to keep her still. He brushed a chin-length section of bangs out of her eyes. "Nope." He told her.

The footsteps increased their pace.

"What?" Her eyes cautioned him.

"No bull's eye."

"Hey! What's going on?" Rivers recognized Nelson's voice. The pace became a canter. "Commanders?" Rivers did not release Wakefield though she squirmed.

"Let me up."

"You're not embarrassed, are you, Judah?" Rivers spoke low enough to make sure he was not overheard.

"Is everybody all right?" Nelson was ten feet away.

"You could never embarrass me."

"Is that a challenge?" Rivers cocked an eyebrow. "We're fine, Chief."

"Let me rephrase." She hissed in his ear. "You could never *mortify* me."

Rivers felt Nelson swaying like a tower over them. "Well, snap to, or something." Nelson sputtered. "We have a development. Looks like you two have a development as well."

Rivers snorted at the station chief's attempt at a military order. "You can't order us to 'snap to or something.' However, I bet, if we both ask nice, Commander Whallop-The-Enemy will release her prisoner."

"You attacked the commander?" Nelson's jaw dropped low.

"I did not. Okay, maybe I did." She shrugged and backed off his lap, pushing against his thighs for support. "He startled me." She lowered her hand from her position over him. "Keep your sternum and core straight as you pull up."

"Now you tell me." Rivers aligned his hips and shoulders, bunching his thigh muscles and arms to rise with his partner's help. "What's the development?"

Nelson was studying Wakefield's demeanor. To shield her from scrutiny, Rivers stepped into the chief's line of sight and repeated his question. "Let's walk."

"There is a second room paid for by one of the brother's credit cards. I asked one of the clerks to run his number through their computer."

"Maybe he brought his wife and kids along." Rivers slowed them down for Wakefield to catch up after retrieving her coat.

"More likely his mistress. I called both rooms. No answer either place."

"Maybe the ringer is off. I understand that is a common occurrence." Wakefield gave the men a blank look.

Nelson held her look for a moment and then resumed his pace. "Perhaps it is that simple, but I want you two there. We're going in." Nelson made eye contact with Wakefield around Rivers again. "I am sorry for your loss, Commander. Dietz told me, but asked that I let him deliver the news."

40

The trio stood at the front entrance when Chad hailed them. He loped across the street. His baggy clothes and stringy black hair, when combined with the black Kevlar vest with no markings and the heavy-duty pistol strapped to his waist, created an amusing paradox.

"When did they start giving guns to children?" Rivers teased the younger man.

"Yesterday," he quipped easily, "when the adults could not finish the job without help."

"Congratulations, Chad." Wakefield stepped between the two before the playful insults degraded. "I understand you were assigned to help the presidential team with sweeping."

"Where are your men?" Rivers leaned around her shoulder.

"Well," Chad looked down, "I don't think congratulations are in order. But thanks. I am searching cupboards, mailboxes, windowsills, flagpoles, and garbage containers for explosives. And you're not *supposed* to see us, Commander." Chad gave Rivers a funny nose twitch that made him look like a rabbit to Wakefield.

"Anything suspicious?" Rivers sounded almost eager. With his explosives background he probably would love to get his hands on some bomb to de-rig. It would be better than all this paper pushing and dead-end chasing.

Wakefield tilted her head to include the two men in her field of vision at the same time.

"I haven't seen anything." Chad smoothed his long hair.

"What's the chief concern?" Rivers moved along side and looked back at the hotel where they were now stationed.

Chad lifted his arm to point behind them. "The Kempi's street-side windows."

Wakefield joined the men in viewing. There were over a hundred possible crow's nests just on first glance.

"There's 168 windows, 126 rooms to account for. In both security checks, no one with more than level-three risk was registered."

"You're kidding. Wakefield has at least level four." Rivers looked sideways at her without moving his head.

Was he joking? He'd better be. Though with my record...

"Wakefield is not a guest in the hotel, sir." Evidently, Chad could not tell if he was funning either. "However I have a message for her."

Wakefield watched Chad unzip his vest and reach into his top pocket. "From Yates." He smiled. "He said he was sorry he didn't get to say good-bye, but he would like you to come visit him in London." The younger agent passed the card to her. "That's his address, phone numbers and e-mail." Chad paused. "I think he really liked you, ma'am."

"Doesn't everybody?" Rivers voice sounded like the growl of a lion beside her.

She saw Chad's thick eyebrows shoot up. "Oh, not me, sir. I don't like her." Wakefield couldn't see Rivers' face, but she imagined it to be fierce as Chad took a tentative step back.

"You don't?" She acted hurt. "Why not?"

Chad licked his lips twice before he could begin to stammer. "I, well, I didn't mean it like that. Of course, I like you. I am just not attracted to you."

Wakefield stifled her laughter. This felt good to her soul. "So you think I am ugly?"

"Oh, no. You are hot. It's just that, um, well, you are so old." His lips pulled back revealing straightened teeth. His eyes widened and he licked his lips again. "I mean, so much older than me. Ugh. That's not right either." Chad's eyes begged Rivers for a lifeline.

Rivers shook his head. Wakefield wished she could see his face without making it obvious.

"So, now I am an old hag. Is that it?" Wakefield touched her hands to her hips.

The door opened behind them. "Commanders," Nelson called in a tired voice. "Quit harassing my agent. Mr Wellingham, you've delivered your message, get back to work."

Chad expelled his breath. "Gladly, sir," he squeaked, already stepping backward off the low curb.

Wakefield could not contain her laughter. "See you later, Chad."

Kempi Room 411
0500 hours

Azure Tiger returned to the blinds of room 411. He watched a harried director organizing the men to move bleachers from a lorry to set up on either side of the *Steigenburger Berlin Hotel*'s entrance. He leaned into the glass pane. Further down *Ku'damm Strasse* the police were already cordoning off the traffic.

"My, what eager beavers we have." He lifted his left arm. "We have five more hours."

The man in front of the flagged hotel across from his perch waved his hands around outrageously, pointing out the orchestra area to a man carrying what had to be a tuba case strapped to his back. The director ran wide-spread fingers through his long gray hair that looked full of static the way it stood out wildly from his head.

"Reminds me of my hairpiece." He chuckled as the director tried to pat his hair back into place as a slim violinist approached. It still looked electrical. "I have the same problem, man."

Azure Tiger watched the U.S. Secret Service plainclothes security team sweep the three-block area. They spoke into their wrists and tapped their ears. A third of them were dressed as early morning joggers. The assassin rolled his eyes at their white sneakers. He could give them a few tips about blending in.

He reached to the right of the window where a black box sat on a small side table he had moved into place. He jiggled the knob on the radio receiver and turned the volume clockwise. American voices invaded the quiet room. Curt answers to short questions seemed to be the order for the morning.

"Awe, man!" A disembodied voice groaned.

"Report, Bluebird 16."

"It's nothing."

"What do you see, Bluebird 16?"

A chuckle choked over the air. "This is Bluebird 17; 16 is whining because the hotel bakery disposed of three-quarters of a turtle cheesecake right where he was searching."

"It was perfectly good cheesecake, and they trashed it."

"Five-star service means no day-old cheesecake, Bluebird 16, don't you know that?" Azure Tiger assigned this voice to the dispatcher.

"On my salary? Are you kidding?"

The white noise of slight static went on for a full three seconds. It was followed by five taps on the mic. Azure Tiger cut his eyes to the side. Something was up. He turned and looked hungrily at the boxy radio on the table.

"This is nest to all birds. I have just received word: Eagle is ahead of schedule, by one hour."

"Ah," the assassin tucked his lips into his straight teeth. "Mr President will be here at nine o'clock." Azure Tiger swallowed. His mouth watered for this kill. He was just spared one-fifth of his wait.

"Somebody should let the M.C. know."

"Canary 12," the identification came over the waves. "I'm on it."

Kempinski Hotel
0440 hours

"He gave me a passkey." Nelson said.

"So I guess that gives us our operational strategy." Rivers watched Wakefield purse her lips. She seemed to have slipped into her agent role with no trouble. Her face was determined and clear. She was a woman of many masks. He looked at her eyes. They jumped from place to place, cataloguing and aware. They betrayed her calm exterior. She did not like going in without options.

"We will visit one room, then the other. Together. What are the numbers?" Rivers looked to Nelson.

The station chief's eyes bagged with lack of sleep, but he was sharp enough to need no notes. "Rooms 768 and 327. Start with the lower floor. Escape from the higher one will take longer."

"Agreed." He and Wakefield spoke together.

Nelson slapped the shoulder of the dark-headed agent who was on elevator duty. "Watch for third or seventh floor activity."

The agent nodded without speaking.

Nelson opened the stairwell door for Wakefield to go first. "Wait." The call came from behind them. Faulkenburg hailed them with an open hand while performing a stylized speed walk that looked duckish.

Rivers cleared his throat, "Save us from people trying to maintain dignity by not running or yelling in an emergency.

"Sorry," the manager breathed. "I thought I had better go with you, so I can apologize, in case you burst in during the middle of something." He smiled tightly.

"Come on," Nelson waved the man to follow. "But please, stay in the hall until we clear you."

Rivers drew his sidearm as they climbed the stairs to demonstrate the reason without cold words. From the Bulgarian's highly arched brows, Rivers' calculated move had the desired effect.

Room numbers were not posted on a sign and attached to the doors of the Kempinski Hotel. Each door's identification was clearly etched in flowing script into the wooden surface above a flowering vine Rivers did not recognize.

Nelson rapped firmly on the solid door. It made a dull thud. Wakefield called out, "Housekeeping," in German, followed by English.

No response. No movement.

Nelson unzipped the black leather binder he had been carrying under his arm. He unwound a cable to about nine feet and turned on the five by seven flat screen in the case.

Rivers took the camera end of the cable and threaded it under the door. Five inches. He had to press his fingertips into the plush carpet to move the cord. He panned the interior left to right.

"Entryway is clear. We can't see the bed though." Wakefield whispered above him. "Nice display contrast," she complimented Nelson's equipment.

"Withdraw, Commander." Nelson spoke. "Let's go in." Rivers pulled the cable out.

He heard the electronic lock release with a click. He stood and pushed the long, metallic handle down. He was glad neither of the others challenged his going first. The door stood open an inch. Wide enough to check for a safety chain. Holding the pistol at his right ear, pointed toward the fourth floor, he chambered one round.

In a practiced burst of energy, Rivers entered the room. He leveled the gun at his shoulder. The closed bathroom door did not have a telling crack of light. The blinds threw silvery streetlamp shadows on the wall. The curtains were open.

One of the other three flipped on the overhead light. He preferred to work in the dark.

The bedspread lay smooth.

Rivers bent his elbow to raise his weapon toward the ceiling. "All clear."

Wakefield sighed. "768."

Rivers hid the roll of his eyes as the Bulgarian did his own sweep of the room. Apparently, he found everything to his satisfaction, for he trotted along behind the three of them to the stairwell. The manager's natural coloring had faded into a pasty green.

41

"**D**oesn't it seem a little odd to you, Mr Faulkenburg, that a man has paid for two rooms in your hotel, yet is not in either one of them?" Nelson looked back into the room.

Wakefield watched the black-haired man shrug his crossed arms. "Who knows what a man is thinking."

She was trained to read body language. This man's demeanor screamed covered defensiveness. Maybe it was just nerves. Maybe he knew more than he was saying.

"I've got to interview some of the maids before they start their rounds." She moved around the others standing in the hall. An idea occurred to her. "Mr Faulkenburg, would it be possible for me to see the penthouse before I leave? My friend was telling me about how opulent it is."

She suddenly felt awkward when Rivers and Nelson turned their eyes on her.

"Sorry, beautiful sailor, the penthouse is occupied. Perhaps the Englishman will check out before you have to leave town." He raised his eyebrows lightly. "I will call and you can come have lunch with me, hmm?"

Wakefield returned his smile. "That would be generous of you, Mr Faulkenburg." She did not exactly say yes.

"An Englishman, you say?" Nelson's eyes seemed to pierce the Bulgarian. "What is the man's name?"

Wakefield felt, rather than saw, Rivers tense as they waited for the reply.

"A gentleman from London. Wonderful customer. James Yates."

"But...but Yates." She was speaking, but was not sure what she was trying to say, or to think.

"Yates left for London yesterday morning." Nelson raised his chin and looked down his nose at the man who was his same height.

"No. He is here. I assure you, one does not forget to check out of a 2000 euro per night penthouse."

Wakefield felt light headed. *What? Weird.*

She looked to Rivers and then Nelson. They were looking at each other.

Maid Readyroom
Kempi Sub-basement
0519 hours

Tatiana was right. Wakefield felt her heart quicken like it always did when she stepped into a battlefield. The Guatemalan women looked like they belonged to a gang, down to the matching white kerchiefs they tied on their heads. There were four women that stuck together. The Kempi housekeepers rushed around to meet the day.

Wakefield watched from the doorway as the mammoth Lupe-Maria shoved two women out of her way at once. She elbowed a hefty unnaturally red red-head in the ribs, and the ample flesh of her backside threatened to knock a slight, gray-headed woman off her feet. Lupe-Maria's tent-uniform billowed around her as she backed her cart closer to the doorway. She did not bother looking behind.

Tatiana caught Wakefield's attention as she peeked out from her locker. She winked one coal-colored eye, as if to say, "I warned you, good luck."

"Excuse me," Wakefield jumped right in, raising her voice over the women's clatter.

Lupe-Maria turned her bulk around faster than Wakefield thought possible. "You aren't supposed to be down here." She left her cart and waddled closer. A gap spaced her front teeth. Her girls, admittedly much smaller, moved in behind her.

Wakefield had to bend her neck back to look at her, the woman stood so close to her. *She might be taller than Rivers*, Wakefield decided. It was definitely time to start throwing her own weight around.

She leaned forward inches from the olive-colored house who wore a Kempi apron. She touched a warning finger to the woman's upper chest, an inch below her collar bone. "Take a seat." Wakefield copied her Basic Training instructor's tone that implied, "do what I say, or become guacamole."

Lupe-Maria did not look as though she wanted to comply, especially in front of all her colleagues that she had intimidated into submission.

"This is not about you," Wakefield whispered in Spanish as she brushed between two of the Guatemalan women.

She switched back to German. "I am Lieutenant Commander Wakefield of the United States Naval Intelligence. I'm working with our CIA to uncover a man who is trying to kill our president in a few hours. I need your help." She used her best inspirational voice on the woman who stood in various states of dress. One by one they finished buttoning up their dresses and dropped, back to back, on the long wooden benches in the center aisle.

"Sit." Lupe-Maria growled. The few women who were still standing because the seats were all taken, actually dropped to the concrete floor at her command.

Wakefield felt her cheeks start to bunch. She squashed the grin. Lupe-Maria had them well trained, even if it was through fear. "I have found that maids have better access to and more knowledge of what goes on in hotels than anyone else." A little flattery never hurt. "Has anybody noticed any people who..." Wakefield repeated the whole list of characteristics that she had assigned to Azure Tiger over the weeks she had been working on the case.

The 47 women on duty stirred. Some looked at each other, some looked down. No one looked at her. A woman with short, black hair sitting next to the laundry chute elbowed the woman next to her.

Lupe-Maria surprised Wakefield, speaking first to offer information. "Alejandra, Marta and I were just saying the other day that we all have a room where no one sleeps. Sure someone comes in everyday and throws back the covers and throws the towels on the floor, but there is no trash. The television control is always in the same place."

"The suitcases have never been opened." Alejandra added as she pushed back the kerchief on her forehead with wide-spread fingers.

Wakefield turned slightly on her heel to look between the two women. "Were rooms 327 and 768 involved?" Three black heads nodded dumbly.

At that, the floodgate was beaten down by each woman trying to best the last with her strange guest stories.

Wakefield was able to pick out one over the next 25 minutes that, while it did not sound case-related, it did peak her interest. A wrinkled woman in her late forties raised her hand. "I have had a similar experience in the penthouse. The last few weeks it has been rented to the same man." Wakefield waved her hands to shush everyone. "The man, I did see him once, he was dreamy for an Englishman. Not that pasty skin." *She had to be talking about Yates, but why would he have been here for weeks?* "Everything neat as a pencil when I arrive. Bed tidy, shower wipe down, toilet seat clean." She raised her thin eyebrow knowingly at the others. "The garbage be bagged outside door."

Wakefield could feel her eyes growing larger as her head lowered with incredulity. She owed them some explanation, she knew. Finally, a small giggle escaped. "I'm sorry." She tried to flatten her grin. "I am friends with Mr Yates of the penthouse. And I had no idea he was so…so…"

"Freakish?"

The voice was from behind her. Rivers had found her this time. "Perhaps that is a little strong." She wondered how much he had heard. And when had she lapsed into English? "A meticulous perfectionist." *Why had she said a few weeks? She must have misspoken and meant days.*

Wakefield watched the atmosphere in the room change. The women straightened their posture, more smiles appeared. Hands straightened uniforms and smoothed back hair. How did he do it?

"Is there such a thing as an *un*-meticulous perfectionist?" Rivers' voice put him closer behind her now. She had not heard his movement.

"Yes. Me." She heard a covered snicker from the left corner.

"I beg to differ." He whispered right behind her now.

"Ladies, may I introduce my partner, Lieutenant Commander Rivers." He must have made some funny gesture behind her, because the whole group burst into giggles. "Get out here so I can see you, mister." She reached back and blindly found his hand. She pulled him up even with her.

"Now back on point." A young woman with shy eyes raised her hand from her seat on the concrete. "Yes?" Wakefield waited for her to speak.

"German okay?"

Wakefield nodded.

"I have the earth floor." The girl's German was halting at best, though understandable. "Room zero-one-seven is same as other rooms. All clean, no work. But only two of three days. Crazy." She shrugged. Judah wrote down the room number.

"I have a suite that looks like hell broke loose. One of the filthiest I have ever seen." The speaker's nose looked like a beak. "And I have seen some. There was also a gun in the table."

"Room number?"

"489."

Another half hour passed and Wakefield had a list of 35 or 40 rooms to research, a sore back, and a stomachache from laughing so hard at the strange habits of Kempi guests.

The elevator dinged closed and Rivers pressed the lobby button. "Thanks." She leaned against the shiny wall. "You loosened them up well." She reached over to pat his forearm. "As soon as you showed up, all the girls were anxious to talk."

42

Dietz crushed his third paper coffee cup and slammed it with the others in the trashcan beside his desk. "Ugh." He swore under his breath. "Where are they? Why won't they answer their phones? They are supposed to keep them on their persons, that's why they are portable."

He sat in the pool of light spilling from his desk lamp. The gas logs on the right wall hissed. He picked up the black handset and dialed the fourth floor in hopes that if he did it personally, it would make a difference.

Four rings before the answering service picked up and a pleasant female voice that he did not recognize asked him to leave a message.

Dietz tried Nelson's cell and Rivers' SatFone. Nothing.

He groaned and stomped his foot twice under his desk. "You all know I *hate* to be kept in the dark." He warned the three people who were not present. "This debrief will be reminiscent of the Spanish Inquisition for all three of you."

He shook his head feeling ready for a shower. He was pretty sure he smelled overripe, too. "As soon as this fiasco is through."

"Room service." A tiny tuxedoed man announced in English at the door to Faulkenburg's office. Rivers looked at Nelson then his partner who was slouched on the sofa in the manager's office. "We didn't order anything."

Nelson was quick to follow with, "What have you got?" He tossed his half-size magnifying glasses on the manager's desk that he had commandeered hours earlier when he tired of the spinning chair.

"Herr Faulkenburg sent this up for you. Coffee and a light breakfast." The server wheeled in his cart and began to set up by the window without prompting.

While Rivers watched, the small man uncovered servings of porridge, sausage, brochen, butter, chocolate spread, and cheese slices. He set up a half cantaloupe filled with diced fruit for them to serve themselves. He sensed Wakefield perk up at the mention of coffee. The server hid the silver dome lids under the gauzy curtain on the cart.

"This is a light breakfast?" Rivers felt drawn to the colorful plates and heard his stomach rumble.

"Mm. It smells delicious. Please send our regards to the cook and Herr Faulkenburg." Wakefield reached over him for the silver carafe of coffee.

The laser printouts of the history of each room did not make exciting breakfast reading material. "Hey," Rivers smashed his bite of cheese and brochen to the inside of his cheek and brushed a crumb from his chest. "All of Einstein's brother's rooms are on this list, along with the mistress's room from earlier."

"A quarter of all the rooms in the hotel are on this list, Commander." Nelson's ran his fingers through his hair and sighed.

"I wish we could just evacuate the whole hotel and look every person in the eye." Wakefield popped a grape in her mouth. "But where would we put them and how?"

"I could pull the fire alarm." Rivers frowned. *It wasn't a bad idea.*

"But the courtyard and street could not hold 1500 people, especially with the band setting up. It would drive the secret service guys mad." Wakefield shook her head.

"Well, we have to do something." The white walls and colorless furnishings of Herr Faulkenburg's office were closing in on his mind.

"I think he has to make the next move." Wakefield reclaimed her seat on the sofa heavily.

Rivers could not believe his ears. "His next move is going to be a double shot to the heart of the President of the United States." The bile rose in his throat just saying the words out loud.

"I hate to take sides," Nelson tapped the white oak desk top with a manicured fingernail, "but I agree with the commander."

"Which one?" Wakefield and Rivers spoke simultaneously.

Nelson chortled in the back of his throat. "Rivers."

Wakefield seemed to press her back further into the overstuffed cream-on-cream tone sofa as she crossed her arms. "Well, do you have any bright ideas on how to smoke him out?" She seemed to think twice about her sharp tone and added a more submissive, "sir."

Nelson nodded and reached for the phone on the manager's desk. Rivers noted with disgust that it was also colorless. "It is time to check in with the boss." Nelson dialed the touch-tone buttons with a pencil eraser.

"Dietz," Wakefield whispered the name.

Rivers could not tell if it was a good whisper or a bad whisper. Her posture and features ambiguous to him. She never said anything to point to her loss, but occasionally, he caught an unguarded expression of fresh pain. The responsibility gnawed at him. "I will make this right for her," he vowed silently. David was pushed back into the padding of his chair with the forcefulness of the place the vow was birthed from.

The chair squeaked under the pressure, so he knew he had not imagined it. Slowly David released his breath in a sniper's controlled, silent, hidden way.

A memory as vague as a déjà vu tickled his mind. When had he been in this place in his spirit before?

David stilled his body, controlling his breathing as he'd been taught by LT Rudd so many years earlier in BUD/S. Only his eyes moved as he scrolled through his memories looking for a time when he had felt the strength of an emotion—almost a mandate—like this before.

People still jabbered around him and part of his brain catalogued it all—he even responded correctly to a couple of benign questions Nelson asked him around the phone tucked under his chin. But David's spirit was unsettled.

Memories flited across the screen of his heart. The young boy he had spared and who had then given away their position in Kosovo. The explosion that had destroyed two SEAL families, Tom's and Mikey's. Their faces and their wives' faces flashed in his mind.

The peace he felt when first coming into Jesus' arms at 19 years old washed over him. His identity in his family. The love and security he felt there. Among his team. The what-ever-it-takes, invincible-SEAL substance charged through his veins. Was it an antibody or a pathogen? He'd never made a determination before, because it was both. How was this vow functioning in him now, an antibody or pathogen?

Filasek's bearded face flashed, his now-dead wailing-wall buddy. Judah hugging him good-bye in the convoy-truck. His promise to Filasek in that moment.

No compromise. No release. I'm a man of my word. It's who I am. The thoughts were so strong David was sure he had whispered them aloud. Yet, Nelson still spat instructions into the phone, and Judah still stirred her coffee while closely following Nelson's side of the conversation with some sarcastic, not-quite-under-her-breath commentary from the sofa, so he supposed he had not.

David stared at Judah, her face going back and forth from its current "conversation" with Nelson to those long minutes when he stitched her cheek back together. He had swallowed the emotion of that day in a big SEAL gulp, but it revisited him in the oddest moments.

He couldn't shake the rage he felt at Filasek for hurting Judah. Sometimes he had to nurse that rage and give it vent so it wouldn't overwhelm him.

But what was this old-new feeling, uneasiness, in his heart? *I protect that which I love. I think I love her.* Filasek may have had some luck escaping justice in the past, but he'd never had a SEAL come for him. *I will find him, and I will set it right for her.* Rivers doubled down on the vow.

Why now? Is this right? The questions briefly flitted across his mind, but he dismissed them. He was distracted by the "I think I love her" recognition and all it was rearranging in his heart.

Kempi Hotel
Room 411
0550 hours

Azure Tiger bayed back and forth in front of the window wall. His long limbs hung loose on his upright core. His feet padded the marble floor, each step light, yet shifting his weight with precision ease. T.S. Eliot's smoke cat could have learned from his moves.

A gray line streaked the horizon.

He stopped to check the evidence. He trotted at the same animal pace to the bathroom. The flip of a switch swathed the room in blinding light.

The clear glass with the bottom lip print of Judah Wakefield shined on the countertop. A second glass, unmatched of course, kept it company. He could see his own finger print on the crystal. The lotion he had used still sat on the counter.

In the bedroom, the covers were mussed and the sheets pooled to the floor on one side. A single strand of blond hair lay like an undisturbed queen on the pillow he had dented to the right depth with his own head. The second pillow lay discarded on the carpet.

It was perfect.

If there was only a way to get her prints on something immovable in the room, it would be ironclad.

"Filasek will live to regret this assignment." The India-born man swore. Then he laughed. "Maybe he won't."

287

43

"**W**here have you guys been?" Dietz's voice assaulted Wakefield's ears from the speakerphone on the far side of the office. "I've been calling for hours."

Judah grimaced as she remembered turning off the SatFone after their conversation. "Sorry," she called out. "That was my fault."

"Where are you and what's going on with POTUS?"

"Um," Nelson cleared his throat. "This is an unsecured line, sir." The announcement told the director of counterintelligence that they would have to talk in code.

Wakefield pushed away from the cream-colored couch as Nelson explained the situation. Her voice hurt trying to project across the room while she was tired. She leaned down and rested her elbows on the white oak desktop. "Have there been any developments on the backward money trace, Dietz?" She was counting on them finding the killer as he took the shot. Putting the man who was behind the hiring out of commission was what she craved.

"Actually, some. Roger broke through the Swiss cheese and went back 87 bounce-accounts all over the world. I'll e-mail you the list if you'd like. He traced it as far as Athens, Greece to an account that was open for 10 days in the name of a man who has been dead since 1947."

Rivers twirled a pen through his thick fingers. "Talk about dead ends." Rivers huffed as he tossed the pen onto the desk.

"Probably. But I'll send a Company man to view the bank's tapes. If they have any."

Rivers straightened up. "Why don't you cut off the credit cards of the Munich guys. If fact, let's tip off the front desk of their hotel. Maybe they know where to reach their boss. We will get an operator to flag any calls from Munich here."

"Interesting," Wakefield thought aloud. *At least it was something.*

"At least it would be something," Rivers spoke her thoughts. He had not done that in a while. She could not stop the slow smile tugging at her lips.

"Give it a try, Commander. You've got Wakefield to back you up if you decide to go breaking into someone's hotel room."

They all three exchanged looks and decided without words not to tell the director that they already had. "Mr Nelson has been enjoying field duty, too, Dietz." Wakefield offered the older man a teasing wink. "He knows how to do more than push paper."

"I know. I wouldn't have recommended him for my replacement if he was not salty."

Nelson squared himself professionally in Herr Faulkenburg's chair. Wakefield did not miss the way his chest puffed slightly and his eyes lit up at the compliment from his boss. She made a mental note to mention it to Dietz. Later.

Tegel International Airport, Berlin
Airforce One
7:45 AM

"Mr President, you can't leave. You will arrive too early." Michael Hanratty, the youngest man to ever head a presidential public relations office stood blocking the airplane door. He gripped a pen in his left hand and a clipboard with a schedule columned next to a checklist rested inside his curved forearm.

"The early bird gets the worm, as they say." The U.S. President touched his freshly shaved jaw. "I am ready to go, so I am going." A touch of humor played at his lips. "They don't call me 'Eagle One' for nothing."

Hanratty sighed and shook his head, his spiky gelled hair not budging a fraction of an inch. He stepped back as the president moved toward the door. "But, sir." Hanratty's eyes dove for his checklist and he readjusted his earpiece connected with the M.C. "The timpani player has not yet arrived. And the people will not be there to greet you. Low numbers will not create the look we—I—was going for. That is if the camera crews are even there yet."

The Secretary of State, approached from the left passageway. "Hanratty," the deep voice of a movie villain thundered at him. "Are you standing in the path of your president because some poor German musician overslept and is late for work?" the secretary's face darkened and his fudge-colored eyes widened.

"Yes, sir. Uh, no, sir. I don't know." Hanratty felt his knees locking. Some days he wished he was back in grad school and had never heard of this job.

"Which is it, son?" The president's mouth quivered and his tiny lips disappeared altogether.

Is he laughing? This is not a laughing matter. "Um, the timpani player, he is French—"

"Ah, the French." The president's head rolled back as he looked toward the ceiling. "It seems there is no end to the trouble the French want to cause me." He touched his forehead as if to alleviate a coming migraine.

Hanratty stood a moment in indecision. The Secretary of State stared at him. He felt as big as a clove of garlic in a swiftly closing press. "I don't want him embarrassed by a small showing. The European press—" He shook his head. *There, it was out.*

The president let loose a low chuckle. It sounded borne of a lifetime of political service. "After all these months, you still don't know me, do you, Michael?" He sounded almost disappointed.

Hanratty felt his jaw disengage. He stepped to the side and unlocked the hatch for his boss to step through. He did not know that George W. Bush was aware of his first name.

"The president does not embarrass that easily." The Secretary's deep voice echoed in his head as they watched the proud-shouldered man descend the iron grate stairs to the U.S. Marine in dress blues waiting with his right hand one inch above his right eyebrow. "It is my personal opinion that he only puts up with the fanfare because it offers him the opportunity to hear the individual American's story personally. The man chooses his battles, and he is not going to object to a piece of red carpet and a woman's chance to sing the national anthem when he wants his nation's and the United Nations' support to free oppressed people groups from the strangle-hold of horrific regimes."

"Excuse me," Ms Jamison, a presidential speechwriter tapped his shoulder. He would recognize her voice anywhere. When he turned sideways, her light brown and highlighted bob was in perfect order, as always. "I need to run over a few last minute changes with the president." She lifted a perfectly arched brow.

"Sorry." Hanratty backed out of her way. Ms Jamison was a mighty asset to his team. He had not met anyone better with words. Her phraseology had the potential to sway a nation. He watched her trim, black-suited figure descend the stairs. He hoped that one day *his* words would sway her—to go out with him. Away from all the presidential circus noise.

A steady stream of people followed her. Twenty-two in all. They piled into the five black Excursions waiting on the tarmac.

Hanratty adjusted the phone earpiece again and spoke to the downtown director. "We are leaving the airport now. I hope you are ready for us."

"We'll have to be. Gotta go," was the short reply.

44

Faulkenburg's Office.
0755 hours

Rivers hung up the phone by dropping it the final three inches into the cradle. "He's on his way."

"What." Wakefield could not help yelping. "He's way early." She glanced at her watch. With the travel time to the *Steigenberger Berlin* from the airport, she weaved her head slowly, counting, the arrival would end up being another 25 minutes ahead of schedule.

Nelson scooted up to the edge of his seat. "He is probably just as anxious to have this done as we are."

"Maybe." Rivers shrugged. Wakefield knew the president was unconvinced. "But I am sure he realizes that entry into the hotel is not the only risk. Azure Tiger is an experienced assassin—"

"You don't need to tell me that, Commander." Nelson interrupted and huffed out his breath.

"He has the potential to be anywhere he wants to be, to look like anyone. He could shoot during the speech tonight on live TV, or walking down a hallway, or if the president ventures out onto his balcony, or even walking past a window."

Rivers sounded taut. Even in Afghanistan Wakefield did not see him this stressed. It dawned on her, in the desert, he was moving; he was doing something. Here, he was stuck, waiting; he could not be proactive like the SEALs taught him to be.

"Commander, we've been over this before." She tried a reassuring voice. "He will take his shot from the crow's nest. He has never broken his M.O. before. Inside the hotel, the president has been routed to avoid any two-story views. Azure Tiger will shoot while the target is outside and from the high ground."

Rivers stared at the white carpet. "How can you be sure? How do you know you have all the intelligence and history on this guy? Why isn't it possible that he might change this time?"

"It is my job to be sure, to get inside his head." She told him with more confidence than she felt. "I have studied him for ages. He is sitting up in his carefully chosen nest right now. Probably rechecking his bullets and getting hungry, rehashing his escape plan." She walked over closer to Rivers' haunt next to the window. "We have both been where he is. You know what it is like." She shook her head and ran her fingers through the ends of her blond hair.

She could use a brush. A shampoo would be better. Sleep and a shower would be best. Her dry contacts were beginning to stick painfully.

"Yeah. And I prefer that end to this waiting around. Our action is contingent on whatever he decides to do. Reaction." Rivers paced. "I hate it."

"Your control issue rearing its head again?" she asked softly. Undying personal issues seemed to be the theme on this mission. She remembered how soothing it felt when he prayed for her. Perhaps now was the time to return the favor.

Rivers stopped in front of the south window. He looked like the picture of Sampson in her white, childhood, zip-around Bible as he placed both hands on the insides of the window frame.

Remembering the outcome of the strongman's pillar-pushing day, she placed her hand just above the center of his back.

"Are you sure you two have only been partnered up once before?" Nelson's voice railroaded from the desk. She had briefly forgotten his presence.

She felt Rivers' intake of breath in her hand. His voice was a rich vibrato. "We have a bond that goes back a thousand generations, sir."

The words touched a deep part of her belly. The bridge of her nose tingled. She felt her eyes fill. *How could I have been moved by Yates' smooth delivery of romantic words?* Her mental picture of the Englishman and his kisses faded to dim color next to the vibrancy of the truth in David's assessment. He was right. There was already a commonality and a depth to their relationship before one date. Her heart could never achieve that connection with the kind and handsome James Yates.

She ducked inside his raised left arm and softly prayed so that only God and the two of them could hear. "God give your son, David, the strength to trust you to be in control of all things. Bring peace to the jumpy places inside. You are a good God and can be trusted with our best interests. Jesus, thank you for the gifts and abilities that you've entrusted to him."

She sighed and slowed her speech. She did not want to continue with the words she felt she was supposed to pray next. "Continue to hone those skills, that he might serve you in the fullness of your plan."

Wakefield smiled at the sound of Nelson shuffling papers that did not need shuffling.

Rivers dropped his chin to rest, momentarily, on the top of her head. "Thanks," he breathed.

Kempinski Room 411
0810 hours

He checked his watch again. His stomach rumbled. There was time. He dialed room service. A fat American cheeseburger, French fries and a large Coca Cola in honor of the soon-to-be-dead American president.

Azure Tiger's lips curled back. The tension of the wait brought almost the same high that the kill produced. Forty-five minutes to go. Time to implement the first phase.

The food would arrive in 20 minutes. He walked to the window. Just enough time to find the diversion he was searching for.

The window latch was cold to his touch. He slid the glass left. Wind eddied into the room. "Mm. Smells like snow."

He left the wooden slats in place. The radio relay of the little plain-clothes ants below kept him in the protected loop. "All clear" sounded from every station. At 0825 the final sweep would begin.

"Each team move one position clockwise on your sheet." The instruction crackled over the system to all the teams of two on the ground.

Azure Tiger checked his copy, downloaded from the secured Internet site. "Hm. That puts Bluebird 16 and 17 at the west dumpsters. Perfect location for a body dump."

He scoped the men as they made the change in position. "They're good. I'll give them that." The assassin whispered to the stock of his .50 caliber Browning. There was no joking among the ranks now. The Americans sweeping the area stuck to business.

He squeezed one eye shut as a young man with scraggly black locks walked into his cross hairs. "Get a haircut, man." Azure Tiger encouraged him disparagingly from five stories up. "You look like a girl."

He pivoted the scope further right. The gathered crowd shivered in heavy coats on metal bleachers. The M.C. coached them off mic, but his bass voice boomed the distance to Azure Tiger's open window.

Two men dressed in solid black, ex-marines he guessed from their disciplined stance, scanned the two hundred people who waited for the president's arrival. Of the two hundred ticket holders, he knew that 39 were children. A day that they would describe to their grandchildren: January 25, 2002. A Black Friday. Maybe.

He ran his clarifying scope past the striped blinking police blockade to the thousand or so people that filled the sidewalks as far as he could see. In some places, they spilled into the streets. Droves of uniformed policemen kept the streets passable.

He focused again on the Secret Service teams. Number sixteen of the Bluebird team looked to be arguing with his partner. His hands were tense on his hips, his jacket slung open, despite the chill. It showed a white T-shirt with an emblem at the left breast. He lowered the scope from the man's face and the blue words came into focus: Kansas City Little League Coach of the Year.

"How honorable of you, Coach," he spoke to the man, "to become a martyr for your president. I hope your kid appreciates your sacrifice."

Two gray-green dumpsters squatted side by side. Coach pointed to his partner and the one closest to the road, then to himself and the other. They began to climb.

Azure Tiger felt of the atmosphere outside his window. He checked the flags and signage for breeze movement. Three, maybe four kilometers per hour.

Coach reached the lip of the garbage container first. He straddled it as his partner swung his leg over the edge, facing away from the *Kempi*.

Azure Tiger focused on the base of the slower man's skull. He was in need of a haircut *and* a dye job. The new growth was largely laced with gray.

The Browning was set to deliver two bullets with one pull. The metal trigger rested comfortably under the crook of his first finger. Exactly halfway between the tip and the first joint.

He braced his right foot sideways behind him. The silencer added to the kick back. And he would prefer to shoot prone. But the roof was completely out of the question. Coach grimaced at something his partner said.

Azure Tiger pulled the trigger.

He refocused the crosshairs before the bullets had found their mark. Only a half an inch adjustment on the barrel.

The cross hairs met between the E and the A in "League" on Coach's shirt. Before his face had time to register surprise, death had hit him square in the chest, twice.

Both bodies fell into the refuse of the gray-green temporary coffins.

He pulled the muzzle inside the window. "Ah." He exhaled long, counting off the seconds. "Three, four, five." He scanned the crowd below him. People were moving, of course, but none in a great hurry, and none in the direction of the fallen men.

The assassin turned the volume knob on the radio to the right and picked up the mic. "This is Bluebird 16," he said. "We've got something." He added a dose of fear to his voice for good measure.

"Go ahead Bluebird 16." The dispatcher's voice flowed into room 411.

"We are in the east side dumpster, second from the last. Nest, request you send the bomb squad." He dropped his voice. "But don't get too close. Seventeen and I triggered the motion sensor. It is pretty sophisticated. The clock is counting down, sir. Eighteen minutes."

"Do either of you have experience in explosives?" The dispatcher's voice hiked up an octave.

"Seventeen is shaking his head, sir." The assassin played out everything exactly as he had planned two days earlier. "And my experience is limited to red wire/black wire. Sorry, sir. This is serious." Azure Tiger pulled the tiny mic away from his mouth and smiled. Then he brought it back. "I don't want to die today, sir."

"We will see that you don't, Sixteen. Sit tight."

Azure Tiger dropped the gun to his side and replaced the microphone. He straightened his back. "I'll do that," he whispered. This was fun. "Huh! Interactive assassination. Maybe I'll sell the idea to a gaming company."

45

John Edwards, affectionately known to his crew as Ed, was today referred to as "Nest." He worked from an unmarked, new delivery truck two blocks east of *Steigenburger Berlin Hotel.* Instead of bread crates, the delivery truck was packed with two million dollars' worth of state of the art communication systems and video surveillance and recording equipment.

He could barely view the corner of the dumpsters where two of his men were trapped with a vicious-sounding bomb.

He reached a hand out to flip a toggle upward. His voice would now carry to all 78 men simultaneously. "We have a situation at the east dumpsters. Position 1-3-6. Men with explosives expertise proceed to this position. Do not approach within a 20-foot perimeter. A motion sensor has been activated. We will make decisions on site." Ed tucked a finger between his black turtleneck and his throat, and tugged it forward. "Bluebird 16 and 17 are inside with the bomb." It suddenly felt stifling inside the back of the truck.

"I have another hail from 16, Ed." The voice came from behind him. The two men, plus the driver, George, monitored all the equipment.

Ed flipped the toggle back. "Go ahead, Bluebird 16. This is Nest." He had a sinking feeling in his stomach. The reheated pizza he ate for breakfast tumbled over and over.

"I think the device has a sound sensor, too, sir. The little yellow lines seem to measure sounds from outside, the crowd, my voice even. Please pass that on, quickly."

The guy sounded scared. Ed looked up Bluebird 16's profile on the computer while he switched the toggle back up. "Men, we have a sound sensor to fight as well. I want my most experienced guys on this: Mitchell, Flannery, Jones, this means you. The rest of you stand back, ready to assist."

Ed twisted the mic away from his lips. "George, pull us back another two blocks. Just in case." The pressure in his shoulder was beginning to build. He reached up with his right arm to massage the old wound.

He pounded his sternum and swallowed hard. *I will never eat pizza for breakfast again,* he promised his digestive system.

Kempinski
0828 hours

The white walls felt like the inside of a ball. Rivers could not focus on anything, as if a ping-pong match, back and forth, was being played out in front of his eyes. Why do we have to stay in here anyway? "Can't we monitor the house computer from the lobby? Nobody is checking in or out right now."

Nelson stretched slowly. "I don't see why not." Rivers found himself at the door before the station chief had finished his sentence. "Your phone on?" Nelson asked as Rivers opened the door.

He patted his waist where he had clipped it. "Yes." He glanced at Wakefield who had her feet up on the couch. "Let's go partner. Back to the land of color." He stayed only long enough to see her feet slide to the floor and her hand wave him away.

"I'm coming, Dorothy." Her voice carried out into the hall.

That was funny. Rivers snorted. Four steps later, the little song beeped out from his phone. *Anchors Aweigh.*

He spoke hastily, "Rivers," before the second phrase of the song played.

"Commander, it's Chad." The young agent's voice sounded strained. He was talking too fast. "There is a bomb across the street in

299

the east dumpsters. Edwards is not planning to evacuate the people. There are too many. Will you come?"

Rivers felt the flash-heat of adrenaline hit his extremities. The colors of the hall only served to distract him. "On my way."

"There are sound and motion sensors, Commander. Be careful."

"That's brilliant. What happens when the band starts to play?" Maybe Azure Tiger had deviated from his mode of operation after all. Something niggled at the back of his mind.

"What's brilliant?" Wakefield asked from the hall behind him.

She is learning to walk as silent as a SEAL. "I just got an invitation to join the bomb squad. They need an expert." He grinned.

He smacked his phone off and watched her face blanch. She sucked in her breath. She gave a sad smile. "And you wrote the book. We'll hold things together here. Go save Berlin."

"Here you go." He tossed her the phone. "Keep it safe this time, huh?"

The morning air stung his face. *The temperature must have dropped 15 degrees since we were out here earlier.* He sniffed. "Smells like snow."

Digging in his pocket as he jogged, he pulled out his military ID. If these Secret Service people were worth their spice, he would not be able to get close to the scene without it.

Kempi room 411

Azure Tiger held his weapon like a ready sentry. He watched the men scramble from all over. "So a quarter of you consider yourselves explosives experts. Too bad there is no bomb. That could be fun. Twenty bomb experts blown up at once."

A familiar figure exited below him, pulling on his coat. "Rivers!" the assassin edged back from the window. He narrowed his eyes at the man's figure. "What are you still doing alive?"

Azure Tiger raised the gun to view the SEAL's disappearing back through the clarity of the scope. "Never trust a Greek thug to do an

Indian Royal's work." He lowered the weapon to his side. He would not risk the turkey and dressing for the apple cake glaze. The deadline for Rivers' death was past anyway, he excused himself the small mercy.

Kempi Lobby
0833 hours

Five long, black SUVs paraded down *Ku'damm Strasse.*

Cheers rose from the sidewalks of people. "He's early." Nelson's eyes widened and he raised his left arm, wrist up. Glancing at Wakefield and then back to his watch, she watched the decision form in his eyes. "You stay here and keep watching the computer." Wakefield watched him bolt for the lobby doors without looking back.

Alone, she looked around. One of the front desk clerks filed paper work and another clinked away on an adding machine with his back to her.

Herr Faulkenburg had moved back into his office at the same time as they had walked out. "How did I manage to be the one left behind? Again." She asked the computer screen.

Wakefield raked her hair back into a ponytail as she monitored the screen listing of patrons' breakfast orders, long distance calls and pay-per-view orders. An exciting 1,022 guest rooms. She glanced up every few seconds to watch the slow process of the presidential parade.

"Nelson must have been able to keep him in the vehicle. That is one conversation I would have loved to hear," she mused. "But those SUVs are only bomb-proof to a point.

The computer twittered at her. She had programmed the alert to sound on any of the 50 questionable room's activity.

"Four-eleven." She ran her tongue over her teeth wishing for her toothbrush which was still out in the rental car. "Wasn't that one of the Einstein brothers?" She ran her finger down the numerical list. It was registered in the name Dovlata.

A few clicks on the keyboard brought up his entire room history. He had reserved the room 2 January. Checked in on 18 January.

"A full week ago." Her voice bounced softly off the terminal. "Until now, no calls, no room service, no missing towels, no replaced soap."

The computer automatically updated the file with the man's order. "A hamburger with American cheese, fries and a Coke," she read. "That sounds awfully American, especially for breakfast." Her heartbeat quickened. Why would an American be ordering room service instead of being outside to greet his president?

She flipped the counter map of the building around to face her. She easily found 411. "Street side, and five floors up. It fits the profile."

She picked up the phone and dialed the restaurant. "Hold the order for room 411. I need to take it myself." She ordered the man who picked up the call.

"It left the kitchen moments ago."

Wakefield slammed the phone down on the run.

She had the cell phone; Rivers was not available. Nelson was gone. "I'm the one with no back up and I get the bad guy. Bad-guy, maybe." She corrected herself, but it was just a formality. She felt that little niggle of confirmation that she usually felt when the end was near.

She scribbled the room number on a piece of scratch paper she plucked from the shelves under the desk. She added a scrawled J.A.W. for Rivers and left it next to the terminal. "I'm checking out a lead. Room 411." She called to the filing clerk.

She grimaced. It was unorthodox, but it was the fastest way. She leapt up on the counter top and nimbly scrambled off the four-and-a-half-foot customer side. "Tell my partner when he comes in."

A light touch confirmed that her pistol was still at her back as she sprinted in a beeline for the elevator bank. A well-dressed mother and child emerged while she was 15 yards off. She decided not to draw her weapon until it was necessary. "Thank you, God, for perfect timing." She slipped into the elevator as the doors were sliding shut. Only one other person occupied the ascending room. The seven button was already lit when she punched the four with her middle finger.

"Hurry, hurry." She urged the lift cables. She tried to ignore the prying eyes of the gentleman in a fedora who stared at her fidgeting in the reflective brass door.

After an eternity, the doors released her. She dashed left.

The server had parked a silver service cart outside a door and was straightening the fabric covering the sides.

Wakefield broke into a jog when he began to rise. "Wait." He turned toward the noise, his hand poised to knock. She was just about there. "I'll take it in." She softened her voice as she got closer.

The baby-faced server lowered his hand but did not budge from the doorway. "You must sign for the food."

"No problem." She snatched the receipt from the boy's hands and scrawled her name on the bottom. It was illegible even to her.

The young man studied the up and down scratches. He turned it sideways and then back again. "What does it say? I can't read it."

This is unbelievable. "It says my name, Judah Wakefield. Now get out of here," she hissed at him. "I'll deliver the food for you. It's okay. I know the manager, Herr Faulkenburg."

Wakefield saw the boy's knees lock. *Not now, kid. Just be a slacker and go back to the kitchen.* "But I don't know Herr Faulkenburg." He crossed his arms and planted his feet. "Why are you so anxious to—"

She didn't allow him to finish. She drew the pistol from her waistband under her shirt. Careful to keep her aim from him directly, she waved the gun in the air. "Go back to the kitchen." Concern turned her voice into a low rumble. "There is an international assassin behind that door and you are about to get caught in friendly fire, because I will shoot you thorough, if I have to."

The boy's eyes bugged and his cheeks turned a mottled pink.

"Go on," she gestured back toward the lifts with her pistol. The tuxedoed youngster ran like a gangly antelope.

Unclipping Rivers' phone from her waist, she dialed Chad's number from memory. "Get Commander Rivers. Tell him I need back

303

up. Room 411. A-Sap!" She whispered the instruction into the phone and cut off the connection before his reply could alert the occupant of the room.

Surprise would offer her the upper hand. She pulled out the passkey. The silver cart slid to the side in silence.

If she was wrong, she could always bring the food inside and apologize.

She slid the keycard into the metal lock.

The light flashed green.

She inhaled deeply. *One, two, three*, she counted off.

The handle pushed down under her left hand. In her right, she cocked the pistol and held it close to her ear, pointing toward the ceiling.

She pushed the door in a half inch at a time to check for a safety chain. *Very bold of him*, she assessed.

The sounds of the crowd outside drifted to her ears. *His window was open?*

The door swung wider to the left and she leveled the gun, sweeping the room from right to left as the door left her uncovered.

Target kneeling by window. Heavy gun. Sniper scope. No one else in the room.

A sliver of light fell across the man's eyes.

Wakefield lowered her weapon a minute amount. "How did you know where?" She watched his bony index finger squeeze the trigger.

46

Rivers ran across *Ku'damm Strasse* and down to the first alley east of the presidential reception area. In the distance he saw a convoy of black SUVs coming. The M.C. must have seen the same thing, because the red carpet was being unrolled as Rivers rounded the corner.

A hand immediately pushed into the middle of his chest. Not hard enough to injure his ribs, but he could feel it.

"Lieutenant Commander Rivers, Navy SEALs," he spoke authoritatively and flashed his ID at the man in a jogging suit. "Where's the bomb?"

"Follow me," the fake jogger said. That was easier than Rivers had expected.

The men were creeping one foot in front of the other. They obviously took the motion sensor very seriously. The orchestra strains grew louder with last minute warm up runs. "What are they saying?" Rivers asked a young man over the music and cheering. Twenty or so agents were milling about. Mostly loners, some in pairs.

"Nothing. The men inside won't answer our hails."

Rivers kept walking at regular speed. He noticed that the alley was paved with concrete instead of cobblestone, making his movements easier. "Hey," he yelled to the three men when he was close enough to be heard over the orchestra.

The tallest of the three was closest to him. He put a finger to his lips.

"If the band did not detonate it," Rivers shrugged, "It's not sound sensitive. And I don't know of a device in the world that can be attached to a bomb and can sense movement through metal."

The three men straightened up as he spoke. They nodded sheepishly. "Who're you?" The closest man asked with a guarded expression.

"Rivers. Navy SEALs. Who is in charge here?"

"I am. Flannery." The man with British teeth and too small lips held out a hand. But Rivers was already walking away.

"Flannery, I'm going to take a peek over the side. Either back your men out, or come help."

"I'm with you. Normally I'd argue, but you've already proven right, so I won't." Flannery touched his mouth self-consciously.

"Good man." Rivers nodded. He would have hated to have a jurisdictional war while a bomb was counting down. "Who's inside?" Rivers gripped the metal container 10 inches above his head.

"Bluebird 16 and 17."

"All right, Bluebird 16 and 17," Rivers called over the edge. "I need you to call out if you are alive. Kick around, make some noise.

No response.

Only two explanations entered Rivers' mind. One, there was a gun to one of their heads and they would not risk the noise. Or two, they were unconscious or dead already.

No time for equipment to be brought in. The president was pulling up now.

Rivers tightened his grip and began to pull his body weight up with only the strength of his arms.

Fifteen inches up, his ribs screamed all the way.

He smelled the rotting food as he inhaled after the exertion.

Rivers focused on his white thumbs pointed toward each other. The rim needed paint. He categorized the contents in a fraction of a second.

His foot to the wall of the container helped push him back so he dropped to the concrete.

"All clear." He jutted his chin toward the dumpster as he spoke to Flannery. "No bomb, no men. Only garbage."

Flannery nodded once. He lifted his left wrist to his mouth and began speaking to dispatch. He waved five men over to double check the garbage. "The rest of you, over to the west side dumpsters. Double time."

Rivers weighed having left Wakefield with Nelson against searching out the rest of the bomb threat.

"Come on," Flannery called over his shoulder to him. "You waiting for an invitation?"

Rivers pushed off the concrete, jogging after the group. He glanced at the Kempi tower across *Ku'damm Strasse*.

The M.C. smoothed his wiry hair. He heard the "all clear" piped through the comm system in his left ear. The orchestra director knew to commence his final eight-count to establish rhythm as he touched the handle of the president's vehicle.

Armed marine guards in their creased dress blues formed a three-deep line on either side of the scarlet runner leading to the podium. The sound of heels clicked sharply in the breath-holding quiet.

The door handle felt icy to his ungloved fingers. The heavy door opened without a sound.

It was as if the president was privy to the unannounced count. He started out of the Excursion with his right foot. The M.C. smiled inside at the lime green striped black wool socks the president wore with his dress shoes and suit.

The U.S. President's foot hit the ground at the imaginary eighth beat. It appeared that his standing began the music, though the conductor's back was to the procession.

The M.C. allowed an outward smile at the precision. "*Magnifico!*" he pronounced. He could not have pulled that off if they had practiced 500 times.

The six marine guards saluted stiffly to the opening notes of *The Star Spangled Banner*. Leading the melody was a brass trumpet.

The shrill sound split the air. Even the guest of honor looked up. The six notes hung for two blank seconds before the trumpeter repeated them with the backing of a full orchestra.

The result was magnificent.

The sound held the majesty one might imagine in the Second Coming. George Bush raised his right palm to wave at the crowd that was jostling to its feet.

Marines in tandem escorted him forward. The marching steps now lost in the beating of the drum, the singing of the violins and cellos, the screaming of the brass instruments. Alongside people clapped and whistled.

When the trumpet began the home stretch, the M.C. could pick out the Americans in the crowd. They were the ones singing along, "Oh say does that star spangled banner yet wave..."

The president touched his hand to his heart, thin lips mouthed the final words along with his people, "and the home of the brave."

The M.C. felt a bubble of delight rise. While he did not equate the U.S. leader's arrival with Christ's triumphant return, he knew a successful presentation would guarantee him a pick of the best jobs in the future.

Room 411

The trumpet sounding startled both Wakefield and her target.

The shot came off the large weapon. She watched him brace against the heavy kick back.

"What is going on Yates?" Her mind strained to make sense of her friend's presence. "Why are you here? How did you know?"

She moved her gaze from his blue eyes down. She found the .50 caliber weapon now pointed at her midriff. A thin wisp of smoke floated upward from the muzzle. A gun of that size at this range, she calculated a hole in her body the size of Miami.

"I came to say good-bye, Judah."

She brought her aim back to his temple. "Are you going someplace?" her mind and her heart argued over finding Yates here. *I saw him pull the trigger.*

She saw the curve of his lips start upward. She studied him as he laughed at her and her little pistol, faced off against the sniper's weapon of war.

His laugh turned to a snarl and a mask fell over his features. The whites of his eyes looked yellow for a second before disappearing into slits. His jaw thrust forward unnaturally.

The music from the window swelled.

His voice sounded deeper than she remembered. "You are going where I am going." He growled as he took a step toward her. "I see now why Filasek dislikes you so. You show up at the most *inopportune* times."

"No." She raised her chin. "James, Azure Tiger, Dovlata, whatever you want to call yourself, you and I will end up in very different places." As Wakefield continued to stare into the man's eyes, unafraid of what lie beneath, she felt the connection with the spirit world.

Jesus, speak through me, she prayed.

Spirit or natural, the gun pointed at her flesh was very much in the physical world.

I will be your strength, Judah heard the words echo in her mind. She had one second to realize that it was not the scripture she had always hoped to hear if she ever found herself in this situation. What she wanted to hear was, "You will live and not die."

She flashed back to the words spoken in the church in Halle. "God deals in purposes we've never dreamed of."

Gritting her teeth and sucking in her breath, Judah pointed her gun to the ceiling, and dropped the bullet out of the chamber. She flipped the safety into place. Not taking her eyes from the challenging stare, she tossed her pistol on the bed.

She would not threaten. She would not reason. Judah rolled her lips over her teeth once more and ordered him firmly, as she would a subordinate. Her tone was not one of antagonizing, but one confident in her authority. "I command you to put down the weapon in the name of Jesus Christ."

47

He kept seeing the chipped concrete replay in his mind. He had never missed a target before.

Her coming in threw off my concentration, he excused himself. He would take another shot. He laughed at her gun. *Sure, she is a crack shot, but no one in her right mind would take that shot. Not when the retaliation is so imminent.*

Who does she think she is, ordering me around like one of her swabbies? "I will do what I want, when I want, so just shut your pretty face."

The music softened for a moment before building again.

Keeping his face and body toward her, he backed over and turned up the volume on the radio blindly. A fast glance through the blinds showed that the bulk of the Secret Service men were moving to the west dumpsters. Ignoring his current pest, Dovlata sidestepped left to watch the little insects below scurrying at his bidding. He could not stop his smile as he hid his body against the wall and peeked out the window.

The noise from behind him was bothersome. "Shut up, woman! And stay where you are." He whirled around. Wakefield's advance had stopped. But she would not shut up.

"Or what? You'll shoot me with the same gun as you just used to kill the president? You will put the gun down, now." Her eyes seemed to fasten him to the wall.

He shook off her stare and stepped toward her again. The corner of the bed was the only obstacle between them. "I don't need a gun, Judah." He tossed it on the bed; hers bounced with the heavy displacement. "You need to know that you are not leaving this room alive. Are you sure you don't want me to use the gun? It would be less painful."

"I've been shot before." She tossed her long ponytail to the side and slid one foot forward a few inches. "It is *not* less painful."

"Then you were not shot in the right place. I said don't move." He emphasized forcefully.

"Why are you doing this, James?"

"I am not James." He spat on the carpet thinking of the pasty faced Brit whose identity he had borrowed after he had buried him. He glanced back at the window and then focused on her face.

Just pick up the gun and kill her, he told himself.

"I don't want to," he argued, glancing at the progress of the presidential procession down the red stripe of carpet. "If I wanted to, she'd be dead. I am in control of this situation, and I don't want to hold the gun right now. I have to accomplish the objective first."

A flash of heat rolled through his body. The music was winding down. The dorks outside waned patriotic as they burst into song. *How pathetic.* "The blasted country of your birth will never support or accept you," he scowled at the singers out the window. "Your country will condemn you!" His voice felt rocky in his throat.

He mopped his forehead with both hands. "It is turning into an inferno in here. God! Why won't that woman shut up?"

Because I sent her to speak to you.

The assassin violently shook his head. "Ugh, that hurts. Not you again." He put a hand to either side of his temple and continued to shake as he bent at the waist to cushion the pain.

"I do not hear voices in my head!" He felt the words rip from his throat as he tried to shake the voice loose.

You've been hearing voices in your head for years. Even Mine on occasion. I am the One who offers you the way out.

"The coward's way." He spat again as if he were cursing in Ancient Israel.

A breeze floated in through the window. "A fan in hell," he sighed. He lifted his long curls off the back of his neck to feel the coolness.

"Come over where it is cooler," invited the wind. "I will give you eternal peace for your soul."

"Peace is a lie. There is no peace. Only a bit of coolness for you to enjoy." The sound came from the window, a low voice that seemed to override all the noise from before.

The assassin reached for the long sleek gun on the bed, but could not focus enough to move his feet. When did the wind acquire a voice? And why was the wind arguing with the voice that could not be shaken loose from his head?

"Come closer," the wind invited. "You have earned it. Come to the window."

He picked up leaden feet one at a time. "I have to see the target. Kill the target." He despised the weak echo of his voice among the more powerful ones.

The wind felt soothing. All the voices diminished as the wind blew over his ears.

"To swim in the coolness." He nodded. "My whole body needs to be cool. I am so hot."

He fixated on the tiny man below. His gray suit fluttered in the cooling breeze. His blue tie floated up from the clip, and the leader's hand smoothed it back into place. He was not sweating. He was outside, in the coolness. The man adjusted the trio of microphones to the proper height and began to speak.

Azure Tiger looked directly down. A ledge. An easy stretch allowed him to sit on the brick in the coolness. His skin cooled, but his insides still burned. He gulped the air into his lungs. *That should help.*

His eyes fixed on the man at the end of the red carpet.

Dead. "He should be dead. Why is he still moving?"

He brought his arms up to take the shot. No rifle.

Azure Tiger looked at his hands. Deep lines showed through the red. "Where did the blood come from?" The assassin rubbed them together. It got worse. "Sticky."

Let Me wash the blood off.

"Not you again." He cringed. "Just leave me alone!" He groaned gutturally.

I made you.

"I made myself."

Come in. Let Me make you clean. Let me be your Father.

"I'd rather be filthy and burn in hell before I have another father who shames me. I will not come in. I like it where I am."

The little man speaking turned to leave. "He's getting away!"

Azure Tiger pushed the blinds to the side. "No. He is supposed to die now. On TV. On the red carpet."

A hand touched his shoulder. He shrugged it off.

"Finish the mission," the wind whispered.

He brought his hands up. "You cannot take these weapons away." They dripped with red.

The red would look nice against the target's crisp white collar.

"Fly. He's getting away!" screamed the wind, no longer cool and soothing, but demanding.

He brought his hands down to the brick and kicked against the wall like a diving board. Solid and sure.

The target's head came closer, but the angle was wrong.

The wind laughed. It was low in his ears. "I win. I win." Coolness rushed over his body.

"Now I'm cold."

"Not for long," the wind promised.

The world dropped to black.

48

R ivers heard feet pounding in the concrete alley. A different pitch than the music. A pitch he was used to listening for.

He looked up to see Chad charging toward him, hitching up his britches as he ran. "Sir. Sir!" Chad's arms flailed about his head like a drowning man. "I've been looking all over for you. Wakefield needs back up in room 411. She has a lead on Azure Tiger."

Well, now the entire population of Berlin is aware. "Did she take Nelson with her?" Rivers loosened his grip on the dumpster and shuffled his feet quickly toward the Kempi.

"Nelson is over with the president." Chad huffed as he hung his head forward leaning from the waist. His breathing sounded ragged. Rivers guessed he had been running for some time. How much time had lapsed?

"You guys take this." He looked to Flannery. "I've got an emergency." Glancing at the loitering men, he spotted three capable-looking men. He pointed. "You three, with me," he ordered and took off.

The crowd stilled and the president began his greetings. Good, he was speaking, that meant he was still breathing.

The SEAL stepped off the curb with his left foot and skidded to a halt. Something caught his attention. Something out of place.

He snapped his head back.

He watched with horror as a man climbed out a window five stories up. The curly hair looked familiar.

He recognized Yates' lithe body. "He's supposed to be in London." Rivers calculated half on the sidewalk, half in the street. The map of the Kempinski came up in his mind. That window would be just about right for room 411.

"God, let her be okay," Rivers breathed the prayer as he took off at full speed. His elbows and knees pumped like pistons. Rushing adrenalin staved the pain that should have encased him from his rib injury.

Six running strides into the street, at an angle in line with the front door, Rivers jerked himself to a stop again.

Yates began to plummet.

His loose cotton button-down fluttered as he glided downward. It was the only movement. He did not rake the air or backpedal. He had the pasture of floating even as he sank to the earth.

Bush was no longer speaking. The crowd clapped in a dull roar that undulated in Rivers' ears.

The SEAL followed the line of the fall. His eye stopped at the second story. A striped gold and black vinyl canopy stretched over the doorway. Rooms 411, 413 and 415 were in a direct line above the awning.

Rivers heard the sickening snap as Yates' legs, head and left arm crashed into the canopy frame. His body disappeared, and the vinyl ballooned under the pressure.

It was too much. The canopy split, depositing Yates' body, butt first, onto the cobblestone fifteen feet below.

Rivers retraced the fall line to the window. Wakefield's white face looked down. Her mouth was open in a silent scream. Her eyes extended. She'd seen everything.

Wakefield or Yates? Rivers mind screamed at him to make a decision.

Room 411

Wakefield pulled her head back into the relative warmth of room 411. If she never saw another evil man die, it would be fine by her.

The smell of the cheeseburger and fries she left in the hall made her queasy. She placed a hand on her stomach and forced the bile back.

How would it look to have a Naval Intelligence officer throwing up on the scene?

The sound came over the radio to her left as she faced the open doorway. "Sparrow 8 to Nest. Man down in front of Kempi entrance. Send ambulance immediately."

Four seconds passed before the dispatcher came back. "Nest to Sparrow 8. Screamer on its way. One of ours?"

"I don't know, sir. Looks like a hotel guest was pushed out of a window."

Wakefield saw the tiny mic on the table with the receiver. "Nest. Lieutenant Commander Wakefield, Naval Intel, here. Downed man is Azure Tiger. He jumped from five stories."

"*The* Azure Tiger?" came the disbelieving voice. "I thought he was a myth. How did you get this freq, Intel?"

"I *am* Intel." She tried to laugh but could not find one. "Send a mop up crew. Forensics, too. Kempi room 411."

She could hear the ambulance a few blocks away. She grimaced at the thought of the emergency techs trying to break through the crowd and traffic barriers.

Wakefield categorized the room as she had not been able to do with Yates standing against her. "Whew," she blew out her breath and closed her eyes for a fraction of a moment of relief. "It's over."

"Actually." She smiled at the familiar masculine voice coming from the doorway. "It's not."

Her eyes flew open. *Speak*, she begged him without words.

"He still has a pulse. If he makes it, there will be a trial."

"He's not dead! How did he survive that fall?" She felt her knees buckle under her.

"How'd you figure it out?" Rivers walked in and stood next to the bed staring at the weapons.

She moved her glance from her partner to examine a felt-lined gun case open on the carpet. "Room service." Judah pointed to the door. A shard of white poked out of a crease in the gun case lining. "Do you have gloves?" she stepped closer, magnetized.

"Sure, why?" He pulled a leather pair from his pocket and slapped them against his palm.

The noise startled her. "I want to see that." She pointed out the corner of white. It was definitely paper.

"He's not dead." Rivers shrugged. "It's not a crime scene." She noted that Rivers pulled on the gloves anyway.

She looked up sharply. "Yes it is." Didn't he know? "He shot Bush."

"There was no shot."

She shook her head. "I saw him take it."

"No one went down." Rivers countered and mirrored shaking his head.

"I saw the recoil." Wakefield crossed her arms and stared at her partner over the empty gun case. *What's wrong with him?* "Did he miss? Azure Tiger never misses."

The radio noise caught their attention as Rivers reached out to touch the paper. Together they looked at the squawk box. "Nest, Canary 10. We have two D.B.s in the west dumpster." The words were slow. And hard to absorb.

"Are they ours?" The dispatcher sounded past the point of caring whether he followed radio protocol or not. The dread in his voice said that he suspected who they were.

Wakefield looked at Rivers. *Had there been a bomb after all? And I pulled him away from it.*

"Bluebird 16 and 17. They're pretty messed up. A couple of what's gotta be .50 cals each." Judah captured Rivers' blue-green eyes, understanding what the transmission meant. "As if it would take more than one," Canary 10 sounded disgusted.

"This room just became one half of a murder scene," she mumbled.

The sound of sliding paper brought her attention back to the gun case. "You can't tamper with evidence," she gasped. Rivers was a SEAL, what was he thinking?

"I'm just looking at it." His brow wrinkled. A crease down the center of the page showed that the paper had been folded in half at some point. His eyes narrowed, he turned the paper sideways and then flipped it to the back. Then back to the front. Brought it closer to his face.

The constant movement made it impossible for her to focus on it. "What is it?" She dropped to her knees next to him.

"A fax." He turned it upside down.

"Yes, I can see that." She grabbed his forearm. "Hold it still, will you. What does it say?"

He turned it right side up once more. He shrugged. "It's Greek to me."

She pulled his arm closer to her, not wanting to transfer prints to the paper. "Hm, me too." Judah pursed her lips. They felt dry. Then she grinned over at him. "Fortunately," she raised her fine eyebrows at him comically, "I speak Greek." She tittered. "I've always wanted to say that."

"Amazing." Rivers breathed. Wakefield could not interpret the expression on his face as he looked at her. She lowered her head, not breaking their eye contact. "I should marry you."

She closed her eyes and reopened them. Yes, she had heard right.

She shook her head trying to get him to break out of his trance-like staring. "No way." *He has the weirdest timing.*

"Why not?"

Yes, why not? She asked her mouth that had spoken without permission. "You haven't even asked me on a date yet." *There, smart Alec.*

319

The elevator door pinged.

"Will you go out with me?" She was suddenly aware that she had not removed her hand from his forearm.

"You'll have to ask my dad. He approves all my dates first." *See how you deal with that.* She felt the challenge in her eyes move to her cheeks.

"He suggested a steak and swing dancing. Hurry up. What does it say? Somebody's coming."

She willed her heartbeat to slow down. The wind blew in through the open window. She shivered. "It looks like a hit list. Some instructions at the top." Her fingers pressed white into his skin. "Oh, my." She read it again. Her Greek was still such that she had to translate it into English before it made sense. And the names were spelled phonetically.

She had hoped to never see that name again. "How careless." She pinched her bottom lip.

"What is it?" he hissed in her ear.

"It's signed Arafeh Filasek."

"Intel?" An American voice called into the room, out of sight. "Clear?" Wakefield jerked her head up and scrambled to her feet.

"Come on in." Her voice cracked and strained. "All clear."

They rose from squatting on the carpet. When she looked at Rivers again, the paper was gone as were his gloves.

A crew of seven men and one woman, all wearing black Kevlar vests and ball caps swarmed into room 411.

"Dietz, first." Rivers brushed her ear as he whispered.

"It is freezing in here." One of them said. He walked to the open window and set down his tackle box of equipment. "Is this where he jumped?"

"That would be it." Wakefield wet her lips.

"We'll be downstairs getting some coffee." Rivers announced and with his hand to the curve of her back, propelled her to the exit.

A crewman called out, "Wait." Wakefield looked over her shoulder at the speaker. She guessed his pock marked skin had been the butt of many jokes in his lifetime. "Wakefield, did you touch anything while you were up here?"

She could answer that honestly and still keep Rivers' secret. "I touched the window frame and the radio mic, and of course, the door handle." She gestured with her knuckle to the handle next to her. And the glock is mine."

"All right. We'll get your statement later." He took a 2X3 inch tablet of paper from his pants pocket and flipped it open from the end.

Wakefield pressed her lips together. "Hm-hm." She nodded and then felt the pressure of her partner's hand against her backbone.

49

Dietz looked out the window into the piercing morning sun as the wheels of his 747 touched down. His knees hurt, his hips ached and his back felt like he'd never be able to stretch fully again. He looked at his watch.

Nine hours in coach. "Never again." He grumbled to the double Plexiglas window, not bothering to lower his voice. Who could hear him over the roar of the engines back here?

Air Force One, proudly reflecting the morning light off her sleek planes, towered over the marine guards surrounding her. The huge airplane stood like an untouchable island in a sea of concrete 500 yards from the terminal complex.

Despite his aches, he was glad he hopped the midnight plane to Germany. Eagle One was not as untouchable as his aircraft.

The long wing of his Air France ride cut into his view. *Did wings always bounce so much*? He felt every seam in the concrete as they taxied.

"Please remain seated with your seatbelt fastened…" The flight attendant's voice droned first in English, then German. "Yeah, yeah." Dietz unbuckled his belt just to spite her. He counted the minutes before the president's appearance at the *Steigenburger Berlin*. It would be close. As long as the limo he told Melissa to arrange was waiting, he would make it.

There would be no stop in baggage claim. His two changes of clothes and toothbrush were in the bin above his head. Even the

Director of Counterintelligence couldn't take a razor aboard. It lay in a box somewhere in the underbelly of Dulles Airport.

Ku'damm Strasse
0932 hours

"Listen, Rivers," Judah placed her hand on the commander's upper arm to slow him. He turned his blue-green eyes to her. She begged herself to ask him about his earlier statement. *What did he mean?*

What if he was kidding? Her elated heart liquefied. The silence stretched too long. "Thanks." She finally spoke. "For taking me to the hospital. I need to check on Yates."

He shrugged. "You didn't want coffee. Where else is there to go?" He resumed the lead on their walk to the rental car. The sidewalks teemed with people dispersing from the presidential remarks. Most of the conversations Wakefield could hear were about the suicidal man, not the greetings from the American president.

At the car Rivers offered her the keys with a raised eyebrow. "Thanks. I think I'm fine to ride this time," Judah smiled.

St Josef Krankenhaus
Baumerplan 24, Berlin
1012 hours

Nelson paced the tile hallway of the drab hospital. He decided there was a universal code for hospitals to dress in puke-green paint with cream-colored floors.

Sitting still made his insides quake. He'd be running to the bathroom if he wasn't careful. Doctors and nurses whizzed around him. Orderlies wheeled patients by him.

He turned to the sound of his name. The navy officers were headed straight for him. They were the last people he wanted to talk to. Their quick pace ate up the distance, and they looked determined. The woman even more so than the SEAL. Not surprising. He had heard that she was in the room when the assassin jumped.

"Have you heard anything?" She called before coming into range. No greeting or anything. The scar on her cheek stood out against her pale skin garishly.

"How did you let things deteriorate to this point, Commanders?" He addressed both, but only had eyes for Wakefield. The SEAL had been disarming a bomb, for Pete's sake.

She looked shell-shocked. He grabbed the elbows of both officers and pushed them in front of him into the small waiting room where he had been obliged to wait.

Rivers shrugged his hand off and glared at him, briefly. Then he sauntered to an orange molded chair.

Nelson dropped Wakefield's arm. "You had a gun, Commander. Why doesn't our assassin have a bullet in his brain?" Red threatened at the edges of his vision.

Wakefield took a shaky step back. Her face lost even more color. She looked left at the floor, and he could see her throat move as she swallowed.

"Lay off, Nelson." The warning came as a growl from Rivers' direction. "The man is in custody. The president is still alive. What do you care?"

Should've figured he would defend her. Nelson turned his head and set his jaw at the SEAL who lazed back in his chair like a giraffe. His long legs sprawled out into the middle of the tiny room taking up too much space. "The man deserves to be dead."

"Jeez. It is only a matter of time. Give the man a fair trial and then we'll let you pull the handle." Rivers' curled-lip expression made him feel like a bug.

"Do you have any info on Yates. Um, the assassin?" Wakefield corrected herself.

Hmm, sounds like a little triangle was beginning to form. No wonder she didn't shoot him. Dereliction of Duty, here comes Wakefield. Nelson cut his eyes to the woman and then to Rivers quickly. The SEAL did not seem concerned. About anything. "Nothing more than the EMT's eval. He has two broken legs, and a broken left wrist. Every one of his ribs is cracked, which I can tell you is very uncomfortable. A concussion, a ruptured spleen that they are taking out now, and a smashed tailbone, besides a myriad of cuts and bruises."

"Huh," Rivers grunted and looked at Wakefield. "Not bad for a five story fall."

"How long before we know if the surgery is successful?" she looked up with a glimmer in her eye. "A ruptured spleen is life threatening."

"Wakefield was a corpsman before she joined Intel." Rivers explained the unusual knowledge.

"Maybe another hour." He shrugged. The nurse had not said.

"You ready for that coffee yet?"

"Maybe some tea." Wakefield sank into an orange chair as Rivers stood. "If you can find some."

"I'll go harvest some in India if I have to."

His attempt at humor fell short. Too soon and too reminiscent of Azure Tiger's home port.

"I can't believe none of us put together the English accent with India. British Imperialists in the 1700's introduced their language and customs there, actually indoctrinated the people." Nelson said.

Rivers walked to the door without offering to get anything for him.

"Wakefield, I did some checking since I've been here." Nelson tapped his handy, clipped to his belt. "There really is a James Yates in British Intel. He was reported missing by his sister nine days ago in London. I guess the assassin took him out sometime in November, which is when his sister last heard from him and when this guy showed up at the Kempi."

She frowned sadly. "So basically, everything he told us was a lie." She stared at the floor. "At least we should be able to track down our money for our expense account." Her eyes got large and she did not look up. "You didn't know about that, did you?" She winked one eye closed as she glanced up.

"It is probably better for your career if you don't mention it." He still felt roiling anger at her, but there was something likeable about her at the same time. He felt his stomach lurch again. "I am going to walk."

50

Wakefield twisted uncomfortably in the plastic seat. Alone, again, she waited and this time, prayed. She did not like the questions that were coming. Her soul cried, deeply. She bent over and rested her elbows on her knees. Her head fell into her hands.

"Why didn't I know?" Her lips smashed together. "Why didn't You tell me?" She closed her eyes; humiliation waved over her.

"God, I don't understand." Her words sounded muffled in the confines of her lap. "This wasn't supposed to happen. Things were going so amazingly." The bridge of her nose began to sting. "I mean I have heard about demons submitting to your name. I've seen it happen in healing services and deliverance sessions, but not...never when it was a life-threatening situation." Footsteps approached the doorway. The gait sounded like Nelson. He ambled by every eighty-four seconds.

Judah scrunched her fingers through her hair and pulled it forward to let its length cover her confusion. "Father, I didn't think he would jump out the window. I would have done something else if I had known that."

Something other than that which I asked of you?

The words permeated her swirling mind. A single tear dropped to her black corduroys. "No, I guess not. Not when you put it that way." She thumbed away the errant tear. "I can't believe he lied to me like that. I really liked him."

So did I.

"Did?" Wakefield sat up slightly. "Does that mean he is dead?" She felt the rate of her breathing increase, but it came in short huffs. Her mind took her back to the church in Halle. Melody again told her, "Sometimes we just can't see what God is up to."

No, he is alive for now. I am tired of asking him.

"Asking him to follow you? Does that mean it is too late for him?" Wakefield felt herself begin to choke. This was by far the oddest conversation she had participated in. She knew it was not rising from within herself. Yet, it came so easily.

Oh, because of my mercy, I will ask him once more before his time is fulfilled.

"Would you rather not?" The tone she heard sounded like it would cause him pain to be rejected again.

It is my great pleasure to offer mercy.

"Oh." She sniffled as she head footsteps again. Two sets. "I choose to trust that you know what you are doing." She blew out her breath and her spirit buoyed slightly within her.

Rising, she went to investigate the noise. She tossed her hair up again into a scraggly, half-pulled ponytail.

Rivers was walking with Dietz toward her. Rivers put her paper cup of tea into his left hand and pumped the director's right as they continued toward her.

Both men wore smiles, she could see now.

"Dietz! You came!" *Blast protocol.* She trotted down the hall to hug the director of counterintelligence.

"Director Dietz! What are you doing here!" Nelson's voice echoed from behind her.

Silence reigned a moment. The four looked at each other.

Dietz answered. "The same reason you are. Checking on our boy. I just talked to a nurse. He's still in surgery." He looked to the three to confirm.

"He's going to live." Wakefield reached up to trace her collarbone. She probed her heart. The guilt was gone.

"Good." The three men said together. Rivers sounded thoughtful and Nelson relieved. It was Dietz's vengeful tone she didn't predict.

"Do you have some inside track with the physician?" Dietz eyed her.

"Sort of." She reached for her tea, signaling the men she did not wish to be interrogated. She sipped the liquid. *Lukewarm. How long has Rivers been gone?*

Hotel Askanischerhof
Ku'damm 53, Berlin
Friday 25 January 2003
1214 hours

Rivers keyed open the door to Wakefield's room and stepped back into the hall. He yawned, ready for some rack time. The door swung in under her slim hand. He held out her overnight bag. She didn't reach back to take it. "David." Her voice carried a slight tremor. "Somebody's been in here."

"Get back." His senses jumped to full alert. They had heard that the four men in Munich had checked out of their hotel. Maybe it wasn't over yet. Was there a fail-safe plan from whomever had hired the tiger?

Rivers dropped Judah's bag, and pulled her by the shoulders back into the hall. He went inside. Funnily enough she didn't protest.

Bathroom clear. Main room clear. The closet door stuck as he pulled it, then opened freely, clear. Under the bedskirt only needed a vacuum to the platform. He examined the bedside phone. No bugs. Behind the side table there was nothing. He flipped back the lip to her suitcase on the floor. "Everything looks all right to me."

"Yeah, I see that. It was just a feeling when I walked in."

A low chuckle erupted. "Everything is fine, except this." He pointed to the color-coordinated rows of rolled clothes. "You said you were *not* a meticulous perfectionist."

"I suppose you might see it as a little carried away. But hey, everything I own is in this hotel room now. I have to stay organized."

Her dimples dug into her cheeks as her lips turned down. Her gaze did not leave the tidy rows in the black suitcase.

"I suppose I can afford to indulge you." As they chatted he catalogued her micro-expressions to assess her capacity to carry the stress load.

"What happened to Joe? My cat." She looked up. Her sea-blue eyes held steady.

His stomach dropped. *I hope she did not want to take the body home.* "I buried him in the wildflower garden in the *Kempi* courtyard. I hope you don't mind."

Her eyes turned down at the corners. She looked rather relieved. "Not at all." She sucked in her breath sharply and reached for the wall, but kept speaking, as if he could not see that she was dizzy. "I've never had someone bury the dead for me before. Thanks." Her fingertips whitened as she fought to keep her balance.

He wrapped his fingers around her upper arm. "Sit," he commanded.

"I'm fine, just overtired. Probably low blood sugar. I'm too tired to eat though."

He was unsatisfied with her answer, but her lips were melded. "Lie down then. I'm going to crack the door between our rooms." He chuckled lightly at the way she looked up at him through her lashes from her seat on the bed. "It's avant-garde, I know." He couldn't resist teasing. "But it is an avant-garde kind of day." He went for the door before she had a chance to argue. "Call if you need anything."

"Aye, aye, sir." Her voice was playful, but more telling was that she did not seem bothered by his meddling.

That's a start, he decided and winked at her.

From his room, he called out, "Cool. They replaced the window. It's nice and warm in here."

51

D ietz moseyed into the opulent suite that took up the entire top floor. The suite of the Steignberger Berlin Hotel was certainly fit for a president. A directional plaque at the door pointed to the left for the private pool, Jacuzzi, steam room, and exercise equipment, to the right for the living quarters and sundeck, straight ahead for the conference room, dining room, office and library. Dietz frowned, the stress of being a world leader was not without its perks. Dwarfed by the high ceilings, massive marble pillars and life-size, full-body paintings of by-gone German war heroes, Dietz spied a bevy of black-clad Secret Service men outside one of the doors. The president was obviously conducting his business today from the library.

Bush's graying hair had been trimmed in the past few days. A tiny white line showed around his neckline against his tanned skin. He held the phone to his ear nodding. He waved the loitering Dietz inside.

"Yes, yes." His Texan tenor played pleasantly off the books in the room. "Thank you again." His genuine gratitude was unmistakable.

"Director," Bush offered his hand to Dietz. "Thanks for coming. Care for a bottle of water?"

"Love one, Mr President, thanks. Why am I here?" he didn't care to waste time on pleasantries if he was going to be fired over the morning's transpirings.

"I wanted to thank you. I understand Azure Tiger is down for the count."

"Yes, sir. He won't be on the job market again, Mr President."

"Tell your people a job well done. I told you there was nothing to worry about."

"But, sir," Dietz felt his eyebrows shoot up. "You...you were shot at."

"He missed." It sounded so simple from Bush's lips

"Two men are dead."

His face dropped sad. "I do regret that. I've already been on the phone with their families. They died as heroes, giving their lives for their country, for me." Dietz watched Bush turn his bottle of spring water covered in condensation in his hands. "As I told those men's wives and mothers, I will do my best to live up to the privilege of that honor."

Hotel Askanischerhof
Rivers' Room 407
1639 hours

Rivers' eyes flashed open. He saw the white bumpy ceiling of his hotel room. There was the sound again.

The soft mumblings of a female voice that had awakened him. Is Judah *dreaming?*"

He rolled up to a seated position and stole over to the connecting door, open about four inches. From this vantage point, he could see her sitting up against the headboard with the covers pooled at her waist. Her neck was bent awkwardly away from him. She pulled her fingers through her long hair.

"The hardest thing is that all dad's things are gone. Everything I had left of him...I'm sure the girls have some pictures that I can have copied, but I can never replace the uniforms, the duck that he tried to carve when I was seven." Her laughter was without mirth. "Yeah, but I think I'll leave the cradle with you for safekeeping until I need it. If you don't mind."

He closed his eyes, feeling a piece of her pain.

"I just want to come home for a little while, Momma. It's all too much for me right now." Her voice broke. It split a chasm in Rivers' heart.

"I already talked to my C.O. and the judge in my article 32. I have 30 days leave on the books. Can I come home for a couple weeks?"

Her sigh was deep. "Thanks. I'll have to get back to D.C. a little early to reestablish housekeeping. Ugh, that means more apartment hunting. No, no...my renter's insurance should cover everything. My flight will arrive in Minneapolis tomorrow at 1547, um 3:47.

"Oh really? Yeah, I'll call her. Thanks, mom. I love you, too."

Rivers backed away from the door as he heard her replace the receiver. The soldier needed comfort and rest. Her mother would see to her physical needs. And he would make sure she got the emotional rest she needed from the constant struggle against Filasek.

52

Wakefield heard the phone ring 3,000 miles away at her little sister's house in Apple Valley, Minnesota. From her mother's tone of voice, it did not sound like a good, "your sister wants to talk to you."

"Penny? Hey little sis."

"Judah, where have you been?" *Yes, her voice is clearly agitated.* Judah rolled her neck to relieve the kinks.

"I'm in Berlin. Why?"

There was a silence. "With the president?"

Wakefield frowned, she supposed so. "Yes, with the president. Though at the moment he is several blocks away. Mom said you wanted to talk?"

"Yes." Penny drew a deep breath. "First, have you talked to Melia yet?"

"Not since New Year's."

"Mm."

"She's pregnant, isn't she?" Wakefield put the sound of her sister's disapproval next to the earlier word of knowledge.

"Yes, but you didn't hear it from me. You always know." Penelope sighed, as if keeping a surprise from her big sister was the ultimate goal in her life. "When are you going to settle down and have one?"

"When God sends me to the right man."

Her sister sighed. "I hope he hurries up. So what is Berlin like?"

Wakefield raised her eyebrows. "A little congested at the moment." *Does she just want to chit chat? We can do that tomorrow when it is not an international call, and when I get over this sleepless loopiness.*

"Hey, I forgot. I'm mad at you."

Wakefield pressed her back into the pillows and pushed her fingers through the crown of her drying hair. "What did I do?" With Penny it could be anything from buying the brand of detergent she was boycotting to forgetting to send a birthday present.

"What did I do?" Penny mocked. "E-bay ring a bell?"

"Um, no."

"Don't kid around, Judah. I saw the tulips I painted for you for sale on E-Bay."

Wakefield's mind circled, trying to wrap around the importance of the information "What?"

"I mean if you didn't want it, you could have given it back."

Rivers knocked on the connecting door swinging it open slightly under his touch. Judah wiggled up straighter in the mattress, made sure she was covered and waved him in.

Penny was still talking. "I was impressed to see the bid up to $325, but I'm still hacked at you."

Pressing her palm against the mouth piece she told him, "It's my sister, just a second. Penny. Penny!" She had to break in. "Listen I have to go. Call mom and she'll tell you what's going on. Just know that it is my favorite. I wouldn't sell it for a million dollars, because you painted it for me."

"What's up?" Rivers asked from the end of her bed.

"I think we just got a lead in the fire stuff. My sister saw a one-of-a-kind painting from my house for sale on the Internet."

"Somebody took it out of your apartment before they set the place on fire and is now selling it?"

Energy pumped through Judah's body and brain. "It's a long shot, but it's possible." She threw back the covers with her left hand. He started at her movement and started to close his eyes. She looked guiltily at her partner. She knew she was dressed, but he didn't.

Rivers snorted in the back of his throat and rolled his eyes. "Let's go find Dietz."

He still stared, not moving. *I am dressed, I can feel my clothes.* She glanced down just to confirm. She questioned him with her eyes.

He jutted his jaw at her and lifted an eyebrow. She had forgotten she was wearing it. "What could make a stellar naval officer like yourself, sleep in a U.S. Marine Corps t-shirt?" he grinned like he caught her skinny-dipping in the Potomac.

Quietly, she let him in. "I needed to feel close to my dad." She looked at her shirt from above. It looked more threadbare than she remembered. When had the letters started peeling?

"Then you haven't lost everything of his. That's good."

Steigenberger Berlin Hotel
1747 hours

Wakefield sat on the edge of the pink Queen Anne Chair in Dietz's suite. He looked like he had gotten a few hours of sleep since the hospital. He spoke animatedly—well, as animatedly as Wakefield had ever seen him—into the phone.

He sounded confident that, unless the painting had exchanged hands, his team could track down the arsonist and thief. "I realize we don't have jurisdiction, but we have the information and better computer people." Dietz nodded hopefully. "Gather the intelligence and coordinate with the FBI and the local police. Jackson, make sure this gets done by-the-book. I don't want to lose this guy. He burned down the house of one of our own. Call me back."

Dietz turned his attention on her and Rivers. "Sounds promising." Dietz's little black mustache twitched as he smiled. "Jackson had found the painting on E-bay before we were off the phone."

"Did anyone discover Azure Tiger's real identity?" Rivers asked. He draped himself over the chair that matched Judah's. "I realize prints are not going to help. We had those all along, but now we have a face to run through the computer."

"Sorry, you guys must have already gone back to your hotel when the word came." Dietz looked at the curtains. "We didn't need to put him through the computer. One of my analysts who used to be in the India field office recognized him. His real name is Hossien Dovlatabadi, the illegitimate son of the most powerful Maharaja in India. His mother was a white woman. But, I guess *her* genes were stronger than his father's."

"That would explain his skin tone, blue eyes, and curly hair." Wakefield let her back touch the back of the chair as she absorbed Yates' life.

"Apparently, the Maharaja kept him for a time, I think he was six, and then when he married his current wife, he publicly denounced Hossien's mother's claim of parentage, even made the woman change the name on the birth certificate. The boy did not have any of his features. But, the Maharaja felt guilty enough to send him to the best schools in India and abroad. He saw his father only once after being kicked out of the palace."

"How crushing for a young man." Wakefield breathed. It explained a lot about the man she had profiled and about the man she had known. Compassion rose in her breast.

"Don't feel sorry for him, Commander. He made his own choices in life and now has 119 attributed, but unconfirmed, kills. All good men." Dietz voice was hard. She looked into his eyes as he stared at the curtains. His eyes were harder than they had been at the airport in D.C.

The phone jingled. "Dietz," he said shortly. "All right. Um-hm. Yes, Okay." He huffed. "I'll tell her."

Wakefield looked at her watch. Dietz had only hung up the phone 28 minutes earlier. It was too soon for a name.

He hung up. "We have him in custody." Dietz huffed again and shook his black hair. "The painting clashed with his fireplace. He wouldn't name his employer, but he's being held pending charges."

Wakefield closed her eyes and let her head drop back.

Rivers chuckled at the gesture. "I guess that clears you of suspicion, Gunsmoke."

She cracked a smile. "Good thing. The JAG office wouldn't appreciate having to defend me in civilian court at the same time as they are prosecuting me in a court martial."

53

Filasek punched his phone off. The busy signal seemed as constant as his pulse. No news. He'd been watching satellite CNN for nine hours straight. He rubbed his sore back. "Where are the headlines?" He screeched.

Zreik's New York telephone rang and rang. "What is that man up to?" He cursed the young man. "I should not have trusted him."

It was Dovlatabadi's constant busy that was maddening. "I'll kill him myself." Filasek cursed.

Mounting suspicion made him grip the edge of his stucco balcony. "If she got in the way again…" He left the sentence trailing as Wakefield's face swam before his eyes in red. "I will devastate America." His breath came raggedly. "Cut a slash across her heart this time and it will never be forgotten. Death to all Infidels."

All the wasted planning time and squandered resources boiled over. A scream of fury ripped from his throat.

Hotel Askanischerhof
Carpark
1856 hours

Wakefield unfastened her seatbelt. Rivers pulled up the emergency brake in the tight quarters. "Now that things are clearing up, you should be able to sleep, huh?" She looked sideways at him. *How did he know I couldn't sleep?* "What about that steak I promised you?"

A smile grew and she blinked. *He remembered. I wonder if he remembers what else he said that day.* "We'll have it in D.C. when you come to testify at my article 32."

"You've got it." He removed the keys from the ignition and nodded confidently.

"Good. My defense attorney, not to mention the judge, was beginning to think I made you up." She locked the door as she hauled herself up from the mini. "You'll get a call. It won't be until the end of February though."

They entered the lobby of their hotel. It looked shabby after seeing the *Kempi* and *Steigenberger Berlin* for so long. "I'm flying in the morning, out at 0740. Care to drop me off?" She liked his lopsided grin.

"Love to. One condition. I'm buying the coffee this time. And no McDonald's." He raised a dark brow.

They rode the elevator alone. She grinned at him in the reflection. She liked that mirror. She could hardly see her scar at all. Of course, to be objective, she couldn't make out her eyes very well either.

St Josef Krahkenhaus, Berlin
2147 hours

Dietz entered the windowless room located at the end of a long hallway. A burly ex-Army Ranger from the CIA station in Hamburg, closed the door behind him. The click of the lock pleased Dietz, like the clang of prison doors when you are on the right side.

The once world-class assassin lay prone, cast in white plaster, with the exception of his right arm. He used that to mute the television. "I hope you appreciate the private room." Dietz felt the heat of hatred rise to his ears. "It won't last long."

The man's nostrils flared. "Sure. Whatever you say." The cultured British tones sounded cheap coming from such a despicable man.

Dietz stared at the once lithe body destroyed by his abrupt meeting with cobblestone. He felt a measure of justice. Dovlatabadi's head had been shaved, making his eyes appear too large for his gentle features. He looked less like a killer than any man Dietz had ever come across.

"What do you want?"

"I came to tell you what your life will be like from now on." Dietz felt himself smile. This would be pleasurable. "Your entire life, 24 hours a day will be taped." He pointed to the camera mounted in the ceiling of the secure room.

"You will be extradited to the United States as soon as the doctors approve flying with your head injury. You won't make it, at least not according to the papers. A massive brain hemorrhage brought on by the air pressure fluctuations. We just weren't able to save you in the air. I already have the press release written. As soon as you can walk, you will begin your new career. Have you ever heard of a sweeper?"

The injured man's angular cheekbones hardened. Dietz saw that he knew a sweeper was a man who cleaned up government messes. Didn't matter which government. A sweeper was a killer of killers.

"You can't make me." Dovlatabadi spat. "Your whole life will be about me. Someday you will not be watching."

"Oh, I'm not making you. You are volunteering."

The assassin's face froze. "Why?"

"Your mother and half-brother are being picked up," he looked at his watch, "as we speak. I'm assigning you to our Middle Eastern division."

Fear swamped the man's eyes. Dietz liked it. "I'll never blend in there. You know that."

"Get a tan and some Clairol." Dietz replied harshly. "The great Azure Tiger is dead; I'll bring you a headline. You now work for me."

"How long?"

"Until you mess up and get yourself killed. If we deem that you did it on purpose, you family will join you in the Beyond." Dietz gestured widely with his hands.

"Ha! I know better. You can't do that in the USA."

Dietz clamped down hard on the man's one good arm, pinning it to the bed rail. "Buddy, you are not in the USA. You are in the CIA. And I..." He crinkled his eyes and he laughed. "I will be your best friend."

54

Rivers handed Judah back the computer case she would carry aboard the airplane. It was time for her to go through the checkpoint. He had to stay behind. He reached out and touched her soft cheek, covering the scar with his palm. "Get some rest, Judah A. Wakefield."

"Yes, sir." She tilted her head back and then touched the lapel of his khaki uniform. He was dressed for his trip home. "David." She fingered his gold Trident pin, looking a million miles away. "Promise me, you'll get those ribs checked out by a professional when you get home."

"I promise."

She slid her computer through the X-ray machine. A little wiggle of her fingers and she rounded the corner. She was gone.

Rivers' first step felt more like a stagger. "Being alone never bothered me before," he mused while fishing for his SatFone at his waist. "But I sure don't like it now.

"Dietz." He rang the director of counterintelligence's personal cell number. "Get me Wakefield's mother's address."

Driving up to the familiar blue house with the country wrap-around porch that Isaac Graham had built himself offered unexpected catharsis for Judah's soul. She blinked back tired tears. The snow three feet deep in the wide front yard heaped in six- to eight-foot black mountains at the road. She had planned to be home for a family Christmas that year. "I'm only a month late, but," she stopped inside the front door to breathe in the heavenly smells as she took off her wet shoes, "I'm finally home."

"Auntie Judah's here!" Her sister Melia's cry hit the front door. She came around the corner with Lillie on her hip, swinging her little legs happily. Penny followed Justin and little Emma's rampage to the door and joined the huddle.

"So, when's dinner?" Judah asked when she could breathe again. She wiped kid slobber off the corner of her mouth.

"Some things never change." Her mom said from behind the group hug. They all laughed. Even though the little ones had no idea what was funny.

"They're so cute. I didn't know you were coming, Melia."

Her younger sister shrugged. "Threw the kids in the car last night and headed down."

"You have about 40 minutes until dinner, if you want to take a bubble bath and relax after that long flight." Her mom straightened her brown hair that was laced with more gray than Judah remembered.

"That sounds blissful."

"I'll take your stuff up to your old room." Penny grabbed the black suitcase with the blue scarf knotted to the handle. "Mom told me about the fire. Sorry for jumping on you like that."

Judah smiled and ruffled her sister's short curls. "The guy is in jail now, besides, if you hadn't seen the painting, he'd have probably gotten away with it."

Judah heard the doorbell ring as she undressed. Adjusting the water temperature to fill the garden tub for a long soak, she let the water sluice over her hand.

"Judah," a motherly rap on the door interrupted her daydream. "Honey, you might want to come downstairs."

"In my robe?" What was so important that it needed her attention right now?

"Sure, dear. It's just us girls."

Judah closed the bathroom door behind her to retain the steam.

Her sisters' stifled giggles floated up the staircase.

Judah stopped in the doorway. "Oh my word!" She couldn't make her feet work.

On the coffee table sat a gorgeous bouquet of lavender roses. A vase of purple orchids adorned the wide mantel. A crystal bowl of purple daisies sat on the side table by Graham's recliner. A strange looking bunch of purple pompons stuck out of long grasses in a decorative wood vase. A huge bunch of deep purple tulips stretched toward the ceiling from the hearth next to a potted African violet. A bouquet of spring flowers, mostly huge purple chrysanthemums did not have a home yet. A giddy Penny held them.

Each vase or planter was accessorized with a large brown bag of M&Ms at the base. A sealed, lumpy envelope sat on the coffee table by the roses. She ripped through the seal. An enclosed trial-size bag of M&Ms fell into her hand. "To keep in your purse and think of me. Don't eat these." The sticky note said.

The note was much more personal.

> *Dear Miss Wakefield,*
> *Thoughts of you pushed me to distraction today.*
> *Much too dangerous for my line of work. Feel free*
> *to share and enjoy the large packages of M&Ms.*
> *But will you hold on to this small package for*
> *safe-keeping? I believe this is the lauded package.*
> *Please check with the Manufacturer for*
> *authenticity of said package, as I do the same.*
> *Your partner,*
> *David Rivers*

She giggled as she noticed her fingers trembling. She re-read the note with the candy in her palm. She could feel the small chocolate buttons through the paper.

Judah held them up to her closed mouth. She couldn't be misinterpreting this overture. It was too plain.

Could this be the real thing? *Lord*? She could not even finish formulating the words. *You know. Will you tell me? Is this the man you have been preparing me for the last 31 ½ years?*

She was almost afraid to listen for an answer.

No audible answer, no pictures, prophetic or otherwise. She felt a peacefulness in knowing, not what her answer was, but that she *would* know. When the time was right, she would know. *Your plans for me are good.* She felt excitement rise as she pictured an old-man Rivers. *They are to prosper me*, she considered his hazardous job—and hers, *and not to harm me*. She smiled again as she tilted the M&M bag back and forth.

She could contain her excitement no longer, "Hoo-rah!" she yelled, not caring who heard her. It only made her enthusiasm all the more real to hear her cry echo off her childhood home's walls. The place where visions of bridal veils and wedding songs were first practiced.

Her sisters and mother clapped and giggled along with her nieces and nephews.

"Oh dear! The bathwater!" Judah yelped and rushed with the note and candy in her hand, to catch it before the bubbles overflowed.

TO BE CONTINUED...

In book three of the Desert Sailors Series
Grecian Vendetta

Available in late 2016

David Rivers is missing. Following Rivers' vow to protect Judah, David becomes the bait Filasek uses to lure Judah to him, outside of all the protection the U.S. offers.

Judah Wakefield follows the lightest of clue threads to find Rivers, but what she finds is much more than she trained and prepared for. Lies and betrayal in the midst of an al-Qaeda-backed, triple threat to bring the U.S. to its knees, asks for more from Judah than she is prepared to give. With no way out, will she pay the ultimate price to save Rivers and the American people from Filasek's diabolical vengeance?